THE CARE AND FEEDING OF WASPISH WIDOWS

Also by Olivia Waite

The Lady's Guide to Celestial Mechanics

THE CARE AND FEEDING OF WASPISH WIDOWS

A Feminine Pursuits Novel

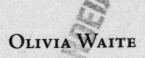

OLIVIA WAITE

AVONIMPULSE
An Imprint of HarperCollinsPublishers

THE CARE AND FEEDING OF WASPISH WIDOWS. Copyright © 2020 by Olivia Waite. All rights reserved. Printed in the United States of America. No part of this book may be used or reproduced in any manner whatsoever without written permission except in the case of brief quotations embodied in critical articles and reviews. For information, address HarperCollins Publishers, 195 Broadway, New York, NY 10007.

Print Edition ISBN: 978-0-06-293182-5
Digital Edition ISBN: 978-0-06-293180-1

Cover design by Amy Halpern
Cover type design by Patricia Barrow
Cover illustration by Christine M. Ruhnke
Cover images © Period Images; © Jannarong/Shutterstock (couch); © Dm_Cherry/Shutterstock (background)

Avon Impulse and the Avon Impulse logo are registered trademarks of HarperCollins Publishers in the United States of America.

Avon and HarperCollins are registered trademarks of HarperCollins Publishers in the United States of America and other countries.

FIRST EDITION

20 21 22 23 24   QGM   10 9 8 7 6 5 4 3 2 1

With gratitude to my great-grandparents—
to Grandpa Lee, for the bees,
and to Grandma Ruth, for the gardens
and also for letting six-year-old me drink
all that caffeinated black tea
which explains why I always had so
much energy for tree climbing.

ACKNOWLEDGMENTS

In writing this book I threw myself headlong into the work of Eva Crane, a quantum mathematician turned legendary beekeeper whose *The World History of Beekeeping and Honey Hunting* has been an invaluable resource and a perpetual flood of inspiration.

Publishing is volatile at the best of times, but never more so than the past few months. I would like to send all my love and gratitude to the writers, editors, publicists, illustrators, booksellers, and librarians who have fought to keep making stories in times when it feels we need them more desperately than ever.

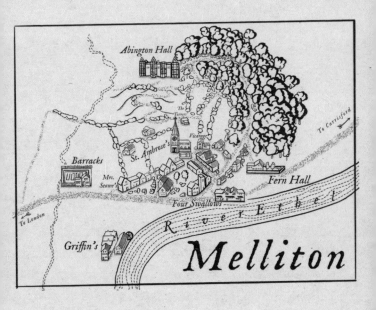

Abington Hall

The Turner's

Vicarage

To Carrisford

Barracks

St. Ambrose'

Mrs. Stowe's

Fern Hall

Four Swallows

To London

River Ethel

Griffin's

Melliton

The publication of a lascivious book is one of the worst offences that can be committed against the well-being of society . . . Let the rulers of the state look to this, in time!

—ROBERT SOUTHEY

The Care and Feeding of Waspish Widows

CHAPTER ONE

May 1, 1820

The corpses were giving Agatha the most trouble. They looked too much like people.

She chewed the end of her graver while she frowned down at the wax, only half-covered with lines carved by the sharp steel point. It wasn't that her son Sydney's notes about the event weren't detailed. They were. He'd been quite gruesomely observant about the whole execution, from the first drumbeat to the last dangle. "Afterward," he wrote in his hurried scrawl, "the hangman cut the bodies down from the scaffold and laid them out for beheading, bare as a row of teeth."

But what *kind* of teeth? A jagged, feral twist of fangs, like a snarl frozen in time? Or more like the matched tombstone set you'd see in the grinning skull of a *memento mori*?

There was a time and place for poetic expression, and it was *not* when you were describing a scene so someone else could make an accurate picture of it. Agatha's efforts to educate her son after his father's death had never prioritized *make sure the boy can convey his ideas in clear and precise metaphor*, but maybe they ought to have.

Thomas would have been so flummoxed, rest his soul.

Agatha had been widowed three years now, raising a boy on the cusp of manhood and running Griffin's print shop and never more than an inch shy of catastrophe. Even something as familiar as copper plate etching, which she'd learned at her mother's knee, seemed only another opportunity for everything to go wrong.

She spun the graver vexedly in her hand and cursed all teeth.

If she were a history painter in the Royal Academy—like the ones whose work she'd so often copied for the *Menagerie*—she'd strive to make each dead man unique. An outflung hand here, over there an agonized crooking of limbs. Careful composition would allow the varying shapes and poses to mirror and counterbalance one another, and create a whole greater than the sum of its individual parts. The viewer wouldn't be aware of this—but they would feel it, deep in their gut.

But this work wasn't high art. This was a sensationalist sketch of this afternoon's hangings for those who hadn't or couldn't attend in person, and the simpler she made it the faster and more easily she could print it. Right now the execution of the Cato Street conspirators was the city's favorite subject, and every hack and handpress owner on the banks of the Thames would be rushing to offer cartoons and etchings and pamphlets. She wasn't even taking the time to sketch the scene beforehand: this design was being cut directly into the smoked wax ground of the plate.

She knew simpler was better, because simpler was faster, and faster meant more sales before the public's ghoulish fascination moved on.

Yielding to necessity, she made the corpses all identical, the line of bodies as stark, stern, and terrifying as sharp metal could slice. *Dead*, those harsh lines said. *Dead, still dead, none more dead, so aggressively dead it borders on rudeness.*

But her artist's sensibilities couldn't be entirely ignored. She found herself drawing the living onlookers as individuals: a tall woman, a fat man, a pair of friends with straw hats and walking staves, come in from the country to see the execution; a child pointing and clutching its mother's hand. Looming over everything stood the tall figure of the hangman, heaving up the first severed head for the mob's approval.

They hadn't approved, Sydney's notes explained. They'd booed and hissed and thrown things at the executioner, crying out against state violence and the tyranny of wealthy, self-interested men.

And no wonder. Everyone knew the government was corrupt, from the magistrates to the House of Lords to King George himself.

Agatha carved the hangman's outlines especially deep into the wax, so the acid would bite deep and the rich black ink would be sure to fill the space thickly. He ought to inspire fear— though he wasn't the man who scared her most in this business.

George Edwards had been second in command of the assassination attempt; it had been his urging that had spurred the plot onward, and his knowledge of Cabinet members' movements that had helped them fix on a time and place.

But George Edwards had been working as a government informer the whole time. He'd only played the part of a co-conspirator. For all anyone knew, Mr. Edwards might have come to witness the execution—might even have stood beside one of the condemned men's mothers in the crowd, offering a polite handkerchief to stem her desperate tears. Just as he'd offered false support to the son now on the scaffold.

Agatha didn't approve of violent revolution. No decent person wanted England to go through what France had suffered these past decades. And the recent Radical War in Scotland this past spring had brought the specter of an uprising far too close to home for the government's comfort. The laws had tightened, because the Lords were scared.

Agatha was no radical, herself. But every time she thought of George Edwards's deception, well . . . it twisted her stomach into knots.

Or maybe that was only the ache of hunger. How late was it?

Agatha looked up from her work for the first time in hours, and realized the shadows on the walls were from streetlamps and not the setting sun. The two Stanhope presses lurked like rooks against the east wall of the workroom, their long wooden arms skeleton-still now that the apprentices and journeyman had gone home for the night. Drying prints were pinned up around and over them, waving softly like shrouds.

Well, technically speaking, not all the apprentices had gone home. The lamplight coming through the back window cast a halo over the dark hair of Agatha's best apprentice,

Eliza Brinkworth, who occupied the spare bedroom upstairs and who was working quietly and patiently at the next table over, adding careful layers of color to a print of Thisburton's latest caricature. Her slender shoulders were hunched, her brow lightly furrowed as she brushed amber and ochre over the cartoonist's dancing fox figures.

Eliza had come to Griffin's with nothing more than a gift for sketching and a will to work. Now, four years later, she had blossomed into an able assistant in both copperplate engraving and woodcuts, and was the swiftest producer of sheet music blocks Griffin's had. The ballads she illustrated had become a reassuringly steady profit stream, as subscriptions to the luxurious *Griffin's Menagerie* ladies' magazine declined under the new stamp taxes. If Eliza had been Agatha's daughter, she would have been an ideal choice to take over the running of Griffin's.

But Agatha had no daughter. Instead she had only—

Out front the shop bell chimed. Then the door between the shop and the workroom opened.

"Hello, Mum!"

Agatha's heart soared skyward on helpless winds of maternal fondness at the sight of her son, returning from Birkett's, where he'd gone to settle the weekly bill for paper. He'd grown so tall and sturdy these past three years, a far cry from the thin and sensitive boy who'd hidden in his room for a month after his father's death. Nineteen-year-old Sydney was windblown and tousle-haired, bouncing with vitality, eyes bright with eager purpose, and just where the hell did he think he was going?

For after that hurried greeting, her son had vanished up the stair, with a clatter worthy of Hannibal and all his elephants.

Agatha frowned in suspicion. "Sydney Algernon Griffin!" she called. "You promised you'd—"

Before she could manage to set her work aside, block his way, and forestall an exit, Sydney reappeared at the foot of the stairwell. He'd changed his brown coat for one of bottle green, and the flush on his pale cheeks spoke of haste and excitement—but also, to his mother's keen sight, of guilt. "Going out again, Mum," he called cheerily. "Back late. Love you!"

"—print this plate—" Agatha managed, but not quickly enough. The doorway was empty, and the chime of the shop bell was the only reply she got.

So much for filial duty.

This was the bane of Agatha's current existence: she couldn't very well leave the business to her son if he was never around to run it.

Her temper surged like a storm cloud, and descended upon the only object available. Her apprentice, whose dark head lifted, and whose creamy complexion went rose red at the sight of her mistress's narrowed eye.

Lord, but weren't the young astonishing? Even at the end of a day so long as this, Eliza radiated keenness and energy. "Break for dinner, ma'am?" the girl piped. "I know it's Betsy's night off, so I could run to the Queen's Larder for a pie, if you like. One pie ought to be plenty for the two of us."

An attempt at distraction. It would not work. "Eliza,"

Agatha said, with careful clarity, "do you know where my son is off to this evening?"

The girl's glance flicked down, then back. "I couldn't say for certain, Mrs. Griffin."

Agatha's voice was cool as a razor. "Perhaps he is attending one of the Polite Society's chemistry lectures."

Eliza ducked her head. "Couldn't say, ma'am."

"A poetry reading? A concert? A play in some theater or other?"

Eliza shook her head.

Agatha drummed her fingers on the tabletop. "Dare I ask whether my son has developed a passion for Mr. Rossini's latest opera?"

Eliza sighed wistfully. "If only."

Agatha snorted.

Her apprentice blushed and bit her lip. "That is—I don't think so, ma'am."

"So." Agatha drummed her fingers again, four tiny beats like a guillotine march. "That leaves only one possibility. Eliza, tell me my precious, precocious Sydney is not bound for the Crown and Anchor, to drink bad ale and cheer for whoever is spouting tonight's most radical nonsense."

"It wouldn't be right to tell a lie, ma'am," Eliza said plaintively.

Agatha pinched at the bridge of her nose to keep her head from exploding in maternal vexation.

She knew part of this was her fault, really. She and Thomas had raised the boy in a print-shop, surrounded by persuasive pamphlets and cases of type waiting to be reordered and rearranged into new flights of rhetoric. Sydney swam in arguments like a fish—but Agatha was worried that only made him ready to be hooked and filleted.

Her voice ground out the old complaint. "I never expected him to be a paragon. He's a young man, after all. It's best to keep your expectations low if you want to avoid disappointment. I just wish his vices kept him more often at home!"

She cocked an eyebrow at Eliza, who was still squirming, even though the girl had done absolutely nothing to squirm about.

Unless . . .

"At least he doesn't seem prone to debauchery," Agatha said, watching carefully. "That's something."

Ah, yes, there it was, the flush spreading from the girl's cheeks to the tips of her ears. It was as good as cracking open her diary to read it in plain ink on paper.

Her son and her apprentice were more than merely friendly.

Not surprising, really. They were both healthy and young—oh, so young! Agatha could remember when nineteen seemed mature and wise and fully grown. It took nearly two decades to reach it, after all. But nineteen looked very different when you looked back on it from the lofty heights of forty-three. And forty-three would probably look green as grass from the cliffs of seventy-five, should Agatha be lucky enough to attain such a venerable age.

Time tumbled you forward, no matter how hard you fought to stay put.

Agatha sighed and looked down at the image on the

copper plate, with its burrs and burnishing. All those little figures, waiting for the acid bath to draw their lines sharp and true. Today they were everything; tomorrow they would be forgotten.

Well. No point in dwelling on the philosophical. Especially not when there was dinner to think of. And absolutely nothing was less philosophical than a steak and kidney pie. "Two pies, actually, Eliza," she said. "Two for us, and a third for Sydney—wherever and whenever he returns."

The apprentice nodded and was out the door in a flash, eager to escape while she was still in the luster of her mistress's good graces.

Agatha rose and threw open the door to the yard behind the workshop, letting the early summer night flood in. She sucked in deep lungfuls, savoring the rare moment of peace.

After dinner she would sink the copper into a basin of eye-watering aqua fortis to let the acid bite into the metal, then polish the rest of the wax away so the new plate would be ready for use when the journeymen came back in the morning. The presses would ring out, and another day's work would begin.

It was good work, constant and familiar, and Agatha liked it. But every now and again, especially in these moments of quiet, Agatha would peer up at the lamplight-dimmed stars and imagine taking her hand off the tiller, even for a moment.

What might it feel like, to not sense Time's drumbeat so close against the back of her neck? What vistas could she see, if she were able to lift her eyes for more than a moment from the rocky road beneath her hurrying feet?

She grimaced. Griffin's would go bankrupt within a week without her.

A print-shop needed a firm hand—Thomas had been steady and brilliant, but not forceful. Agatha had been the one to haggle over prices with the colormen who sold them ink and the stationers who sold them paper; Thomas had collected all the artists and poets and architects and fashion experts whose names graced bylines in the *Menagerie*—but it was Agatha who'd had to arrange payment and proofread their pieces and etch all the embroidery designs, copies of art, and furniture illustrations that made the *Menagerie* so popular among the *ton*. And it was Agatha who penned the scolding letters when a contracted writer let firm deadlines sail blithely by. She was the one who made all the journeymen jump to when she entered the workroom, and whose voice sent all the apprentices scrambling.

Not a ship captain, she thought, nor a steersman: they had set watches and times for rest. No, Agatha was more like . . . the wind in the sails, keeping the vessel on course.

If she ever stopped, it would be a disaster for everyone.

She was still frowning up at the sky when Eliza returned with the pies. And her worry didn't leave her when she got back to work. It haunted her like a little ghost, mournful and insistent, until she blew out the last tallow candle and tucked herself into her bed on the upper floor. It kept her from sleeping deeply, so she heard the precise moment when her son's footsteps thumped out an unsteady welcome on the stairs, to the musical echo of Eliza's answering giggle.

No doubt they thought they were being discreet.

Well, if they were making fools of themselves for love, they weren't the first. The real danger was Sydney's passion for political talk. What would his quiet, self-conscious father have thought about his son's gadding about with silver-spoon philosophers and revolutionaries?

Agatha sat up and punched the pillow.

As for the matter with Eliza, Thomas would have wanted to speak to the young couple directly, but despite the prickings of her conscience, Agatha was content to observe the pair for now. Best not to meddle in the affair until they were further along, or did one another some harm.

Which they probably would.

But secretly Agatha hoped they would make a real match of it. Eliza was sensible and clever, and Sydney for all his faults had inherited his father's good heart and earnest soul. Not that the two of them would be thinking of such practical matters: with them it would be all swoons and sonnets. Not any different from Thomas and Agatha, in their youth.

She only missed love when she took the time to remember it. That was the one thing that had never disappointed her.

She fell asleep to the memory of kisses from decades past, and a pair of hands whose ink stains were twin to hers.

Sometimes Penelope Flood imagined the small spire of St. Ambrose's was reaching up joyfully toward the heavens. Today, however, it felt more like the church's stone foundations were biting deep into the muddy earth.

It was probably the funeral. Famed local sculptress Isabella Abington, descended from Earls of Sufton, had been laid to rest this morning in the vault of her illustrious forebears. Sleeping stone figures of the first earl, his wife, and his son stretched out in the northwest corner of the church, their limbs entwined in cold, bone-white vines spotted with marble bees, some of which still bore traces of ancient gilt. Mr. Scriven, who kept goats up on Backey Green, said that these first Abingtons had been entombed in pure honey, preserving their bodies from decay.

Penelope had always thought this sounded unpleasantly sticky—but then, that sort of thing was to be expected of the dead. *A sticky end* was the phrase that sprang to mind, though probably not on account of the honey.

Penelope didn't know if the story was even true—Mr. Scriven had a way of embellishing a tale if he thought he wouldn't be caught out—but she liked the thought of it. Isabella had, too. The late lady might even have demanded the same entombment, if it weren't a certainty the vicar would have forbidden any such outlandish practice.

Now it was up to Penelope to tell the bees.

Abington Hall sat in stony splendor atop the hill just above St. Ambrose's, past Stokeley Farm and the empty cottage where the Marshes had lived until last winter. From up here you could see all of Melliton: the long ribbon of the river in the west, woods in the east, small hillocky hillocky hills in the north (dotted this time of year in small hillocky sheep), and the misty green of the farms that unrolled southward like a bolt of velvet flung toward the Thames. Cottages and manors and the streets of the town proper threaded these green patches like the veins in a leaf.

Aside from a few rare visits to London and the seaside, every breath of Penelope's forty-five years had been breathed out somewhere in this landscape. Her brothers had left one by one, to take over various branches of the Stanhope family's merchant enterprise. One brother slept beneath a stone in St. Ambrose's churchyard. Her parents had gone to rest there, too, a few years after. Penelope's husband had sailed away with her last brother—so now Penelope was on her own, with only letters to bridge the distance.

If she tried to walk away now, she'd have to leave her entire past behind, her soul wiped as clean as a newborn babe's.

She was far too comfortable here to contemplate starting over somewhere else. Especially when there was still so much work to do in Melliton.

Today's errand at least was simple, if somber. She paused outside the Abington Hall gate to fill her lungs with the good, clean scent of greenery and earth and last night's petulant rain. She'd worn her best lavender gown and a black crepe veil not for the crowd in church, but for this visit. She unpinned the hem of the crepe from where it rested across the crown of her head, and drew it down over her face, tucking it into her neckline so no skin was left exposed. Thick leather gloves didn't particularly suit the mourning mood, but she knew Isabella wouldn't object to her being a little practical.

After all, these weren't Penelope's bees she would be speaking to, even if they knew her.

She tugged open the gate and made her way through the grounds toward the bee garden.

Instead of a modern apiary, the bee garden had six hives in boles—small hollows set into the stone of the ancient wall, each just large enough for the straw dome of a single skep. A fountain in the center of the longest wall sent a burbling jet from a stone face into a larger basin beneath, and provided water for thirsty bees to drink. The grounds were planted with a riot of flowering trees, herbs, and blossoms: apple and lavender and hyssop, cowslips and yarrow and honeysuckle.

The gold-and-black-velvet bodies of honeybees danced from blossom to blossom, bearing their harvest back to their home hives. Insect wings caught the morning sunlight, tiny flashes of film and filigree that dazzled the eye and gentled the spirit.

That gentleness was deceptive, however: in a month or so, summer's bounty would make the bees as lazy and languorous as dowager duchesses, but in spring they were still sharp with winter's hunger and liable to sting anyone threatening their growing stores of honey and comb.

The trick was to be respectful, but not fearful. Bees could smell panic. So Penelope ambled from one hive to the next, knocking softly on the straw coils to get the bees' attention, then murmuring condolences on the passing of their mistress. Each knock set the hives buzzing softly, a small cloud of worker bees twirling up from the hive entrance to see who dared disturb their home in swarming season—but Penelope kept her movements slow and smooth and her voice low, and the bees soon settled again.

When she'd told the news to all six hives she stood by the fountain for a while, pulling the gloves off and tucking them in her pocket.

"Can you check that first hive again, Mrs. Flood?" Isabella asked. The elderly woman was wrapped tight against the winter wind, but her eyes were bright and her mouth set in a stern line that brooked no opposition. "I swear I saw a moth emerge from there the other morning."

It was still quite cool for wax moths, but they could do a lot of damage to a hive if they weren't caught in time, and Penelope didn't want Isabella to worry. So she did as commanded, puffing a little more smoke into the first hive and tilting the skep up so she could peer into the folds of comb inside.

"I see no larva, none of their webs," she called, "and the colony seems strong—plenty of ladies here to fight off intruders." Some of them were hovering around her head and hands as she worked, but the smoke had made the bees sleepy enough that she didn't fear their anger. She murmured an apology for disturbing them anyway—it paid to be polite to bees—and set the hive back down. Carefully, so as not to squash anybody.

As Penelope stood and turned back, Isabella hurriedly put down the edge of the skep, the sixth one, and stepped back as if she'd been caught stealing sweets from the kitchens.

Penelope clucked her tongue. "You know you should let me do that," she chided. A hive was heavy even at the start of spring, and Isabella's strength had been waning all winter.

Not that the sculptress was prepared to admit it. She shook her head back haughtily even now, those dark eyes that had enchanted an emperor flashing with defiance. "Never you mind," she said. "When I can't see to my own hives, you will know I am not long for this world."

And so it had come to pass, as though that proclamation were a prophecy: the chill Isabella had caught at Christmas moved into her lungs, and by April she had been too weak even to leave her bed. Penelope had taken over caring for the hives then, and intended to do so until Abington's heir relieved her of the duty.

She would miss her friend, who'd had so many stories from her travels around the world, but who'd never seemed to scorn Penelope for having stayed so timidly close to home. Penelope had given her extra wax for modeling, and Isabella had let Penelope borrow liberally from her library, never telling a merchant's daughter it wasn't seemly or useful to be interested in mathematics, or Roman history, or wild romantic poetry.

Penelope was still frozen, listening to the buzz of the bees and letting the tears fall beneath the crepe, when someone coughed politely behind her.

She wiped her eyes and raised her veil to find the vicar Eneas Oliver nodding at her solemnly. His black broadcloth looked very black indeed against the tender spring greens all around them. "*Nec morti esse locum*," he intoned, "*sed viva volare sideris.*"

Penelope smiled. "Nor is there any place for death, but living they fly to the stars."

The vicar nodded approval, his white-blond hair floating gently around his ears. "Virgil's fourth Georgic. Of course, my aunt always preferred Ovid. But no one would dare quote lecherous Ovid for a funeral."

"Not even the last books of the *Tristia?*" Penelope protested. "He was so poignant in exile."

Mr. Oliver ignored this, glancing from Penelope to the hives. "Were you reviving that old pagan superstition, Mrs. Flood? Telling the bees?" He shook his head, amused and superior.

"Your Virgil was a pagan, too, sir," Penelope retorted, then immediately regretted it. This was no day to be drawn into old arguments—especially not with the man who'd taught her her first lessons about bees. Her next words were softer. "Miss Abington will be much missed."

"Thank you," the vicar murmured, his voice thickening.

Penelope looked politely away, and for a moment the only sounds were the burbling of the water and the humming of the hives.

Eventually Mr. Oliver said, "I used to come here as a boy. At first for the apples, but later, more and more, for the bees. Old Mr. Monkham was the gardener in those days—he showed me how to approach the hives safely, and how to harvest the honey when autumn came. Every time I talk about sulfur on Sundays, I remember his lessons."

Penelope remembered Mr. Monkham, too. He'd had her older brother Harry soundly whipped once for stealing a handful of strawberries. "Fewer beekeepers are using sulfur these days," she murmured. "It's so wasteful, killing all your hives every year, when there are other methods for getting honey."

"None so traditional, though. And none so in harmony with the ultimate fate of human souls." The vicar brushed aside one golden lady, buzzing curiously around his pale hair. "We mortals end in sulfur, too, don't we? While the best fruits of our labor are gathered elsewhere, by more illustrious hands than ours. And our lives are bounded by larger powers beyond our comprehension."

"Are you saying you like bees because they make you feel like God?" Penelope asked tartly.

Mr. Oliver laughed indulgently. "It helps keep my mind fixed on eternal rewards, if I am in constant contact with creatures so ephemeral as these," he said. "Though there are certainly ways in which tending a beehive and tending a parish are startlingly similar. Both prosper best under the guidance of an educated mind."

They prosper if you keep them, not if you kill them, Penelope thought, but only bit her lip. The fate of the Abington hives was out of her hands.

The vicar heaved a sigh. "But speaking of duty . . . May I escort you back to the house, Mrs. Flood? I believe my sister has laid out a luncheon for the mourners."

Penelope nodded, and they walked through the gardens and into Abington Hall proper, where Melliton society had gathered to mark the loss of their most prominent personage.

People looked up, then quickly looked away again, dismissing Penelope. *Oh,* those lightning glances seemed to say, *it's only her. You know, merchant's daughter, the eccentric one? Wears* men's clothes around, does something with bees, I don't know what. What on earth can one actually do with bees?

These were the cream of the local gentry: the men with gold watch chains and the women in gauzy silks, purchased with the rents from the tenants and smallholders Penelope drank with most evenings in the Four Swallows. Or else these fine folk claimed the profits from the boats other men steered up and down the river Ethel, carrying goods to and from London and more far-flung counties. Even if they'd never dream of opening a ledger themselves, or paying an invoice, or asking what kinds of goods they traded in, or who died producing those goods.

These were the people who thought to have money was everything, but to earn it was a scandal. Penelope's family had enough money to be acceptable, but not nearly enough to make her friendship valuable.

Mr. Oliver nodded farewell and went to murmur among them, using all the correct words and expected phrases.

After the freshness of grass and apple blossom, Penelope found the hall's warm, close mix of scents and polishes and perfumes painfully cloying. She quickly made her way to the drinks on the sideboard, and let the fizzy richness of Mrs. Bedford's cider drive away all other fumes and flavors. The Abington Hall housekeeper was a ten-year champion brewer at the town fair, and Penelope never missed a chance to sample her creations.

Most of the mourners around her were dressed in sober grays and browns and purples as they went through the careful minuet of grieving in public. Smiles reined in, voices hushed, a certain stiffness about the shoulders that said they were burdened by sorrow but not too much sorrow, an embarrassed sort of sadness—as though Death were an acquaintance whose face was familiar but whose name you couldn't quite recall, and you were trying to nod politely as you hurried down the street before they could detain you long enough that you'd be compelled to stop and chat.

Only the family were in the black of full mourning: the vicar, his sister and brother-in-law Viscount and Viscountess Summerville, and of course Mrs. Joanna Molesey, Isabella's longtime companion and friend.

Rather more than a friend, according to the gossips.

Penelope knew that not only were the gossips right, but in this instance they dreadfully understated the case: having spent many hours visiting the two women at home, and hearing about their shared adventures abroad, Penelope was in no doubt that Miss Abington and Mrs. Molesey had loved one another as deeply and passionately as any two people ever could. Mrs. Molesey was an accomplished poet in the habit of reading early drafts of her work aloud, and at home her sly and witty love lyrics were always addressed to an alluring and unnamed *she*, though the published poems often changed the pronouns. When they didn't, they bore the delicate subtitle: *In imitation of Sappho.*

Penelope was not the only one able to decipher such a code, and so Melliton society often moved in uneasy ripples and eddies around Mrs. Molesey, even as they basked in her fame and intellectual luster.

Right now the poet herself sat in splendid isolation on

a scrolled bench against one wall: chin high, steel-gray hair swept back, her face ghostly pale against the black bombazine of her gown. All around her, mourners in pairs and trios kept themselves at careful oblique angles—they knew they couldn't turn their backs outright, not today of all days, but they still wanted not to engage if they could avoid it. As though the palpable weight of her grief were enough to drag all of them down.

Well, Penelope was humble enough in the instep that few of the high-born people in this room really noted what she did. And she wasn't afraid of grief. She plucked a few small morsels from the sideboard and cut directly through the crowd to the bench.

"When did you eat last?" she asked Mrs. Molesey, then shook her head. "Never mind—you should eat something now."

The poet accepted the offering of bread and cold meat, and even nibbled on a corner of a slice.

Penelope's spirits rose. "You can have my cider if you want it."

"No, thank you—I've a thin enough rein on my control at the moment, which spirits would undo entirely," the lady murmured, the rich timbre of her voice rougher than Penelope had ever heard it. One corner of that long mouth tilted up. "Unless you want me to lose all control of my tongue. If I wanted to, I could send up such a shriek as would whiten the hair of every prune-faced hypocrite trying to playact plain and honest sorrow."

Penelope cast an instinctive glance at Lady Summerville,

who was indeed pursing her lips and relentlessly projecting an air of winsomely-carrying-on-through-near-collapse that would have done credit to any ingenue on the stage.

The poet caught the direction of her gaze, and leaned close. "Yes, to look at her you'd never guess how truly eager she is to punt me out of the house and take her aunt's place. She expects to inherit everything, as Bella's only living relative. Well, aside from Mr. Oliver—but he's quite comfortable in the vicarage, I'm sure. He's certainly richer than his sister and her lord, the title notwithstanding." Mrs. Molesey's chuckle was half creak, as though long disused. "I do hope she'll give me time to change before she evicts me, at least. Black is an impossible color for traveling."

Penelope's laugh was helpless and far too loud. It paused all conversation and set every eye rolling her way.

She could see their thoughts as though they were written in the air: *that Penelope Flood again—can she never be serious for a moment?* She took a long pull of cider, blushing painfully, and smoothed at her skirts with her free hand.

The murmur of polite conversation rose up again like the tide.

Mrs. Molesey's smile deepened enough to dimple. "So at least now they have someone else's behavior to cluck about. Thank you, Mrs. Flood."

Her cheeks burned. "It was the least I could do."

The poet took another absentminded bite of bread, and Penelope bit her lip to prevent herself from saying something encouraging about it. Judging by her earlier declaration, Mrs. Molesey was liable to take to fasting just for the sake of being contrary. Her emotions ran volatile, though deep and true. Penelope could just see her reclining on an antique chaise in Grecian robes, head tilted proudly, one hand tragically on her brow, reciting shiversome verses about wasting away until death reunited her with her lost love.

Penelope had loved a few people in her time—but she'd never loved anybody to such poetic heights. That was the one thing she'd truly envied Isabella Abington and Joanna Molesey: not the adventures, not the fame, not even the artistic success both women had found. Maybe they all came as a set, and one couldn't lay claim to a devoted, passionate love without flinging oneself into the world and hunting it down.

Penelope was the furthest thing from a hunter. She should probably resign herself to her fate: furtive affairs and transitory dalliances. And fewer and fewer of those as the years went on. Oh, and an absent husband—so long and so frequently absent that she tended to forget Mr. Flood even existed. And theirs had certainly not been a love match, in any case.

The sweet-tartness of the cider burned like acid on her tongue.

Mr. Nancarrow, the most expensive of Melliton's solicitors, approached the sofa to interrupt Penelope's gloomy reverie. His narrow face was set in its gentlest expression, but there was no softening the sharp angles of his chin and cheekbones. He bowed low and said: "I beg your pardon, Mrs. Molesey, Mrs. Flood, but I must ask you to step into the library with me for the reading of the will."

"Both of us?" Penelope asked, surprised. She'd known Isabella had liked her, but enough to be included in the bequests?

"Both, please," confirmed Mr. Nancarrow.

Penelope drained her cider and followed obediently as the solicitor led the way to the study, collecting Mr. Oliver and Lord and Lady Summerville along the way.

CHAPTER TWO

The library was the primary battlefield in the war between order, as represented by the housekeeper and her strictly trained staff, and chaos, as embodied solely but sensationally by Joanna Molesey. Stacks of books the poet pulled out for use in her writing would be cruelly tidied away before she was finished with them; as a counterattack, she would rearrange selected shelves in unusually frustrating ways and see how long it took Mrs. Bedford to notice the Shakespeare volumes were out of order because Joanna had set them alphabetical by first line, or reshelved the history section in order of ascending length of title.

Today it looked as though Mrs. Molesey was carrying the war: half the Shakespeare was off the shelf and strewn about the room, and Penelope recognized a goodly number of volumes of Byron, Herrick, Moody, Dante, and Donne on the grand oak desk before Mr. Nancarrow shifted them so he could sit with his hands barristerially folded in front of him.

Viscount Summerville immediately sprawled on the sofa with a whoosh of breath like a horse just come from a hunt. He was a mass of muscle and heartiness, from the wind-tousled auburn hair to the ruddy cheeks. His wife took a seat beside him; he shifted to ensure they weren't touching. Not out of any concern for propriety, Penelope knew—rumors said his lordship had a mistress and three children two towns over, and that he spent as much time away from home as he possibly could.

Perhaps that was why Lady Summerville had always guarded her status as if it were rare porcelain. She had a great deal of venom to pour on those who failed to treat her with proper care, as though her position and authority were one chip away from a shatter.

Mr. Oliver pulled out a spindly chair next to his sister, patting her hand solicitously, and Mrs. Molesey settled into her usual armchair as if it were a throne. Her face was serene, but Penelope saw how her hands clenched and unclenched on the riveted plush of the arms.

Penelope made her way over to the window, where she could stay more or less out of the way and steal glances at the garden all the while.

At least it shouldn't take terribly long. The Abingtons had been absurdly rich in prior centuries, when the hall had been built, but the family had been in decline for generations, and now both their fortunes and their family tree were decidedly scanty.

Mr. Nancarrow picked up the papers with a look of dread as if he spoke at his own funeral, not his client's. After the usual introductory statements—Penelope half listened while watching the clouds scudding across blue sky—the solicitor harrumphed a little for fortitude and moved on to the essential clauses.

"Mrs. Abington left behind a sum of two thousand, three hundred and forty-seven pounds, as well as Abington Hall. Fifty pounds will go to Mr. Oliver, Miss Abington's nephew. The house and grounds will go to Lord and Lady Summerville, along with . . ." He took a breath, then plunged forward. ". . . Along with the collection of statues in the sculpture garden."

Lady Summerville sucked in a gasp.

Mr. Nancarrow shut his mouth, flinching slightly.

"*Which* statues?" the lady choked out.

"The ones . . . exterior to the house," the solicitor confirmed miserably, eyes on the printed sheets in his hand.

"The ones where my aunt—where she—with no—with all the . . ." The viscountess's voice vanished into a horrified whisper.

Mr. Nancarrow ducked his head and tried to sink his long chin protectively against his chest. Either that or embarrassment muffled his voice. "The ones your aunt only showed to select visitors here at the Hall, yes, my lady."

"The *erotic* statues," Mrs. Molesey said loudly and with evident savor.

Lord Summerville let out a hum that rose at the end like a curious question.

The glance his wife sent him could have carved his heart into ribbons before he even had time to bleed.

The vicar went cherry red in the face and cleared his throat. "What about the rest of the estate?" Mr. Oliver asked.

Mr. Nancarrow straightened the papers unnecessarily, still hunched as if bracing himself against a coming storm. "The remainder goes to Mrs. Molesey, with affection, in gratitude for her years of faithful companionship."

Lady Summerville's whole body clenched like a fist.

The poet merely inclined her head, evidently unsurprised by this news.

"Along with . . ." Mr. Nancarrow cleared his throat, closed his eyes, and swallowed hard. "Along with a diamond snuffbox of particular sentimental value to them both."

"The Napoleon snuffbox?" For a moment Lady Summerville looked as though she were going to lunge right up from the couch and grab the solicitor by the throat—then she recalled herself and clutched to her husband's arm as if seeking support. He curled his lip but made no move to dislodge her. "Surely not!" the lady cried. "Surely such a valuable and *historic* heirloom should remain with a loving member of the family!"

Mrs. Molesey leaned forward in her chair. "You are quick to name yourself family now, are you? Yet you've visited only twice in the past ten years, though you live only two towns over." She narrowed her eyes. "If that's how family behaves—"

"Ladies, please," Mr. Oliver broke in, in his best Sunday voice.

Mrs. Molesey bit back whatever accusation she'd planned, glaring fiercely at the interrupter.

The vicar went on, tones rolling around the room like church bells. "Perhaps there has simply been some mistake." He rose from his chair and approached the desk, smiling gently and holding his hand out for the will. "Surely you got those bequests confused, Mr. Nancarrow? Surely the snuffbox was meant to go to my sister, and the statues to Mrs. Molesey? They are . . . rather more to her taste, I believe."

The lady in question snorted again at this euphemism.

Mr. Nancarrow's timidity went icy at this affront to his professional competence. "I assure you, Mr. Oliver, there has been no mistake. Mrs. Abington made herself perfectly clear in this point on several occasions." Two spots of red appeared in his cheeks. "Though I beg you to spare me from quoting her remarks verbatim."

"Of course he's not mistaken," Mrs. Molesey said with a sharp little laugh. "What would be the point of leaving me all those pretty statues, and nowhere to show them off? But you, Ann—you have such a charming home, with so many charming corners to fill. You can place Bella's artworks where all your charming friends can admire them."

She laughed harder as Lady Summerville spluttered, and the viscount began to look alarmed at the way his lady's hand fisted tighter and tighter on his arm, pulling the fabric of his coat dangerously taut.

Mr. Oliver saw this and moved hastily, coming around to his sister's side and bending down toward her ear for a fiercely whispered conference.

Penelope edged toward the solicitor, who was mopping at his brow with a handkerchief. Poor man, he must have been dreading this. "Was there a bequest for me, Mr. Nancarrow?"

"Hmm?" The solicitor blinked, then basked in relief at having been asked a simple question in a friendly tone. "Oh, did I not say? I am terribly sorry. Let me see . . . yes. You, Mrs. Flood, are bequeathed the Abington beehives. Or rather the care of them, since it specifies they are to remain at Abington."

"The hives?" Penelope exclaimed.

Mr. Oliver's head came up, and his surprised eyes met hers.

"But . . ." She swallowed her objections for poor Mr. Nancarrow's sake. Yet it was such an odd bequest: the vicar was an able beekeeper in his own right, more than capable of handling half a dozen simple skeps in addition to his own more scientific hives.

What on earth had Isabella been playing at?

She retreated to the window again, uncomfortably aware of the vicar's eyes following her, his expression one of careful, virtuous consternation.

Lady Summerville was whispering in a low hiss like a kettle on the boil, and her husband was blustering back as he tried to free himself from her grip.

Mrs. Molesey was sitting regally back to watch, as if the rest of the party were fools capering to entertain her.

Penelope looked out the window—which had an excellent view of both the bee garden and the maze that held

Lady Summerville's new statue collection—and imagined she could hear Isabella's mischievous laugh on the wind, one final time.

There was no sweeter privilege of motherhood than knocking at dawn on the door of one's self-indulgent son, only to observe when the door creaked open that he was spine-shudderingly, knee-wobblingly, and stomach-churningly hungover.

"Good morning, my dear," Agatha trilled extra-brightly, smugness wrapping around her like a warm, comforting shawl.

Sydney managed a pained whimper in response. Heavens, but he looked like he'd been turned inside out and then back again and his skin no longer hung quite correctly on his bones.

Agatha let her voice turn syrup-sweet. "What say I make you something special for breakfast? Kippers and bacon? Eggs and gravy? Jellied eel in a brandy sauce?"

Sydney's face went from white to green and then gone, as he slammed the door in her face—presumably to have a private tête-à-tête with his chamber pot.

The slam of the door and Agatha's full-throated cackle brought Eliza blinking out of her room, leaning on the door and peering around into the hall. "Ma'am?"

"You'll have to run the shop today," Agatha told her. "Sydney's a little the worse for wear, and I must drive to Melliton with the Crewe silk samples." Yesterday she had set one of the newer apprentices, Jane, to cutting the bolt of shimmering brocade into precise squares, ready to be tipped in with the printed pages and bound with the magazine.

It had been one of Thomas's best ideas, including fabric from all the finest weaving works—not only silks, but wool and chintzes and patterned calicos, and the occasional lush velvet in winter. It also gave them an excuse to solicit advertisements from London modistes, to tempt ladies who wanted something more complex or ambitious than their own needles and skills could supply.

"Of course, ma'am," Eliza said, tucking an errant lock behind her ear. "Will you be stopping over in Melliton?"

Agatha was impressed despite herself: the girl's question had almost sounded innocent. Though she was obliquely asking if she and Sydney were to be left alone for an entire night.

"Absolutely not," she said repressively, and had the satisfaction of seeing her apprentice's face fall just a little. The print-shop always took precedence over romance; it took precedence over everything. "We have Mr. Thisburton coming round tomorrow morning, remember."

"Yes, ma'am." Eliza bobbed a curtsey—an occasional tic from her old life as a maid in the Countess of Moth's house—and hurried to wash her face and dress for the day.

Agatha made her way downstairs to unlock the workroom and let in the half-dozen workers clustered on the threshold. They all streamed in with the dawn, nodding to their employer. Soon the early morning quiet yielded to noise as everyone went about the makeready: preparing formes, woodblocks, paper, and ink for the day's jobbing. Eliza had gathered her tools and a pewter plate readied with musical staves, then settled into the shop front, tidy and smiling and ready to punch notes and hand-engrave crescendos until the day's first customers arrived.

Agatha paused in the doorway between shop and work-room and surveyed her small kingdom, letting herself briefly bask in the sounds of a machine in good working order. The business would probably tick along steadily until evening—but *Griffin's Menagerie* was still the bulwark on which the business stood firm. For now, anyway. And the *Menagerie* had to be printed on the speedier press at Melliton.

So Agatha buttoned up her coat, climbed into the wagon, took the reins firmly in her gloved hands, and made her way northeast.

The roads weren't bad, especially once she got out of the city. The hired horse, Augustus, was a focused, plodding sort of animal, and Agatha had only to keep a little tension on the reins to guide him on the way. The sun was out and the wind was fresh and birds were singing in the meadows and fields on either side.

Agatha cordially loathed all of it.

It wasn't that it wasn't beautiful. It would have made a very salable engraving. Wildflowers and birdsong and all that rot. Such picturesque scenery ought to have been peaceful, according to every poet that she'd ever heard of. The prob-lem was that getting outside London, away from high walls and narrow streets and the press of people, made Agatha feel every inch of the loneliness she usually was so good at distracting herself from.

The wide, blue stretch of sky that arced above only served to remind her that she carried something just as blue and stark and empty inside her breast.

She chewed her lip and distracted herself from the pangs by listing off every color she would use to illustrate the scene: lapis and azure and aquamarine, of course, then lead white, ochre, vermillion . . .

Finally, just when Agatha was about to perish from impatience—roughly an hour—she turned off the main road, followed the drive a half mile more, and turned the last corner before the printworks itself.

A journeyman spotted her from a window and ran out to begin hauling in the bundled silk samples, while Agatha made sure one of the printer's devils saw to the horse's comfort. Once Gus was brushed and fed and cropping happily at the small fenced field to one side, Agatha reluctantly turned toward the building itself.

The Melliton printworks had started life as a flour mill, and there was still something bakerish about the way the light warmed the red brick and wooden beams. Here was where they printed the *Menagerie* and book-length works, as opposed to the single-page broadside prints and pamphlets produced by the London shop. Thomas had built an extra wing on one side of the building to store Griffin's collection of stereotype plates, and converted the central space into a light and airy workshop. Behind the printworks the river Ethel was running high and frothy today, muttering like a mob with a grievance. The same water entered the building through a pipe to feed the ever-hungry boiler in the basement. Agatha had been down there only once, when the steam engine was first installed, but still felt her throat close up when she remembered the sounds and the heat and the hiss of it.

Enough wasting time, she chided herself. There was too much work to be done.

She brushed the dust of the road from her skirts, squeezed her fists for strength, and made her way toward the entrance on the south corner. The windows were wider here, letting in the early summer sun. Those sweet golden rays warmed everything except the hard, icy core of Agatha's heart.

This place, more than anywhere else, reminded her of Thomas, and even after three years it gave her a jolt of grief to cross over the threshold.

It shouldn't have been such a shock, should it? After all, aside from the fact that the press here was steam-powered and therefore faster, it wasn't that much different from the London shop. Roughly the same size, the same smell of ink and metal and oil. The same anxious nods and greetings from journeymen and apprentices and devils, though the staff was smaller and the names were different: Downes and Jarden and the Ashton brothers.

Except Agatha had only ever been here occasionally, until Thomas died. He'd selected the building and hired everyone who worked here, making trips out while Agatha ran things in London. Three years later, it still felt as though they were all of them, Agatha included, simply carrying on temporarily until his return.

She took a seat at her usual worktable, brilliant with light from the tall front windows. Downes wasted no time in pleasantries, but promptly brought her a proof of the next issue as the two young Ashtons went to the stacked manuscripts and began inserting one silk sample near the end of every set.

"Mind you keep the corners neat for the binders," Agatha said, mostly to have something to scold them for. She preferred to keep her apprentices on their toes.

She cast a skeptical eye over the proof but Downes knew his business, and the thing looked as neat as human labor could make it. Some new fashions in curtains, a view of Rome in ruins—copied from a painting Agatha had seen in last year's Summer Exhibition—the next thrilling chapter of a sentimental serial. And at the end of it all the Crewe silk brocade, sky blue bordered with bouquets of wildflowers, lustrous and bright as high summer.

It twigged something in her memory, both painful and pleasant. She frowned forcefully down at the blossoms until her brain dredged up the answer: ah, yes, an old scrap of verse, back from when Agatha and Thomas were newly betrothed—he'd printed the lines for her special, on the sly, setting the type in secret late at night after the shop had closed. Something about *to weave fresh garlands for the glowing brow,* or thereabouts.

Her husband was not, of course, the poem's author.

Thomas adored poetry, but never attempted it himself. This was fine by Agatha, who had neither an eye nor an ear for poetry.

But she did like Thomas—and she liked to be thought of.

Griffin's had published that poet, and the plates for her volume were stored not fifty yards away from where she sat.

"Anything amiss, ma'am?" Downes inquired, an edge of unwonted anxiety in his tone.

"Hmm?" Agatha said, then shook herself. "No, Mr. Downes, just strategizing."

Those poems would make a very tempting little book at this time of year, when love hovered in the air, waiting for young lungs to breathe it in like so many wildflower scents.

Agatha let herself stroke one finger over shimmering brocade before handing the pages back and pronouncing the issue approved. "I'm going to pull some old plates from the back for reprinting," she said. "What's the queue like at the moment?"

"Not as full as I like to keep it, to be honest. We've got ten or so more pages in the new edition of *Celestial Mechanics* and then we're clear," Downes replied. "I'd planned on getting started on some of next issue's embroidery plates, but there's room if you want to add something."

"I was thinking about a short run of Joanna Molesey. That first volume always sold well. And it's close to the Romantics people love these days, without the scandal."

Downes made a face. "You sure people will buy it, without the scandal?"

"Hmph." Agatha pursed her lips, but the corners crept up in spite of herself.

Downes grinned, the inevitable ink swipe on his cheek looking extra dark against that flash of teeth.

Agatha nodded, making the decision final. "We can advertise it as a cure for the ills of this decadent age, maybe."

Downes went back to supervising the print queue, and Agatha crooked her finger at one of the Ashtons, then strode through the door and into the cavernous space of the warehouse proper.

At once several pounds of tension dropped away from her shoulders. This was familiar. This was comforting. This was home.

The high, narrow windows let sunlight fall on the maze of shelves filling the rest of the space. Each shelf was made of sturdy oak, reinforced at the joins, braced in copper as much as possible to carry the weight of the lead stereotype plates. Any printer who ran more than a jobbing press soon amassed their own collection of these, given time: setting type every time you wanted a new edition of something popular was both slow and expensive—with stereotyping, you made a clay or papier-mâché cast of the type, then poured molten type metal into that, and when it cooled you'd have a perfect ready-made plate to hand whenever you needed more copies of a book or print or poem. You could even make corrections and change typographical errors, if you were clever about it. Griffin's had been in the printing business for nearly a century, passing from father to daughter to son and so forth, and for at least the past fifty years they had been storing plates in this same warehouse.

Agatha was a Griffin by marriage, not birth, but her

father had been a printer, and this place always took her back to her childhood and made her feel pleasantly nostalgic. Letters large and small marched backward across the plates as they leaned against one another—rather like tombstones, but tombstones that were certain of their resurrection.

That was the comfort in being useful: it saved you from becoming neglected, or discarded.

Agatha flipped through the ledger on the shelf by the door. *Molesey: Poems, 28.* Far back corner, apparently. Agatha beckoned to the one young Ashton—really, she ought to learn to tell which was which at some point—and led the way back into the maze.

The hum of the river grew louder the farther she walked. It really was sounding quite angry, with an alarming, persistent kind of whine on top of it . . . then Agatha reached aisle 28 and realized that wasn't the river she was hearing at all.

Her heart seized and her blood ran cold.

Bees. Hundreds of them, it looked like, in a mass on the edges of one shelf of plates. Buzzing, darting about, flashing in the sunlight like tiny winged arrows. Wriggling, *crawling*, even over one another—as though they weren't individual creatures at all, but rather some nebulous, amorphous blob of insect awareness.

Beside her young Ashton gasped and began to move forward.

Agatha seized him by the shoulder before he could get himself stung. "Not too close," she warned. "Who knows what could set them off?"

She kept her grip on him tight, even as she peered forward. Yes, of course, as luck would have it, there was a broken window at the end of aisle twenty-eight. The bees must have found their way in through that.

They had been making themselves comfortable here for . . . Agatha didn't know how long. Long enough to have started several honeycombs, obviously—the folds of them hung from the plates for Molesey's *Poems*, long glistening golden curves.

One of the insects buzzed closer, as though scouting for threats; Agatha stepped back, dragging young Ashton helplessly with her.

Agatha reminded herself to breathe, sucked in a fear-chilled lungful, and belatedly worried she might breathe in bees. But the insects seemed mostly interested in their own business, adding more comb little by little to secure their hold upon Molesey territory.

Agatha had had books stolen and pirated before—what printer hadn't?—but to have a book colonized by bees? It was absurd.

No, more than absurd: it was *flummoxing*, is what it was. Agatha was flummoxed. Bewildered, confounded, and absolutely discombobulated. She had no experience to guide her over this obstacle.

Carelessness she could reprimand. Accidents were bound to happen sometimes. But . . . bees? What on earth did a printer do about bees?

Agatha chewed on her lip and told herself to use her

brains. When you didn't know the answer to a question, the first thing was to find out who did.

She knew someone who knew bees. Thomas's elderly mother, Eva Ladler Griffin Stowe: a woman who had given three husbands back to God but kept their names. She also kept a few hives of bees in her garden.

It was somewhere to start, anyway.

Agatha hauled young Ashton back to work, gave Downes instructions to let nobody near aisle 28, and was out the door.

Agatha liked her mother-in-law a great deal, but the time they had briefly shared a home after Thomas's death had been difficult. It had been a relief for both of them when Mrs. Stowe announced her intention to move back to Melliton. Now Mrs. Stowe shared a small house with a spinster friend on the west edge of town. Miss Coningsby managed the house and Mrs. Stowe the garden, so they each had their kingdom.

Agatha didn't bother to knock at the door but simply let herself in through the side gate and walked around to the small walled plot at the back.

There Mrs. Stowe sat, as she always did in fine weather, watching her roses slowly spread their petals.

Her hands were crawling with bees.

Agatha had seen this trick before, but it never failed to make her shudder a little. "Are you sure you should be doing that?"

"Their stings help with the aches." Mrs. Stowe turned her head and the delicate parchment wrinkles of her face folded into a grin. "They don't sting me often, of course, but I appreciate the sacrifice when they do."

She lifted her hands and shook them gently, and the bees detached themselves and flew back to the hive against the low wall at the back.

"So you might enjoy a gift of more bees?" Agatha said, moving closer and dropping a kiss of greeting on the older woman's proffered cheek. "I happen to know of some that are in need of a new home."

"You've seen a swarm?" Mrs. Stowe brightened. "Were they flying or had they settled somewhere?"

"Very settled—they're colonizing the back corner of my warehouse."

"Oh." Mrs. Stowe laughed. "Then they need rehiving. You'll be wanting to talk to Mrs. Flood."

"I'll talk to anybody who knows how to get rid of bees."

"Mrs. Flood knows *everything* about bees." Mrs. Stowe's voice was emphatic with conviction. "What's more—she'll know if someone's in need of a new colony. And she's kind. A little too kind for her own good, probably."

Agatha huffed. "What does kindness have to do with it?"

Mrs. Stowe clucked her tongue, as though Agatha were a stubborn child avoiding her lessons. "Because *you* don't know anything about bees, and you're asking her a favor."

"I could pay—"

"Don't you dare."

Agatha snapped her mouth shut.

Mrs. Stowe's smile broadened. "This isn't London," Mrs. Stowe went on, more mildly. "We don't usually send invoices around when we help one another. And Mrs. Flood has money enough that she doesn't worry about getting more." She raised her elbows to the arm of the chair, steepling her fingers. "You might have to be in Mrs. Flood's debt for a little while, is all. Until you find a way to pay her back in kind."

Agatha shrugged, though even the mention of the word *debt* made her itch between the shoulder blades. She skated too close to that edge too often, and the anxiety of it was rarely far from her thoughts.

But she couldn't just *leave* the bees in the warehouse. It was untenable. That meant the bees would win.

There was only one decision to be made. Agatha steeled herself, and made it. "Where might this Mrs. Flood be found?"

Chapter Three

The Four Swallows tavern stood where Melliton met the river Ethel, and it was the custom for some of the local bee-keepers to take their nuncheon together there on the small pier that stretched out into the water. Penelope had walked her usual southern circuit in the morning, and would circle around the cottages and farms to the north in the afternoon, checking on everyone's hives, but the summer days were long and left plenty of time for a leisurely midday meal.

A willow overhanging the bank offered some shade, its fluttering leaves making the light shimmer in a way that would have been much more pleasant had Mr. Painter not been clouding the air with tobacco smoke from the pipe he was huffing into.

Mr. Koskinen shook his head and took an aggrieved draught of his beer, blowing smoke away from the surface of the liquid before bringing the pewter tankard to his lips.

Mr. Biswas was laughing silently, gray whiskers shaking against his brown skin.

Penelope had started to laugh, too, but it had turned into a cough that left her breathless, with tears leaking from smoke-reddened eyes. "Enough, Mr. Painter! It makes me dizzy."

"Aye," the man said, between puffs on the pipe, "but it makes the bees dizzy, too, doesn't it? Goes to show: tobacco smoke beats wood smoke for tending hives."

"Unless the tobacco makes the beekeeper so disoriented she stumbles and knocks over the skep," Penelope countered with a wheeze. "Besides, it adds a bitterness to the honey. Give me a good base of pine needles and vary the aromatics: lavender for spring, dried roses in summer, orange peel for fall."

"I find puffball mushrooms are best, myself," Mr. Biswas offered.

Penelope was horrified. "Miss Abington always warned me that would kill the bees!"

"No, not if you're careful." Mr. Biswas pursed his lips and confessed, "If you're truly careful, you wrap some linen around your mouth when you use it. For caution's sake."

Mr. Painter went back to smoking normally, and the air soon cleared again. His mouth worked thoughtfully around the pipe stem. "What do you use, Timo?"

Timo Koskinen tilted his shaggy red head and considered the question. He'd been a sailor before his marriage, but now he was perhaps the most learned beekeeper in Melliton: his octagonal glass observation hive was a marvel of engineering, and he'd read just about everything there was to read on the subject.

Perhaps the weight of all that knowledge was a burden, because Timo Koskinen could never, ever be rushed when someone asked him a question about bees.

A swallow darted by, flirting with the surface of the river. Beneath the willow branches a trout appeared, snapping at mayflies that hovered just out of reach.

Mr. Biswas twisted a section of his whiskers idly between his fingers.

Mr. Painter tapped the ash out of his pipe and refilled it, tamping the brown leaf down into a sturdy pack. Likely his own product, imports of which had bought him one of the finest houses in Melliton.

And still Mr. Koskinen considered. Lazily he raised one calloused finger and scratched his weather-reddened chin.

Penelope's attention wandered, caught by the ripple of wind on water and pulled downriver by the speed of the current. So she happened to be looking in the direction of the print-works and the old military barracks when the woman appeared.

She was in close-tailored gray, with streaks of silver snaking through her dark hair and a flush of agitation blooming in her pale face. Her eyes sparkled with irritation; her mouth was a stern slash. Penelope knew at once that when she spoke, her tone would be sharp, and her patience with waywardness thin.

Beneath the collar of her shirt, Penelope felt her neck grow hot.

Oh. Oh, dear.

The woman came to a stop, hands on hips, eyes on Penelope. "Are you Mrs. Flood?"

Penelope knew what she must look like: a round, graying woman in trousers and a man's coat, skin dusted with tan and freckles, hair cropped at her ears, battered old boots, rather plain and potato-shaped in all. Sitting—and drinking—with a group of weathered former sailors in the middle of the day. "That's me," she said cheerfully.

The woman narrowed her eyes. "I am Agatha Griffin. My husband's mother said I might find you here."

"I know plenty of husbands," Penelope replied, and grinned. "Even more of their mothers."

Mr. Biswas sputtered out a surprised laugh, but subsided under the blade of Mrs. Griffin's gaze.

Penelope cocked her head. "It would be Mrs. Stowe who sent you?"

The woman's gaze slid back to Penelope. It had lost none of its steel in the journey. "I need your help with some bees."

All four beekeepers sobered. Penelope drained the last of the ale in her tankard and rose to her feet. "Gentlemen," she said, with a nod of farewell. "Let me know what Mr. Koskinen's answer was."

Mr. Biswas chortled and Mr. Painter gestured regally with his pipe.

Mr. Koskinen swallowed his feelings along with another pull of his beer.

Penelope turned to Mrs. Griffin. "We'll have to stop by

my house first to gather a few things. I live on the edge of the wood, just west of town."

Mrs. Griffin nodded, and Penelope shouldered her pack and began leading the way.

It was a fine day for a stroll, but no matter how sweet the breeze or how cheerfully the birds swooped and sang, Mrs. Griffin's mouth stayed in that set, irritated line.

Penelope liked a friendly silence, but this was not that, and her nerves soon got the better of her and set her talking: "So, where is the swarm?"

Mrs. Griffin didn't answer right away.

Penelope held her tongue and bided her time, step by step.

Wind rustled the grass at the edge of the road.

Finally the woman burst out: "How on *earth* did you know?"

The mix of surprise and anger was deeply satisfying. Penelope wondered if magicians felt like this, after a particularly mystifying trick.

But unlike the magicians, she didn't mind giving away her secret. She settled her pack more firmly on her shoulder and began to explain. "If it was advice you needed for a hive you kept, Mrs. Stowe could have given it. She's a perfectly capable beekeeper. Not much of a walker, though, these days. And if someone had been stung badly enough to send you running—well, you'd have run for the physician, wouldn't you? But you look vexed, like there's something of an emergency. And you've been sent to find me by name. So that means there's a swarm somewhere it shouldn't be, and you need me to find a better home for it. Simple." She whistled a little, to keep from grinning at the affronted look on the other woman's face. "And you never answered my question."

After a moment, Mrs. Griffin gave a decisive nod, and Penelope's chest went allover warm at this tiny sign of approval. "Some bees have got into my warehouse," Mrs. Griffin confessed.

Ah, yes, the print-works in what had been the old Huston mill. Penelope's curiosity pricked up its ears. "There's a swarm among your books?"

"No—among the printing plates."

"Which plates?"

Mrs. Griffin blinked, evidently considering the question odd. "An old book of verses by Joanna Molesey."

"Oh, how marvelous! Which poem of hers is your favorite?"

Mrs. Griffin snorted. "I am far too busy to indulge in poetry."

This answer stopped Penelope's tongue dead as a landed fish.

She was saved from concocting an answer, however, as they were now mere steps from her house. She loaded a few things into a wheelbarrow, along with the everyday tools she'd already had in her pack, and turned down the road that led to the print-works.

The load made it more difficult to carry on a conversation, so Penelope clamped her mouth shut and told herself that if the other woman grew uncomfortable with the silence, that was no fault of Penelope's.

But she felt guilty about it, all the same.

Mrs. Griffin frowned down at the wheelbarrow. "All that just to kill a few bees?"

Penelope stopped dead and dropped the wheelbarrow handles. The wooden legs hit the dirt of the road with an angry *thunk*. "We are *not* killing them."

Mrs. Griffin slowed and halted, her gray skirts swirling around her ankles. "We aren't?"

"No. We are rehiving them." Penelope tapped meaningfully on the curve of the straw skep hive that filled most of the wheelbarrow—much easier to lift and tote around right now than it would be once it was full of comb and honey and slumbering brood. "If you want your bees killed, you will have to find someone else to do it."

"I don't necessarily *want* them killed," Mrs. Griffin retorted. She jerked her head to toss a loose lock of hair out of her eyes. "I just assumed it would be necessary in order to get them out of the way."

"It's not." Penelope took a deep breath, trying to tamp down the anger flaring up in her throat. She felt like Mr. Painter's pipe, pouring out smoke and heat. It wasn't Mrs. Griffin's fault; she just didn't know. "Some bees may die in the rehiving process—they might sting someone, or get crushed. It happens, no matter how careful a beekeeper tries to be. But the *colony* will survive. And that's important."

"If you say so." Mrs. Griffin waited, then frowned harder. "Can we get on with it, then?"

Penelope folded her arms. *She* wasn't the one in a rush

this fine summer's day. "Not until you agree we're not going to kill the bees."

"Fine!" Mrs. Griffin threw her hands in the air. "Though I don't see why it matters, one way or another."

"It matters to me," Penelope said quietly.

The woman shot her a look so searching that Penelope nearly stepped back from the force of it.

Then the anger seemed to go out of Mrs. Griffin all at once, like a lamp being blown out. "Alright," she said, and blew out a long breath. "My apologies, Mrs. Flood. You know your business, of course."

Penelope blinked. "Thank you."

Mrs. Griffin nodded, Penelope lifted the wheelbarrow again, and together they walked the remaining three quarters of a mile to the print-works.

Penelope grabbed her smoker but left the rest of her tools in the wheelbarrow next to the fence, where it was immediately nosed at by a large sorrel horse, lured no doubt by the scent of honey. Penelope patted his neck by way of apology.

Mrs. Griffin waited by the door to the print-works, fidgeting. "If you're *quite* ready, Mrs. Flood."

Penelope squashed the tempting urge to dawdle, just to be contrary. It was coming on noon, and she likely had two hours' work ahead of her. "Show me what we're dealing with, Mrs. Griffin."

Heads snapped to attention when Mrs. Griffin walked in, and gazes sharpened in recognition when the employees noticed Penelope. She nodded to Mr. Jarden and shook the hand of the grinning Reggie Downes. "I hear you've been colonized, Mr. Downes."

"Indeed we have, ma'am."

"This way, Mrs. Flood." Mrs. Griffin was already waiting at the door to the back of the warehouse—goodness, she didn't waste any time, did she?

Reggie Downes rolled his eyes in apology where his employer couldn't see.

Penelope winked at him, then followed the printer into the maze of shelves.

It was a little like a library—but a vast, giant, monolithic kind of library, such as she imagined some race of titans might have built, to memorialize in solid metal the books that had told of their exploits. The plates were lined up in rows, one after another, with only a little space between. Her hands itched to pull one down from the shelf and read it, huge and heavy though they were.

From farther down the rows, Mrs. Griffin cleared her throat. She was standing near the back corner, arms folded, caught in a shaft of sunlight coming in through the nearby window. It gilded the gray hue of her dress and made the silver in her hair gleam like liquid fire. A few errant bees danced in the light around her, small sparks hovering over a larger, hotter flame.

Mrs. Griffin burned with impatience, alternately glaring at Penelope and at something else down the aisle to her right.

Presumably the swarm, judging from the unmistakable

humming of hundreds of bees. Penelope wished she had the luxury of stopping and listening for a while. But even from half a warehouse away, there was no withstanding the force of Mrs. Griffin's expectations.

Penelope walked forward, fighting the urge to kneel like a squire being knighted.

Then she reached the aisle and saw the bees.

Everything else fell away.

As she'd suspected, this colony of bees wasn't a swarm proper: it had been once, but the bees had long since settled and made themselves a hive. A strong one, too, by the look of it—even from six feet away Penelope could make out the round domed cells of drone brood, and the smaller domes where baby workers were growing, and even a few rows of new honey capped off. Well-done of them, so early in the season.

They'd built fresh comb in between the leaden plates, fixed to the underside of the shelf above. Quite as if the bees had only wanted to memorialize their own work alongside Joanna Molesey's. The shelf they'd settled on was chest-high, which was good, since if they'd colonized one of the higher areas it might have been more difficult to wrestle them out without damaging either the bees or the humans trying to help them.

Penelope stepped forward to get a closer look—and stopped as a hand seized her arm. She turned her head. "Is something the matter?"

"I thought . . ." Mrs. Griffin peered at her anxiously, then took a deep breath and dropped her hand from Penelope's coat. The spot where she'd touched burned a little for a moment or two after, then cooled. "I'm sorry."

Penelope tilted her head. "You were afraid I'd get stung?"

"Weren't you?"

"Not particularly." Penelope tilted her head. "But I'm used to bees, remember. I forgot that you weren't." She pulled out her smoker and her tinderbox. "Here's what I'm going to do: I'll start with a little smoke, to make the bees drowsy and willing to be handled."

"You're going to *handle* them?" Mrs. Griffin paled.

Penelope laughed softly. "How else did you plan for them to be moved?"

Mrs. Griffin huffed, but made no reply.

Penelope pulled out her tinderbox and lit the smoker. A few pumps of the bellows later and the funnel was puffing out clouds of sweet white smoke. Penelope brought it close to the colony and puffed at the main mass of bees; the colony clutched a little tighter and wriggled a little slower, as the smoke began to take effect. "It will be a minute or two yet," Penelope said, and went to retrieve the wheelbarrow.

Mrs. Griffin was still there when Penelope returned, wheelbarrow trundling over the stone floor.

Penelope realized that she would have an audience for today's work. "You don't have to stand watch, if you don't like. It's going to take some time, I'm afraid."

The printer grimaced. "I will not feel comfortable until these insects are gone," she replied. "My people know where to find me when I am needed."

Well, Penelope was used to working with touchy, easily

irritated creatures. She puffed a little more smoke on the bees, though, just in case, and wished it would have had the same calming effect on Mrs. Griffin.

Perhaps the printer would be less anxious if she knew what Penelope was doing, and why. "First thing is to make the new hive a welcoming place," Penelope began. She'd brought with her a round straw skep in two parts, like a bell with the top part of the dome sliced off. The inside of the larger part she'd rubbed with a little beeswax, which gave some traction to the straw coils and let the bees know this was a safe place for building comb. She set this on the bottom board and made sure it was steady and wouldn't tip. Next she spread out a plain sheet on the floor—*the better to spot you with, my dear*—and brought out a handful of slender bars made of birch.

"The bees should be well and drowsy by now," she said, turning to Mrs. Griffin. "I'm going to put on some gloves and a veil, since I'll be working quite closely with the comb, but you should be quite safe as long as you stay still and quiet."

Mrs. Griffin nodded once, sharply, and Penelope donned the rest of her bee clothes: sturdy gloves that disappeared into her coat cuffs, and a hat with muslin hanging down from the brim, tucked cozily beneath her coat lapels. "Right," she said, and pulled out her knife. "Now we start cutting out the comb."

She moved forward leisurely and carefully sliced the largest golden wedge away from the shelving. Bees clustered and hummed on the comb as she lifted it, but only one or two took flight in alarm.

Penelope turned the comb back and forth, peering closely. "Ah, there's the queen—see that larger bee, in the center of the cluster? Her daughters are taking proper care of her." Penelope couldn't keep some of the joy out of her voice: bees followed their queen loyally, so moving her was the first step to moving the colony as a whole.

"Now we just . . . rearrange the furniture a bit." Penelope knelt and rested the base of the honeycomb on the sheet, near the larger main section of the skep. A few quick strokes with a turkey feather brushed the bees from the comb to the sheet, where the workers quickly made a defensive clump around their dethroned queen. Meanwhile Penelope took out a large needle and thick linen thread, and whipstitched the upper edge of the honeycomb to a birch bar, being careful not to go through any brood cells. She then rested the bar across the top straw coil.

The honeycomb was now hanging in the center of the skep, just as it had hung from the underside of the shelf.

Penelope grinned. "Time to move our queen." And, slowly, she slipped her gloved fingers into the mass of bees on the sheet.

Behind her, Mrs. Griffin choked.

Penelope kept her fingers soft and her mind serene—some of the older, stranger books said bees could read a beekeeper's thoughts, and Penelope didn't know if this were true but she *did* know that bees were still very much a mystery.

It never hurt to be careful, did it?

She slid her fingers slowly underneath the queen and a few of her ladies, murmuring compliments. A few more workers followed until the palm of Penelope's hand was crowded. Then she lifted and reverently placed the queen and her little court inside the skep, on the bottom board. Soon enough the queen would make her way up the walls and back onto the comb; the rest of the hive as well as the remaining clump on the sheet would slowly but inevitably follow.

Even now, a few had flown out of the skep to tell the others where the queen had gone, and a few other insects were marching determinedly across the sheet, following the scents of honey and home.

Penelope stood and met Mrs. Griffin's wide-eyed gaze through the muslin of her veil. "That's the heart of it. Now we just do the same thing a few more times."

Mrs. Griffin's eyebrows rose and she breathed out a little laugh. "Oh, is that all?"

Penelope was puzzled by the astonishment in the printer's tone. It seemed out of all proportion with the ordinariness of the job. "Yes, that's about it. Not terribly complicated, I suppose."

Mrs. Griffin made a helpless noise in the back of her throat, and leaned against the wall at her back.

Penelope cut down and moved the other three pieces of comb, as Mrs. Griffin watched and fidgeted at the end of the aisle. A few times Reggie Downes came back to murmur some question, and once Sam Ashton came back simply to watch; Mrs. Griffin tolerated the boy for fully five minutes before shooing him back to his duties.

When all the pieces of comb were safely hanging within the skep hive, Penelope delicately scooped up the remaining bees from the sheet and poured them gently along the top bars. The queen had already made it back onto one of the combs, she saw with a smile. The smaller skep lid, once settled, closed off the hive and protected it.

"Now we just give it a little while for the stragglers to find their way," Penelope said, stripping off her gloves and lifting her veil away from her face.

The light had shifted into mid-afternoon richness, and Mrs. Griffin moved nearer to peer interestedly at the skep. "What will you do with the hive?" the printer asked.

"Well, my own garden is not large enough to support more hives than I already have." Penelope's smile widened. "So I thought you might keep it."

Mrs. Griffin's gaze was a lance.

Penelope tugged her gloves off and tucked them into her coat pockets. "Normally I'd offer it to one of the local families, but it's been a very strong year for swarms, and I don't know anyone with hives standing empty at the moment. And the bees chose this spot, so there must be things they like within foraging distance—and when it comes to flowers and forage, you'll find that bees know best."

Mrs. Griffin cast a helpless glance around the shelves in the warehouse. "You can't be suggesting I keep them *here*?"

She sounded appalled. Penelope took pity. "Well, not indoors, of course—but maybe out against the back wall? They would be snug as houses, up against the brick with a bit of roof to protect them from the rain."

Mrs. Griffin swallowed. "I'm not sure I have the constitution to . . . do what you've done today." A wave of her hand indicated the sheet, still spotted with a few disoriented bees.

"Oh!" Penelope shook her head. "It's not like this usually—rehiving is a very particular thing, and something of a specialty of mine. Most of the work with bees is just watching and waiting: check to make sure they're building honeycomb right, check to make sure you don't have pests, check to make sure no one has knocked over a hive. A lot of people set children to tending them, for the day-to-day."

Mrs. Griffin pursed her lips, weighing this new information. "My apprentices have their own work—and I am in London most days . . ."

Penelope shrugged. "If that's all that's stopping you, I could keep an eye on the colony and let you know when something needs doing."

"You would?"

"Of course! It's very little trouble—I only have four colonies of my own, you see, so it leaves me plenty of time to look in on a lot of the other hives in and around Melliton. Make sure all the bees are thriving, help out whenever there's chalkbrood or wax moths, show new beekeepers how to harvest honey and wax."

Mrs. Griffin was staring at her as if she'd started speaking some mystical language other than English. "What would I owe you? Why would you go to such trouble for me?"

Penelope chuckled, even though something about the tenor of the question made a part of her ache with sympathy.

Imagine having to question why someone might offer you a kindness. "Not for you, Mrs. Griffin—we've only just met. I'd do it for the bees, though."

"Because you care about the bees." That said carefully, as though Mrs. Griffin expected it to be instantly contradicted.

Penelope smiled. "Precisely."

Once again, the printer fixed her with that searching look. It was all Penelope could do not to spread her arms and turn around to be inspected.

But then Mrs. Griffin straightened, and her eyes met Penelope's again. "I'll call Mr. Downes in to help."

Penelope had brought a small stool in the wheelbarrow, fortunately, anticipating something like this. Together she and Mr. Downes lifted the bottom board with the skep— gently!—and walked it out through the print-works and around to the side of the warehouse. From here the river was a gentle burble, and the meadow beyond beckoned.

Mr. Downes helped situate the hive, then returned to the print-works. Mrs. Griffin hovered, gazing at the scenery as though she suspected it was trying to pick her pocket. Penelope considered the location. The fences to either side of the property should keep the hive safe from local wild-life, but Penelope made a mental note to come back and build a proper small fence sometime soon. She took down the printer's London address, and gave her own direction in return, promising to write as soon as there were any devel-opments with the hive.

"Congratulations, Mrs. Griffin," she said, tucking the slip of paper into a pocket. "You are now a beekeeper."

"Thank you," the printer said. "I think."

"You're welcome, I'm sure."

When she left, Mrs. Griffin was standing beside the skep, arms crossed and frowning. Still as vexed as before, but puzzlement softened it—she resembled nothing so much as a bee gone out early for forage, who had come back to find the rest of the hive had swarmed without her.

Time, Penelope knew, could work wonders. So could bees.

She couldn't wait to see what effect both would have on Mrs. Griffin.

Chapter Four

Dear Mrs. Griffin,

I write with good news: your new beehive is thriving and the colony is hard at work. I will let you know as soon as your first honey crop is ready, or if any problems arise.

Sincerely,

Mrs. Penelope Flood

Bees were a country thing. Or so Agatha would have thought. But they suddenly seemed to be everywhere in the city: buzzing on the signs for sweet shops and grocer's, hovering over taverns and public houses, carved into the decoration of churches and cathedrals. Even embossed on covers by the bookbinderies, where Griffin's brought their finest manuscripts to be encased in leather and gilt.

When Agatha stepped out behind the workshop three days later for a breath of fresh air, and found herself hypnotized for a quarter of an hour by one particularly fat bumblebee's progress across the stretch of mischievous weedy wildflowers at the back, she threw her hands in the air, gave in to Fate, and wrote back.

> *Dear Mrs. Flood,*
>
> *Thank you for keeping your expert eye on the hive's progress. I admit it makes me a trifle anxious to think of them working away out of doors, while I sit at my desk plotting to make off with the fruits of their labor. Normally one pays wages or offers room and board for that sort of thing.*
>
> > *Regards,*
> > *Mrs. Agatha Griffin*

The reply came two days later.

> *Dear Mrs. Griffin,*
>
> *Well, you did provide the bees with shelter and land, albeit only a very small parcel. Think of them as journeymen, if you prefer, or tenants. Farmers, not factory workers.*
>
> *I should caution you, though, they are liable to resist enclosure with more than usual ferocity.*
>
> > *Sincerely,*
> > *Penelope Flood*

Agatha snickered out loud at that, and was reaching for pen and paper in almost the same instant.

Mrs. Flood,

Clearly bees are more radical than I would have
expected, considering that they are so famous for their
royalty. My son, Sydney, would be delighted to hear of their
democratic sentiments—he is of a rather radical persuasion
himself, though I have every hope he will soon grow out of it.
Nineteen is still young enough to be wrong and recover from
it, wouldn't you think?

Perhaps the next time he announces his intention to hear
one of Mr. Carlyle's seditious speeches in the Crown and
Anchor, I will tell him to go sit in a beehive instead. Surely
that would be safer than letting him stroll so often into that
wasp's nest of anarchists and Jacobins.

As it happens, Griffin's has just received the first finished
copies of a new book on bees written by a very learned
Scotswoman. I am no expert, but the first pages have
intrigued me—I include a copy as a gift, and beg you will
tell me if the book is all grand new scientific revelations, or
the wise observations of ancient generations.

Either one should suffice for an advertisement.

Regards,

Agatha Griffin

Mrs. Griffin,

I write with a somewhat mixed collection of news.
First thing, the Scotswoman's bee book is excellent—very
tart and keen, and solidly observed, though naturally as
a fellow enthusiast I have questions on some of the finer

points. Which may in fact only be down to differences
between our pleasant southern woods and the chillier,
rougher climates of the north. I have a brother near
Edinburgh—I shall write to him and ask. He'll be
delighted I finally have an interest in the weather up there,
which is usually the only thing he manages to get into his
(mercifully short and rare) letters.

Second thing—alas, the bees would have no use for
your son on account of his being unfortunately male. Male
bees, or drones as they are termed, are the largest and most
apathetic of the species. They have but one purpose: to escort
the queen on her mating flight, giving their lives so she may
produce children. The rest of the time they doze on the
threshold of the hive, feasting on honey but fetching none
themselves, ever watchful for predators but incapable of
stinging; they perish with the onset of winter.

Young men are always frustrating, in some way: I
am the only daughter among seven siblings so I speak
from tedious experience. But surely your son has more
purpose than a drone, even if he has not yet perfected the
art of political pragmatism as we wise and stoical elders
have done. Does he help you in the print-shop, or is he a
member of one of the scientific organizations that are so
increasingly common?

There is so much scope for activity in our current
age: even here in sleepy Melliton we have a debating
club, a philosophical society, and a botanical association
(really more of a gardener's gossip club, but marvelously
well-informed). We had a Hampden Club until Lord

Castlereagh's recent acts were passed—and if a few local former members still meet of an evening to share a meal and some conversation, and if their talk occasionally turns to the current debates in Parliament, well, surely they do so in all innocence and with an eye toward the legality and propriety of their behavior. (But don't tell my lord Castlereagh, all the same.)

>*Sincerely,*
>*Penelope*

Agatha read this letter three times straight through, with an increasingly unsettled heart. She had no idea how she was expected to answer it.

It wasn't only the joke about Castlereagh—though, to be sure, every printer and publisher in London this past winter had watched the trial of bookseller Charles Richardson and worried about being arrested and imprisoned next.

Griffin's was a respectable, moderate press—but Agatha's natural caution was currently at its highest peak.

But it wasn't only that which made her pause. Mrs. Flood's conversational tone in this letter, the length of it, and the delicate advice about Sydney, all of which meant she had taken Agatha's earlier letter much more to heart than Agatha had anticipated . . .

This was a letter from a friend, or someone who was becoming a friend, and Agatha had no idea what to do about it.

It wasn't that Agatha lacked friends. Mrs. Pestell at the Queen's Larder was always affable, and Mrs. Barns, the bookbinder's wife, always stopped for tea when she could. But in both those cases friendship had happened on account of existing connections—the way acid bit through a design you'd already carved in the wax. The curve and angle of the relationship was predetermined. Bounded by the lines you'd drawn.

In a word: *safe.*

She had no design where Penelope Flood was concerned. There was no larger purpose in the connection. Agatha couldn't think of a single useful reason to write back.

Except that she wanted to.

But she couldn't think of any reason *why* this should be so. She couldn't think of anything she wanted Mrs. Flood to do for her, besides keeping an eye on the bees, or anything she could do for Mrs. Flood, now that she'd sent the Scots-woman's book as a thank-you for the bee business. It ought to have been something she could put out of her mind until the next crisis came along—the bees stung someone, say, or pests got into the hive somehow. Then there would have been an excuse for a letter.

Not knowing precisely what you wanted from someone—well, that was the surest way in the world of being disappointed when you didn't get it.

No, she thought sternly, even as one hand pulled a fresh sheet of paper in front of her and the other dipped the quill into the ink. She would not write to Mrs. Flood again unless it proved necessary. The days were so busy. Agatha's time would be much better spent keeping up with more urgent correspondence—the Roman antiquarian, for instance, or

Madame Tabot the modiste. She would not write to Mrs. Flood.

Agatha glanced down to find that her hand had kept pace with her thought—but only in part. Only long enough to write *Flood* at the top of the new sheet of paper lying smugly on the desk in front of her.

Paper was expensive. And this was the *good* paper, Agatha's finest stock. Used for the ladies and artists and artisans who contributed to the *Menagerie*, and who would respect her more if she was obviously using high-grade linen paper, not the cheaper cotton stuff.

A whole sheet wasted. Wasted, that is, if she wanted to address anybody *except* Penelope Flood.

Agatha sighed, and yielded, and began writing.

Flood,

Six brothers! My deepest sympathies. I only had one myself. But such a one! Trouble enough for six, I'd wager, and laughter enough for a dozen. We fought incessantly, but heaven help you if you looked at either one of us crosswise.

He's gone now—he died at Lyngør, with the navy. Sometimes I imagine he's really still out there somewhere at sea. I know it's not true comfort, but it gets me through the worst of the pangs.

Agatha scowled down at the paper, her hand itching to cross those lines out. Instead, she dipped her pen again and tried to hastily deflect, as though the earlier paragraph hadn't happened at all:

Do any of your siblings still live close by?

She didn't dare write any longer, for fear of what else she might say. And she'd left off the honorific in the salutation, so she signed it simply:

Griffin

The letter hadn't been sent out an hour before Agatha was ardently regretting every last mortifying word.

How had she managed to fit so much embarrassing material in such a short note? Stale wit, childhood tantrums, and a truly treacly flight of fancy involving a dead relative.

Such a letter deserved to be discarded.

It deserved to be burnt.

Annually, as a caution against similar sins.

It ought to be shown to schoolchildren for the next hundred years to teach them how not to write melodiously in English. Like an anti-Shakespeare, or the opposite of Burke.

It was worse than poetry.

Agatha felt as though she'd wantonly sliced off a piece of her beating heart and sealed it within the envelope. How would Penelope—how would *anyone?*—react to being the recipient of such a gory, messy missive?

She cut the lines of her next engraving extra deep out of pique, and was particularly sharp about Jane's inattention and poor Crompton's perfectly common compositing errors—but her agony only subsided when the Tuesday post brought a reply that was obviously several pages in length.

Agatha tucked it hastily into her skirt pocket, where it smoldered like a banked coal until she could dismiss her employees for the day, send Eliza and Sydney off to the theater, and lock herself in her study with the curtains drawn.

Dear Griffin, the letter began, and set Agatha's heart racing in gorgeous terror:

> *My condolences on the loss of your brother. He sounds like a charming, stubborn, eminently lovable young sailor.*
>
> *It is terribly hard having family at sea. My father was a merchant captain and his sons mostly followed him into the trade—the brother I mentioned in Edinburgh runs accounts for a shipping company there. My youngest brother, Owen, was the vicar here until we lost him some years back. My second-youngest brother, Harry, and my husband are in whaling, and often gone for two or three years at a stretch. They could have been drowned or devoured or anything years ago, and the letter just not reached me yet.*
>
> *They could be dead even as I write this.*
>
> *I think about it sometimes and it chills the breath right out of me. You are right, it is a solace to think that should they perish, I could stave off grief for some short while by imagining them still braving the swells together somewhere.*

At this point the words started dancing and Agatha had to put down the paper to dash the water from her eyes.

It was nothing. Truly nothing. She'd thought she would embarrass herself, and she hadn't. That was all. She'd sent a tender, bleeding part of her heart blithely off on a thoughtless impulse, and such an error obviously deserved to be consigned to the yawning depths of a polite and awkward silence.

Penelope Flood had sent that humiliating weakness back as carefully, cushioningly wrapped as a treasured heirloom. As if Agatha would be incomplete without it.

Her mother-in-law had been right: Penelope Flood was extraordinarily kind. Far kinder than Agatha deserved.

Thinking poorly of herself was familiar, and helped steady her whirling thoughts. She glanced again at the door and read on:

The nearest of my living siblings is my brother, Philip, who married a Welshwoman whose father owned a mine. The rest have scattered in the course of pursuing fair love and fortune. Mostly the latter, to be frank. Only I have stayed in Melliton, in the house where we all grew up. It rings a little emptier now that it's just myself.

Perhaps that's one reason I work so hard to stay busy. There are a number of farming families in the area whom I visit regularly—beekeeping is not very demanding when a keeper has only one or two hives, but as soon as you have moths or mice or foulbrood showing up it is helpful to be able to call on someone with expertise. The families enjoy

the honey and wax their hives produce, I have a chance
to observe how variations in nearby flora affect things like
honey production rates and hive strength, and it keeps me
out in the fresh air and not brooding alone at home.

However, at the moment, I also have the benefit of
a witty and talkative guest: my friend Joanna Molesey,
whose name you'll recognize, has come to stay with
me after the loss of her patroness. She has family in
the north, but some small legal matters—including a
missing diamond snuffbox—require her to remain in the
neighborhood for some indefinite length of time. If you
have a moment to spare, I can tell you the whole story . . .

Agatha read the letter twice more beginning to end, then
folded it back up along its creases. As a businesswoman she
was careful to preserve all her correspondence; such records
often came in handy when disputes arose over payment rates
and deadlines for delivery.

She could not, of course, put Penelope's letter with these.
It was far too personal.

Nor could she put it in the small dresser beside her bed,
where Thomas's letters rested, the fragile stack tied with
a blue silk ribbon. Scraps of delicate poetry he'd found,
printed flowers just for her, lines he'd typeset himself as a
youth—these were also personal, also secret, but not quite in
the same painful way. You *expected* love letters to be intimate
and embarrassing.

What they weren't, Agatha realized, was *specific.*

Thomas had loved words as naturally as breathing, but he was more a collector of them than an artist with them. Or to put it another way: he could take several unrelated pieces on poetry and history and essays on art and the sciences, set them in a compelling and natural order, add illustrations to underscore the meaning, and make the final result immensely appealing and artistic—but he could never have composed any of those pieces himself. His art was in the collection of things, not the writing of them.

When courting Agatha, Thomas had sent her bits of other people's poems because they captured how he felt—but that wasn't the same as writing her a love poem himself. Agatha had always known this on some level—so she'd kept her replies in the same vein. Snippets of things, thoughts pulled out of their natural ground. She hadn't the talent for such collections, not the way Thomas had, but to her great chagrin it had never occurred to her that she was allowed to form her own replies in her own particular manner. She'd assumed she was supposed to fit her style to his.

This new correspondence with Penelope Flood, though, was made up only of the things the two of them said to one another. No contract disputes, no professional relationship to protect, no stolen snippets. Nobody else's words to get in the way.

Agatha had never thought to want that before. But all at once she found herself craving it like a drunkard craving another glass of gin.

To have the space to let her thoughts meander, to be able

to simply say what she thought, instead of having to hunt down the part where someone else had said it better, or said it first, or said something close to it . . . It was intoxicating.

Maybe she was getting ahead of herself. After all, for all she knew, Penelope Flood wrote like this to everyone. With so many brothers scattered around the globe, she must have a great deal of practice in using letters to bridge the gaps of time and distance.

Even if this was ordinary correspondence to Penelope Flood, it was something new and special to Agatha.

And she wanted even more now to write back. She tucked the letter into her skirt pocket, and composed a reply.

Then, to make up for the self-indulgence, she forced herself to turn back to the never-ending work. When Eliza and Sydney returned, she was three letters deep into her correspondence for the *Menagerie*, and only the occasional whisper of paper in her pocket reminded her that she'd taken an hour for something selfish that evening.

Penelope's next reply came enclosed with a pressed flower.

An apple blossom, she said, *from the gardens at Abington Hall. You recall in my last note I mentioned I inherited the Abington hives? There are half a dozen of them, and they sit in a cozy courtyard of their own on the top of Melliton's highest hill. The place has been a bee garden for at least two centuries, if not more, and the plants have all been carefully chosen for apiological delight in every season.*

They are less of a delight to Lady Summerville, the hall's

current occupant. She wishes she could knock down the
ancient walls and put in a modern lawn with a prospect,
and I am old-fashioned enough that this strikes my heart
with all the heavy tones of a funeral bell. Fortunately, Lady
S has not the funds for such alterations. The bee garden
remains safe.

But my heart tells me the detente cannot last. I fear the
most for the apple trees, so ancient and yet so delicate in
their spring finery. Their fruit is the sweetest in Melliton
in the autumn, and it would be a shame to deprive future
generations of the childhood ritual of clambering over the
wall to steal them.

    Flood

Agatha tipped the apple blossom into her palm and peered down at it. Its petals had been perfectly, lovingly pressed of all moisture, leaving it so light it trembled at even the slightest whisper of breath. Most of the flower was white, but the tips of the petals still bore traces of a blush pink that would have been irresistible beneath the summer sky in a hilltop garden.

Clearly, Agatha had the same taste in flowers as bees did.

She carefully tipped the fragile blossom back onto Penelope's letter, refolded the pages, then tucked the latest missive away with the others in her new hiding space: between the pages of a manuscript copy of the Scotswoman's bee book. The bulk of it occasioned no notice sitting on her desk among her other papers, yet it gave Agatha a little frisson to see it and know it held a secret.

That little flower haunted her the rest of the day, hovering on the periphery of her thoughts, pale petals fluttering like wings in the edges of her vision. She found herself idly doodling it in the corner of her sketchbook, when she ought to have been working on other things. There was something alluring about the shape of it—she couldn't help wanting to trace every line of the delicate veining, or use her scribe to follow the curves and points of each individual petal.

A shame it was so delicate. The years were not kind to fragile things.

She reached out for a small stub of boxwood, almost before the thought had completed itself. Soon the table beneath her busy hands was filled with curls and corners and shavings, as she carved away everything but the flowing, flowery outline.

Flood,

Thank you for the apple blossom—it brought a moment of sunshine and good country air into a day that was otherwise a cloudy one. Such flowers are not so easy to come by here in the city, but I have sent you one anyways, at the end of this note. Woodcuts are slowly beginning to grow popular in printing circles—they lack the precision of copperplate, or the dramatic shading of mezzotint in the English style—but I learned to engrave first in wood, and it has always seemed to me the more appropriate material for natural scenes and figures.

More importantly, they last. A well-done wood engraving will let a printer make impressions for centuries,

*long after other kinds of plates have been worn down by use
and the weight of the press.*

*Even if Lady Summerville has her wish, some small part
of your bee garden will survive.*

Griffin

Agatha knew her trade, and had done her work well.
The apple blossom printed at the end of the letter was an
exact copy of the one Penelope had enclosed. She'd even
brushed strokes of pink watercolor onto it, to breathe a
little life into it.

Another piece of her heart, tucked into a fold of paper
and sent into another's possession. Strange, how it got a little
easier every time.

CHAPTER FIVE

Flood,

Forgive the delay in this response—as you may have heard, our long-absent Queen Caroline landed at Dover on 5 June and everything since has been near anarchy. The King is aghast that an entire continent no longer separates him from his wife, whom he decries as unfaithful, Parliament is anxiously debating how much money it will take to persuade her back to Italy, and everywhere the common people (spurred on by the radicals and reformers) are hailing her as their champion. She is William the Conqueror, or Henry VII come to claim his throne—or she is Bonaparte, returning from exile to make one last play for undeserved power. Everyone in the Strand, it seems, has a pamphlet to write, a newspaper to sell, or a crude satire to sketch on the subject, myself included—I've enclosed our latest one from Thisburton, with the Queen as a well-fed and feathered goose, and the reformers as foxes licking their teeth at her approach.

The fox likeness of Orator Hunt is, I think, particularly good.

Reverence for the Queen is suddenly the standard by which public figures are to be judged in the public eye. Lord Wellington was accosted by the throng and forced to declare Caroline innocent—"and may all your wives be like her," he is said to have added. Jubilant mobs have been breaking windows in the palaces of the mighty—unless said windows blaze with candles in her honor. Flags and cheers and laurels greeted the Queen at every point between Dover and London.

The rumors of her infidelity are in all the streets cried down as scandalous—especially considering the King's own well-known penchant in that direction—and her innocence is trumpeted even (perhaps especially) by those who really ought to know better. The city at all hours is full of shouts and songs in the common quarters, while the gentry board their doors and prepare as if for invasion.

In France the revolution began by bringing down a queen; here in England, we may well begin by lifting one up.
    Griffin

My dear Griffin,

Believe me, the evening conversations in the Four Swallows have touched on little but Queen Caroline for weeks. Every proclamation, every public letter she writes is cast over for secret messages to her fellow radicals and revolutionaries—for many of the locals have no trouble

*believing that a woman raised in the lap of luxury is
somehow also speaking to and for poor farmers and artisans
like themselves. The announcement that her name was to
be struck from Church liturgy has offended the more devout
parishioners more than I believe the King realizes.*

*Even Lady S, Melliton's staunchest and most loyal
monarchist, has been heard to murmur support for the
Queen: Her Majesty is a woman wronged, a mother
deprived of her child, a wife denied her due titles and the
respect of her proper rank. Some of this is very difficult to
argue against—though, considering the source, one very
much still wants to.*

*However, it is another queen entirely I must write to
you about. Your hive is nearly ready with their first honey
harvest of the summer! If you'd be able to make your way
to Melliton for the occasion, you might enjoy, as you said,
making off with the fruits of their labor.*

I do hope you'll come.

    Flood

Well, what else could Agatha do but agree? She made arrangements for Eliza and Sydney to run the print-shop for two days, sent a note asking Mrs. Stowe if she wouldn't mind having a guest for a night, and gathered up this month's silk samples to take with her again.

At least she could be efficient that way. Or so she told herself. Though such small economies had never made her heart race or her hands fidget like this before.

The drive to Melliton was even more interminable than the last. But at length it did end, and she pulled up to the print-works beside the river, and there was Mrs. Penelope Flood, in trousers and a man's old jacket, turning from her wheelbarrow to grin at Agatha as she handed the horse's reins over to young Ashton.

Agatha almost had to step back, as that smile hit her with all the force of a blow.

Mrs. Flood's eyes were sky blue. Had Agatha forgotten, or simply not noticed? Her grin was wide and warm, and her gold-and-silver curls tossed lightly in the soft morning breeze.

Agatha gasped through the vise squeezing her chest as the reality stole her breath: this was no longer the face of a stranger, but of a friend and confidante.

"Mrs. Griffin!" Mrs. Flood gave a little laugh and held out a hand.

Agatha took it, unable to resist. Palms clasped warmly together, then Mrs. Flood let go. Agatha's skin chilled at once—too soon. She'd barely had time to register the touch.

"Mrs. Flood," she said. Surely it was the dust of the road that had her voice sounding so low and rough. "So good to see you again."

"You as well. Are you ready to harvest your first honey crop?" Mrs. Flood asked. "Or do you have things to see to first?"

Agatha looked behind her. Mr. Downes had already begun directing the journeymen to unload the silk samples from the wagon. He met her gaze and nodded, dark, curly hair bobbing, to let her know he could take things over from here.

Agatha flexed her hands to stop their shaking and turned back to Mrs. Flood. "Where do we start?"

Mrs. Flood cocked her head. "You change, if you're going to be working with the bees." When Agatha hesitated, Mrs. Flood pulled several garments out of a bag in her wheelbarrow. "I usually borrow my brother's things, as he's near my height, but as you are a fair bit taller, I've brought you some of Mr. Flood's to wear for the occasion."

They were sturdy garments but not shabby: a light sailor's jacket in deep blue, a linen shirt, and a pair of country trousers.

Agatha hesitated, conscious of the weight of her skirts and the eyes of her curious employees. "I am a respectable widow, Mrs. Flood."

"The bees don't care about that at all, Mrs. Griffin," Mrs. Flood said, but then went on in a quieter tone. "I understand if it seems improper—but bees have a terrible habit of getting caught in skirts and petticoats, and stinging one badly in self-defense. Better to be safe, if a little eccentric, than to suffer so much unnecessary pain. And the bees don't know you yet—when you're better acquainted, you'll be able to dress more as you're used to doing."

Agatha accepted the clothing with hands made awkward by novelty. "Better safe than stung," she said, more bravely than she felt.

Mrs. Flood laughed, and Agatha's heart jolted to hear it. "Exactly right."

She changed in Mr. Downes's office. It was odd, undoing

the buttons on her brown cotton and putting a man's long shirt over her light stays. The jacket buttoned high but hung rather loose, and the trousers bagged down to the knees and tucked easily into the tops of Agatha's own leather boots—which were tough enough to deal with London cobbles, and so could probably weather a day or two on the soft earth of Melliton's roads and fields.

She met Mrs. Flood back behind the print-works, where the morning sun sparkled on the waves in the river. Every step across the turf felt like a new one, with no long panels of fabric swirling around her as she moved.

"I haven't worn trousers since I was a girl," she explained, swinging one leg back and forth experimentally. "Sebastian—my brother—used to lend me an old pair of his so we could sneak out into the city at night."

Mrs. Flood chuckled. She was leaning against the brick wall, one leg bent, the smoker dangling from her hand as she idly pumped to keep it lit and puffing proudly. "Hopefully this afternoon's work will involve a trifle less mischief."

"Only larceny," Agatha replied. "As promised."

Mrs. Flood laughed again, the sound finding a thrumming echo somewhere deep in Agatha's belly. "Let's begin."

Mrs. Flood was already wearing her gloves and a hat with a veil; she instructed Agatha how to tuck the fine muslin tight—but not too tight!—at the neck, and began pumping the bellows of the smoker more frequently while Agatha pulled on a pair of thick gloves. The muslin veiling her face was very fine, and only seemed to cast a light morning mist over the scene before Agatha's eyes.

"First thing to do when harvesting," said Mrs. Flood, "is to smoke the bees. It takes a few minutes to have an effect." She placed the spout of the smoker near the hive entrance and puffed out long jets of white smoke.

Scents of grass and herbs rose up, tickling the back of Agatha's throat almost enough to make her cough. Already the few bees she saw were moving lazily, staying close to the hive entrance and disappearing into the straw coils of the skep.

Mrs. Flood placed a hand on top of the skep's upper portion. "You saw the basic skep hive before; once the bees had taken to their new home I made some modifications so the honey is easier to get to." She lifted the top bell of the skep and the segment came away.

Agatha gaped behind her veil. Now sitting on the top of the hive was a glass jar, about the same size and shape as a gas lamp's globe. Honeycomb coiled inside it and pressed up against the walls, a golden, living labyrinth spotted with laboring bees. Beneath the jar, a flat wooden circle with a hole cut in allowed bees to scurry up and down between the main hive body and the jar.

Enchanted, Agatha moved closer. The glass was, as Mrs. Flood had promised, almost entirely full—she could see the capped honeycomb chambers where the sweetness was safely stored.

"It's a good sign, this much honey so early in the season."

Agatha swallowed a gasp of surprise. Mrs. Flood was at her elbow, her veiled head inclining toward the bees as fondly as a mother watching over her children.

Sunlight caught the muslin of her veil and made it glow like a saint's halo.

Agatha had to force her gaze away, or else she'd never stop staring. She turned back to the honeycomb, and the bees who even now worked to cram more wax and sweetness into every nook and cranny.

"I've seen such jars for sale in the market, every summer and fall. I thought they'd been filled by people—I didn't know the bees did all this," Agatha replied, her tone hushed. She felt . . . reverent, admiring, in a way she hadn't on that first day. These weren't invaders any longer: they were *her* bees. Tenants, Mrs. Flood had said, and now Agatha could see exactly what she meant.

Mrs. Flood's breath rippled the muslin as she explained. "They're not quite as common as plain skeps, but they've got two great advantages: first, they let a beekeeper actually observe the bees at work, which is the best way to learn about them; and second, they let you take honey without having to slaughter the entire hive."

"The *entire* . . ." Agatha blew out a breath, and tried again, more calmly. "Is that done often when stealing honey?"

Mrs. Flood's hat and veil bobbed once, sharply. "Very. Traditionally you hold the skep over burning sulfur until all the bees drop off. You get more honey that way, since you don't have to leave any for the bees to live on during the winter—but it's wasteful. More than wasteful: it's cruel. And I'm far from the only beekeeper who thinks so."

"Then why do it?"

Mrs. Flood puffed a little more smoke over the hive before she answered. "Tradition. Change is difficult, and beekeeping is ancient. And a lot of cottage beekeepers can't afford the glass for this method—not when the straw skeps are so much cheaper. It does take a little more specialized knowledge to get the bees to fill the jars properly. The sides need to be rubbed with wax first on the inside, for instance. Otherwise the bees will just slip off and never leave anything there for you to harvest. There are a few other hive designs trying to solve the problem, but most of them are available only to the scientific classes: your gentlemen beekeepers and lady gardeners and such. Mr. Koskinen has quite a fine one; perhaps he'll let me show you someday. Still, every year people bring out more new designs—because many other beekeepers and scientists hate seeing the same awful cycle over and over again, every year. Capturing wild swarms in the spring, only to kill them all in the autumn. Never letting a colony grow or thrive from year to year, or trying to learn how it is they make honey, or uncovering the secrets and mysteries of the hive."

Agatha blinked. "Mrs. Flood, that was almost . . . poetic."

Mrs. Flood laughed, though there was a bitter note in it this time. "I know by now that isn't a compliment, coming from you."

"It ought to be."

Mrs. Flood's head snapped up, and toward Agatha. The veil seemed suddenly more opaque than before.

Agatha felt her face flush, and hoped it wasn't obvious beneath the muslin. "Maybe I simply don't have the necessary capacity for poetry, to understand its true merits."

"Maybe you simply haven't encountered the right poem," Mrs. Flood countered. She angled her face to peer down into the hive entrance, blowing lightly on the few bees still buzzing there, then straightened.

A knife appeared in her hand, long and sharp; she offered it to Agatha handle-first. "Would you like to do the honors?"

Agatha grasped the knife, made sure it was steady in her gloved hand, and took a deep breath. Under Mrs. Flood's direction, she placed one hand on the top of the jar to steady it, and slid the knife blade between the lip of the jar and the wooden board beneath. It cut cleanly through the base of the honeycomb, and Agatha tipped the jar up and stepped back.

Mrs. Flood was ready with a new vessel to place atop the hive, then showed Agatha how to blow away the few bees remaining in the jar in her hands. They spun irritatedly into the air and made brief, angry orbits around Agatha's head before returning to the security of the hive.

Mrs. Flood waved her gloved fingers at them as they departed.

A bit of cheesecloth tied tight around the neck of the jar came next, and then Agatha was officially possessed of what felt like several pounds of rich, golden bounty.

"Congratulations," Mrs. Flood said. The two veils between them hid most of her smile from Agatha's eyes, but it was there in her voice, as lush as the honey weighing down Agatha's hands.

Agatha stood there with her hands full of wealth, in Mr. Flood's borrowed clothes, and realized she wasn't ready to go back to ordinary life. She wanted more of . . . whatever it was they were doing here. The two of them, together. "Is that it?"

Mrs. Flood stiffened, then turned away to set the skep dome back on the hive to protect the empty jar from sunlight and rain. The laughter had fled from her voice when she finally replied, "It's really not that difficult a task."

"No, I meant . . ." Agatha sighed and set the honey down at her feet. Her gloves came off next, and the veil with them. Color returned to the world around her, painfully vivid, searing her eyes for a moment before they recovered. "You said you have other hives you look after, around Melliton. Couldn't we . . . couldn't I help you with that?" She tugged on the cuffs of Mr. Flood's jacket. "I'm already dressed for it, after all."

Oh, it was hard to tell what Mrs. Flood was feeling, behind that muslin veil. But then she lifted it, and her mouth was solemn, but her eyes glowed. "I would like that," she said. "Very much."

Agatha bent to pick up the honey jar again. Relief made it weigh half as much as she'd thought before. She felt she could have lifted the world, if she'd been asked. "At your service, Mrs. Flood."

Mrs. Flood's mouth crooked at the corners. Those blue eyes moved leisurely down from Agatha's face, to the blue jacket, to the loose trousers, and the leather boots. Then away.

Agatha shivered, as if the sun had ducked behind a cloud. *You're wearing her husband's clothes*, Agatha reminded herself, and felt extremely queer about it.

They bundled Mrs. Griffin's dress and petticoats into a cloth bag and added it to the gear in Penelope's wheelbarrow. They made a brief first stop at Mrs. Stowe's house, so Mrs. Griffin could leave her things there for the night.

Mrs. Stowe was deadheading her roses. She took her daughter-in-law's masculine attire in stride and admired the honey, before Mrs. Griffin went inside to ask Miss Coningsby where best to put her things.

"I'd have introduced you years ago," Mrs. Stowe said, "if I'd known you could make my daughter-in-law a beekeeper so quickly." She sent Penelope a sidelong wink that made the heat flare up in her face.

Mrs. Griffin returned before Penelope could reply, and Miss Coningsby waved shyly to Penelope from the kitchen window. Then Penelope and Mrs. Griffin were off again.

It was a good day for checking the hives: clear but crisp and not too hot. The spring blooms were yielding pride of place to summer flowers, scents of lilac and cherry blossom fading in favor of lavender and rose. Penelope introduced Mrs. Griffin by name to each cottager—and, just as carefully, to each beehive.

The printer's eyebrows rose sharply the first time Penelope did this, but over time Mrs. Griffin lapsed into quiet amusement at what she clearly had chosen to perceive as an eccentricity.

They made the whole south circuit together, from Knots Down past Ilford Hall and into the wood. It was the opposite of the order Penelope usually walked it, and it gave her the odd sense that she was winding a clock backward and making the hours run the wrong way round. If they kept this up, she imagined the two of them growing younger and younger with each step—Mrs. Griffin's hair turning rich black and Penelope's gold, the creases at the corners of both their eyes and mouths smoothing away, aches and pains and stiff joints loosening as limbs grew lithe with youth again.

Then the wheel of the wheelbarrow struck a rock and jolted Penelope right to her teeth. She stopped for a moment to shake the tingle from her hands, as the full weight of her forty-five years thumped down on her.

Well, it had been a nice daydream while it lasted.

"Shall I take over pushing that for a while?" Mrs. Griffin asked, cocking an eyebrow.

Penelope shook her head. "Oh, no, it's nothing—I was just distracted for a moment."

They resumed their walk, and Penelope tried to keep her mind from wandering by fixing it on her companion.

Of course, this risked another kind of distraction.

Agatha Griffin strode with her hands clasped behind her, head tilted back, dark hair balled at the base of her neck. The deep blue of John's old coat suited her, especially as the climb up the road into the wood brought out the roses in her cheeks and made her breathe rather hard.

At your service, Mrs. Flood.

Oh, would that were true. Or better yet, the other way around—Mrs. Griffin was very obviously what Mrs. Stowe called the managing sort, and in past liaisons Penelope had thoroughly enjoyed being, as it were, managed.

Not that this was a liaison. It still hovered well under the protective aegis of *friendship*. Some of it Penelope would have been tempted to read as flirtation from other sources, but despite the growing warmth in her letters, Mrs. Griffin seemed more skittish than seductive. Penelope had not missed the way she tugged at the cuffs and collar of her borrowed coat, or how she starched up whenever Penelope brushed cautioning fingertips over her elbow to guide her down a turn of some of the less obvious paths.

Probably just a passing fancy on Penelope's part. No doubt it would vanish soon enough.

After they left the fourth cottage, whose busily buzzing hives only needed a little trimming of the grass to keep the entrances clear, Penelope turned to her companion. "You know why I talk to the bees, don't you?"

"Because there's more bees around here than people?"

Penelope laughed, even as she shook her head. "So they know who we are. The more familiar bees are with a beekeeper, with their scent and their movements and their voice, the less fuss they make when the beekeeper approaches them. Or, say, starts shuttling hives around, or removing comb, or any one of a hundred other things that would make wild bees turn on you in outrage. You stop being a threat to them, in short."

Mrs. Griffin tilted her head. "That . . . actually sounds quite sensible." She quirked her lips. "Familiarity breeds contempt, as they say."

Penelope shook her head. "Familiarity breeds trust, Griffin."

"So long as you don't expect them to talk back."

Penelope chuckled. "Of course I don't." She cast a sly look at the other woman, from the corner of her eye. "I do recite my favorite poems to them, though. Pastorals, usually."

Mrs. Griffin's mouth twitched. "It's a wonder they don't try to sting you for that alone."

They walked on.

Mrs. Griffin frowned lightly, the toes of her boots scuffing the stones out of the road and out of her way. "Does Mr. Flood help you with the bees when he's not at sea?"

Penelope adjusted her grip on the wheelbarrow handles. "He did, once or twice, when we first met," she replied, smiling to remember. John had frowned at the bees as though he suspected them of teasing him by flying in curves and squiggles rather than straight lines. "But he's at sea for such long stretches, and he mostly only comes back home in the winters, when there's very little hive-work to be done."

Mrs. Griffin kicked another rock. "How long have you been married?"

"Oh . . . ten years this August."

Mrs. Griffin's gaze was carefully pointed elsewhere. On the grassy banks, on the treetops—anywhere but at Penelope. "No children?"

Penelope laughed before she could stop herself. "No children, no."

She waited breathlessly for the next question—fully ready to drop her usual hints about her intimacy with John, or rather the lack of such—but Mrs. Griffin's curiosity had apparently exhausted itself for the moment.

Only the birdsong filled the air between them for the next quarter mile.

Afternoon waned into evening. Because they were moving backward, the south circuit terminated where it usually began: Penelope's home on the edge of the wood, just where it met the main road. To the west were the farmlands and high street; to the east the road wound through a mile of semiwild woodland until it split and sent tendrils to each of the larger estates that lay in a long curve on the wood's far side.

And here, where road and wood and farmland all met, on a slight rise looking over the river, was Fern Hall, two centuries old and still in the prime of its youth, as buildings went. Light from the lowering sun cast it red against the shadowed trees behind. Stone and wood, plaster and paint, glass and a small garden—but what Penelope saw when she looked at it wasn't the structure of the house itself.

She saw all the places where her family wasn't.

The Stanhopes hadn't built Fern Hall—that was some other clan, whose name Penelope had sadly forgotten—but as soon as Alexander Stanhope had purchased the place it had become the center of the family's world, a combination home and storehouse and navigational reference point.

Even now, with her siblings and their children all scattered to the far corners of the map, Penelope could feel the presence of all those long-loved objects pull at her like the tug on a compass needle: the embroideries her mother had sewn onto chair covers and sofa cushions, the papers her father had stored in the study, the bedrooms still full of toy boats and schoolbooks and outgrown, outworn clothes that had passed down from sibling to sibling.

Penelope had never been able to shake the thought that despite the distance between them all, if she tried to throw any of these things away, five brothers would descend on her in an instant with shouts of the most strident objections. She had, by default, become something of a steward for the memories of her siblings. The one remaining root that held the family tree in familiar ground.

She had conceded only this much: she had moved everything out of one bedroom to make space for Joanna to stay. Penelope was still fighting the urge to confess it all to Michael in a letter—she'd fretted and flinched as Daniel the footman and George the gardener had moved hobbyhorses and emptied all those bookshelves. As though her brother would hear the ruckus all the way across the ocean in Canada.

According to Mrs. Braintree, the Stanhopes' stalwart cook and housekeeper, their guest was having one of her *feral days*, as she termed them, and had retired to her room with a request that she not be disturbed for anything short of fire, flood, or cold-blooded murder. (Presumably, with the latter, she'd either want to watch or offer tips for how to hide the body.) "I am sorry you won't get to meet her," Penelope said. "She's still very much in mourning for Isabella. I'm sorry you never had a chance to meet *her*, either."

Mrs. Griffin's eyes turned thoughtful. "Mrs. Molesey was her companion, you said?"

Penelope met her gaze boldly and directly. "For thirty years. After Isabella's husband died, they traveled together and shared a home." She wasn't quite courageous enough to put it more plainly than that—Mrs. Griffin was a Londoner, and certainly didn't seem inclined to a too strict observance of propriety, but people could always surprise you.

Some secrets weren't Penelope's to reveal.

Mrs. Griffin's gaze widened in understanding.

Penelope braced for the worst.

But all the printer did was say: "It's so difficult to lose a loved one. I hardly knew myself in the first days of my widowhood. Please convey my sympathies to Mrs. Molesey."

Somewhere, deep in Penelope's breast, a knot she'd only barely been aware of untied itself. She breathed a little easier for it.

It made her feel briefly bold, so she squared her shoulders and asked Mrs. Griffin: "Would you like to come for dinner at the Four Swallows with me?"

To her small surprise and vast delight, Mrs. Griffin blushed and said yes.

Chapter Six

Agatha had never seen Mrs. Flood in skirts before. Granted, they'd only met twice now, but Agatha was mortified to realize that after the first shock she'd assumed Mrs. Flood wore men's clothing perpetually, and not only when she was minding bees.

Instead, Mrs. Flood stepped out of her house in a cinnamon frock, the color bringing out the gold lights in her short curls and turning the hue of her eyes into something like sapphire.

She looked, in a word, delicious, bobbing forward to lead the way through the deepening twilight.

Agatha could only follow helplessly, in the plain gray dress and a faded paisley shawl she'd changed into at Mrs. Stowe's. If Mrs. Flood was a rare spice, savory and sought after, Agatha was a lichen scraped off some dismal northern crag. She had never felt so ancient.

Respectable widow, indeed. She almost wished for the blue coat back again: at least it had some color to it.

Dear god, when was the last time she'd cared at all about her appearance beside the usual category of *Are there stains on this skirt?* or *Is this sleeve going a bit threadbare at the elbow?* Not since . . .

She almost stopped walking as realization staggered her: not since Thomas. And, before Thomas, with Kate. The two times in her life she'd spent ages before her mirror, turning this way and that to check the fall of a gown, the line of a seam, the placement of a necklace or ribbon. She clenched her hands together and for a moment felt the ghostly pressure of the wedding band she hadn't worn in two years.

She was so distracted by the revelation that before she realized it, she walked into the Four Swallows and into a raging battle.

Halfpennies were flying through the air like musket fire. They pinged against the floor and off the wall behind a chestnut-haired woman standing in the front corner. One tan hand held a drooping sheaf of ballad sheets. The other was raised to snatch flying coins out of the air. Any she caught she tucked into the deep front pockets of her overskirt, which bulged with rolled-up broadsides, lyrics, and songs. Behind her a boy of ten or so scurried about, gathering up fallen coins. He had the same chestnut hair, but skin a shade paler than his mother.

Agatha batted one poorly aimed halfpenny away from her face, and started as a hand tugged on her elbow.

She turned to see Mrs. Flood laughing and shaking her

head. "Looks like Nell's performing tonight—come on, we'll be out of range in the back."

Once past the front cluster of the audience the crowd calmed somewhat. Agatha nodded at Mr. Downes and a few other pressmen at the long central tables, sharing drinks and food and conversation. Another group in one corner was playing cards; a solitary figure at the bar was hunched over her ale with a book in her hand. Agatha recognized the other three beekeepers from her first meeting with Mrs. Flood, sitting variously around the room.

Agatha and Mrs. Flood found an empty pair of chairs against the wall. The barmaid brought two foaming tankards and promised them pasties, as the ballad singer's voice rang out to start her next song.

Agatha took a swallow of beer and paused, blinking. "This is quite good."

Mrs. Flood leaned back, radiating smug local pride. "Has the poor beer you find in London taught you that every tavern waters down its ale?"

Agatha snorted, then lapsed into silence. She couldn't remember the last time she hadn't hurried over a meal, trying to get back to work as quickly as possible. But there was no project waiting for her at the end of tonight. Nothing left undone, nothing hovering anxiously over her shoulder. It made her feel restless, and she shifted in her seat.

The girl came by again with the pasties, and Agatha was relieved to have an excuse for being tongue-tied. It helped that the pasty was at least as good as the ale, if not better: curried mutton with onion and peas.

They did not have the corner to themselves for long: Mrs. Flood seemed to know everyone, or everyone seemed to know her, and soon Agatha had been introduced to brown-skinned Mr. Biswas, Mr. Koskinen all pale and red-haired, his curly-haired wife with intelligent eyes, and two young men, tall Mr. Thomas and broad-shouldered Mr. Kitt. Mr. Thomas lived on half pay from the army, and Mr. Kitt half pay from the navy, and between them both they cobbled together a household and argued affably over whose turn it was to buy the beer. Mr. Biswas owned the Four Swallows— "named for my tattoos: one swallow for each crossing of the Equator," he'd explained, one hand tapping proudly on his barrel chest—and like any good host he rose every so often to make the rounds, checking in on the clusters of sailors and farmers and the few solitary drinkers, putting an oar into a well-worn argument, ducking into the kitchen to confer with Mrs. Biswas.

It was not that Agatha was bothered by all the noise: London had a way of making noise comfortable that Agatha had long embraced. But Agatha had spent the whole day out of her element, and now she faced a group of friends whose shared jokes had long since carved grooves and furrows into one another's metal. She watched Mrs. Flood lean over her tankard, laughing at Mr. Thomas teasing Mr. Kitt, and wondered how to fit into the picture.

A peal of notes rang out, and the whole group turned back

toward the ballad singer at the front of the long room. Nell had pulled out a small guitar and was tuning it carefully. A sense of excitement visibly washed over the crowd, expressions rippling like waves beneath the gust of a new wind.

Agatha cast a sidelong glance at Mrs. Flood, whose cheeks were flushed with anticipation and whose eyes were bright as stars.

When she caught Agatha staring, she winked.

Agatha's face flamed.

She was saved from having to say anything by the start of Nell's song:

> *"Come listen, friends, and hear the tale*
> *Of a gay young pair of lovers*
> *They had no care for any fair*
> *Unless 'twas one another.*
>
> *They wed one bonny summer's day*
> *And deemed the match successible—*
> *But the lass was seen to turn pure green*
> *When he wore his Inexpressibles!*
>
> *As he walked up and down the town*
> *Every maid's eye turned to goggle*
> *At calves and thighs of marvelous size*
> *All in those buckskins coddled."*

The sly gesture Mr. Kitt made while singing along with *coddled* made Agatha snort half a tankard's worth of ale up her nose. Listeners hooted approval. More halfpennies rang out against the wall.

Nell grinned acknowledgment and the song went on:

> "She chose her day of vengeance well,
> By her spouse it went unguessable:
> In she did stride, he almost died—
> She wore his Inexpressibles!
>
> He hollered up and down the lane
> A-cursing her uncladness
> She shouted higher, 'It's your attire
> That drove me to this madness.'
>
> Whene'er the row began to fade
> Another shout revived it
> When dawn appeared, the town crept near
> To see who had survived it.
>
> The wife emerged all bathed in smiles,
> Her joy quite irrepressible
> Sprawled out in bed, poor husband said:
> 'She wore out me Inexpressibles!'"

Half the crowd was shouting along by the end, from the young farmers' wives to the old salted sailors. The piece was clearly a local favorite—Agatha'd heard and printed a great many ballads in her time, but never this one. She cheered and clapped until her hands ached, and when Nell's son came around with the broadsides she pulled out a halfpenny of her own and asked him for a lyrics sheet.

He shook his head. "That's one of Mum's own. Never been printed. I've got 'Jenny of the High-Way' or 'The Milk-Maid's Complaint,' if you like." He brandished samples of ballad sheets and caricatures, some plain black ink, others painfully bright with cheap color.

Agatha glanced down at the sheets, and with a little start realized many of them were Griffin's printings, from the London workshop. She glanced at Mrs. Flood. "Can I ask you for one more introduction?"

Mrs. Nell Turner gave the guitar over to her son and shook Agatha's hand. "A pleasure to meet you, ma'am."

"The pleasure is mine," Agatha replied. "But I have to ask you—how did you come to sell Griffin's broadsides here in Melliton? I wasn't aware we had any wholesalers outside of London."

"My husband works for Birkett's," Nell explained. "He brings me the latest ballads when he comes home on his days off."

"When he remembers," the younger Turner muttered.

Nell cuffed him softly on the shoulder.

Agatha pulled her sketchbook and pencil out of her pocket. "I wonder if I might interest you in a more direct arrangement . . ."

A quarter of an hour later Agatha had the lyrics to "His Inexpressibles" jotted down to be set and printed, with more generous payment terms and a new wholesale arrangement for Griffin's other broadsides, signed with both her name and Mrs. Turner's.

"That was kind," Mrs. Flood said, as they waved farewell to their companions and stepped out into the night.

"Kind?" Agatha snorted. "It was business. I plan to sell 'Inexpressibles' all over London. And just wait until the plagiarists catch wind of it—they'll be singing it in Ireland and Scotland by summer's end, I promise you. And neither Mrs. Turner nor myself will ever see a penny of *those* sales."

"But she will see quite a few more pennies now, thanks to you."

Agatha snorted again, but more softly. "Save your compliments for when I've done something altruistic, and not merely mutually beneficial. I plan to profit off Mrs. Turner's clever songs, make no mistake."

The pub-deafness was wearing off, and she was suddenly aware of how sweet and musical the night was, here just on the edge of the lantern light. The river murmured a lullaby, and the wind sighed harmony in the willow branches.

"Mmm." In the dimness, Mrs. Flood's smile was a thin line of gold where the light touched her lips. "Does this mean you'll be coming to Melliton more often?"

"It might." Agatha's throat was dry, adding a low, rough note to her voice. "If Mrs. Stowe will have me."

"I'll have you, if she won't."

Agatha sucked in a breath.

Penelope Flood turned her face skyward, taking the measure of the moon to see how far along the night had gone. Moonlight and lamplight mingled on her cheeks, silver warring with gold.

On nights like this, standing beside a woman who looked like that, it was extremely trying to remain a respectable widow. Agatha clenched her hands so tight her knuckles creaked.

Mrs. Flood sighed. "I'd best be heading home. Good night, Griffin."

"Good night, Flood," Agatha replied. She spun on her heel and strode down the lane, letting the night wind put distance between herself and temptation.

CHAPTER SEVEN

The post had been busier than usual in the two days Agatha'd been away. There were letters from the musical reviewer in Paris and the hotelier from the Alps, along with others whose handwriting she didn't quite know by sight. So much paper, speeding back and forth over land and sea—and it never ended.

The *Menagerie* was their bread and butter, Agatha knew—but it still felt stiff and unnatural, like an old suit of armor she had to squeeze herself into. One that pinched at the toes and creaked at the elbows, because it had been made to fit someone else.

She shook herself. Clearly spending too much time with the poetical Penelope Flood was having an effect on her. Suit of armor, indeed. They were words, that was all, simple words on plain paper. Something she'd been doing for three years now.

Three endless, awkward, embarrassing years while she paged through etiquette guides and letter-writing manuals to find ways of saying what she meant in phrases that didn't sound as blunt and impatient as she felt. It was a dance Thomas had excelled in, but which Agatha had always abhorred. She always had to look up the references, and never felt comfortable adding any unless they came direct from the manuals or etiquette guides. She lacked the will for wordplay or allusion or quotation—or else she lacked a certain fluidity of mind.

Something that youth would be far more adept at, Agatha realized.

She stared thoughtfully at the towering stack of letters and came to a swift, self-serving decision: she would delegate. Was this not precisely what apprentices were for? "Eliza," she asked the girl working at the table by her side, "how would you like to take over some of the *Menagerie* correspondence?"

"Me?" The apprentice looked up from her music plate, her surprise a most imperfect mask for her eagerness. "Write to the lords and ladies?"

"Not yet—let's start you with the artists and musicians." Agatha sorted through until she found the most recent letters from the music reviewers who frequently sent pieces in for the *Menagerie*. "The experts and professionals. They're quite a bit more entertaining than the lords and ladies, I assure you."

Eliza accepted the letters as though they were as fragile as baby birds. "Then why do you want to be rid of them, ma'am?"

"Well," Agatha started, and stopped in horror when she realized she was blushing. Good god, blushing at her age, how mortifying. "To be perfectly frank, I need to make time to travel back and forth to Melliton more often. Say, once a week instead of once a month."

Eliza stared.

Agatha's cheeks went hotter, and her mouth flattened into a steely line. "So our first wholesaler outside town is well stocked," she insisted. "And there is always something in the queue that needs proofing. And I'll be able to check on my beehive, too, of course." She realized she was close to babbling, and snapped her mouth shut.

"Of course, ma'am."

Eliza murmured obediently enough, but Agatha shriveled in her soul to see the question marks still hovering in the girl's dark, curious eyes. She hurried to change the subject. "Let me walk you through the first one, and show you the book of sample letters . . ."

Still, even the embarrassment of a secret attraction to a married woman didn't stop her from visiting Melliton again a week later. And the week after that, and the week after that, until it became an accepted part of the rhythm of her life.

Mr. Downes developed a nervous habit of twisting one bit of hair endlessly between his fingers, until it became clear that despite her more frequent appearances his employer spent as much time out of the print-works as in it. Agatha took to carting her sketchbook with her, since Mrs. Flood only rarely needed a second person's help; the sketchbook's scenes of London life and famous landmarks began to alternate with country views and cottage scenes and detailed studies of bees and wildflowers. Agatha also brought with her the profits from the first "Inexpressibles" run, new ballads for Mrs. Turner to sell, and whiled away evenings with the crowd in the Four Swallows or with Flood and Joanna Molesey at Fern Hall, before heading back to the solitary darkness of Mrs. Stowe's spare room. When needed she would hire Gus and cart the *Menagerie* issues back with her, but most times she found a seat on the stagecoach, which was appreciably quicker and cheaper.

The blueness of the sky no longer seemed so empty, arching above her on the journey.

Agatha had sold all of Thomas's things after he died, and so she walked every circuit in a pair of Mr. Flood's cast-off trousers and the same blue coat. She was growing quite addicted to the freedom of long strides free of clinging skirts, and in the lack of pale petticoats to be brushed clean of mud and dust after a long day's walk.

Nor was that the only change. The differences between city and country, once so stark in Agatha's perception, began to fade. People were roughly the same in both places, after all, underneath the regional trappings of apparel and accent. She'd been foolish ever to think otherwise. Just like in London, people in the village argued, they teased, they worked, they loved.

And: they fucked. Because even lurid artworks, which Agatha had always thought of as a vice particular to the city, could be found in quiet, homely Melliton—provided one knew where to look.

It was her fourth circuit. Penelope Flood had walked with Agatha to show off her personal beehives at Fern Hall:

two skeps with glasses on top, and an extremely scientific design by a Swiss apiculturist which Flood referred to as a *leaf hive*. This structure was a series of tall rectangular frames with glass sides, all joined with hinges at the back so they could be closed up tight, or fanned open wide. They looked, in fact, precisely like the pages of a book, connected at the spine and spread out in front. Instead of letters and lines of words, however, each glass-covered "page" was alive with buzzing, building, crawling, cleaning bees, packed so tight that in many places you couldn't see the comb beneath.

Agatha remembered when that would have made her shudder. Now, she put one wondering hand on the glass and smiled to feel the heat of an active hive.

The whole structure was placed under a small red-tiled roof to keep off the wet, but which had the effect of making it look like a shrine—even before Agatha noticed it was overlooked by a small replica of the Medici Venus. A souvenir that had been brought home by one of Penelope Flood's many seafaring brothers in his youth, the beekeeper explained, while Agatha sketched a fascinated study of the leaf hive in swift, precise lines.

Flood also pointed out the queen, larger than her commoner daughters but still hard to spot amid the thronging, buzzing crowd.

"Do you get a great deal more honey from this hive?" Agatha asked, as her pencil added the velvety insect shapes.

Flood tilted her head. "Well, yes, because it holds more bees. But in a skep you can use glasses, with wires to keep the queen below, so the honey harvest is a simpler process.

With the leaf hive, I have to close off the passages between the two halves until the first half is empty of bees, so I can harvest honey unimpeded, and I still have to cut through the sides where the bees have glued it in place and then . . ." She checked herself with a wry twist of her mouth. "It's complicated, shall we say."

Agatha snorted softly. "So I see."

"However . . ." Flood went on.

She was using her storyteller's tone, which made Agatha automatically lift her eyes and still her pencil, curiosity chiming irrepressible notes inside her.

Flood stroked the side of the hive possessively. "The leaf hive's great advantage is that it lets a person observe every hour in the life of a hive. Larval hatchings, the building and capping of comb, queens' duels—"

"Duels?"

"Oh yes—when a new queen hatches before the old one's set off with a swarm, the two bees will hunt each other through the hive. They pipe for one another, calling out threats, until they meet in some dark corner of the comb and then . . ."

Agatha was riveted. "And then?"

"And then: slash! Stab!" Penelope Flood's mobile mouth was a mournful twist. "You can only ever have one queen to a hive."

Agatha cast a newly anxious eye on the bees in front of her. "They sound almost as vicious as Jacobins."

Flood laughed at that. "Not quite so bloody as that, to be honest. More like . . . Elizabeth and Mary, Queen of Scots. Only one head can wear the crown."

"Have you ever seen a queens' duel?"

"Not myself—but plenty of naturalists have, and written descriptions in some detail. We are in a great age for beekeeping, you know. There have been great advancements made these past few decades; they've made harvesting honey more productive and more pleasant, for both bees and humans. It's about understanding the true nature of bees, and working with that nature instead of against it."

Agatha looked again at the queen, basking in a circle of her daughters, their small front limbs combing her attentively. "You mean, because bees are so well governed by their queen, it means they are governable by beekeepers?"

Flood's lips thinned. "Some keepers think so. For myself, I find that bees do best when left to govern themselves as much as possible. A keeper is there to provide help, not to impose a human's notion of order. Because as much as it looks like a monarchy, a hive does not depend on any individual bee, not even the queen—on her own, without her attendants or her drones or her daughters, she is nothing. And she keeps nothing for herself. The colony shares everything."

"But surely the queen is needed to make more bees," Agatha said. "Even I know that much."

Flood's grin was a revolutionary slash. "On the contrary: if a queen dies, the workers will simply raise themselves another. The lineage may be broken, but the colony endures forever."

Agatha stared at the hive, and all its miniature architecture on display. Brown and ochre, spring green and bright gold—after she counted the tenth different shade in the cells of the comb she was compelled to ask: "What do the different colors mean?"

Flood looked up from her notebook, where she was penciling observations of the leaf hive. She smiled to see Agatha all but pressed up against the glass. "The colors tell you what kind of plant the bee visited," she explained. "Different plants make different kinds of honey."

Agatha could only stare at all those tiny hexagons, brilliant and beautiful as a church window. "How do you keep them separate?"

"You don't. The bees do, when they find something that's blooming well. Cherry and plum trees, heather, raspberries. They take as much as they can from one plant before moving on to the next." Her smile widened. "It's a good deal more fun if I show you."

That was how Agatha found herself in Penelope Flood's honey larder, sitting at the low table with a half dozen jars of honey awaiting her pleasure. "Start with the wildflower," Flood urged, and held out a spoon.

Agatha took it warily, careful not to let her fingers brush Flood's. The metal was warm from her hand, though, which was almost as bad for Agatha's peace of mind. She took up the jar of wildflower honey and spooned up a small dollop: light amber, very clear.

It tasted, as she'd expected, like honey. Sweet and delicious. "Very nice."

Flood's smile turned impish. "That was from one of the

hives near Backey Green," she said. "Now: this is from Mrs. Stowe's garden."

This jar was slightly darker amber, with a mist of crystallization. Agatha scooped up a bit from the still-liquid part and put it on her tongue—and stopped. Still sweet, still honey—but the flavor was now a darker floral, almost perfumed, with notes underneath that were almost bitter. "Oh," she breathed. "Oh, it's so different."

"Your mother-in-law grows mostly roses and thyme," Flood said. "You see how it affects the flavor?" She talked Agatha through more varieties: heather honey and apple blossom and a strong, herby one that came from the deepest part of the woods. "Honey is never all one thing," Flood explained, while Agatha curled her tongue into the bowl of the spoon to get the last layer of sweetness. "It's lots of little bits, which together make something unique."

Agatha licked her lips. "Which honey is yours?"

Flood blushed a little and slid forward the darkest jar, almost ruby in color. "The woods near here are full of blackberries, so that's mostly what my bees bring home."

This time, Agatha filled the entire spoon. Flood gazed avidly as she raised it to her lips and opened her mouth.

Agatha swallowed, thick honey sliding lazily down her throat. She closed her eyes, sparks bursting against the back of her eyelids as one lush flavor after another poured through her. Sharp greens and deep purples and the tang of berries. The sweetness lingered on her tongue and clouded the air around her as she breathed out on a helpless, hungry sigh.

She opened her eyes just in time to see Penelope Flood's throat work as she swallowed, hard.

Agatha wondered what it would taste like if she and Penelope—

No. Mrs. Flood was a married woman. Agatha clung to her respectability by the thinnest of threads. "Thank you," she said instead, and hated how stilted it sounded to her own ears. "I had no idea that the location of a hive could make such a difference."

Flood's blue eyes cut to Agatha, sly and suggestive. "Would you like to see the oldest hives in Melliton?"

And that was how Agatha came to see the gardens of Abington Hall.

"The skeps are replaced as needed, of course," Flood said an hour later, barely out of breath even though Agatha was still panting from their quick ascent up the hill path. "But the boles have been home to bees for who knows how many hundreds of years. So I like to think of them as the same hives, in essence, if not in actuality."

Agatha could only nod, her voice not yet trustworthy. It was one of the first truly hot days of the season, hissing with crickets. She sucked in lungfuls of sweet, apple-and-herb-scented air while Flood walked the small enclosure, sweeping clear the doorways of each of the hives. The bee garden was pleasant enough—but the tall windows of the hall looming up beyond it were dark even in the daylight.

Agatha couldn't shake the feeling those windows were watching her.

Flood caught the direction of her gaze and shook her

head. "Viscount Summerville has gone north for a bit of shooting," she said, "and his lady has gone to London, so is not here to trouble us. Not that I don't have a duty to see to these hives, considering Isabella left them to my care." She cast Agatha a sidelong glance, and even beneath the bee veil the curve of her lips made Agatha go breathless all over again. "So it's also a perfect time to show you what else Lady Summerville inherited."

The metal of the side gate latch was far too hot to touch barehanded: Agatha felt it even through the thick leather bee-keeping gloves, before she swept the muslin veils away and bared her face to the sun. She followed the beekeeper through the gate and around the first few bends of a hedge maze Agatha hoped she wouldn't have to navigate out of on her own.

By the third turning she was breathless again, and so disoriented that she was glad the bright heat of the sun in the sky above told her for certain which direction was up.

They turned one more corner and found themselves in the middle of an orgy.

Agatha wasn't prudish; she'd been a wife and was mother of a son, and Griffin's had occasionally taken commissions for the sort of private engravings that banished one's prudery forever. But it was one thing to consider licentious poses on paper, from behind the safety of the frame—it was quite another to stand inches away from a sculpted satyr who was life-size in all ways except the one where he was enormously larger than life.

"Goodness," Agatha said, and blushed to the roots beneath Mr. Flood's broad-brimmed hat.

Flood's answering grin heated her skin nearly as much as the sunlight did.

Was it possible to perish from a combination of arousal and embarrassment? Agatha cleared her throat and fought for something like aloofness, turning her eyes back to the satyr as the lesser of two temptations. Well, for a given definition of *lesser*, at any rate. "How would one even walk?"

"Quite carefully, I should imagine," Flood said with a laugh. "Especially going around corners."

"I fear for his fellow pedestrians."

Flood cocked her head. "The nymphs don't appear to be complaining."

And indeed, the lithe figures scattered around among the hollyhocks and peonies looked every bit as louche as the satyrs. Admittedly, with more realistic physical proportions. Some were plump and sported dimples in cheeks and elbows; some were slender as birch trees with merely a whisper of bosom. The closer Agatha looked, the more each one felt . . . specific. The sculptress had not just captured the likeness of a model—she'd been recreating the forms and faces of people she knew deeply and well.

That realization was more shocking than the satyr anatomy, quite frankly: you felt that to look at any figure was to interrupt them at a most private, pleasurable moment.

The couple lounging in luxury at the center of the scene was even more easily recognizable—particularly to anyone who'd been engraving and publishing satires during the wars. "Good lord," Agatha choked, "don't tell me that's—"

"Bonaparte," Flood confirmed.

"A little more apart would have been appreciated."

Flood cackled.

Agatha squirmed and gaped at the statue of the former emperor sprawled on a tiger skin, in all his natural glory.

The beekeeper's voice was fond, as though discussing an old friend. "He's dressed—well, not so much dressed, but depicting Bacchus, of course. You should see the one of him as Mars that Wellington brought home: it's nearly twelve feet tall, which puts most people's face right about . . . well, you can guess where."

"Good *lord*."

Agatha yanked her gaze away from the emperor's glory to peer at the woman lounging at his side, hair crowned with stars, and a lingering sadness in her large eyes. She was covered in a flutter of drapery, which was as good as a nun's habit in this setting. "And that's Josephine as Ariadne, I expect."

"Very fitting, don't you think? Parted from her first love, then raised up to glorious heights by the second."

"Oh, a very apt allusion. I expect this was sculpted before the emperor divorced her? Bacchus would have been ashamed to do any such thing."

Flood's expressive lips twisted. "Bacchus has no need of heirs, though, does he? A mortal monarch does."

Agatha sobered. England had too recently lost the heir to the throne, the much-loved young Princess Charlotte. She had died giving birth to a stillborn son, only a few scant weeks after Thomas's heart had given out; in Agatha's personal anguish the country's prolonged, widespread grief for the young someday queen and mother had been both a comfort and a torment.

Comfort, because it had given Agatha a very handy excuse for tears when she was in a most fragile state.

Torment, because it turned the world into a ghastly mirror, showing a mother and son being mourned when she was a mother with a son, in mourning. There had been no escaping, no recourse from reminders of loss. Even now, looking up at another lost queen, it cut too near the bone for Agatha's comfort.

She reached out and grasped Flood's elbow as if it were a lifeline. "Show me a different one," she said.

Flood looked down at Agatha's hand, then up again with a smile. "This way. My favorite is in the center of the maze."

Flood's favorite statue was a pairing: a dryad and a water nymph. The dryad was mostly tree below the waist and in one arm high above her head. The other stretched down as she leaned toward the water nymph—whose own legs vanished into waves and froth, though her arms reached up, eager to twine with those of the dryad.

The figures were almost, but not quite touching: fingertips inches from grasping, lips parted for a kiss but still a breath away from meeting.

That sliver of space cut through Agatha like a knife. "Oh," she gasped, and pressed her hand against her heart. "That's Joanna Molesey, isn't it?" For the water nymph's long nose and hungry eyes were the absolute mirror of the poet's.

Flood nodded once, sharply. Her voice was reverent, as though they stood in a cathedral. "The dryad is a self-portrait.

Isabella sculpted this when she was much younger—right after she'd met Joanna and Mr. Molesey for the first time."

"Did her husband . . . ?" Agatha had to stop and clear the roughness from her throat. There was so much hopeless yearning in those figures that it made her want to weep. "Was he very angry about it?"

"According to Isabella, Mr. Molesey looked at it and said: 'Oh, how sweet, the nymph and the dryad want to be friends even though they abide in different elements.'"

Agatha looked at those reaching hands, those parted lips, and back at Flood. "*Friends?*" she blurted, and pointed at the water nymph. "This statue does not embody *friendship*, Flood. That nymph is literally melting below the waist, and the dryad is doing the opposite of whatever Daphne does whenever Apollo catches up to her. Honestly," she said, folding her arms, shaking her head, "you could not come up with any clearer signal of sensual encouragement than opposite-Daphne."

Flood was laughing at this helplessly, silently. At length she gasped, "You are an artist, Griffin: you're fluent in this language. The late Mr. Molesey was very much not."

Agatha made a rude noise for Joanna's deluded, departed husband and turned back to the statue. "It's lovely of course— and rather scandalous—but what makes it your favorite?"

Flood got herself under control with a final chuckle. "Partly that it is so beautiful. And I love the curl on that wave, and the bend in the branches. It makes me think of the best kind of pastoral poetry. But also . . ." She paused, biting her lip. "This is going to sound horribly sentimental."

Agatha waved this aside. "You've already mentioned poetry. We might as well bring sentiment into it."

Flood's eyes creased at the corners, whether from the bright sunlight or from the difficulty of putting her thoughts into proper words, Agatha didn't know. At last she said: "Isabella sculpted this because she fell in love with someone she shouldn't, and she couldn't act on her feelings even if they chanced to be returned. Art was her only way of grappling with the situation. It's a moment of perfect hopelessness, captured in stone—but it's not the end of the story. So when I look at this statue, I can almost . . . look past the pain and see beyond to all the years and the happiness they had together. They had no idea they had all that to look forward to. So the statue, you see, means something more, something better than what the artist originally put into it. And that strikes me as a sort of miracle."

She cast Agatha a shy smile, knowing she had offered something tender and fragile, ready to laugh at herself if that's what Agatha chose to do.

Agatha did not feel like laughing. She felt lightning-blasted, rooted to the spot. Mr. Flood's old coat felt stiff and brittle, like a layer of bark that had encased her tense shoulders and awkward arms.

Someone else's wife, she reminded herself. *Someone else has already claimed her hand, so yours must stay at your side.*

But oh, it was all she could do not to reach out.

"Did you ever show Mr. Flood this statue?" she asked instead—then silently cursed her too-sharp tongue.

If Penelope Flood thought the question too probing, it

didn't appear to trouble her. "I did. 'Very Greek,' he called it."
Flood's smile widened, two dimples winking into view in her
cheeks. "And now, whenever I look at it, I am going to recall
the phrase 'opposite-Daphne.' Which I never could have pre-
dicted before, either. So you see: truth, as well as beauty, is in
the eye of the beholder."

Agatha managed a choked laugh, but beneath her borrowed coat an unspeakable thorn had burrowed into her
chest, and she knew it would ache for some time yet.

CHAPTER EIGHT

The Four Swallows was buzzing on the night of 6 July, and it was all on account of the news. Penelope shouldered her way through to the bar to get a round for herself and Griffin, then squeezed up next to the printer on a bench to hear Mr. Biswas read aloud from the latest edition of the *Times*.

A secret report had been presented in the House of Lords: the summation of two green bags' worth of evidence against Queen Caroline's fidelity and character, collected without her knowledge by spies for the king and his government. Naturally, since it was a secret report, everyone was talking about it.

The Queen had composed a petition to the Lords asking that she be permitted to speak in her own defense; instead, Lord Liverpool had presented a Bill of Pains and Penalties.

"Adultery," Mrs. Koskinen murmured, translating the legalisms. Her plump white hand squeezed her husband's arm in distracted outrage, and her red curls bobbed as she bounced. "He's been accusing her of being unfaithful for a decade now."

"If she is, it's no wonder," Mrs. Biswas grumbled. "Not

like George has ever done anything to endear himself to his wife. He didn't even write to tell her when the Princess died. Her own daughter!"

"She's a wicked woman," mutter Mr. Painter, huffing out clouds of smoke from his pipe. "The whole thing is an embarrassment to the nation."

Mr. Biswas continued to read from yesterday's paper in a clear, carrying voice. His eyes went wide as he scanned ahead and reached the heart of the matter: "*A Bill to deprive her Majesty, Caroline Amelia Elizabeth, of the title, prerogatives, rights, privileges, and pretensions, of Queen-consort of this realm, and to dissolve the marriage between his Majesty and the said Queen.*"

"Dissolve the marriage!" Mrs. Koskinen gasped.

"Divorce," Mr. Painter confirmed, in heavy tones. "Though it's not the usual way such things are done."

"Can he force one through like this?" Mrs. Koskinen demanded. "Surely the Church will have strong objections—and the people won't allow it—there's been one mutiny already in the King's Mews on her behalf—if the army rises up to defend her—"

Her husband put his large hand over hers, and she bit her lip and subsided.

"The Lords are responding now," Mr. Biswas went on. "*Earl Grey said that it must appear to be a very great disadvantage to the Queen to have allegations made against her by the committee, and a bill afterwards laid on their lordships' table, and placed before the public, for a considerable time before she was allowed to be heard.*"

"Quite right," Mr. Kitt responded. "Any other criminal on trial has the right to speak in his own defense. Should not our Queen, if she is to stand accused?"

"The King will never permit it," Mr. Biswas responded. "Nor his friends in the Lords. It would give Caroline a chance to describe George's even worse failings—under oath, in the public record, ready for any and all scribblers to put into tomorrow's caricatures." He caught himself and his brown cheeks went ruddy. "No offense intended to present company, of course."

"None taken," Griffin replied pleasantly, toasting him with her ale.

Mr. Biswas continued reading the argument from the Lords, Mrs. Koskinen hanging on every syllable.

Mr. Kitt leaned over to speak to Mr. Thomas, Griffin, and Penelope. "It's an absolute godsend for the radical press—they're now free to attack the King all they like under cover of defending the Queen's good name."

"My son Sydney nearly had an apoplexy about it yesterday morning," Griffin said wryly. She was looking rather regal herself, to Penelope's eye, in a dress of lilac linen, the light fabric a concession to the summer heat. It made the gray in her hair gleam and her eyes shine like jet in the firelight. She tilted her head thoughtfully. "As for myself, I feel terribly uneasy about the whole business. Too many people are calling for too many others to take up arms."

"Do you believe the Queen is guilty, then?" Mr. Thomas asked.

Griffin snorted. "As if half the Lords haven't done everything they're accusing her of, and more. As if the King himself hasn't been parading mistresses all up and down the country since long before his royal father died. What does guilt even mean, in such a context?"

"You'd think the King would have better followed his father and mother's example," Mr. Kitt added gently. "They were the very picture of a happy English marriage."

"This can't be only because they are unhappy," Mrs. Koskinen said. "He was content to leave her alone when she was in Italy."

"He sent spies!" Mr. Biswas cried.

Mrs. Koskinen folded her arms. "It seems to me that what he wants even more than a divorce is to not share the power of the Crown."

Arguments multiplied. Volume doubled. Mr. Biswas and Mrs. Koskinen traded words at impossible speed, while Mr. Koskinen's brow grew more and more craggy with dread. Mr. Kitt and Mr. Thomas were leaned close together, whispering blond hair against brown, barely enough space for a breath between them, both men's faces troubled and pale.

Her friends had always argued in the Swallows, but this was more than friendly teasing. People were becoming actually angry. Penelope leaned against the back wall of the tavern, seeking comfort from the wall's sturdy bulk.

After a moment, Griffin angled toward her, firelight licking across her face. "Everything alright, Flood?"

Penelope bit her lip and shook her head. "It shouldn't have to come to this. It should be easier to sever a union when the parties make one another so evidently miserable. Even if she was tired of Italy—why can they simply not live apart, as so many couples do?"

"Because he's King and she's Queen," Griffin said grimly. "And they both want everything that means."

"So he has to brand her publicly as faithless and depraved, and the Lords have to all vote on whether they agree. And for what? Spite and pride."

"And power," Griffin countered. "Even if she's not crowned, as long as they're married, she can be used as a cudgel against his ministers. Good English loyalists who wouldn't pick up a radical paper to light their kitchen fires with will champion Caroline, because they can do so without feeling it makes them disloyal. You heard Mr. Kitt: the radical press will support the Queen because they oppose George, not necessarily because they believe the Queen to have done nothing wrong in Italy."

"Who cares what she did in Italy?" Penelope burst out. "If George doesn't want her, why should it matter that somebody else does?"

Griffin's dark eyes were hot as coals as they pinned Penelope in place. "Would it have mattered to you? If you had someone who—who wanted you, and your husband was an ocean away, would you have taken any happiness you were offered, no matter how illicit?"

Penelope laughed painfully, for that struck too near the bone. Griffin wasn't to know how Penelope dreamed of unbuttoning the high prim collar of John's coat to press hungry lips against the printer's neck; how often she imagined Griffin's slender form trapping her against a tree in the heart of the wood, while Penelope's hands shoved that blue coat off the dark-haired woman's shoulders.

Even now, hearing Griffin's voice turn stern and steely like that made Penelope want to fall to her knees and do anything the woman commanded her to do. The more licentious the better.

Her friend wasn't offering anything like that, no matter how much Penelope wished she would. Agatha Griffin was far too respectable for that sort of dalliance.

Penelope turned her tankard around on the table, leaving dark wet rings on the wood. "I would have to think about the consequences of any indiscretion," she said. "How many of my friends and servants have been paid to inform on me? How many eyes are watching me, prepared to exploit any errors or sins or moments of weakness?"

Griffin sucked in a breath so sharp it sounded as though she'd been stabbed. Slowly, she leaned away, both hands clutching her cup hard enough that her knuckles shone white against the pewter. "Indeed," she said, refusing to meet Penelope's gaze. "A husband's power knows very few limitations, even when he is not a king."

Penelope knew she'd said something hurtful, but couldn't think what. They sank into a private, awkward silence for two, while all around them people argued over adultery.

Inevitably the Turner boy came around, hawking caricatures and cartoons about the scandal.

Mr. Painter turned up his nose at the whole set, and went outside to smoke in peace. Mr. Biswas set aside the *Times* to buy a sheet of the cheapest paper, splashed with the brightest colors. The image showed Queen Caroline as a luxuriant, fluffed-up chicken, the feathers of the headdresses she favored carrying down to clothe her squat, round shape. Beside her a towering rooster in Italian costume bowed chivalrously over her hand, while in the background various foxes in Liberty caps pilfered the henhouse of all its eggs. Scrawled names of radical writers floated above their heads like smoke from revolutionary bonfires: Cobbett and Carlyle, Hone, Brougham, and Hunt. *Lord Sidmouth* was written above a turtle in a constable's costume, but it was clear he'd arrive too late to apprehend the thieves.

A COCK IN THE HENHOUSE, read the caption.

Mr. and Mrs. Biswas snickered; Mrs. Koskinen rolled her eyes and resumed whispering anxiously into her husband's ear about possible legal wrinkles in the coming debate.

Penelope put her face into her tankard, drinking deep to hide her disquiet.

"That's one of Thisburton's cartoons," drawled Mr. Kitt, peering over Mr. Thomas' shoulder to look. "You put out a lot of his work, don't you, Mrs. Griffin?"

"Some, though not this one," Griffin admitted. She looked less pained now, but she still wasn't meeting Penelope's eye. "I'm not sure any one house could print *all* of them—he's rather prolific."

"He spends himself all over the place," Mr. Thomas added.

Mr. Kitt elbowed him; Mr. Thomas squawked out a laugh, and Griffin rolled her eyes.

Mr. Kitt groused, "It's easy to be prolific when you draw

satires for both sides of any question. Doubles your audience in one stroke: you draw something pro-Parliament, then something just the opposite."

"That doubled audience is perhaps what makes him so valuable to work with for us printers," Griffin put in, with a wry twist of her lips. "Or so I keep telling my son, whenever he makes that same point."

"Kitt would prefer the man confine his talents to the reformers' side of the argument," Mr. Thomas explained.

"Quite so," Mr. Kitt confirmed. "As it is, Thisburton seems to have more fondness for money than political convictions."

"Perhaps because one cannot eat political convictions?" Griffin suggested.

Mr. Thomas chuckled into his ale, as Mr. Kitt made noises of mingled amusement and outrage.

Penelope thunked her tankard down on the table. Beer sloshed over her wrist, but she didn't care. "I agree with Mr. Kitt," she declared.

"I'm a little surprised," Griffin said at length. "I'd have thought you'd be more likely to appreciate a pragmatist, when it comes to the question of putting food on the table."

"I daresay Mr. Thisburton is in no danger of starving, or even running short of work," Penelope bit out. "And I think it's certainly practical to say that his playing both sides of an issue might hinder our progress. The man has a great talent, and through his work he has the power to influence opinions in such a way as to sway the people to one belief or another. He ought to be deliberate about how he applies that influence, if he cares about the fate of his fellow countrymen. He treats it like a game—but one only he can win, while the rest of the nation loses." She shook the liquid from her wrist, and folded her arms with finality. "You cannot get a ship to go anywhere by blowing on both sides of a sail."

"Hear hear!" Mr. Kitt said.

Griffin's smile was slight but sincere. "Trust a sailor's wife to think of it in nautical terms."

"Trust a sailor's wife, full stop," Penelope replied, and felt the tightness in her chest ease a bit when Griffin laughed in response.

The whole country had already been stirred up by the Queen's return. Now the introduction of the Bill of Pains and Penalties struck the island like lightning, inflaming the populace to new flashes of fury. Agatha could barely keep abreast of what was happening. Revolution was called for in the taverns, while in marble halls, titled lips whispered the same word as though it were a curse to conjure with. Everyone had an opinion, but nobody *knew* anything. Anxiety clouded the air more than the fog ever had.

Every time Sydney left the house, Agatha wondered if today was the day the uprising would start, and Sydney would be the one marching at the front with the banner. Making himself a proper target. She wondered if she'd ever see him again, and even though she knew she was being ridiculous, her heartbeat stuttered in her chest. Radical papers praised the recent civil wars in Naples, Spain, and Portugal, while soldiers arrested radical writers and seized their print-ings in bulk; Peterloo and Cato Street were revived in the public imagination; Tory papers complained that the rabble would take up arms, and the soldiers would refuse to con-front them, and good English patriots would be slaughtered in their sleep by pitchfork-wielding mobs, or beheaded by the guillotines that were surely being erected on every village green and in every London square.

Each time Sydney came back, he'd found another writer begging Griffin's to print a pamphlet whose rhetoric could get them fined, arrested, transported, or worse.

Agatha rejected most of these offers outright—Griffin's had a reputation as scientific and artistic, rather than radical or political—but with the streets in such turmoil, sales of picturesque landmarks and tranquil tour scenes were suffer-ing. Something had to bridge the gap.

"A broadside edition of one of the Queen's letters, then," Agatha yielded with a sigh.

"At least it's not technically sedition, to reprint the words of the Queen," Eliza offered.

"Not until she's divorced, anyways," Agatha muttered. "Though if that happens, I expect we'll have larger matters to worry about."

Sydney's face lit up at the thought of speaking out and getting his message heard—any message, even if it wasn't as fiercely radical as he might have hoped. "I'll set the type myself, if you like, after the workmen have gone home. That way nobody will know where it came from."

Agatha snorted. "You think the journeymen don't know

every nick in every piece of type we use? But it's a good precaution, all the same." She narrowed her eyes. "Do you even remember how to compose type?"

Her son only grinned. "I'm sure it will come back to me."

It did, to his mother's mingled pride and irritation. Late that evening, with the shop quiet and the streetlamps flickering orange outside, Agatha cast a practiced eye over the finished forme: the bundle of leaden letters and bits of wood, tied up tight with twine to hold all the smaller pieces together. They'd pull a proof to check for errors, but any decent printer could decrypt the backwards letters in the composing stick by the time they finished their apprenticeship, and Agatha's practiced eye spotted no mistakes.

It only took two people to operate the iron Stanhope press, so Agatha let the young people do the bulk of the work. Sydney set the forme in the galley, and the galley in the press-bed; Eliza skimmed the congealed skin off the top of the ink, and used a knife to spread a thin liquid layer on the glass-topped table next to the press. A single sheet of paper went into the tympan, atop layers of cloth padding to soften the blow of the plate; the frisket came down to protect the edges from ink, its cut-out center square framing and presenting the blank page like a yeoman holding a snowy sheep in place for shearing.

Eliza daubed a thin layer of ink onto the letters of the forme, filling the air with the dark, lush scent of oil; Sydney lowered tympan and frisket onto the bed, and pulled the rounce—a bar that slid the whole arrangement into the heart of the press.

All that was mere preparation: now came the moment of truth.

A single pull of the long central lever brought the flat, heavy platen down with a thump Agatha felt from her heels to her heart. She flinched internally, and hoped the noise wasn't audible to anyone in the street outside.

Normally it was her favorite part of the process. The instant when all the layers of padding, paper, ink, and type were squashed together—and something new came out.

Sydney pushed the lever back, turned the rounce, and opened the frisket. There it was, in black and white, shining wetly: the words of Queen Caroline to her subjects and supporters. Sydney held it out for Agatha's approval, suddenly and adorably shy.

Agatha's heart softened. He'd looked just like that the day he pulled his first proof out of the press, as a young apprentice. It had been Thomas he'd handed it to then, of course.

How fast the years went by, when you had worries to keep you busy.

Swallowing her nostalgia, Agatha eyed the proof, pronounced it good, and hung the paper up to dry. Eliza was already daubing the forme with another layer of ink, and Sydney slipped another page into the press. Another thump, and a new broadsheet to hang from the lines strung across the top of the workroom. And so on, as the minutes spun by.

Press-work made for a comforting rhythm—like the beating of a very large, very slow heart. Agatha hung up another broadsheet and paused to read through a few sentences, taking in the meaning now rather than simply looking for mistakes. "'General tyranny usually begins with individual oppression.' This is much more radical stuff than I would have expected from any monarch."

"They say William Cobbett wrote this one," Sydney said, his hero's name lingering on his tongue like a benediction. "According to Prestwich, who dined with him privately the other evening, Cobbett sees the alliance between the Queenites and the radicals as a natural bond: both have been oppressed, exiled, punished, and spied upon by the government, merely for asserting the rights to which they are legally and morally entitled. If we can harness popular support for Caroline, we might be able to push through actual changes—they say now that Cobbett has her ear, we might get her to support the expansion of suffrage, or even more reforms . . ."

He went on in this way for some time, laying out elaborate plans of negotiation and leverage, most of which were rhetorical, and all of which had at least seventeen separate steps yet were somehow both inevitable and predictable.

It made Agatha feel as though the very stones beneath her feet couldn't be trusted to stay steady.

She remembered what Penelope Flood had said about Thisburton: *He treats it like a game.* All the arguments and the strategies and even the enthusiasm: it was about winning, about scoring points and defeating opponents and being the person who was the most right. Sydney and the young radical men followed political debates the same way their aristocratic nemeses followed horse races—and whenever they talked about revolution, the assumption was that they would be ones on top at the end.

You could almost hear Robespierre laughing from the other side of the guillotine blade.

"Tell me," she blurted, to banish the image, "if you could alter one thing about government—only one thing, but you could change it instantly, without having to argue with anybody—what would you change?"

"Just one thing?" Sydney thought about it for the whole time it took to print another copy of the Queen's address. "I'd revoke the sedition and libel laws," he said at last. "Because a free press is the key that helps you unlock every other door. You can't change what you can't openly talk about."

"Not the vote?" Eliza asked, using one forearm to brush her hair back from her forehead. "I know the press is important, but if the people in power have no reason to listen to you—and unless you're electing them, they don't—how is disenfranchisement any different from censorship?"

Sydney pulled on the press-arm, grunting a little with effort. "So you'd institute universal suffrage: give every man the vote."

"Man *and* woman. Otherwise it's not really universal, is it?" Eliza coolly rolled out another layer of ink for the daubers.

Sydney chortled. "And they say I'm the radical one!" He grinned. "Sorry, Mum. You're outnumbered."

"Don't mind me," Agatha said dryly. "I'm just a cranky old woman with no vote, biding my time until death. The future is yours to worry about."

"So what would you change?" Eliza asked. "Just one thing."

Agatha took the newest broadsheet, and pinned it up for drying. The other sheets fluttered as the string vibrated, billowing like the sails of a ship. She thought of a sailor's wife with gold-and-silver hair, and her husband somewhere far across the sea. Her throat felt tight with the unfairness of it. "I'd make divorce simple. And cheap."

Both Eliza and Sydney stopped, the former with daubers raised, the latter with a fresh broadsheet in one hand. The heartbeat rhythm of the press stopped with them.

London had never sounded so quiet.

Belatedly, it occurred to Agatha that her son might take that as a glancing reference to how she'd felt about his father. But what was she to do? She couldn't tell him: *Oh, don't worry, it's only that I'm lusting after my friend who is inconveniently married.*

She plucked the broadsheet from Sydney's hand and hung it up with the rest. How convenient that the stretch of white paper and black ink hid her face for a moment. "I only mean to say, look at all the fuss currently, on account of one unhappy marriage," she said, too loud in the silence. "Imagine if the King and Queen could simply agree to part—perhaps we wouldn't be standing on the precipice of a revolution."

"Perhaps we need a revolution," muttered Sydney, glancing at Eliza.

"Perhaps," said Eliza tartly, "we need *several*."

Sydney grimaced at that and chewed his lip—a habit he'd inherited from his father, that showed up when he was most anxious. Agatha hadn't seen him do it in a while now, she realized—for all her own worry about the state of the nation and the tenor of the times, Sydney had been nothing if not eager to throw himself into the fray. If he'd been able to choose what Griffin's printed, he'd have been right there on the radical edge with Cobbett and the rest of them.

What was the use of keeping the press going for him, if he was only going to use it to get himself jailed or worse? She knew he was old enough to make his own choices—but did they have to be *these* choices?

Agatha's heart was a wriggling worm in her breast. She groped for a change of subject. "How have you been getting on with the *Menagerie* correspondence, Eliza?"

Her apprentice shrugged. "It's not that different from the wholesalers, to be frank. They make offers of things to write, and they ask when they're getting paid, and they apologize for articles that turn up late or go missing, all that kind of thing. I expected them to talk more about—I don't know, about the things they're writing the articles about? I thought we'd be discussing art, or music, or fashion, about what all those things mean and how to do them well." She shook her head, adding more ink to the forme. "Then again, it's clear they have money and education, so maybe they can tell that—well, that I don't. Our critics write for people who can afford to buy paintings, or sit in a box at the opera. Not for someone who pins up an engraved print or sits in the stalls."

Sydney pulled extra-hard on the press-arm, making the plate thump doubly loud. "What about someone who knows the melody of every popular ballad in London? And who learns new ones as soon as she hears them?"

Eliza went allover pink. "Those are just tunes. Easy enough to learn by ear."

He shook his head. "Doubt any of your music critics have learned half as many."

Eliza's eyes were lowered, but the curl at the corners of her lips showed how pleased she was. Sydney went back for more paper, the tips of his ears turning red.

Behind the drying broadsheets, his mother rolled her eyes and hid a smile.

At one hundred sheets, Agatha declared the work enough for now. Eliza sponged the ink from the form and then the glass, while Sydney tied the forme up again and set it in a drawer for tomorrow night's work. They'd have to wake early to pull the dried pages down and bundle them up before the workmen arrived.

As Eliza had said, it wasn't technically sedition—but this was not an argument Agatha was prepared to make in any official legal capacity. Better to avoid the authorities' notice altogether.

They trooped up the stairs, and to bed. Agatha diplomatically took no notice of her son's hand, straying briefly toward Eliza's for a single soft touch, a silent good-night.

They all went separately to sleep—or so she hoped.

CHAPTER NINE

The summer sun beat down on the Melliton high street. Agatha fancied she could hear the flagstones of the main square sizzling, and had a sudden anxious vision of the stack of broadsheets in her hand bursting spontaneously into flame.

"It'll be cooler in the woods," Flood assured her. The hives had been well tended for the past few months and any damaged skeps replaced, so the wheelbarrow was no longer an everyday necessity: today, Flood carried slung over her shoulder a bundle with the smoker and its fuel, and a few other small tools of the beekeeper's trade.

Agatha shifted her grip on the lyric sheets to let the air cool her hot palms. "Then let's hurry, after we stop at Nell Turner's."

The Turners lived one turn off the high street in a cottage ancient as the hills, whose venerable thatch was almost entirely moss. The lane passed the door as if reluctant to linger, and spent itself in a wheat field behind a low fence; the crop stretched to the foot of the hill beyond, silky and yellow-green as newborn envy.

Agatha expected Flood to knock, but instead the bee-keeper went past and around to the garden at the back of the house. This was a functional potager, worlds away from either the ornamental labyrinth and extensive kitchen garden of Abington Hall or even Mrs. Stowe's cozy cottage roses. Cabbages, onions, radishes, lettuce, and celery, with smaller patches of various herbs, climbed up everywhere out of the dark earth. And in the middle, on a small stool just like the one behind Agatha's print-works, a new skep hive, straw gleaming like gold, young worker bees entering and leaving as they went about their tireless honey production.

Mrs. Turner was defending the onions ruthlessly against the encroaching weeds, and looked up with a start as the two women approached. "Mrs. Flood! Mrs. Griffin!" she exclaimed, springing to her feet and brushing the earth from her hands. "Is there something amiss?" She glanced at the hive, then back at Flood. "I haven't been doing anything wrong with the bees, have I?"

"Not since I checked yesterday afternoon, Mrs. Turner. We won't keep you long." Flood's cheery voice allowed no room for embarrassment, and Mrs. Turner's hands lowered. "We were just stopping in on our way up Backey Green."

"Do you have somewhere I could set these?" Agatha hefted the bundle of broadsheets she carried: a second printing of "Inexpressibles," plus two other new ballads specially selected for Melliton tastes.

Mrs. Turner wiped her hands clean on her apron and led them into the house.

Inside was all low ceilings and dark wood beams, and the heat from the hearth where that evening's bread was baking. The furniture in the main room seemed as old as the house, but the bread smelled wonderful and the wood of the floor had been scrubbed within an inch of its life. A tumbled pair of beds, one large and one small, could be seen through a doorway in the next room—Mrs. Turner hurried over to pull the door shut with an embarrassed squeak of the hinge. "So," she said, "they've been selling well in London?"

"Faster than most," Agatha confirmed. She set the new broadsides down on the long central table, paper and ink covering the scars in the wood. "I've been told by Griffin's resident ballad expert that you probably already know melodies for the other two?"

Mrs. Turner cast an eye over the two new sets of lyrics, and nodded. "I have something that will suit."

Agatha clasped her hands, trying not to sound too eager. "I was also wondering if you had any more original songs I could persuade you to let me print."

"It would be a pleasure," Mrs. Turner said affably. "Just as soon as you deliver the latest payment."

Agatha was confused. "But . . . Mr. Turner came by and collected it earlier this week. Eliza mentioned it."

Flood's sunny smile faded, and Mrs. Turner set down the broadside with a small, pained sigh. "I see." Her mouth had gone tight, her eyes anxious. She smoothed her skirts over her knees, and folded her hands. "I would ask you to deliver any payments to me personally in the future, Mrs. Griffin. If that is possible."

"Of course . . ." Agatha said faintly, cringing internally. How foolish she'd been not to have considered before that Mr. Turner might not have been the most reliable custodian of the money his wife had earned. Even if he did have a right to it, according to the common law. At least he had not received the total sales amount, only the most recent quantity. Agatha cleared her throat. "You have my word that all future monies will be put directly into your hands, Mrs. Turner." Mrs. Turner nodded but still looked tense and wary; Agatha couldn't blame her one bit.

"What song are you working on now, Nell?" Flood asked.

Mrs. Turner's expression softened as she looked at Penelope Flood. "I'm fiddling with something about Jack Calbert's ghost."

Flood chuckled in delight. Agatha's ears perked up. "Whose ghost?"

"I suppose it's *ghosts*, plural," Mrs. Turner said, and some of the warmth came back into her golden skin. "Since there's a whole shipful of them."

Agatha's laugh was a surprised burst of sound. "What?"

The ballad singer straightened in her chair, shaking tension from her shoulders. "When the Armada sailed from Spain to overthrow Good Queen Bess, the navy harried the Spanish ships out of the Channel as the winds forced them north. They fled up along the coast—all except one ship, the *Florencia*, which had taken too many English cannonballs broadside. The galleon sank to the bottom of the sea, just past the mouth of the Thames. The navy kept pursuing the surviving Armada—but one sailor by the name of John Calbert marked the *Florencia*'s final resting place in his journal."

Mrs. Turner by now had fallen into a well-honed story-teller's cadence, and Agatha found herself leaning forward in anticipation, one elbow on the table. If her heart kicked up in a quicker rhythm when Mrs. Flood grinned and watched for her reaction, surely that was only because the tale was so exciting.

Mrs. Turner went on, her voice low and playfully mysterious. "The Armada sailed up around the north coast of Scotland. Supplies were running low, ships' hulls bound with cables to hold the rickety planks together. Winds drove them onto the Irish coast. Every hull shattered and sank. England celebrated a Providential escape—and John Calbert came home a hero. He married, had children, and came to live at Melliton, alongside so many other sailors and retired navy men. When he died fifty years later, he left his journal to his grandson Jack.

"Jack was a sailor on a merchant ship. He was also a smuggler, though one clever enough to know how dangerous—and short—a life that was. When he saw the map in his grandfather's journal, he thought of Spanish doubloons and colonial emeralds, though the *Florencia* was a ship fitted for invasion, not one sailing back rich from conquest. He showed the map to his crew one winter night, at midnight in the pub—though it was called the King's

Arms, then—and they made a plan to sail out and search the wreck for treasure.

"The only other person there that dark night was the barkeeper's daughter, Molly, Jack's betrothed. She begged him not to go—said it was too risky, the shoreline rocky and treacherous with currents and shifting sandbars. Especially in wintertime, when the sea was murderous cold.

"Jack only laughed, and promised he'd be at her side again by Christmas. He and his eight—or six, or eleven companions, depending on who you ask—set out the next morning. They found the spot on the map, and Jack went down in the diving bell. When he came up, he swore he'd found the wreck, and it would make all of them and their wives and children rich.

"But a storm came up, and dashed their boat against the rocks. Cold water and the sea floor below them and a storm above . . . not a single man survived."

Even in the warmth of the room, Agatha shivered.

Flood's hand brushed her elbow, then away.

Agatha caught her breath.

Mrs. Turner's eyes glinted as she continued her tale. "All the Melliton families grieved the loss of their sons. Molly's father hung black bunting from the walls and closed the tavern on Christmas Eve. But just as he and Molly were heading up to bed—or in other versions, just as St. Ambrose's bell struck midnight—someone knocked three times at the door. One—two—three."

Agatha jumped, as Flood's knuckles rapped the table at each count. Flood, troublemaker that she was, only grinned.

Mrs. Turner leaned in, voice low and urgent. "Molly opened the door, ready to shout down whoever was disturbing their mourning. And there was Jack—laughing, prideful, handsome Jack, with a spectral greenish glow about him. 'Didn't I tell you I'd be back by Christmas?' he asked, and strode into the tavern. All his men trooped in after, ghostly green, their clothing ragged, their salt-roughened voices calling for meat and ale and pudding. Trembling, Molly and her father brought out everything they'd saved for their own Christmas dinner. They spread the table as well as they could, and then hurried up the stairs and didn't come down until morning. But when they did . . . they found the room swept and the kitchen scrubbed, as if the feast had never happened. And in the center of the table was a gleaming, golden stack of Spanish doubloons."

"Nine or seven or twelve of them, depending on how many ghosts," Flood added.

"I like nine," said Mrs. Turner. "A proper folklorish number, is nine."

"And that's why the Four Swallows is always closed the night before Christmas," Flood finished.

Mrs. Turner nodded to confirm. "Molly married and she and her husband ran the pub after her father passed, and so on down through the family until Mr. Biswas married Molly's great-great-great-granddaughter, and they renamed the tavern the Four Swallows."

"There are people living today," said Flood, "who will swear they've seen an eldritch green glow about the place on Christmas Eve—and heard the sound of ghostly voices singing."

Mrs. Turner let out a skeptical snort. "People enjoy frightening their neighbors, Mrs. Flood."

Flood pursed her lips and tilted her head primly. "Jack Calbert's ghost is more benevolent than frightening, I always think . . ." Flood caught Agatha's eye and popped to her feet. "And now there are other hives we must see to— good afternoon, Nell."

Agatha murmured her own farewell, and they left Mrs. Turner shaking her head with a wry smile on her lips.

Flood led them eastward, along the fenced field. Wheat stalks swayed in the breeze, protective spikes at the top gleaming like strands of silk. "The Turners used to farm here, when this was all commons," Flood explained, waving her hand at the acres and acres of future harvest. "But Squire Theydon—he's the other magistrate, along with Mr. Oliver—bought this whole piece up during enclosure. And Mr. Turner had to look elsewhere for employment. Mr. Oliver was all for sending him to the workhouse at St. Sepulchre's, but Miss Coningsby knew someone at Birkett's so Mr. Turner ended up there. He rooms in a boarding house during the week, but makes sure to come home to take Nell and Arthur to church of a Sunday."

"So he remembers church, but he tends to forget his wages in town on Fridays," Agatha guessed.

Flood's mouth pinched. "It's disgraceful of him. Imagine having a husband who disregards one so completely. I'd be hungry to be noticed, too, in her place."

Agatha looked at her sharply, but Flood's face was turned up to the sun, untroubled. Perhaps that wasn't an allusion to

Mr. Flood at all. Perhaps Flood's husband wrote marvelous letters, enough to bridge the gap of his long absences.

Perhaps Flood was simply loyal, and Agatha was pining hopelessly.

The path led them into the wood, then cut north and sloped upward. Agatha knew the route by now: they would emerge from the high wood outside Abington Hall, then turn west and walk down the soft meadows of Backey Green, where Mr. Scriven's goats and hives coexisted in cordial mutual disdain.

For now, it was a relief to be in the cool, dark shadows of the trees, with bird calls echoing in the branches. Flood's hair looked more gold than silver here, as she strode forward with easy swings of her legs in her brother's baggy trousers.

Agatha's heart was less serene. "Does Mr. Flood often send wages home?" she asked.

Flood nodded. "He and Harry both do, though not directly to me. Whenever they make landfall they both send money to Nathaniel in London: he's head of the company— Stanhope and Sons, right there on the letterhead—and he takes in the profits from every venture and redistributes them to the shareholders. Of which I am one."

One of the tight worries banding Agatha's heart eased a little. "Your father set that up, I assume?"

Flood's smile was sly and more than a little smug. "We're a merchant family, Griffin—we know how to take care of our own. I wouldn't call us wealthy—"

Agatha made a noise of disbelief. "Wealthy folk always say that."

"—but we enjoy a very comfortable living." She took another couple of steps, boots scuffing the dirt in the road. "That's why John married me, you see—only family members can be shareholders."

She spoke breezily, casually, but Agatha felt that fact strike her like a blow to the belly. Her feet walked on, while her brain went floaty with the realization: Penelope had been married for her fortune. "And John wanted to be a shareholder."

Flood nodded, eyes on the path. "He and Harry wanted to get a ship together—Harry would captain, and John would come along to manage the books and cargo. He's extremely good at it. Has a very efficient head for risk and figures, John does."

"So . . ." Agatha swallowed against a dry, gravelly throat. "So it was not a love match, then."

Flood snorted and shook her head, gold curls bouncing. "Not on his part or on mine." Her voice softened, and her eyes gleamed as they rested on all the greenery around her. "John was terribly relieved, though. He and Harry are . . . close. Now they're family in the eyes of the law."

Agatha's breath hitched when she caught Flood's meaning, but she schooled her features swiftly back to nonchalance. She'd been trusted with a secret, here in the greenwood, and she had to let her friend know such trust was not taken lightly. "I'm glad they found their way to happiness," she said, and paused a moment. "Only . . ."

"Only what?" Flood's face was tilted up, watching the play

of light through layers of leaves and branches. Gaze directed away, until the topic was not quite so dangerous.

These were delicate waters.

Agatha watched a slender beam of sunlight pass over the planes of her friend's cheeks. It caught on the soft hair at the corners of her mouth, and the creases that spoke of the years she'd survived. The sight plucked the words from Agatha's throat, unbidden: "Only it seems to be such a sacrifice for *you*, Flood. You deserve better than second place in someone's affections. You deserve to know what it's like to be loved by someone who worships the very earth beneath your feet, who adores you for yourself alone—and just what the hell is so damned funny?"

For Flood had stopped walking to double over at the waist, hands braced on her knees, hooting with helpless laughter until the only sound she could make was a strained wheeze.

Agatha planted her hands on hips. "Are you quite done?"

"Oh, Griffin!" Flood shook her head and wiped at the corners of her eyes. "I've lived forty-five years in the same small town. Of course I've been loved—or had a good few fucks, which is what I think you mean—it's just that none of them were from my husband, that's all."

"Well," said Agatha, feeling grumpy and puritanical. "Well, good. That's good." So Flood didn't feel terribly restricted by her marriage vows. Agatha had known plenty of couples who took them as a suggestion rather than a law, and it had never bothered her before.

It bothered her now—but not for any of the tedious reasons someone might declaim from a pulpit. No, Agatha was troubled because Flood made it all sound like a lark, when Agatha had been tying herself in sullen knots about it.

She didn't even know if Flood preferred women or men or both. And she couldn't ask without risking the loss of a friendship that had become impossibly dear to her. Vital, even.

And she remembered what Flood had said in the Four Swallows: *I would have to think about the consequences.* Agatha couldn't risk doing anything that might jeopardize Flood's standing in Melliton.

Flood's smile turned fond. "You are sweet to worry about me."

Agatha grumbled and tugged at the cuffs of her coat. "Glad I amuse you."

Flood's eyes cut toward her, as they began walking again in unspoken accord. "You must have loved your Thomas very much, I take it." She kicked a clod of earth off into the underbrush. "People who married for love always want everyone else to do the same."

How did one sum up twenty years of marriage in one answer? Agatha had been trying since the day of the funeral, and had never yet succeeded.

She was suddenly desperate for Flood to understand.

"We were devoted to each other—but we didn't start that way," she began slowly. "Our fathers knew one another. They'd worked together on a few books, even. His father pointed me out to him as someone who might be worth marrying, and so Thomas came courting. It wasn't quite an arrangement, but pretty nearly. I'd certainly never noticed Thomas before—had an eye at the time for the flashier types, your silver-tongued rascals and scoundrels and such. Thomas was quieter. Self-effacing. But I wasn't pretty enough to have many suitors, so I had to look carefully at any who turned up." She curled her hands in the pockets of her coat, unable to keep from smiling at the memory. "Other boys brought ribbons and thimbles and such, cheap trinkets they could carry easily and could give out to any girl who happened to be handy. Thomas brought tea—good tea, the kind you wouldn't ever feel like you could buy for yourself even if it wasn't just about the cost. It was . . . It was something you could save up, and keep to yourself—or could share with the household, if you chose."

Flood's smile blossomed. "And I bet you thought of him gratefully every time you made a pot."

Agatha laughed. "I certainly did. Much more strategic a courting gift, in the end."

"Strategic—but kind, too." Flood smiled, her eyes far away down the path ahead of them. "I wish I could have known him."

Agatha's face felt like cracked glass, a pane about to shatter. "He'd have loved you." She swallowed hard. "You could have talked about poetry together, and saved me from it."

Flood's laugh rang out like birdsong as they emerged from the wood. The great stone front of Abington Hall glared at them, distrusting all merriment.

From this approach, the shortest way to the bee garden

in the back took them through the hedge-maze. Agatha followed Flood through the turns—and nearly bumped into the beekeeper when she pulled up short in the heart of the maze.

"How *dare* she . . ." Flood hissed.

There was more venom in her voice than Agatha had ever heard before. Alarmed, she stepped around to Flood's side to see . . . nothing.

But a very new nothing. A great and palpable emptiness where once the paired statues of the nymph and the dryad had stood. Flood growled at the space, buzzing with fury.

Agatha's jaw tightened with dismay. "Lady Summerville?"

Flood nodded sharply, hands clenching into fists.

Agatha looked around again at the nakedness of leaves and lawn and the pebbled path. "Where do you think she moved them?"

"I'm not convinced she only moved them," Flood said. "I fear she destroyed them."

Agatha went icy with realization. This wasn't simply about the loss of a beautiful object. This was an attempt to destroy every intimate thing Miss Abington had thought and felt most deeply. It was vicious, and cruel, and very, very personal. And if Agatha could see that, how much worse must it be for Penelope Flood? She'd found such hope in that statue.

Agatha was shocked at her own eagerness to lash out at anyone who dared destroy Penelope Flood's hopes.

"She had every right," Flood was saying angrily. "I know she did. Those statues were left to her by Isabella. I heard the terms of the will, from the lawyer's own lips. But Lady

Summerville never appreciated the sculptures, and never would. I cannot for the life of me think *why* Isabella did it."

The last sentence was almost a cry, a sound of pure and baffled pain.

Agatha lifted a hand, paused, then tentatively rested it on Flood's shoulder. "Lady Summerville may have been within her rights to move the statues—or destroy them—but you're allowed to despise her for having done it."

Flood's eyes glittered ominously, somewhere between fury and tears. She shook her head. "Times like this I wish I were the sort of person who could sustain anger. I'm like a candle: I burn, and then I melt, with little light and no heat to speak of."

Agatha's fingers tightened convulsively. "I think you're one of the warmest people I've ever known," she whispered.

Flood's left hand lifted up and covered Agatha's, pressing it hard against her shoulder. Fingers interlaced at the tips—not quite grasping, but not separated, either.

"Thank you," Flood whispered. "I'm going to find out what happened. I have to know." She turned her head, and Agatha saw that silent tears had made silver paths down her cheeks. The beekeeper's gaze tangled with hers, eyes blue as the center of a flame.

Agatha burned, and knew it for what it was.

Then Flood stepped away and jammed her hat on top of her head again. The muslin veil came down, hiding her face. "Shall we see to the hives?"

"Of course," Agatha replied. When what she wanted to say was: *While you see to the hives, I'll be at the hall, setting the whole miserable place on fire in the name of thwarted, impossible love.* Her breath rattled like a tinderbox in her lungs.

As though one would offer arson instead of a bouquet, to win a lover's heart. High crimes were probably better suited to a betrothal than a mere courting gift: you couldn't just start burning things down in hopes the other person found it romantic. You'd want to be sure.

At present, Agatha was sure of only one thing: Penelope Flood deserved more than she'd been given.

CHAPTER TEN

The Queen's trial began in August. The country talked of nothing else. Scientific discoveries, foreign wars, significant agricultural developments, even the most ghastly deeds of criminals and murderers—all these were ignored in favor of endless dissection of the minutiae of the Queen's daily life in exile, as described in detail by newspapermen transcribing the words of the government's witnesses. These folk, servants and sailors mostly, sat for days on end answering questions put to them by the Lords, who flocked like ominous black-robed ravens. *Was the Queen ever alone with this man? How was she dressed? How was her manner?*

Since so many of these witnesses were Italian, many of whom had little to no English, the trustworthiness of Italians and servants as a class became a contentious touch point of the overall debate.

Mrs. Biswas's reading of the *Times'* accounts became an every-evening event in the Four Swallows, with the whole pub ready to cry out in protest or mockery, whichever caught their fancy in the moment. To some it was a meaningful political event that would have repercussions in future elections and parliamentary proceedings; to others it was the closest thing to theater that could be had for the price of the beer you were going to buy, anyway.

It made for tumultuous nights, and during the days Penelope was more than usually glad to be so often out of doors and on her own. Though, if she were being brutally honest with herself, the solitude of beekeeping was less soothing than it used to be.

What a change a few short months could make: where it had once felt odd to walk the bee circuit in reverse with Agatha Griffin at her side, now it was the old, original method that felt strange and wrong. Penelope was focusing so much on the person who *wasn't* there as she walked along the high street that it took her a few minutes to notice how many more people there were around her than usual.

Some of them had white sashes or rosettes, the insignia adopted by Queen Caroline's supporters. Some had banners and handmade bunting. And they were all walking in the same direction: the rectory.

Penelope lengthened her strides until she caught up to Mr. Thomas, in his broad-brimmed hat. "What has Mrs. Koskinen arranged now?" she asked. Somehow the woman was able to gather people without the authorities learning about it beforehand—Penelope had yet to figure out how she arranged it.

"A protest," Mr. Thomas replied. His creamy complexion was unusually flushed, and his blond curls were flyaways where they stuck out from the hat. "We're going to demand Mr. Oliver restore the Queen's name to the liturgy."

Penelope's lips pursed. Striking Caroline's name from beside his in the Anglican church service had been one of the ways George had publicly insulted his wife and assaulted her privileges in recent months. It had been an unpopular move, angering the normally royalist churchgoers as well as the radical Queenites.

Penelope thought it was, in a word: *mean*. Kings ought to be above meanness—that was the whole point of them, wasn't it? If they were supposed to be superior to other folk, then they should be *better*. Her resolve solidified. "I don't suppose you mind if I join in?"

"The more the merrier, of course," Mr. Thomas replied, tipping the brim of his hat.

So Penelope turned left instead of right at the village square, and joined the crowd now gathering outside St. Ambrose's rectory.

She had been in a riot before, of course. Nearly everyone in Melliton had. There had been demonstrations after the killings at Peterloo last year, and bread riots during the long years of the war before that. Riots were a proud country tradition, and long practice had worn them into a comfortable pattern: you showed up, you shouted and waved a banner or two, you went home once you'd made your point. Perhaps you did a bit of conscientious liberating of property—Penelope remembered one such occasion, when the mob had seized Squire Theydon's corn from a Sweden-bound ship. They had sold it at once to local farmers and villagers at traditional prices, they'd given the squire his profits afterward, and nobody at all had been hurt. It had all been very disciplined and neatly organized.

When you didn't have the vote, sometimes you had to take what power you could grasp with your own two hands.

An action against the vicar, though . . . That was unusual. Mr. Oliver was an unrufflable man, happy to trust that the Lord knew best even in the midst of the fiercest disagreement. His sermons were as bland and easily digestible as porridge: you never could say you enjoyed them, exactly, but they seemed hygienic in some indefinable way. They made you feel good about being good without you having to do anything at all.

Penelope and Mr. Thomas reached the space in front of the rectory and stopped, on the edge of where the crowd was thickest. The building itself was humble and cozy, a plain two-story stone cottage with a luxuriant garden Mr. Oliver always referred to as "a little Eden."

While more people thronged up around and behind them, Penelope craned her neck, looking around at all the familiar faces. There were plenty of the local reformers and radicals she expected—Mr. Thomas, Mrs. Price the baker, but also Mr. and Mrs. Wybrow and Mr. Northcote and his son—but those familiar ranks were bolstered by a number of women she was used to seeing only in the pews at Sunday services. Mrs. Galloway, whose cousin was a baronet, had her hands demurely folded and a white rosette pinned to her bodice; Mrs. Plumb the mercer's wife and her daughter

Felicia, twisting her hands excitedly in her skirts; old Mrs. Midson, who used to be a governess, peering around at the crowd as if she would be administering an exam to everyone at the end of the riot.

Griffin had been right: the Queen's cause had much broader support than any radical or reformist Penelope had seen. Not even Orator Hunt had gotten so many of Melliton's middle-rank citizens out of their parlors and into the streets.

These were not only the poorer folk whose happiness rose and fell with the price of bread or corn: these were village wives of traders and merchants with comfortable incomes, finally roused to anger by George's repeated injustices to his royal wife.

When Mrs. Koskinen judged the time had come and the crowd was good and thick at her back, that stout-hearted lady marched up to the rectory door, knocked sharply, and called out: "Mr. Oliver! The farmers and freeholders and good people of Melliton want to talk to you!" Then she stepped beside her husband, who stood silent and immoveable.

It was a few moments before the vicar appeared, tugging at the sleeves of his hastily donned jacket. He took in the mob arrayed before his door with one quick glance, counting names and faces as Penelope had, but his smile was everything polite and self-effacing. "Good afternoon, friends. What can I do for you?"

The leader tilted her head back and pitched her voice to carry. "We want the Queen's name back in the liturgy."

"Hear hear!" Mrs. Price called.

The crowd rumbled in support, like a wave breaking on the shore.

Mr. Oliver's smile never wavered. His eyes darted left, and widened when he saw his own deacon standing in the lane, a white sash wrapped around his stocky torso. "Mr. Buckley?" he said, in a voice shaky with surprise and betrayal.

"We want the Queen's name back in the liturgy, sir," the deacon called staunchly, folding his arms and nodding at Mrs. Koskinen as the crowd cheered him on. "We want to pray for both our rightful sovereigns, as we ought to. It's the right and Christian thing to do."

Mr. Oliver spread his hands. "Unfortunately, the Church disagrees."

"Who are the Church?" Mrs. Koskinen demanded. "The bishops? Or the common folk?"

"Both, I'm sure," Mr. Oliver said calmly.

"Then let the people pray for their rightful Queen!"

"The Dissenters pray for her!" Mrs. Midson called out.

Two red spots appeared in the vicar's cheeks. "The Dissenters must apply to their own consciences in the matter," he said, a little more tartly. "My duty is less flexible."

The whole crowd scoffed at this, and objections rang out.

"The Queen!"

"Aye, the Queen!"

Mrs. Koskinen raised her banner and shouted: "The Queen forever, the King in the river! The Queen forever, the King in the river!"

The crowd took up the chant. Penelope cupped her hands

around her mouth and shouted the slogan along with the rest, doing her part to add to the sound.

Mr. Oliver's mouth was now a thin, unhappy line. "I cannot do what you demand!" he cried, a tinny echo drowned by the voice of the mob.

"The Queen forever, the King in the river!"

Penelope widened her stance and prepared to stand her ground for the next hour. This was all very much part of the pattern: it left one with a sore throat next day, but that was all. Eventually, things would wind down. They always had before. Mr. Oliver was a magistrate and knew how this game was played—he was already reaching into his coat for the text of the Riot Act, the reading of which would fix a time for the crowd to disperse.

Then Felicia Plumb threw a stone.

It was not a large stone, but it was well-aimed, flying straight and true toward the rectory. Penelope watched it arc through the air, and for the first time a trickle of fear iced through her. The window on Mr. Oliver's right shattered, raining glass down on the shrubbery beneath. The sharp sound cut through the shouting, made every throat pull in a surprised breath—then the voice of the mob redoubled, half in fear, and half in delight.

The crowd broke and ran.

Mr. Oliver yelped, ducked inside his door, and slammed it shut. Half the people in the lane dashed forward, Mrs. Koskinen included, grabbing up more rocks and hurling them toward the remaining windows, slipping around to all sides of the house.

The rest of the mob scattered in fear, pelting away down the dirt road and into the safety of the side lanes. Mr. Buckley was hollering for everyone to stay calm; Mr. Thomas was shouting more radical slogans and waving his hands fiercely in the air. Glass cracked and shimmered in the sunlight. Someone screamed, someone laughed, and absolutely everyone else shouted louder.

Penelope pressed herself against the rectory's low garden wall and clung to the stone like an anchor to avoid being swept away.

When there were no more windows left to break, the tension eased. Mrs. Koskinen brandished her banner in triumph and led the mob away toward the pub singing. Their voices took a long, long time to fade from Penelope's ringing ears.

Penelope walked as softly as she could around the low wall, and waited a good ten feet from the door.

About five minutes later, Mr. Oliver's door creaked open. The vicar poked his head out, his eyes wide and watery, his face wan with fear. He started when Penelope waved, and craned his neck around, as if he could see around corners to survey the whole of the rectory.

"It's alright," Penelope reassured him. "They've all gone down the pub."

"Ah." Mr. Oliver straightened, and sighed. "I was rather worried there, for a moment."

"I thought I might help you sweep up the glass," Penelope offered.

"Yes." The vicar swallowed, his Adam's apple bobbing up and down convulsively. "Yes, that's very kind of you."

He retrieved a broom and a bin and together they knocked the glass shards from the leaves and swept it up from the ground as best they could. The rich scent of loam rose up around them; the vicar kept his garden well-tended.

Mr. Oliver cleared his throat. "I was surprised to see Mrs. Koskinen at the head of such a group," he said, his eyes fixed on the work his hands were doing. "I never pictured her as a rabble-rouser. She's such a soft and feminine little thing."

Penelope was suddenly, awkwardly conscious of the heft of her body, and the trousers bagging at her knees and tucked into the tops of her boots. She ignored the prickle of embarrassment in her cheeks, tugged on her gloves, and worked on prying the larger glass pieces out of the window frame, tossing them in the bin with the rest of the debris. "Mrs. Koskinen lost her cousin Beth at Peterloo last year. Sabered by one of the Yeomanry."

Mr. Oliver grimaced. "I see. Such a waste of a good soul."

Penelope didn't know whether he meant Mrs. Koskinen or her cousin. She couldn't think of a way to ask that didn't sound rude, so she bit her lip to keep quiet and plucked at more glass fragments.

They moved slowly around the house from window to window. "How is your guest faring?" Mr. Oliver asked. "I hope she is finding a little solace now that the first shock has passed?"

Penelope paused, looking down at the shard of glass in her gloved palm. "It's only been three months. Nothing to set against thirty years."

Mr. Oliver brushed a tangle of leaves and glass and soil into the bin. "Three months is three times longer than Achilles grieved for Patroclus."

"Perhaps," Penelope retorted, "but at the end of the month Achilles stormed back into battle with murder on his mind. Joanna is not quite at *that* pitch of mourning."

Mr. Oliver chuckled, but Penelope couldn't share his amusement. She kept turning his reference over in her mind: Did it mean he *knew* about Joanna and Isabella being as good as a married couple? He had to, didn't he? Most of the countryside knew, after all, or at least suspected. Surely the vicar, with all his learning, couldn't have missed so many clues and rumors? Achilles and Patroclus were famous for their friendship, but to anyone who knew how to read the signs it was definitely *that* kind of friendship. The kind that got men whipped or transported or even hanged. Romantic friendship. Passionate friendship. Very often naked and desperate to fuck each other friendship.

Perhaps he felt differently about men loving men, than about women loving women? The vicar's long-ago words to her brother whispered in her memory: *Men of that sort might find life in the city more to their taste.*

Had Mr. Oliver really meant it like that? Penelope couldn't be sure. The uncertainty tied her stomach in knots.

Because if he disapproved of Joanna and Isabella, of their decades-long devotion and fidelity, which broke no laws at all, how much more easily would he disapprove of Penelope's more transitory, flagrantly carnal affairs? It wasn't only her current lust for Mrs. Griffin, that secret that beat like a second heart beneath her breastbone. She'd been eager enough to act on her past desires.

And Penelope was a married woman. Yes, her marriage was unconsummated, an arrangement rather than a union, and no, she still couldn't have married any of the women she had loved over the last ten years—but it still wasn't *good* that her vows had been broken beyond repair before the wedding cake had even gone stale.

If Mr. Oliver knew, he'd want to send her away, too.

Sometimes Penelope felt she deserved every last drop of the world's scorn. She *knew* what the rules were, but rather than openly flout them, she'd merely hidden her affairs behind locked doors and light smiles and plausible excuses.

No wonder all those lovers had left her, in the end. Passion was for the bold—and Penelope'd never been able to fling herself from the cliff while screaming *Damn the consequences!* She valued the town's opinion a little too much.

She dropped the last shard from the window frame into the bin. "Has Lady Summerville found the Napoleon snuffbox yet?"

Mr. Oliver made no reply at first, his pale hair waving in the light summer breeze. "I have not asked her," he said eventually. "My sister has been so often in London."

Penelope frowned at the back of the vicar's head. "That snuffbox was a particular bequest."

His tone sounded pinched. "I was there when the will was read, Mrs. Flood. I remember."

"I'm sure that having it will go a long way toward helping Joanna move on," Penelope tried. For all she knew, it might be true.

"Are you so eager to hurry your guest out of your home, Mrs. Flood?"

Penelope blinked. "No, I . . ."

"I should think you would be happy to be less alone in that great empty house of yours. Too much solitude can be poisonous to the delicate female constitution."

Penelope flinched, then was instantly relieved the vicar hadn't seen her reaction to his words. *He didn't mean it like it sounded*, she told herself firmly. *He's had a difficult afternoon. Anyone would be snappish in the circumstances.*

If you cry for such a petty reason, you have no one to blame but yourself.

The vicar brushed the soil from his hands and stood, staring into the empty windows of the rectory. "I'll bring it up the next time I see my sister," he said, "but if she hasn't found it yet there's nothing more I can do."

Penelope held her tongue, telling herself sternly that such consideration was more than she deserved.

CHAPTER ELEVEN

Lady Summerville returned on Tuesday, Penelope wrote to Griffin, *and immediately paid for new glass for the rectory windows. She also invited me to tea—a singular occurrence—and for one brief, shining moment I really did believe she'd located the snuffbox, and had invited me over because it stung her pride less to give it to me than to hand it directly to Joanna herself.*

But when I arrived at Abington Hall I found it wasn't a social occasion: it was a political luncheon.

Lady S and a few other of the Melliton fine ladies had composed an Address to the Queen: they read it aloud and asked the rest of us women to sign it, and invited anyone who wished to go with them to London at week's end to present it to Queen Caroline at Brandenburg House. I think Lady S is practicing her political hostessery for the day when her husband inherits the earldom and its seat from his father.

*She dodged all my inquiries about the snuffbox, alas.
Joanna is growing restive about it, and mutters about
making a formal complaint to our local magistrate, but since
that is also Mr. Oliver, I have no hope that will make the
situation less awkward for any of us. It will all be an awful
muddle until someone relents.*

*But! For what may be the first time in my life, I am
excited about the prospect of a holiday! It's been years since
I've been to London, and I am both elated and terrified at
the idea. The presentation itself will take the better part of
a day, but I plan to do some exploring the evening before—
dare I ask you to spare some time to show me the city, as an
inhabitant and a trusted expert?*

*Would you object to my staying with you as a guest for a
night or two? The other ladies have been offered hospitality by
friends of Lady Summerville's—but I would feel much braver
about the whole adventure if I knew the person whose roof I
would be sleeping under. I know it's an awful presumption to
invite myself and you have many demands on your time.*

But could I, all the same?

Penelope chewed her lip and wrinkled her nose at the page.
It was an unusually rambling letter, even by her admittedly
loose standards.

But if she dithered over word choices and rephrasings,
she'd never post it at all.

She signed it, folded it, and sent it at the earliest opportunity.

And received this beautifully brief note in prompt reply:

> *Flood,*
> *You will always be most welcome. Come whenever you please.*
> *Griffin*

It was broad daylight when Penelope read those lines, but she shivered like it was a starlit evening and the invitation had been purred into her ear. Of course Griffin hadn't meant it like *that*—but Penelope couldn't resist wishing that she had. And imagining what Griffin might ask her to do next.

There was no use even thinking about such impossibilities. But they haunted her dreams for the next three nights, until the afternoon she packed her things, marched up to Abington Hall, and spent a rough and rackety hour bumping over the roads and into the heart of England's capital city while making the smallest of talk with Lady Summerville and Mrs. Midson, who was far too eager to entertain them both with tales of her great-nieces and -nephews. Penelope suffered through several amusing childhood traumas and was grateful to be let off with her luggage outside a gemlike building a-glitter with windows, where a sign proclaimed Griffin's Print-Shop in stern, sober letters.

Even just standing outside was making Penelope's heart race—or maybe that was just the proximity of so many people, moving so quickly, through narrow streets with buildings that towered far higher than the ones in Melliton did. If she craned her neck, she could see a sort of park around the corner; the sight of trees steadied her and reminded her to breathe.

She regretted it almost instantly: London certainly lived up to its reputation where smells were concerned.

Thus braced, she shouldered her bag, opened the door, and stepped into the shop.

The odors here were a distinct improvement from the street outside: books and ink and the crispness of paper. Griffin's storefront was a light and airy space, full of color and creamy paper and picturesque prints. Tables full of leather-bound books and urgent-looking pamphlets, stacks of manuscripts ready for binding, sheets of the latest ballads—she spotted "Inexpressibles" straight away—the richly hued latest issue of Griffin's *Menagerie* displayed to advantage, and high skylights letting in what brave sunlight managed to make it this far.

Surveying it all from behind a sturdy cherrywood counter was a boy the very image of Agatha Griffin. Same dark hair, same hawklike stubborn nose, same rich brown eyes. Those eyes lit as he smiled and hurried out from behind the counter to greet her. "You must be Mrs. Flood! I'm Sydney Griffin—it's a pleasure to finally meet you."

"And you as well, Mr. Griffin," Penelope said.

"Please, call me Sydney." They shook hands, his pumping eagerly up and down. Penelope hid a smile. He had all of Agatha's energy, but had yet to acquire her wariness. "Mum tells me you're in town to present an address to the Queen?"

"Along with quite a few of the women of Melliton, yes."

"That's marvelous! I hope I'm still so active in support of reform when I'm as old as you are."

Penelope blinked.

Sydney Griffin went on: "Oh, but where are my manners? That bag must be weighing you down—let me take that upstairs to Mum's room for you. She's in the back, of course, but I'm sure she won't mind if you go right on in. It's through that door."

Before Penelope could gather her scattered wits, the boy had relieved her of her bag, hefted it as though it were nothing, and vanished up the stairs. To his mother's bedroom, as he'd said.

Which, apparently, Penelope would be sharing with Griffin.

She hadn't considered that, when she'd invited herself to stay. She'd imagined she would be displacing Sidney, or one of the apprentices. But Griffin had told her to come, anyway . . .

Maybe there was some misunderstanding. She hadn't left Melliton in so long, her nerves couldn't settle. Nothing was familiar, so nothing was trustworthy. Penelope brushed her hands anxiously over her skirts, then told herself not to be such a ninny and went through the door Sydney had pointed out.

She'd been in the Melliton print-works, so she knew something of what to expect. But just as the city was more densely packed and compressed than the countryside, the London branch of Griffin's enterprise was a busy, cozy center of perpetual motion. There seemed to be far more people and prints and presses than the small size of the room could hold. It was barely possible to breathe; not even the tall windows at the back, thrown open to let in as much air as possible, could banish the industrial smells of metal and sweat and a persistent chemical tang.

"Mrs. Flood?" A girl with brown hair pulled tight into a knot at her neck sat at a table punching musical notes into a block lined with staves. She smiled shyly. "I'm Eliza Brinkworth. Her apprentice. Mrs. Griffin's just finishing up outside." She waved at a door that let out to a small yard in the back.

Penelope followed this direction and found herself on a small patch of a yard: hard-packed ground, high walls all around, yellow-green moss lurking in the corners and on the shadier stretches of stone. And, against the far wall, a table for the etching and cleaning of plates. Agatha Griffin was wrestling with one of these: wiping the plate with a cloth, buffing it clean of ground and mordant with turpentine, then a water wash. A thick leather apron marked with scrapes and scores was tied around her neck. Her sleeves were rolled to the elbow, and her hands were strong and work-roughened. For a moment the copper in her hands caught the afternoon sun with a flash.

Penelope was dazzled, and drifted forward helplessly.

She didn't think she'd made a sound, but Griffin must have heard something, because her head snapped up and those brown eyes drank in Penelope, standing there gaping. Creases folded the soft skin at the corners of Griffin's eyes and mouth as she smiled. "Welcome to London, Flood. How was the journey?"

"Worth it," Penelope replied.

Griffin laughed, set the plate on the table to dry, and rolled her sleeves properly back down to her wrists. Penelope squelched a sigh to see forearms vanish behind cotton again.

Griffin frowned lightly down at the gleaming metal. "I had hoped to get one more plate finished before you arrived—and there's two more jobs to proof, and another set of Thisburton caricatures to color . . ."

"Oh," said Penelope, and swallowed hard against a wave of dismay. "I understand. I'll just wander a bit on my own then, and then meet you back here later?" She twisted one hand around the other, the fine leather of her traveling gloves so much thinner and less protective than what she wore for beekeeping. "Is there somewhere nearby you recommend for an early supper? I was too excited to eat much before setting out."

Griffin cocked her head, her expression turning from frustrated to wry. "Flood, how long has it been since you visited London? You mentioned it had been a while. How long *precisely?*"

Penelope thought for a moment. "1804? During the war, certainly—I came to spend Christmas with Edward, and I distinctly recall he insisted on reading battle reports aloud over breakfast every morning."

Griffin shook her head. "So many years? The city might as well be an entirely new place to you." She untied the apron from around her neck, and hung it on a peg beneath an overhang of roof. There was a mischievous gleam brightening her eyes, and a sly tilt blooming on her lips. "Letting you wander around like a babe in the wood would be downright irresponsible. After all, I have a duty as a hostess, do I not?"

Penelope's heart was a bubble, rising eagerly up through the water to bob on a sunlit surface. "What about all your work?"

Griffin's long mouth crooked in a devious smile. She looked evil and stern and Penelope shivered to see it. Anticipation ripened Griffin's tone into something rich and alluring. "Oh, I think we can find someone to take care of the work."

She marched through the doorway, eyes seeking out and finding her apprentice. The girl shot up from the bench, and Penelope wouldn't have been at all surprised if she'd saluted.

Griffin took this obedience in stride: "Eliza, when Crompton is done with the Thisburton prints, you start the color work and have him begin printing the Egerton plate."

The girl straightened her shoulders. "Of course. Is the Egerton finished?"

"It's drying in the yard; should be ready when you need it."

"Yes, ma'am."

Griffin cast Penelope a smile over her shoulder. "That's the bulk of it sorted." She settled a bonnet like a helm on her head, then tugged her gloves tight over her hands like a general arming for battle. A lovely, sinister kind of mirth came over her. "Just one more thing to do . . ." She marched back into the storefront, Penelope trailing irresistibly after.

Sydney looked up from the counter, then blinked at his mother's attire. Griffin strode for the exit without a moment's pause. "I'm going out, my dear," she announced blithely. "Make sure everything's closed up properly, and don't bother to wait up—we won't be back 'til quite late."

Penelope caught one glimpse of Sydney gaping like a hooked fish before she scurried out the door to keep up with the longer-legged Griffin. The engraver strode purposefully around the corner until the shop windows were out of sight—then spun on her heel and put her hands against her mouth. "Oh dear," Griffin said, shoulders shaking. "Oh *dear*, that felt far too good. I almost didn't make it through with a straight face."

Griffin, Penelope realized with delight, was *laughing*. She couldn't help grinning back. "What have you done to your son, you awful woman?"

"Nothing he hasn't well earned, I promise you." Griffin pushed away from the wall, brushed her hands together, and cocked a head. "Well, Flood? Which shall we start with: fun, or food?"

"Food," Penelope replied. "Definitely food."

Griffin led her through crowded streets, weaving around slower walkers and darting down convenient shortcuts. Penelope was used to walking, but the press of people and the endless, ever-shifting, and indescribable smells made her breathless as she hurried to keep up with the printer's sure strides.

Finally, Griffin led her to a tavern whose door was set several steps lower than the street; even from outside, the smell of roasting meat and bread and sauces made Penelope's mouth begin to water.

Inside, everything smelled so tasty that Penelope in her hunger was hard put not to start gnawing on the back of a spare chair. The place was unimpressive to look at but spotlessly clean, and quieter than the usual tavern; everyone seemed engrossed in their meals. Griffin ordered for them both: turtle soup and fish to start, followed by partridge pie in mushroom gravy. To drink they poured a cider that fizzed tart and sharp to keep Penelope's palate clear as she tucked in, and later, to pair with the pudding, a sweet port that went right to Penelope's head. She sat back with a sigh and set her fork down with a wistful regret that she had no room for more.

Griffin was at her ease, canted sideways, one elbow up on the back of her chair. The other hand spun the stem of the port glass on the table in front of her. Her eyes were liquid as wine in the low light. "Well?"

Penelope didn't hold back. "That may be the single greatest meal I have ever had."

Griffin grinned. "I thought you'd approve. Walcott's is one of the best-kept secrets in London."

Penelope leaned forward. "What other secrets can you show me?"

Griffin froze for an instant, her eyes flashing gold in the candlelight. "That depends," she said, raising her glass to her lips. The port shimmered like rubies. "Would you prefer something edifying, or something decadent?"

Penelope watched Griffin's throat work as she swallowed

the last droplets of rich, heady liquor. "Decadent. Definitely decadent."

Griffin's answering smile was a wicked, wordless promise.

Penelope's pulse leaped, and she wondered what she'd let herself in for.

In the eyes of most decent folk, Agatha knew, Vauxhall was the absolute pinnacle of public London depravity. It could be the ruin of any high-born debutante who dared wander down its shadowed lanes and elude her chaperone in search of the sultry, sordid pleasures of the flesh.

But Agatha and Flood were two middle-aged women free from the rules of high birth and fortune. They had no peerless pearl of reputation to safeguard.

Even if they had, Agatha thought it might be worth a little ruin to see the brilliant lights reflected in the sparkle of Penelope Flood's blue eyes. They shone almost silver in the darkness, pools of liquid light as she tipped her face back to watch the fireworks bloom and burst against the night sky above.

A lithe woman in a dazzling costume, crowned in feathers, danced down an endless tightrope above them as colored stars popped around her. Penelope gasped as the rope dancer twirled on one foot, seemingly unconnected from earthly gravity. She looked liable to fall at any moment and yet she danced on, the spangles on her costume flashing in defiance as she drew gasps and cheers from the riveted crowd below. Beautiful and untouchable.

Agatha looked away from the rope dancer as Penelope Flood laughed in sheer joy.

Beautiful. Untouchable.

The liquor had long since gone to Agatha's head—not only the port with dinner, but the burnt champagne she'd bought for both of them from a stall in the pleasure gardens. She felt as though she stood on a part of the world that was turning faster than it should, the ground itself threatening to sweep her unsteady feet clean out from beneath her. When the rope dancer's finale was done, she and Penelope meandered through the grounds, past fountains and musicians and the private rooms where the gentry held their masquerades. Diamonds flashed on a debutante's wrist as she toyed with the ties of her mask and leaned close to whisper a secret into the ear of a giggling, glittering companion.

Flood tugged her down to be heard above the crowd. "Have you ever been to a masquerade?" she asked.

Agatha shook her head. "It's expensive, and I have no genius for disguise," she replied.

"What?"

Agatha leaned closer.

Flood tilted her head obligingly.

Agatha's lips could almost—just almost—brush the edge of Flood's ear. "I have no—" she began to repeat, but got no farther, as a laughing body bumped into her from behind.

She staggered forward, taking Penelope Flood with her.

Flood's gasp of surprise spurred Agatha into action. Her hands came up automatically, catching Flood by the elbows and steadying them both against the press of bodies in the darkness.

It took her a moment to realize they'd stopped moving. Agatha's face was buried in Flood's hair, curls sweeping her eyelids and cheeks and tickling her nose. Flood's hands were clutching Agatha's shoulders, and she huffed out a little laugh, her chest rising and falling as the sound echoed through her body and into Agatha's.

Agatha turned her head, brushing her lips against Flood's temple. It was *not* a kiss. It was a wordless worry, a touch seeking reassurance. It had nothing to do with how sweet Flood felt to hold, or how good she smelled: bergamot and violets. "Are you alright?"

"I am now." Agatha felt more than heard Flood's sigh as Penelope tilted her head up with a smile. Her eyes flickered with torchlight, and her cheeks were rosy with excitement. Agatha felt the earth spin away ever farther beneath her—

The diamond-decked debutante laughed again, and the spell was broken.

Agatha dropped her hands and stepped away, tugging at her cuffs, smoothing her dress, face flaming in a way not even the champagne could explain.

Flood blinked, and shook her head. "Perhaps it's time we went home," she said.

Agatha nodded, and they left the pleasure gardens behind.

Now they lay in Agatha's bed, wrapped in darkness deep as velvet—and Agatha couldn't sleep.

Penelope had no such trouble. She had all but passed out as soon as her head touched the pillow and was now snoring softly, a homely, intimate sound that made Agatha's heart ache and her fingers twist in the sheets to keep from reaching out.

Strange to hear another person breathing in this room again. Dangerously tempting to have someone so close. The single hardest part of widowhood for Agatha had been learning to sleep singly: no one to steal warmth or blankets from, no one to talk to in that sweet, safe time between getting into bed and slipping into slumber. No one to simply *be there*, whenever Agatha woke up on the wrong side of midnight from some half-remembered dream. The loneliness of the bed she'd once shared with Thomas had felt like an insult to her very soul, and she had never really grown resigned to it.

But now that emptiness was filled with the round, cozy form of Penelope Flood, sailor's wife and beekeeper and Agatha's dearest friend.

Her presence reshaped the bed's intimate geography: the extra dip of the mattress, the unwonted tension in the blankets, the ebb and flow of the currents in the very air around them. Agatha's eyelids grew heavy, and the looming prospect of unconsciousness kicked up her heart into a sudden panic.

What if she fell asleep, and let down her guard, and they woke up entwined? Her arms around Flood's waist, one of the other woman's thighs sliding between her own? Warm breath and tangled hair and thin sheets and soft skin . . .

She could all but hear her friend's teasing snort. *Been that long since someone shared your bed, has it, Griffin?*

And Agatha would have to pretend to laugh, and let Flood go, and feel weak and desperate and pitiful. Flood might have asked for secrets, earlier in the evening—but only as a game, a brief diversion. *A good few fucks*, she'd said, and that was fine for some, but it was not a game Agatha was suited for, especially not with people she wanted to keep as friends. She had too great a tendency to devotion.

Even when that devotion wasn't wanted.

So Agatha rolled onto her belly, tucked her hands firmly underneath her chest, turned her face to the wall, and prayed for a sleep like death.

Chapter Twelve

The sermons were wrong. Hell wasn't fire and brimstone. Hell was a dress of soft white muslin, laced tight around every dip and curve of sturdy Penelope Flood. All those snowy, delicate folds just waiting to be ruined by clutching, ink-stained fingers.

The only color Flood wore was a bright green rosette, pinned high on her shoulder in honor of Queen Caroline. It stood out against all that white like an emerald on ermine.

The beekeeper tied off the last lacing on her bodice and swirled the skirts back and forth experimentally. Petticoats shushed and settled. She shook her head and tucked one curl behind her ear. "Who on earth thought wearing this much white in sooty London was a good idea? I thought it was a joke when Mrs. Koskinen first suggested it—and I was stunned when Lady Summerville offered to fund the fabric purchase." She frowned. "I fear I know too well where she got the money."

"At least she's doing something with it for the common

good." Agatha's throat was dry and aching from yearning; she had to take a long swallow of tea before she could speak. "And it isn't like they're asking you to do field chores, Flood. It's a procession. A spectacle."

"Papa always said people went to London to make a spectacle of themselves," Flood said with a small laugh. "I guess he was right."

"You look absolutely splendid."

Flood's head whipped up, a blush rising in her cheeks.

Agatha's fingers curled tight around the china teacup. She kept her tone brisk, pointed. "And spectacle can be an advantage: I should have no trouble spotting the Melliton ladies when you arrive at Brandenburg House today."

Penelope's blush bloomed further, so lovely that Agatha had to drop her eyes and struggle to keep her breathing even.

Lady Summerville had settled upon a meeting spot and arranged for a number of open carriages, to transport the women of Melliton in style along the roads to the Queen's residence. They would all be wearing unrelieved white, with no ornament other than the green rosettes. Already Agatha's fingers itched to draw such a scene, and she had to admit Mrs. Koskinen's idea had been rather a good one. It was going to be impossible to miss their group, no matter how large the crowds.

Flood gulped down a hasty breakfast and took her leave. Agatha checked on Sydney and Eliza—who were adamant that everything had gone just fine yesterday evening, no problems at all, no surprises, no matter how many times Agatha asked them about it in new, more cunning ways.

The young folk were demonstrating competence. She was secretly, suspiciously proud, and trusted it not at all. Today would be another test for them.

Agatha left them her list of instructions and set out east to see the Queen.

Brandenburg House sat like a temple at the top of a small hill fronting the river. Its pale stone facade rose lordly over the teeming, colorful mass of humanity gathered in the cleared space around it.

Agatha had expected the crowds, and the noise, but she had not expected things to feel so . . . festive. Yes, there were banners being waved and political slogans being chanted—but there were also food stalls and peddlers and ballad sellers wandering the throng, making a fairly solid profit, from what Agatha could see at a glance. A clutch of boats on the river were bringing an address from the assembled watermen of London: their boats were decked out with ribbons and garlands and all manner of bunting, and surrounded by smaller rowboats and skiffs holding lords and ladies and society folk who'd come out this fine afternoon for a bit of excitement. Beaver hats alternated with summer bonnets and liberty caps; imported silks brushed up against printed calico and homespun.

There were so many women. More than at any election or procession or celebration Agatha had seen. White rosettes and handkerchiefs fluttered everywhere.

Agatha pulled out her sketchbook and made a few hasty impressions of the event for later refinement into proper etchings. Such a crowd meant it would be an hour at least for the Melliton coaches to make the journey by road. She sketched a few scenes to pass the time. One of the watermen disembarked and made his way through the crowd with an escort, holding a document in front of him. Agatha followed in their wake, until they reached the doors of the house and turned.

The man with the address read it out in a carrying voice, then offered it to a soberly dressed gentleman at the door, who made a courteous reply on behalf of the Queen. Vows of mutual support were made in staunch, patriotic terms.

It had all clearly been arranged in advance, but like a play well acted, it was stirring not in spite of, but *because* it was all so deliberate. It was as formal as a funeral—or a wedding.

She was high enough on the hill by now that she was able to catch the first appearance of the Melliton procession as they rounded the bend in the road. The coaches trundled through the crowd, white-clad occupants waving, proud and lovely as a bevy of swans in flight. The coaches wound slowly up the hill as the masses of people parted, and the Melliton women stepped out and spread out before the Queen's residence like a wreath of lilies.

Agatha peered at them, trying to distinguish Flood's figure in that sea of white, when a woman in a Caroline-green cloak took a position at the head of the group. She whirled the cloak off her shoulders—and the extra-bright glow of her gown showed off precisely how much dust the other women's white frocks had picked up on their journey.

This, of course, had to be Lady Summerville.

She handed the cloak to a companion, received in return a piece of paper, folio size, and began to read: "We, the ladies of Melliton and surrounding environs, approach your Majesty with that reverential feeling due from the Subject to the Sovereign . . ."

Agatha pulled out her sketchbook and began doodling, as the flattering Address went on and on.

Lady Summerville was on the thin side, with skin like cool marble and deep gold hair. Her dress was perfectly neat and perfectly tailored—silk, Agatha judged from the drape, not the muslin or linen the other Melliton women wore. The viscountess looked as though she'd just stepped out from the frame of one of the fashion plates the *Menagerie* so often printed.

"The principles and doctrines now advanced by your accusers," Lady Summerville was proclaiming, "do not apply to your case alone, but, if made part of the law of this land, may hereafter be applied as a precedent by every careless and dissipated husband to rid himself of his wife, however good and innocent she may be . . ."

Agatha grimaced. So that was why Lady Summerville was so determined. In defending Caroline, she defended her own marriage rights as the wife of a peer. Particularly one who, according to Penelope, would be divorced in a trice if her husband had been able to afford it.

Not terribly altruistic of her, of course—but Agatha had to wonder: Was self-interest the worst motivation, if it resulted in improvement for everyone? Perhaps Sydney's favorite philosophers were right. Perhaps revolution was really only a matter of getting enough people's individual motivations to flow in the same direction, at the same time.

She finally spotted Penelope, standing tall in the sunlight, her hair shining like an angel's halo. The effect was entrancing and Agatha's pencil moved almost of its own volition, recreating the earnest lines of Penelope Flood's face, her lofty gaze, the generous lines of her figure as she stood there in support of her Queen. She looked sweet and honest and loveable, the very picture of virtue.

As she finished her sketch, Agatha gazed down the hill, in awe of the sheer number of people who had ventured here. It was busier than Vauxhall had been last night. The moralists might spend their time railing against the licentiousness of rope dancers and mollies and all the folk of any sex who offered pleasure for payment—but tyrants and politicians like Lord Sidmouth knew the truth: this daytime crowd in front of Brandenburg House was much, much more dangerous.

Here were hundreds, perhaps thousands, of people, most of whom weren't permitted to vote in elections, but who had come to demonstrate to their government and their monarch that they would not be overlooked or ignored. They proved that they mattered by showing up in droves.

For the first time since Waterloo, Agatha felt her soul billow with national pride. Maybe the crowd had the right of it. Maybe something could change this time, without the need for bloodshed.

Surely the powerful would *have* to listen, when so many voices were crying out.

It had been so long since she'd had a hopeful thought about politics that she stood rooted to the spot for quite a few minutes, turning it over in her mind.

Lady Summerville finished her speech to applause and a few shouted attempts at wit, which fortunately were too far away for Agatha to hear clearly. Certainly Lady Summerville's address was a more florid speech than the one the watermen had given. The sober gentleman at the door accepted it all the same, and offered a response in much the same vein.

And that appeared to be that. The ladies in white began to mix with the crowd, and Agatha strode forward to find Penelope Flood. She was talking animatedly to a small brunette woman with a sallow complexion and a thoughtful air. Agatha paused, not wanting to interrupt.

"Are you with the *Times?*"

Agatha was rather taken aback to find herself being addressed by Lady Summerville, who was eyeing her sketchbook with suspicion. "I'm with Griffin's, your ladyship."

The lady's lips pursed. "As in Griffin's *Menagerie?* I would not have expected this gathering to appear in a magazine whose audience consists entirely of society ladies."

"There appear to be quite a few such ladies here, your ladyship," Agatha said, with a wry little bow of her head.

Lady Summerville reached out for the sketchbook; Agatha pulled it back instinctively. The viscountess bristled. "I insist you show me any drawings you have made of me," she said. "There are far too many scurrilous scribblers muddying the waters these days with cartoons and caricatures. Making your betters look ridiculous by exaggeration—you haven't the right to do that to decent people."

"Have you ever objected to anything you've read in the *Menagerie*, your ladyship?"

Lady Summerville scoffed. "I am not in the habit of reading such frivolity—I have more important concerns with which to fill my time."

"Your ladyship?" Penelope Flood stepped in with a smile. "May I present Mrs. Agatha Griffin, who owns the printworks on the outskirts of Melliton?"

"Charmed, I'm sure," the viscountess said, sounding anything but. She did not hold out a hand.

Penelope coughed slightly. "Mrs. Koskinen and I were thinking everyone might like to have something to eat before we begin heading back." She indicated the curly-haired woman and her husband, who was staring around narrow-eyed at the London crowd, as though he expected some urchin to steal the very lint from his pockets as soon as he dared to blink.

"If you think it's necessary," Lady Summerville said, and waved a hand. "I'm sure I can trust you both to handle such mundane matters, now that the real work is done."

"Thank you, your ladyship," said Penelope, in a tone much more polite than the one Agatha would have used in her place.

Mr. and Mrs. Koskinen between them herded everyone toward the pie sellers, and Agatha fell into step beside her friend. "Congratulations on the procession," Agatha said, and showed Flood the sketch she'd made of her. "I was thinking of putting it out as a print to mark today's events—without your name attached, of course. Unless you object to your likeness being sold?"

"Not when it's so flattering. And so significant historically, of course." Griffin snorted. Flood laughed and curtsied as sweetly as any debutante. "My dear Griffin, may I trespass on your hospitality for one more night? We've been invited to a dinner this evening by Mrs. Hannah Buckhurst, of the London Female Reform Society. I expect it will run very late indeed." She leaned forward, a light smile playing at the corners of her mouth. "You should come, and bring Sydney and Eliza as well—Mrs. Buckhurst gave me four tickets."

One more night lying still and stiff beside Penelope Flood might be the very end of Agatha. On the other hand, Flood being disappointed—or sleeping elsewhere—was its own kind of torture.

And if forced to choose between two evils, Agatha knew she would always choose whichever evil let her enjoy the company of her friend. "I am entirely at your disposal," she replied.

"Good," Flood said, and looked around with eyes alight. "Now where did that pie seller get to? I am absolutely famished."

Agatha steeled herself for one more day of blissful torture, and let Flood buy her a pie.

CHAPTER THIRTEEN

They stopped by Griffin's to collect Eliza and Sydney for the dinner—Sydney's face blazed up like a Guy Fawkes bonfire when Penelope handed him his ticket. "We're going to the Crown and Anchor?"

"Are we?" Penelope blinked down at the slip of paper in her hand, and yes, there it was, in inescapable block lettering. THE CROWN AND ANCHOR, ARUNDEL STREET. "So it seems."

Griffin snorted. "Do you think Lady Summerville will deign to show up to an establishment of such infamous character?"

"I doubt it," Penelope replied, still staring at the printing. "The viscount would never countenance his wife visiting a tavern."

"Oh." Griffin's mouth flattened in dislike. "Oh. It's no fun mocking her for his meanness."

Penelope sighed. "I doubt she'd come even with his

permission—she always was as staunch a Tory as you'd ever see."

"A Tory at the Crown and Anchor," Sydney said wonderingly. "Can you imagine?"

Eliza snickered. "It'd be like walking downstairs one morning and seeing the King in the kitchen."

"Or a goose at Gunter's," Sydney replied.

"A wet hen in Westminster Abbey."

"A hyena in Hyde Park."

"Enough!" Griffin said. "Hurry and dress, or we'll be late."

The young folk scampered upstairs to change out of their ink-stained work clothes; their elders more sedately followed suit.

The Crown and Anchor was the most notorious of London's radical public houses. Penelope had formed a vision of what to expect from the place: low ceilings and smoky corners, spilled ale wetting the straw on the floor, furniture that looked like it had been used as a barricade during a war—and not by the winning side.

Instead, the four of them were set down in front of a sober-faced building that took up the bulk of a city block on Arundel Street, squaring off against St. Clement's Church and hard by the Inns of Court with all their studious, thirsty barristers. After showing their tickets, Penelope and her guests walked into a foyer flanked by elegant columns, ascended a broad stone staircase, and found themselves in the Great Assembly Room.

Penelope gasped.

There were marble fireplaces. There were arched windows, stretching at least two stories high, and a musician's gallery supported by another row of columns. The ceiling was a lofty dome of carved and decorated panels, and from the center of the dome hung an enormous glittering chandelier. You could have fit a thousand bodies in the space and still had enough room for everyone to dodge safely out of the way should that chandelier come crashing down.

It was absolutely spectacular, and it made Penelope's heart quail in her breast.

The one thing she'd gotten right was the volume. The high ceiling gathered conversations and sent them back tripled to all the barristers, merchants, musicians, manufacturers, weavers, newspapermen, lace makers, caricaturists, physicians, scientists, poets, painters, booksellers, and tradesmen under its elegant curve.

Long tables had been set for the dinner, and people were already claiming the seats nearest the raised dais where the night's speakers chatted. Penelope spotted Mrs. Buckhurst and the other women of the Female Reform Society, wearing white silk sashes and green rosettes. There was wealth here—not the wealth of the landed and titled aristocracy, but the wealth of a new, ambitious, indefatigable class who never let a good opportunity pass them by.

Sydney was ecstatic, but trying manfully to suppress it. He waved to a friend, offered Eliza his arm, and vanished into the throng.

Penelope twisted her hands in her skirts and wished she could slip through the parquet floor and get away. She'd come thinking she would have a drink and an argument, as she was used to of an evening. But this grandeur was the opposite of the Four Swallows in every respect. It was a temple of Radicalism and Reform, and it wanted only the most devoted acolytes to sip from the font of its wisdom.

Griffin's hand touched her elbow. "Are you alright?"

"I think I preferred Walcott's," Penelope muttered.

Griffin's mouth quirked. "So do I." She smoothed a hand over the skirts of her navy gown—dark as an ink blot against all the marble and cream and color of the decor.

The fidget said she was uncomfortable, too. Penelope felt a stab of indignation that Griffin should feel unwelcome anywhere. Bravery she hadn't been able to summon on her own behalf rose up to release her from paralysis.

She slipped her arm into the crook of Griffin's elbow. "Come—let's find a place before the whole dinner's devoured."

They found seats beside Mrs. Koskinen and a young woman with dark red hair—and just in time, as Mrs. Buckhurst rose and called for attention not five minutes after Penelope finished piling her plate with roast meat and slightly singed vegetables. Her guess about the night's rhetoric had been spot-on, at least: there were speeches made about rights, and toasts to the usual political figures, and even a few rousing songs that had Griffin wrinkling her nose even as Penelope lustily joined in.

Later, once the subscriptions were solicited and the final toasts made to Liberty and Reform, Mrs. Koskinen introduced the young woman as her cousin Miss Crewe. "Have you been to many dinners like this one?" Penelope inquired, leaning forward to be heard above the crowd.

"Not as many as I intend to." Miss Crewe's mouth was an absolute rosebud, even when pursed in wry amusement. She'd spent the speeches listening intently while methodically cleaning her plate, and even now was mopping up the sauces with a bit of bread. "But I was raised on reform, hearing arguments around the family table. My mother founded the Carrisford Weavers' Library and Reform Society last spring." The petals of her lips curved bittersweetly. "She would have been glad to see the crowds at Brandenburg today."

Ah, Penelope remembered. *Mrs. Koskinen's cousin, killed at Peterloo.* "Are you continuing her work with the Society, Miss Crewe?"

Miss Crewe paused with her fingers on her bit of bread. "That depends, Mrs. Flood: Are you a government spy?"

Penelope choked on her beer.

Miss Crewe nibbled daintily on her morsel of bread. Quite as though she accused people of being police informers all the time.

Perhaps she did.

Penelope got her breath back, and managed half a smile. "If I were," she said, "I surely would deny it."

"Of course," Miss Crewe agreed. "But the manner of your denial would be telling." Her lips quirked, and her eyes sparkled. "In fact, it was."

"And just what did it tell you?" Penelope inquired.

Miss Crewe swallowed the last of her bread and folded her hands demurely while she considered. She was quite a pretty girl, and her hands showed the marks of labor: visibly calloused in places, strong and sure. A silk weaver, Mrs. Koskinen had said.

At last, Miss Crewe sighed. "Your answer tells me that you're just as my cousin has described you, Mrs. Flood—very earnest, and very kind."

Penelope pinkened, and sought a less squirmworthy subject. "I wonder if you can explain to me something Mrs. Buckhurst said in her speech . . ." she began.

The silk weaver was a font of information, even more than Sydney, and Penelope listened avidly until Griffin jogged her elbow some time later.

"Flood." Agatha Griffin's face was luminous, bright with so much joy and awe that Penelope's heart gave a little kick and knocked the breath from her. "I've just learned something wonderful. Is there a chance you're ready to leave?"

"Quite." It had been a lively evening, but politics was exhausting work. They made their farewells to Mrs. Koskinen and Miss Crewe. Then Griffin took Penelope by the wrist and began towing her through the crowd toward the stairway.

It's just so we don't get separated, Penelope reminded herself. And then a treacherous thought followed: *She doesn't want to lose me.* "What about Eliza and Sydney?" she stammered, bumping from stair to stair.

"Oh, I already told them we were leaving. They're young—they'll be up until dawn with the rest of the political crowd. And they're well able to find their own way home when they're ready." The engraver cast a sly glance back over her shoulder. "I'm getting too old to see sunrise from the wrong side without a terribly good reason."

"I can think of one," Penelope said automatically, then bit her lip as the heat rose in her cheeks.

Griffin snorted, but she didn't let go, not even when they reached the relative freedom of the stairs. They walked down, past endless debates in other spaces—admittedly, less magnificent ones than the Grand Assembly Room. It was a relief to emerge into the cool evening air, as the first few stars began sparkling in the lilac curve of the sky.

In the chill, Griffin's fingers around her wrist felt like the warmest thing in the world.

The printer towed Penelope south down Arundel Street, to the banks of the Thames, where the law courts kept their halls and libraries. The buildings here were ancient, frosted over with white stonework and narrow, imperious windows.

Griffin slipped a couple of coins to a gatekeeper, who obligingly let them into a court that led to a garden, then another garden, turn after turn until Penelope began to feel like she'd stepped into a fairy maze from a folktale and they'd never find their way out again.

"Good thing I had that barrister draw me a map," Griffin muttered, and pulled out her sketchbook. Pages of women in white and green flashed by, then a penciled path in an amateurish hand. Griffin took a few more turnings. "Left, then right, then two more lefts, and . . . ah. Here we are."

Penelope looked around. They were in a small pocket courtyard, a timeless bubble of peace in the center of the city. The branches of an old willow sifted moonlight and shadow into ripples on the ground, and the sound of water from quite close had Penelope peering around for the unseen fountain.

Griffin dropped Penelope's wrist—her absent fingers left behind a cold, lonely little band of air around the skin there—and pulled the willow branches aside like she was raising the curtain on a Drury Lane stage.

The fountain Penelope heard was underneath the willow tree: a small tilted basin that poured water into a curve around its roots.

Also underneath the willow tree: Isabella's nymph and dryad.

Penelope was afraid to move. Surely she must be dreaming. As long as she didn't move, she would never have to wake up. She held so still her muscles began trembling with the effort of it, as her eyes traced every line of the familiar marble. "It wasn't destroyed," she whispered at last. "I can't believe it. It wasn't destroyed."

"A barrister by the name of Mr. Loveney told me about it," Griffin said softly. "He bought it from an art broker here in town, not three weeks ago."

Penelope let out a breath, far too light and fragile to be a laugh. "And put it *here?*" *Here* meaning *the legal heart of the kingdom.* But also *here* meaning *in this magical, sheltered space.*

Penelope's mind could not take it in.

Griffin's smile was slow as moonlight. "Isabella Abington was a sculptor of no small renown. It will take more than a year for the world to forget her."

Penelope let out a sob and flung her arms around Griffin's neck.

The other woman went instantly pokerish.

Penelope assumed it was only surprise. She would not be put off: her arms tightened. "Thank you," she whispered. Tears spilled over her eyelids and down her cheeks. She pressed her face harder against the taller woman's shoulder, hoping the dark color of the fabric would hide the telltale dampness. She swallowed hard. "I don't care how many years pass: I will never, *ever* forget that you brought me here. Some kindnesses leave a mark, you know. Like a scar, but the reverse."

Griffin's arms came around Penelope's shoulders— carefully, as though she feared Penelope might break. Her hand patted Penelope's curls once. Twice. "You might bring me around to poetry yet, Flood," she said gruffly.

Penelope let herself hold on for one more long, shuddering breath, then reluctantly pulled away.

Griffin fussed at the fabric of her gown, her blush apparent even in the moonlight's silvery rays. "Home, then?" she asked.

"Home," Penelope said on a sigh. As though it were the truth and not only a wish.

The Queen's Larder pub on the corner was in full carouse when they returned, but inside the print-shop all was peaceful and still as they undressed for bed. Penelope settled back against the pillows, frowning up at the ceiling. "Did Mr. Loveney tell you which art-broker he purchased the statue from?"

"He did not. Sydney introduced us, though, so I'm sure it wouldn't be difficult to find it out." Griffin had pulled a nightdress on first thing, and was wrestling her stockings off underneath the skirts.

It was charmingly prudish of her, especially after all the mutual unlacing they'd just done, and it made Penelope instantly begin wondering what else was underneath that billow of fabric. She knew she oughtn't let herself think of it—but it had been such a long and trying day, she simply didn't have the strength to keep her imagination in check.

She'd be more virtuous tomorrow, she promised herself, and fixed the sight of Agatha Griffin's ankles in her memory.

Griffin put her stockings to be washed before she lay down carefully on the other half of the bed. Blankets pulled up to her underarms. Hands folded over her chest like a funeral figure on a monument.

It made Penelope feel half-feral by way of contrast, so she made a bit of a show of nestling into the pillows and blankets, like a creature burrowing in for a long winter's hibernation.

Griffin peered down her long nose at Penelope. The stern effect of this was rather softened by the long black-and-silver braid of her hair, which looked temptingly soft and strokeable. "Why do you want to talk to the art broker?"

Beneath the mounds of bedclothes, Penelope attempted a shrug. "Only curious."

"You aren't going to talk him out of buying the other statues, are you?"

"Certainly not," Penelope said loftily. "I'm just happy to know they aren't being smashed or broken or burned, or anything like that. It's actually a relief to see one making its way through to an appreciative collector."

"You might buy one or two yourself, you know."

"Ha—I couldn't afford them. Not even one of the smaller satyrs."

Griffin winced. "None of those satyrs was particularly *small*, Flood."

"Besides, where on earth would I put him?"

"Where would he fit?"

Penelope chortled, and Griffin went red. Her eyes slid away toward the wall, her mouth tightening.

Penelope's amusement faded. "Thank you again for letting me stay. I hope it hasn't been too much trouble for you."

"No trouble," Griffin said, still looking at the wall.

Penelope screwed up her courage. "I'd like to return the favor, next time you come to Melliton."

Griffin glanced at her then—a swift, piercing look that dried any other words on Penelope's tongue. The printer's gaze slipped down to Penelope's mouth, then away. Penelope worried she'd erred somehow, but then . . .

"I'd like that," Griffin said, and some of Penelope's anxiety eased away. "I've worried I'm intruding too much on Mrs. Stowe and Miss Coningsby's privacy. They each prefer a bit more solitude than my visits have been giving them." She yawned, working her shoulders deeper into the pillow behind her as her eyes fell shut once more.

Penelope settled cozily onto her side, her blanket-burrow warming slow and steady as an oven. "Then it's settled," she said. "You can stay with me and Joanna and give us advice on how best to approach the vicar about the snuffbox. She's frustrated enough that she's concocting . . . plans. Or rather, schemes, the more dramatic the better. Bribing the household staff to filch the item. Sneaking into Abington Hall when the family's away and rifling through cabinets until she finds it. Hiring a brilliant thief from the great criminal underbelly of the metropolis, who arrives in Melliton in disguise." Her lips quirked. "And who then ends up murdered, forcing Joanna to unmask the real killer to clear herself of the crime."

Penelope paused, waiting for Griffin to snort or scoff or otherwise comment on the absurdity of this.

A light snore was the printer's only response. Her lips were slightly parted, her hands still folded tight on her chest. As though if she didn't keep them there, her heart would escape clean out of her breast.

Or maybe that was just Penelope's imagination again. She buried her face in the pillow, and told her own heart to behave.

Chapter Fourteen

The print of Penelope Flood at Brandenburg sold through two printings before the public's attention moved on. Agatha found this immensely gratifying—not only for her skill as an artist, but also for the way Flood blushed whenever Agatha gently teased her about it.

Summer became fall, and the drones began dying.

"Typical," said Joanna Molesey. She was wearing black striped with red, which seemed to help her feel more herself again. "The men perish young, and the ladies trudge on toward winter."

"Plenty of women die too young." Agatha swirled her glass so the last drops of wine chased each other around and around in the bottom of the bowl.

Joanna's eyes flashed. "In the race of man, too many hurry to the finish," she proclaimed.

Agatha rolled her eyes. "Please don't write poetry in public. It's not decent."

Joanna laughed and improvised a second line, her voice falling into cadence like a falcon finding the updraft.

Agatha protested a little more, but only to be contrary. She'd been fully prepared to find the poetess a cynical, tempestuous, sharp-tongued termagant—and Joanna was all those things, without a doubt, but she was also witty, warm, thoughtful, and fiercely principled. She raged out of love, and that lit some answering spark in Agatha's soul.

Agatha now stayed at Fern Hall whenever she came to Melliton. She would stop by her mother-in-law's and see if Mrs. Stowe and Miss Coningsby needed anything—Mrs. Stowe's joints were aching as the weather grew colder, but that was nothing new, and Miss Coningsby was quietly but earnestly relieved to have the house to herself again.

So now there was a small guest bedroom that was essentially Agatha's own space in Penelope Flood's house. The blue coat and old trousers lived in a chest of drawers there, having long since become Agatha's, and with them were stored a few other articles the engraver had brought along for convenience's sake: a cake of her favorite soap, a spare set of underclothes, and a light wool gown. Just essentials. Not like she was joining the household. Not like she really, truly *lived* there.

So what if her room directly adjoined Penelope Flood's? It wasn't as though Agatha spent any time in bed imagining what Flood was doing on the other side of that wall. In a bed that must have smelled of her, sprawled out warm and soft and sleepy-eyed, as the autumn moonlight danced through the window and spilled onto the antique carpet . . .

Agatha stopped her thoughts before they could betray

her further, and set her wineglass down with a sharp *click*. "Have you had any luck with the Napoleon snuffbox?" she asked, though she already knew the answer.

"None," Mrs. Molesey confirmed, with a twist of her lips. "I think our dear vicar has actively begun avoiding me. I caught a glimpse of him from the window when I came up the lane, but when I knocked the housekeeper told me he'd just gone out." She snorted. "Out the back door, no doubt, as though all Hell's minions were in pursuit."

"As if you'd need minions to bedevil anyone," Flood teased.

Mrs. Molesey only huffed in irritation. "I'm horribly tempted to shout at him about it again—but he'd only say again he'd ask his sister, and then we're right back where we started." She made a curt, cutting gesture with one hand. "I might as well waltz down to Westminster and shout at the king."

"They'd arrest you for sedition," Flood chuckled.

"Treason is beginning to look attractive," Mrs. Molesey murmured darkly.

Agatha fiddled with the base of her glass, remembering Brandenburg. "People do shout at the king, though. Pamphlets. Letters." She smiled, thinking of Mrs. Turner. "Ballads."

Mrs. Molesey sat straight up in her chair. "Ballads, you say?"

Agatha clapped a hand over her mouth as the phrase "Oh no" escaped between her fingers.

Mrs. Molesey leaned forward avidly. "Rhyme and meter and melody, you mean. Just the sort of thing a poet is expert in."

Flood chuckled, and refilled Agatha's glass. "Now look what you've done."

"Please, Mrs. Molesey, forget I said anything," Agatha grumbled, and swallowed half the new glass in one go.

"It could be quite a challenge for a poet," Joanna said thoughtfully, "considering the last name."

Agatha frowned at her, but had to ask: "Whose last name?"

"Lady Summerville's, of course," Flood explained. "Summerville's only the title. The viscount's family name is actually Spranklin."

"It's *what?*" Agatha half shrieked.

"If it weren't for the courtesy title," said Joanna, "she'd be Mrs. Archibald Spranklin."

"Just try finding a rhyme for that," Flood said, with relish. "I dare you."

"Oh," said Mrs. Molesey. She rolled the syllable off her tongue, like the word was some rich and savory delicacy. "If it's a *dare*, then . . ." She rose from the table. "I'm going to get started, while the muse is still singing with fury. Good night to you both." She strode out the door and up the stairs, spite crackling in every limb and line of her.

"Now you've really done it," Agatha sighed.

"You're the one who brought up ballads," Flood said, and giggled into her wine.

Agatha Griffin, it transpired, had severely underestimated both Joann Molesey's swiftness of composition, and the lengths to which she could be motivated by pettiness. The very next week saw Griffin back in the Four Swallows, choking on her ale, while Nell Turner sang at least six different lines that rhymed with *Spranklin*, three of which were obscene, and all of which were insulting.

Penelope grinned at her friend, as the crowd roared for Nell to sing it again. "Nobody but yourself to blame, Griffin!"

"*Crankling* isn't even a real word!" Griffin sputtered. She set down her beer and shook her head. "I'm just surprised the authoress didn't come down the pub herself to hear it performed."

"Oh, she'd never," Penelope replied, as the third verse got an even bigger laugh the second time around. "She hates reading her poetry in public. Very much a creature of the pen, our Mrs. Molesey." She smiled, as a hail of pennies rained down on Nell as she bowed her thanks. "But she knows how to reach an audience."

The ballad became the hit of the Four Swallows, and before long it could be heard on the lips of shopkeepers, customers, and children going about their business on the Melliton lanes and byways. When asked who'd written it, Nell only smiled and answered: "A lady." The gossip moved so fast, and caused so much uproar, that three days later Penelope was unsurprised to find her breakfast interrupted by the vicar himself, with his cheeks very flushed and his cravat hastily tied.

"Is that daft Mrs. Molesey up?" he demanded.

Penelope had been about to stand and say a polite good morning, but such a question in such a tone rather made her knees go shaky, and she stayed in her chair. Lord, but would she ever not cringe at a quarrel? "She hasn't come down yet," she said soothingly, and gestured at one of the empty chairs. "But if you'd like to join me, Mr. Oliver?"

"I'm afraid I have no appetite, Mrs. Flood," he sniffed. But he sat down, anyway, and accepted the cup of tea Penelope poured for him. His mouth was flat with displeasure, his face hastily and indifferently shaved. "I assume you've heard this scurrilous ditty that's been making its way through our virtuous town?"

Scurrilous ditty? Penelope bit her lip to keep her mouth from showing her amusement. "I heard Nell sing it, yes—and Miss Coningsby's nephew has learned all the words by heart, she tells me."

Mr. Oliver scowled into his teacup. "My poor sister can hardly bear to show her face out of doors, for fear of that devil's chorus."

Penelope was not quite quick enough to turn her laugh into a cough.

Mr. Oliver narrowed his eyes.

Penelope quickly stuffed half a piece of toast between her lips, hoping the marmalade would at least give her mouth something better to do.

Mr. Oliver fixed her with his gravest expression. "It verges on slander, Mrs. Flood," the vicar warned.

The toast went gritty and dry in Penelope's mouth, marmalade notwithstanding. It scratched her throat as she swallowed it down. "Surely not," she rasped. "If memory serves, the lyrics are very clear about all the things that the fictional Lady S does *not* indulge in."

"A nefarious dodge," the vicar declared.

Penelope was either going to laugh or cry. She wasn't sure which.

Mr. Oliver set his teacup down and leaned forward, lowering his voice to a confessional mutter. "My sister is considering laying a formal charge against the author. As the local magistrate, I'd be forced to investigate. Possibly even to have the writer arrested. Or—since the writer is hiding behind anonymity—we might arrest the performer."

Penelope was suddenly painfully aware of the weight of the cutlery in her hands. Silver and pewter—cold, heavy metal. She clutched her fingers around it so the silver wouldn't fall and make too loud a clatter against her plate.

Mr. Oliver's voice lowered still further. "It might be best if Mrs. Molesey were to spend some time in London. Getting a few new gowns or trinkets, perhaps, or taking a change of air before the winter snows set in and muddy the roads."

"You're sending her away?" Penelope blurted.

"I'm saying she might find the metropolis a more congenial environment at the moment," Mr. Oliver said. He leaned back, nose and chin high, a tight, false smile twisting his mouth.

It was the same solution he had for every problem, Penelope realized. Send the troublemaker somewhere else. Keep Melliton comfortable. Sending Mr. Turner to London for work, paying to move the Marshes to St. Sepulchre's workhouse when their harvest failed . . .

And of course, the conversation that had sent Harry away, semipermanently, and which made it so awkward on the rare times he and John returned home.

Regret burned low in her belly, a sickly ember that never went entirely out.

She had tried to argue with Harry, when her brother had told her what Mr. Oliver had said to him. What he'd implied, rather than saying outright. Penelope had protested that Harry must have been mistaken, that Mr. Oliver had always been so friendly, that he couldn't be so friendly to Penelope and so cruel to her brother. It didn't add up. It couldn't be true.

She knew better now, but it killed her a little that she ought to have known better much earlier.

At the time, Harry had laughed harshly, and then had been on an Arctic-bound ship by the end of the month.

And now it was Joanna Molesey who was to be pushed out. Even though she'd lived here for decades, and was one of the most accomplished poets in the country.

A flare of rebellion licked up within her soul. Isabella would never have stood for this.

Penelope raised her head. "All Joanna wants is the Napoleon snuffbox," she said. "It's hers by right, according to Isabella's will."

Mr. Oliver spread his hands. "I must be honest with you, Mrs. Flood: the snuffbox is missing."

Penelope's eyes narrowed skeptically. "Missing?"

The vicar's mouth was a prim, hard line. "Nobody has seen it—and they have searched, no matter what Mrs. Molesey thinks. It is an unfortunate circumstance, to be sure . . . but no good can come from so much anger and hostility. We should extend more grace to one another, so these petty, worldly divisions do not foster deeper wounds in the soul of our little society." His pale eyes were steely, unflinching. "My sister has been very insistent that the snuff-box is not in her possession. It would take only a very little convincing for her to make a formal complaint of theft."

"Theft?" Penelope sucked in a harsh breath.

"If Mrs. Molesey took the snuffbox before the will was read, it could indeed be construed as theft under the law. How could she be sure it was really her property, after all, until she had heard it from Mr. Nancarrow?" He steepled his fingers in front of his mouth, a schoolmaster with an intractable pupil. "It would be so much easier—for everyone—if this didn't become a matter for the petty sessions."

Penelope trembled, and felt that rebellious little flame flicker and snuff itself out. She wasn't Isabella—she hadn't the nerve, or the social weight, to make the vicar yield to her will. Bitterness filled her mouth like smoke as she said, "I'll speak to Mrs. Molesey, Mr. Oliver."

His smile returned like the sun cresting the horizon. "Thank you, Mrs. Flood. I know I can always count on you to do what's right."

Half of Penelope's soul basked in the praise, even as the better half withered with shame.

CHAPTER FIFTEEN

Agatha stepped out of the workshop into the store to find Joanna Molesey, dramatic as ever in a crimson coat with touches of black, bent over the front counter beside Eliza and Sydney. The trio had a paper spread out in front of them, which the poet was quickly filling with lines in her fluid, hasty hand.

"Now then, what did you say the prosecutor replied—?" Mrs. Molesey looked up and straightened. "Ah, Mrs. Griffin! How lovely to see you again."

"Mrs. Molesey," Agatha replied, with a nod. She'd known the poet was leaving Melliton for the city, thanks to a letter from Penelope, but . . . "What brings you to our humble premises this lovely morning?"

Mrs. Molesey spared one brief glance for the gray drizzle outside the front window, then fixed her eye on Agatha and set her shoulders. "Rage, my dear woman—sheer rage, which must be expressed or it will poison me down to my very bones."

"Mrs. Molesey came to see our selection of ballads," Eliza hurried to explain.

"Your apprentice was extremely helpful," Mrs. Molesey added. Confidence poured from every line of her fine clothes, and nodded with the plumes on her rain-dappled hat. "I was just on the point of asking how much it costs to have a small batch of broadsides made up?"

Her smile was portrait-formal, all assurance and serenity and lofty condescension.

It didn't fool Agatha for a moment. "If you're thinking of printing that one about 'Lady S,'" she said repressively, "you'll have to find another shop."

Mrs. Molesey cocked her feathered head. "You don't need the work, in these uncertain times?"

"There's no payment you could offer that would balance out the distress such a job would cause Penelope Flood."

The poet smiled, and there was a knowing gleam in her eyes. "You are a very ardent friend, though you've known her but a little span of time."

Agatha crossed her arms and said nothing.

The poetess sighed gustily, as one long-suffering and much maligned. "Well, it speaks highly of you to refuse on such a principle—but I must do *something*. I am full up of fire and riddled with words like arrows, and no pleasing target to shoot them toward. At least, until now." She plucked up the paper from the counter, and flourished it. "One of the ballads Eliza showed me. I was intrigued by the subject but disappointed by the composer's expression, and sketched a few lines based on some other popular tunes."

"It's really quite good," Eliza added. "Better than most of the ones going around."

"And it's about the witness testimony in the Queen's trial," Sydney put in. "You know how well Queenite ballads have been selling for us—especially with the Lords on recess while they prepare final arguments. Everyone knows that now is the time to speak as powerfully as they can in Queen Caroline's defense."

Mrs. Molesey smoothly put in her oar. "Things at home have been far too quiet; it's bad for my nerves. If you'd like to bring these two young people to dinner tonight in Gower Street, I'm sure we could work out a few more verses." She widened her eyes, her expression all innocent hopefulness. "Perhaps even one or two more songs, to sell as a set?"

Three earnest faces beamed at Agatha, afire with purpose and the determination to engage in a war of words.

The printer sighed, recognizing a losing battle before she bothered to fight it. "As long as we don't print the 'Lady S' piece." She pursed her lips in resignation, while Sydney whooped and Eliza beamed. Mrs. Molesey's knowing gaze awakened her suspicious soul. "Would you be publishing this under your own name, Mrs. Molesey?"

"Heavens, no." The lady's eyebrows shot up into her hairline as she pretended shock. "A sophisticated lyric poet like Joanna Molesey, publishing common tunes for the unlettered public? What would Mr. Wordsworth say?"

"Or his sister," Eliza said with a snort.

"Tempting as it is to try and shock the pair of them, we'll need a pseudonym," Mrs. Molesey went on, gaze growing distant. "Something—irksome, but not fatal. Feminine. Caustic. Irrepressible. A spur, not a sword or a spear."

"Mrs. Mordant?" Eliza offered.

"Grandmother Gossip," Sydney added.

Mrs. Moseley shook her head. "Too gentle. We want something sharper."

Agatha thought of bees, and stings—but bees put her in mind of Penelope Flood and her kind heart. Yet there was another creature that could work . . . "The Widow Wasp," she blurted out.

Mrs. Molesey's head snapped around at once. "*Yes*," she said, like the voice of an oracle. "Yes, that will do."

The poet took the three of them to Walcott's for dinner, and by dessert there were three more absolutely vicious ballads and parodies of popular tunes for Sydney to begin setting type for the next day. Eliza worked up a few small illustrations: the Queen herself, London as a wasp's nest, a very sharp-limbed wasp-lady with lacy wings that folded around her like a shawl, and striped skirts that belled below the waist before narrowing to a knife-like stinger. Agatha set aside a few reams of paper and had the whole set made up as a chapbook.

She'd expected it to sell; it was perfectly pitched to the tenor of the times.

She had not expected it to sell out the first day. They scrabbled to print more that evening: those sold. They printed a third run, twice that of the first—people bought that, too, and before long you couldn't walk more than one mile in any section of town without hearing one of the

Widow's songs being sung out on a street corner or from a patron-filled tavern.

Pirate editions sprang up like mushrooms from the less ethical presses, to Agatha's grim resignation and Sydney's blazing indignation ("How dare someone copy Eliza's woodcuts!").

He was mollified somewhat when some of his favorite radical philosophers and thinkers began dropping the Wasp's lyrics into the pages of *Medusa* and *The Republican* ("Carlile quoted my line about the green bags!").

Even Catherine St. Day, Countess of Moth, had heard the ballads. She had come by Griffin's to arrange the printing of her foundation's next volume, a treatise by a lady chemist. "Lucy will not stop singing them! Particularly the one that made use of a tune Mr. Frampton had composed," she relayed, eyes twinkling. "He found himself on a walk through Westminster, surrounded by people singing his melody, but with lyrics he'd never heard before!"

"I hope it wasn't too disconcerting—I didn't realize he was composing now," Agatha replied.

The countess nodded. "He works up one or two songs a year: they supplement the income from his teaching and working on his mathematical—"

She was interrupted when Eliza burst into Agatha's office without knocking. "Ma'am, there's soldiers—"

Agatha was up and around the desk and striding into the storefront before she had time to reflect on the prudent course of action.

Eliza was right: there were three soldiers, their red coats

blood-bright in the sun spilling in the windows. "Mrs. Agatha Griffin?" said the one in front, whose coat was a more vivid officer's scarlet, rather than the thick madder dye sported by the other two.

"That's right," Agatha said, sending an anxious glance at her son.

Sydney was standing behind the counter, rigid and tense as a piece of metal under strain. His eyes were as cold and angry as Agatha had ever seen them.

The soldier flourished a piece of paper at her; Agatha took it and discovered a writ of seizure.

It was very official: signed and sealed. Her gut twisted, and sweat broke out on the back of her neck.

She was so shaken she missed most of what the officer said next—except for the words *seditious libel*, which made her snap painfully back to awareness. "We aren't here to harm anyone. We have orders to take away everything by the Widow Wasp," he said.

The officer's eyes stayed on Agatha, and his face was manfully expressionless—but not so the other two. One was eyeing the window glass with gleeful intent; the other was letting his gaze roam across the many watercolors, scenic prints, and loose manuscripts stacked everywhere in the shop.

Everything here could either break or burn, Agatha realized with a chill. She was surrounded by destructibles, her body the only thing between these soldiers' weapons and the roomful of vulnerable people behind her—and the men in front of her looked weathered enough to have seen action during the war. They'd know a thing or two about destruction. About violence. About hurt.

She froze, unable to protest or call out a warning or even move. One droplet of sweat slithered from her neck down beneath her collar. She fought not to shiver, painfully aware of the light, ticklish movement.

"I beg your pardon," came an icy voice from behind her.

Agatha turned her head stiffly and saw the countess standing in the doorway, one hand braced gracefully on the doorframe. She was not a tall person, but the fineness of her clothing and the steel of her posture could not have said *aristocrat* any clearer than if she'd had it written on a placard and carried above her head by a troop of liveried servants.

The lead soldier bowed and regarded her warily. "We are here on the King's business, ma'am."

The countess was looking down her nose at the officer, despite being the shortest person in the room. "I am the Countess of Moth, and of course you must carry out your orders," she said smoothly. "To the letter—and no further."

"Yes, my lady." The officer's mouth went thin, and his two subordinates shuffled themselves slightly more upright.

The countess turned to Agatha. "Where are the Wasp's songs?"

Agatha pointed at the central table, full of what broadsides and lyric sheets and chapbooks they still had.

"And are there any in the back?" the countess asked.

"Only the plates," Agatha replied. "We'll fetch them for you."

"Would you be willing to let one of us walk around to

check that we have everything, ma'am?" the officer hurried to inquire.

Oh, suddenly it's asking permission instead of barking orders? Agatha thought, but out loud she only said, "Sydney, please show the officer around the workroom. To prove to him we are holding nothing back." She couldn't leave while these men were here. She was rooted to the spot, heart racing.

Sydney's eyes glittered dangerously.

Agatha tried to use her own eyes to transmit silent, urgent motherly messages. *Please*, she begged wordlessly, *please don't.*

Her son came around the counter, looking grim. "This way, sir," he said, and led the officer through the door into the workroom.

The two subordinates began gathering up the Wasp's songs, piling the paper in a handcart they had brought with them. The countess moved to stand beside Agatha, a silent, supportive presence.

Agatha kept one hand relaxed at her side, but hid the other in her skirts, so as not to show the soldiers her clenched fist. Heavy hands grasped smooth pages, crinkling them. Chapbooks piled up in the handcart, covers bending, pages creasing, the rustling of all that paper being occasionally broken by the occasional sound of a single page tearing.

It made Agatha flinch every time.

One of the soldiers noticed, and broke into a grin.

Agatha took a slow, deep breath and prayed for endurance.

The countess cleared her throat pointedly, and the soldier returned to his task.

Hours or seconds later—Agatha found it impossible to tell—Sydney returned with the officer. Eliza followed them, eyes wide and cheeks pale.

"That appears to be everything," the officer said, avoiding the Countess of Moth's stern gaze. Instead he turned to Agatha. "I sincerely hope we won't have cause to visit you again, Mrs. Griffin."

His eye flicked to Sydney, and then back.

As a looming, unspoken threat it was wildly effective: Agatha felt the mettle of her soul buckle like cheap tin. Promises, apologies, defensive words bubbled up on her tongue like the froth from a dose of poison.

Before she could choose any of them to speak aloud and damn herself forever, the soldiers turned and marched out, carrying fifty pounds of Griffin's most profitable stock with them.

The countess pressed one hand against Agatha's arm. "I'm so sorry, my dear. Lord Sidmouth is determined to make trouble for everyone—the Polite Science Society has had more than a few lectures cancelled for lack of a permit, under the new laws. If they come again, send Eliza for me at once." She nodded to the apprentice, and slipped out of the shop.

Agatha still couldn't find her voice.

Sydney could. And did. He cursed, so loudly that beside him Eliza started and shook. "We can have another fifty broadsheets made up by this evening," the young man began. "The chapbooks will take a little—"

"No!" Agatha cut him off. "Out of the question. We're not selling any more of the Wasp's work."

"What?" Sydney yelped. "Why?"

"Did you miss what just happened?" Agatha snapped. "The King's own soldiers came and took them all away. Do you take that as an encouragement to *continue* flouting the libel laws?"

Her voice was rising in pitch and volume, and through the open workroom door Agatha could see the apprentices and journeymen gathering around to listen.

Eliza's eyes were wide and white at the edges. "Maybe we should've published 'Lady Spranklin,'" she murmured.

Sydney's jaw set mulishly. The dangerous glitter was back in his eyes. Maybe it had never left. It sparked like a knife blade against flint. "Soldiers means we've been noticed," he said. "We're speaking loudly enough that they had to react. That means what the Widow Wasp says matters. Why would you want us to stop just when we're starting to get what we wanted?"

"Is this really what you wanted?" Agatha demanded. "What if the Countess of Moth hadn't happened to be here? What if they'd destroyed the shop, smashed the presses, harassed our workmen? Or you, or Eliza? What if they decide to bring charges, and put us on trial?"

"They can't jail all of us!"

"They don't have to jail all of us," Agatha shot back. "They only have to jail some of us, and frighten the rest."

Her son folded his arms, looking every inch of nineteen. "I'm not afraid."

"Well, I bloody well am!" Agatha shouted.

Everyone froze.

Agatha sucked in a deep breath, but she was too far gone to stop now. "I am frightened for you, and for myself, and Eliza, and for every single person who works here. I'm scared for the shop—what your father and I worked our entire lives to build—but above everything else I'm deathly afraid that you're so selfish you would *choose* to put all of that—all of *us* in peril, just for a few moments' acclaim from your reckless, radical friends!"

Sydney stepped forward. Agatha realized with a bit of a shock that he was a good six inches taller than her. She'd known that, of course, but somehow it constantly slipped her mind. His voice was low and furious and the unshakeable conviction there nearly splintered her heart to pieces. "Mum, you've run Griffin's for nearly three decades, in the heart of one of the greatest cities in the world. Aren't you angry when rich, powerful men try to tell you what you are and aren't allowed to print?"

"That kind of anger is a luxury I do not have," Agatha said bitterly. "Not when I am trying to ensure that we still have food and shelter and clothing. I want us to be *safe*."

Sydney scoffed. "There are greater things than mere safety, Mum. Happiness. Liberty. Justice."

Agatha yearned to shake sense into him. "But all those things *start* with safety—don't you see? How can you be happy if you aren't certain where your next meal is coming from? How can you fight for justice if your hands are trapped in chains?"

Sydney only shook his head. "How can you fix a broken world if you can't talk about where it's broken?"

"Talk all you like," Agatha said, "so long you print none of it on my presses." She slung her gaze around, pinning every single person in place so they understood this edict applied to all of them.

"You're making a mistake," Sydney insisted.

"It's my mistake to make, because it's my press," Agatha returned. "That's what liberty gets you."

"That's what cowardice gets you!"

Agatha gasped, then snapped her mouth closed. Hurt and fury raged like two wolves within her, tearing at each other.

Sydney huffed, then turned on his heel and stalked out of the store. Walter and Crompton looked grim; Eliza was twisting her hands and biting her lip; Jane the apprentice looked to be on the verge of tears.

All those eyes, reflecting Agatha's own pain and frustration back to her, multiplied . . .

Now the anger overwhelmed her, surging up and overflowing the banks of her soul. "Whatever's next in the queue, get it done," Agatha snapped.

Everyone leaped into motion, some hurrying back to the press or worktable, others moving more slowly as if unsure of the very floorboards beneath their feet.

Soon only Eliza was left in the shop, still wringing her hands. "We only wanted to help," she murmured.

"You can help by doing what you're told," Agatha said. "Why don't you catch me up on the music reviews for next month's *Menagerie*?"

Eliza whispered an inaudible *yes ma'am* and hurried out

to get the latest letters. Agatha was truly alone now, as the gray rain murmured worries against the windowpanes, and the large central table stood bare and glaring in the middle of all of it.

The shop bell jangled suddenly as the door opened and a customer came in, beaver hat shining and kid gloves protecting his hands. His face was all excitement—until he took one look at Agatha's face, blanched, turned around, and strode right out again into the wet.

The printer snarled silently at his back, but it did nothing to relieve her feelings.

CHAPTER SIXTEEN

Penelope was too anxious to sleep. Normally this would have been a cause for frustration—but it was autumn, and time to prepare the hives for the winter's rest. Which meant making sure both the skep hives and the glass observation hive were free from the depredations of wax moths, who devoured the comb.

And *that* meant staying up several nights with the light traps. So, for once, a little anxiety was more helpful than otherwise.

After weeks when she'd demurred and remained in London, Griffin was finally returning to Melliton, and had promised to sit up and keep Penelope company during one of the long watches. Griffin had written Penelope about the Widow Wasp, and about the soldiers' visit to the shop, and in addition to all Penelope's worries for her friend's livelihood and safety, well . . .

She also worried Griffin would blame Penelope for the ugliness. It was a selfish little worry, a miniscule flaw she ought to have been able to ignore, like a hangnail of the soul. She worried at it until it was raw and red and angry.

After all, Penelope was the one who'd introduced Agatha to Joanna Molesey in the first place. Penelope's failure had therefore directly led to the catastrophe: if things with Mr. Oliver and Lady Summerville had been properly sorted out in Melliton, there would have been no need for Joanna to remove to London, and she would have never started writing those ballads with Sydney and Eliza.

Penelope felt like she'd failed everyone, and they were simply too kind to mention it.

Plus, there was the matter of yesterday's letter from Harry, tucked in her bureau just across the room, making her squirm with a shallow, cowardly dread.

Griffin arrived mid-afternoon, and Penelope tried to assuage some of her guilt by presenting Griffin with a truly overwhelming amount of food at tea. "Seedcake? Sandwiches? Ginger biscuit?"

"Lord, no," Griffin said, leaning back to sip at her tea. She looked more worn today than when Penelope had seen her last: the lines on her face more deeply carved by tension and tiredness. "I stopped for one of Mr. Biswas's curried pies on the walk over. I've missed them terribly."

"You can't get curry in London?" Penelope said.

"I can. It's not the same." Griffin took another sip of tea, her eyes lowered.

She was deflecting—which, Penelope realized with a flash, she wouldn't have done if she were feeling angry at

Penelope. No, Agatha Griffin wasn't the sort to hide irritation. If she was upset at you about something, she would make certain you knew.

Some of the tightness in Penelope's chest eased at this. She picked up a ginger biscuit, and let the spicy-sweet flavor burst on her tongue. It tasted like relief. "I'm sure the curried pies have missed you, too."

Griffin went utterly still.

Penelope swallowed the last bite of biscuit, and her eyes darted helplessly over to the bureau. She should tell Griffin about the letter, at once. Get it all out in the open.

Instead, she stood up. "Shall we set up the light traps, then?"

Penelope always set up three traps, each of which consisted of a lantern fitted over a small box with slanting sides: fluttering moths were drawn in to the light, then funneled by the box shape into the hollow darkness beneath. A small switch in the watcher's hand was useful to knock down stronger flyers and larger specimens who might have otherwise escaped. Penelope would gather all the fallen the next morning and bring them to the Four Swallows—Mr. Koskinen swore that wax moths made the best lures for fly-fishing.

She and Griffin had the lanterns lit by the time the sun vanished; three small lights on the lawn, pushing back against the twilight. Daniel the footman hauled two cushioned chairs out—more comfortable for long hours than garden benches—and Griffin and Penelope wrapped themselves in blankets against the autumn chill.

The sky drifted from pink to purple to navy blue, and the first brave stars came out.

The moths came with them, dancing toward the lantern lights, wings looming large against the glow and casting flickering shadows over the small space of Penelope's apiary. She left the larger, fancier types alone—they weren't a threat to the bees—and focused on using little flicks of the switch to knock the pale, mottled forms of the wax moths down into the box. One by one, moth by moth, as the breeze whispered warnings in Penelope's ears. It was far too late now for wildflowers, so the breeze carried only the earthy, *memento mori* scent of fallen leaves from maple, ash, and hawthorn trees in the forest behind Fern Hall.

Griffin reached into her coat and pulled out a flask. "I brought a little something to help us keep warm."

She handed it over, and Penelope took an experimental pull.

Brandy rushed over her tongue, strong and sweet with that alcohol haze that settled into one's throat like steam. She swallowed appreciatively. "This is good."

"It was Thomas's favorite," Griffin replied. She settled back against her chair, woolen shawl wrapped around her throat. "French. Hard to come by during the war, unless you wanted to pay smugglers' prices for it. We hadn't bought any for a few years, when he died." She took the flask back, tipping it up against her long mouth. "So I drink it now in his honor."

Ah, yes, Griffin's lost husband. Did she still pine for him, in the secret places of her heart? Penelope felt heat prickle in the corners of her eyes, and tilted her head up as she stared at the stars. But they offered her no clear answers, only a cold and distant glitter. "You must miss him awfully."

"If I could wish him back, I'd do it in an instant," Griffin replied. "Though there would be some awkwardness, I expect. He'd notice all the ways I've changed in the past three years. So many days, so many hours, and I had to figure out how to get through each one without him. It . . . left a mark, you might say."

"A crucible transforms the metal," Penelope replied.

"Just so." Agatha took another long pull of brandy, tongue slipping out to catch one errant amber droplet from the silver rim of the flask's mouth.

Penelope felt heat clench low in her belly. It was the brandy, that was all, sucking the air from her lungs and sending that lick of flame through her veins.

She reminded herself they were speaking of Griffin's late husband. And grief. Penelope was far too familiar with grief.

"I know precisely what you mean," she murmured. "It's so easy to think you're living your life as the same person you always were. You don't notice all the new little thoughts and feelings you've had, hour by hour, each one turning you slightly this way or that—until he comes back at the end of the voyage and you notice how far out of alignment you've become. Things you didn't even think were important enough to say aloud, but taken all together they accumulate."

A short silence. "When who comes back?" Griffin asked carefully.

Damn.

So much for secrets. Penelope shifted in her chair, and flicked another moth away from the light and into the darkness. But there was no graceful way out—only the direct way, straight through awkwardness into whatever lay on the other side. "My husband, John. And my brother, Harry." She kept her eyes fixed so tightly on the flame that the rest of the world faded into darkness. "They wrote to say they'd be back at Christmas."

"That's good," Griffin said. "Isn't it?" She cocked her head, lamplight gleaming off the silver hair at her temples. Her eyes turned cold as the stars overhead. "Forgive a blunt and indelicate question but: Does Mr. Flood expect to share your bed when he returns?"

"Lord, no." Penelope let out a short burst of a laugh, that settled into her chest like lead. "He'd be horrified if I even suggested it."

"How very flattering of him," Griffin returned, her voice dry as the desert. She reached out one booted toe and knocked a moth into the box nearest her. "So why is it a problem?"

Because I know I'll feel mortified if my husband and the woman I'm desperately lusting after are sleeping beneath the same roof. "Because I wanted to invite you and your family to come stay with me for the Christmas holiday."

Griffin considered this. "And now you won't have the room?"

Penelope swatted at more moths. "No, I just . . . I wasn't

sure you'd still want to come, if Harry and John were here, too. You've never met them, after all." She sighed. "This isn't at all how I imagined our conversation going."

Griffin sat up, hands gripping the arms of the chair. "Flood, do you like your husband? I know you don't love him—but do you enjoy his company? Do you find him a pleasant, sociable man in general?"

"I do."

"Do you think he'll dislike me, or Sydney? Or that we'll dislike him?"

Penelope snorted, and carefully poked the fuzzy back of a lunar underwing to move the creature away from the trap. "Oh, he and Sydney will take to each other like two political ducks. John has very definite opinions about the Combination Laws that he will be only too happy to expound upon at some length."

"Then is it your brother who's the problem?"

"No, damn it all, it's me!"

Griffin snapped her mouth shut, blinking. The silence of the night slammed down again, leaden and thick.

Penelope blew out an exasperated breath, and lowered her voice again. God, she was bad at untangling things. The secret of what she most refused to say burrowed beneath her skin like a worm in an apple.

But she had to try and explain *something*: Griffin was looking at her too closely, and Penelope had never been very good at subtlety or subterfuge. "When I was young . . ." she began, swallowed hard, and held out her hand.

Griffin gave her the brandy at once.

Penelope took a long draft, and braced herself. "When I was young, the house was always full of people, all of whom were older and bigger and busier than me. So I got used to just . . . going along with someone else's idea of what we ought to be doing at any moment. Didn't matter whether it was my mother, my father, any of my siblings. Or later, the vicar or Joanna or Isabella. I found myself behaving a little differently, depending on who I was with and what made it easiest for them to overlook me, or be amused by me, or not ask me to leave. The more I loved someone, the more I worked to please them—and the harder it was for me when pleasing one person meant disappointing someone else."

Another flick of the switch, another moth into the box.

Griffin's mouth had gone somber, the lip of the flask resting thoughtfully against one lip.

Penelope went on. "I wasn't conscious of this for a long while, of course—and then I assumed it was something everyone did, if I thought about it at all. One by one, my siblings moved away. Owen died, then my parents. I started doing the bee circuit, as more and more families struggled to keep their homes. I got used to being on my own, to being myself. And then I married John."

Griffin held out her hand; Penelope passed over the brandy.

She continued her story as Griffin raised the flask to her lips. "We only lived together for six months, but it was unpleasant in a way that took me at least that long again to understand. I had never been half of a pair before—not the kind of pair people could acknowledge, anyway."

Griffin choked on the brandy.

Penelope chewed on her lip. She certainly wasn't going to get into *that* tonight as well. One shameful confession per evening was more than enough, thank you very much. She hurried on. "Every time we went out, to church or the Four Swallows or anywhere, someone would make a perfectly ordinary remark—I knew how a wife was supposed to behave to her husband, and I knew how John and I behaved as friends, but because those things were different I wouldn't be able to do anything. It was like my heart was a rope pulled in two directions at once. It tied me right up: I couldn't move; I couldn't speak. So I'd sit there, silent and sweating into my delicate Sunday gloves. For six months' worth of Sundays."

"That sounds terrible," Griffin said.

"It was." Penelope pulled the blanket tighter around her shoulders, fending off the night's chill. "It was easier with friends, somehow—you introduce your friends to each other, and then they become friends, and you don't get pulled apart. But a husband? There was . . . a sense of being watched, as if every word and gesture meant something different and particular than what I intended. As if all my eccentric behavior reflected on him, too. It froze me right up, and I could tell John noticed and felt hurt by it, and then he and Harry left—but the next time they came back it happened again, but worse. It was years before I was able to put words around what I felt was happening."

"That you weren't good at being a wife in name only?"

Penelope stared into the burning heart of the light trap. "That I don't always know who I am supposed to be."

Griffin, bless her, didn't scoff. She turned this over, while moths blissfully flirted with the flame. Blades of grass stood out sharply in the flickering, ghostly night. "What about those lovers you mentioned? Was it different with them?" One corner of her mouth lifted. "You were very emphatic about having been fucked, Flood."

The way her voice turned low and smoky on the word *fucked*—it made Penelope want to rub herself against it like a cat, and set up a thrumming heat low in her belly. "We were always discreet," she said. *And all women,* was the thing she carefully didn't say. "It didn't feel like the same pressure, even when we were together amid larger, louder groups. Nobody knew, so we weren't . . . *considered* in the same way."

Griffin snorted. "Because nobody ever notices illicit love affairs."

Penelope laughed in spite of herself. "There wasn't much time for anyone to notice anything: they were all very brief liaisons. Maybe I only have trouble with long connections." She sobered. "Maybe I'm just not the sort of person who inspires a lifetime's worth of passion."

"Rubbish," said Griffin.

Her answer was swift, her voice was firm, and her certainty was palpable. Penelope went all over red, thrumming with the sweet shock of that single word. She was unspeakably glad the darkness and the flickering light would hide her reaction from the woman who'd caused it.

"You've been unlucky, that's all," Griffin went on. As though she weren't tearing down the foundations of Penelope's carefully built-up solitude. "You are extremely kindhearted and sweet, Flood—but you're also observant and cautious, two things that aren't often found in the kind of person who lets themselves get swept up in reckless love affairs. Especially where . . ." She paused for a moment. "Especially where there is good reason to be cautious."

Penelope felt turned into a statue, stiff as marble and leached of color.

Griffin leaned forward. "Do you know what I think?"

Penelope shook her head.

Griffin's eyes were bright with anger. "I think you let your brother and his beloved overwhelm you. I think you so wanted to help them, in whatever way you could, that you sacrificed your own happiness for theirs."

Penelope shifted in her seat. "Marriage was never in my future."

Griffin made a wordless noise rejecting this statement.

Penelope felt a flicker of temper, shoring up the unsteadiness of her voice. "Marriage as it is practiced in England is not made for women like me."

Griffin openly scoffed at that. "Don't be ridiculous, Flood: you are one of the sweetest, strongest, truest people I have ever met in my life. You worry about everyone's happiness. You want the best for all your family, friends, and neighbors—even the ones you don't like. And I don't know if anyone's told you this in a while, but you're lovely to look at. On top of everything warm and wonderful about you, you are absolutely beautiful. I can't imagine a single reason—"

"It's because of women!" Penelope exploded.

It was a harsh cry, close to a shout, and it made Griffin rear back in her seat.

Cheeks burning, Penelope lowered her volume back to a whisper. Her voice was just one more shadow in the darkness. "All my life, I have only ever loved women. And I cannot marry a woman, under English law. So it didn't seem to matter much if I married somebody else. For practical reasons." She heaved a frustrated breath, furious to have lost control. "So."

The silence stretched out, and Penelope's nerves stretched with it.

Her mind helpfully offered up all the awful possibilities Griffin could say in response. The best Penelope could hope for was a new and permanent awkwardness: *The less said the better*, perhaps, or the terrible *I suppose it's none of my business, really.*

The worst thing would be the unmistakable moment where a friend withdrew their friendship while you watched. To see a warm smile fall away, a bright eye turn cold, and to know there was no going back to how it had been before. Penelope had seen it happen half a dozen times in her life, and it never got any easier to bear.

She squared her shoulders and braced herself, as the other woman stared off into the distance. No doubt she was stunned by the truth Penelope had revealed. No doubt Penelope had now officially ruined everything.

"If you could . . ." Griffin asked slowly. "If you could have married any of the women you loved—would you have?"

It was as though she had asked the question in some language other than English: it took far too long for Penelope's slow brain to chew through the question. She thought back over her past, with the usual twinge of self-chastisement. "They often went and married someone else instead," she said at last. "Emma Koskinen, for example, after our brief summer passed."

Griffin squeaked in surprise.

Penelope chuckled. "I imagine I should have felt more upset about that—but she and Timo were so much better suited, and he was so serious and fascinatingly Swedish, and I was twenty-one and blissfully gay. We all stayed friends, quite easily." She stretched her legs out, crossing and uncrossing them at the ankles. "Friends have always been more valuable to me, anyway. I've never wept over losing a lover; I've always regretted losing a friend." She kept her eyes very fearfully on the lanterns and added: "I should regret the loss of your friendship more than anything in the world, I think."

She didn't look around, not even when Griffin spoke in a voice so low and husky Penelope could practically feel it against her skin: "You'll always have my friendship, Penelope Flood. There's no question about that."

Penelope blinked and blinked into the lantern light, determined not to cry.

Griffin cleared her throat and went on talking. "As for the question of Christmas, the answer's quite simple."

Now Penelope did glance over. "It is?"

"You'll invite us to stay for the holiday, and I'll be very

charming to your husband, and if I see you becoming stiff or awkward or anything like that I'll just turn to you and say, *Maybe we need to check on the hive by the print-works*, or some other such excuse, and you won't have to be stuck." She tilted her head. "If you think that might help."

It *was* simple, when Griffin said it. Simple—but not small. Penelope felt hope rise up, a fountain overflowing its banks. "You'd do that for me?"

Griffin snorted, the sound bright and joyful in the darkness. "Of course. We're friends, Flood."

Could it really be that simple? Penelope had stewed in dread and guilt about this for the better part of a decade, but Griffin sounded so matter-of-fact about the whole thing. As if it was something she was happy to help fix.

For one warm, golden, glowing moment, Penelope basked in the hope that she wasn't broken, that her secret flaws were overlookable, that she could throw open the welcoming doors of her heart and having something other than the cold wind answer.

"Besides," Griffin added, "after the Wasp business, it will do us all good to get away from London for a little while."

Golden hope vanished, smothered under shadowy wings. This wasn't about Penelope, not in the way that she thought. She was only one of many things on Griffin's mind.

She wanted to be so much more important to Agatha than that.

Realization would have knocked her legs from under her, if she weren't already sitting down. Good lord, when had she gone and fallen in love with Agatha Griffin?

And how did she not realize earlier, when she might have properly nipped it in the bud? It was in full flower now, a dark, dangerous rose unfolding in the heart of her, petals climbing up her throat and threatening to spill from her lips.

She knocked down another moth, breathed in the scent of the dying year, and hoped winter would take pity and freeze that love all the way down to the root.

CHAPTER SEVENTEEN

Before Agatha could contemplate Christmas, and having to be civil to the man whose wife she pined for, there was work to do: the Queen's trial was coming to its conclusion.

The verdict, when it came, raced through the city like a fire: the Pains and Penalties Bill had narrowly passed. The Queen was guilty.

The Lords were, however, still arguing about the whether or not to keep the clause mandating divorce, which would thrust the Queen from her throne and title. Agatha, etching another scene of Queen Caroline sitting stiffly in the dock, wondered how the woman bore the weight of so much naked cruelty. To be so loathed by your husband that even a continent's distance wasn't far enough; and now, out of pettiness and selfish power, to have him shine the worst possible light on the private details of your life and household.

It was public humiliation on an imperial scale, and it lit a sick, slow-burning flame in Agatha's heart that no amount of distraction or discipline seemed able to snuff out.

It was one more appalling outcome of the risk every wife took when she said her vows and handed herself over to a husband's legal rule. Agatha had loved being married, mostly—but she couldn't deny that there were times she felt much more secure as a widow than she had during her marriage. Loving and kind as Thomas had been, Agatha was a pragmatic person, and she'd been well aware Thomas's kindness had been just that: a kindness. Not something Agatha had a legal claim to. To have the bearability of one's existence depend on whether or not one's spouse was inclined to be generous, well . . .

She had trusted her husband. But not the law that gave a husband so much power.

She thought of Penelope Flood, whose husband was not unkind, but that didn't seem to help. Flood found her marriage uncomfortable, and took all the blame for that feeling upon herself.

Agatha dug the graver doubly hard into the wax, her heart bubbling like an acid bath as she sketched in the angry shapes of the men in Parliament. The curling wigs and crowded benches looked like storm clouds, swirling with chaos.

This treason wasn't anything like Cato Street. Queen Caroline hadn't attempted to murder anyone. She'd only dared to return to England and remind her husband she existed. And now the whole engine of the government was turned against her, simply because her husband—one man— wanted out of an unhappy marriage.

The unspeakable, unbearable *unfairness* of it all seethed in her breast like a canker. She silently cursed King George's name, along with all self-serving, neglectful men.

Men like John Flood.

Agatha carved away another line: another lordly figure asking primly prurient questions of a likely bribed informant. Agatha was only a printer's widow; she had no vote, no power. There was nothing she could do to help the poor Queen now.

Sydney burst into the workroom, collar askew and face flushed despite the November chill in the air. He declined to meet his mother's eye—since the argument, they'd stepped too carefully around one another, as if avoiding the shards of something precious lying broken in the space between them. He made a face and announced to the room at large: "They're keeping the divorce clause!"

Crompton shook his head, and one or two of the journeymen muttered cynical disappointment. Small Jane's eyes were wide as she looked to Eliza for guidance.

Eliza was watching Sydney intently. "So there's to be another vote, in the Lords?"

He nodded.

Eliza's mouth set in a thin, angry line.

Sydney cast a defiant glance at his mother. Agatha could guess why. One of the Widow Wasp's most popular songs had been a parody of the old tune "Once Again I'm Vainly Dreaming," a ballad depicting Anne Boleyn's last thoughts before King Henry sent her to be beheaded. The original was melancholy and nostalgic, a woman condemned by her husband, hearkening back to the days when love was fresh and young.

In the new ballad, Queen Caroline's faux-wistful asides comprised a long, long list of King George's many scandals and failings and insults as a husband. The lyrics were bitter and pointed and side-splittingly funny.

It was the ballad Sydney was proudest of, and it would never be more apropos—or more saleable—than right now.

"There's another caricature caption to be composed, if you please," Agatha said coolly.

Sydney's expression soured, and he stomped across the room. His hands were shaking as they pulled type from the cases and slid it into the composing stick. Every tiny chink of metal on metal was like a barb sinking into Agatha's bruised heart.

She held her tongue, though her throat burned with words unuttered.

As soon as the day's work was done, Sydney vanished for the evening, and was still not home when Agatha fell into a fitful, irritated sleep.

On the new vote, the bill again squeaked through—but so narrowly that Lord Liverpool grudgingly retracted it before it could be sent to the House of Commons. Everyone knew—and if they didn't, the papers soon told them—that this was because such a narrow margin meant the bill had no chance of passing the Commons, where the radicals had stirred up every friend and supporter to the Queen's cause.

It was over. The Queen would keep her husband and her throne.

The country triumphed as though a war had been won. More so, even—the grand celebrations after Waterloo were now entirely eclipsed. Bells rang out from church steeples and Dissenting chapels throughout London. People flooded the streets, singing and crying, "The Queen, the Queen!" and hurling bricks through the windows of the papers who'd printed articles and letters against her. At the Crown and Anchor, radicals drunk on more than the tavern's best ale loudly and indiscriminately toasted the Queen, the King, the army, the navy, Thomas Paine, George Washington, and every revolution. Fireworks and firearms and even cannons went off at such frequent intervals that the rich pulled their curtains shut and trembled in fear of the guillotine, imagining every cart and carriage rolling past was a tumbril coming to bear them to their doom. Insulting effigies of the Italian witnesses and the lordly prosecution were burned on street corners, and guillotine flags with ominous slogans waved from pubs and taverns across the city.

Penelope's next letter showed that Melliton had rejoiced just as loudly as London.

> Everyone from town trooped down to the rectory again to demand the vicar ring the church bells in the Queen's honor. Mr. Koskinen ran up the steeple and pulled bell ropes until dawn broke. I don't think anyone for ten miles round got any sleep that night, but everyone was as merry as midsummer, anyway.
>
> Lady Summerville held a tea at Abington Hall, to celebrate having banished the specter of aristocratic divorce. Fine ladies congratulating one another on all their hard work. I slipped out into the garden maze and found all the satyrs and Napoleon gone—only Josephine remained, sad and solitary.

Please go visit the nymph and the dryad for me, won't you? I need to know at least those two are still safe.

More statues sold? Agatha dashed off a quick inquiry to a few of the art brokers she knew from the *Menagerie*. Perhaps Napoleon was somewhere she could take Flood for a visit. Maybe somewhere with moonlight and a fountain and a concealing veil of leaves . . .

She was interrupted by a knock at the door; she put down her pen and craned her head to see Sydney standing there, a pamphlet in his hand and sheer misery in his face. "What's happened?" she asked.

In answer, he merely handed over the paper, which had *A Letter from the King to his People* emblazoned across the top. "It's lies," he said. "Self-serving, unjust lies. And it's selling out on every corner in the city."

"Oh," said Agatha on a sigh. So the backlash had begun. There would be as many pieces against the Queen now as there had been before.

Sydney all but collapsed on the bench at the foot of Agatha's bed. "I really thought they were all listening," he said. "The Lords, the people—everyone. I thought we were getting through. Damn it all, I thought something was going to *happen*." He slapped an emphatic palm down on the padded bench top.

Agatha set the pamphlet aside and patted her son's shoulder. "It rarely does," she said. "I'm sorry."

He blinked. "You knew? How did you know?"

Agatha pressed her lips together. "I've seen it before, of

course. Happens all the time in this business. The upward sweep and the crash afterward. Sometimes it's bigger, sometimes smaller. You'll get used to it eventually."

Sydney's horror was gradually giving way to a dawning recognition. "All the time?"

"All the time. Though—this was rather a large one. It's not always quite so excessive. And it's particularly hard when you care deeply about the matter the storm is centered on." She smiled softly. "Which you do."

Sydney was staring as though he were bobbing in unruly seas, and Agatha held the only lifeline. "How do you bear it?"

She could only shrug. "Strong drink?"

Sydney let out a broken laugh.

His mother clasped her hands against her knees. "You focus on the things that are important. The people you know. The work you do. You take the anger that burns inside you and put it to use, so your heart doesn't devour only itself."

Sydney sucked in a sharp breath. "Has anyone ever told you you ought to write poetry?"

"Careful, my darling son." Agatha laughed. "I will cut you right out of the will, see if I don't."

"Do you think . . ." Sydney paused, looking grumpy, and for a dizzying moment Agatha felt as though she were looking into a mirror. Sometimes she forgot he was as much her son as Thomas's.

Sydney's voice was soft, but steady. "Do you think if we'd kept going as the Wasp, things might have been different?"

Agatha bit back the urge to tell him not to be foolish. That was the fear talking, and fear had almost ruined things between herself and her son. "I'm not sure," she admitted, and saw Sydney's eyes widen in surprise.

Her cheeks went hot, but she pressed on. "When your father was still with us, Griffin's was much more focused on the arts and sciences. The *Menagerie* was everything. He was part of the political conversations—but distantly, as a listener more than a speaker or a publisher. The political jobs you've brought in to offset the stamp taxes have been financially sound choices, it's true—but I don't have a good sense yet of how to balance the risks and the rewards in the political sphere. Until I do, I am likely to want to avoid the larger risks, if I can." She plucked at the nothing on her skirt. "Even if it means doing something rather cowardly."

Sydney rose and walked over and bent down, his lips brushing her cheek. "I'm sorry I was so angry," he said. "If it helps, Eliza's been raking me over the coals for a week now, for sulking when you were just being protective." He rolled his eyes, giving Agatha a precious moment to dash the water from her own, unseen. "Don't tell her I told you that. She'll never let me forget it."

"I won't," Agatha promised. She let her lips curve upward knowingly. "Is there . . . anything else you feel you should tell me? About Eliza?"

Sydney went so red it was all his mother could do not to laugh. "I don't know what you mean," he mumbled, and escaped soon after.

Agatha turned back to her letter with a knowing smile. Penelope would enjoy hearing about this . . .

CHAPTER EIGHTEEN

Penelope woke at dawn two days before Christmas, even though she could have slept later: the slumbering hives didn't need looking at for a few days yet. The day lightened from black into a dull, leaden sort of gray, where clouds hung low like surly eyebrows and the air put clammy fingers down the back of one's neck.

Penelope prowled around the house, counting the seconds as they ticked past on the clock face.

It got so bad that Mrs. Braintree started making broad hints about illness and fever and dosing Penelope with something from her terrifying stillroom. (Mr. Scriven said her great-great-grandmother'd been a witch in the old days.) Penelope allowed herself to be gently shooed out of the kitchens and back to the parlor by one of the new maids, hired for the holidays.

But finally, after ages had passed, it was late enough that Penelope could take her handcart to the Four Swallows and meet Agatha, Sydney, Eliza, and all their luggage in the main courtyard where the stage had deposited them before continuing along the road north to Carrisford.

The young folk were looking around with skeptical eyes, and Penelope had a pang of concern that they were not seeing Melliton at its best. Hopefully the holiday would bring the kind of cold, crystalline snow Penelope loved most, the kind that silvered every edge and turned the houses and crofts and cottages into rolling, icy fairylands.

But then she looked over to see Agatha Griffin taking a deep breath, shoulders lifting and a tightness in her face smoothing into something like happiness.

Penelope's heart warmed in helpless response. "You can put your luggage right in the cart," she said.

Griffin grinned. "I will—but let Sydney push the thing, if you please. He needs more wearing out than you do."

Sydney made an affronted noise but grinned and took up the task willingly enough. Eliza tossed her bag on top of Griffin's and sent Sydney a pert look.

Penelope gave the boy directions, and the whole group began moving east toward Fern Hall. Sydney and Eliza quickly drew ahead, talking constantly the whole time. Griffin watched them thoughtfully. "Two entire weeks away from the shop. I haven't done anything so self-indulgent since—" She bit her lip, cheeks flushing. "Never mind."

"Don't hold back, Griffin," Penelope said cheerfully. "Tell me all about your hedonistic past, where you never take even a fortnight away from work."

"Pot calling kettle, Flood. How many beehives have you visited this morning?"

"None," Penelope returned. "I was saving them all for you."

Griffin went even pinker. Her booted toes scuffed at a rock in the road. "Will Mr. Flood be joining us?"

Penelope's expansive mood withered somewhat. "He and Harry are spending one more night with Michael in Wales before they come east." She sucked in a lungful of cold, wet air. "They'll come bearing gifts from Christopher, and Lawrence and his wife. But for tonight, it's only us."

Griffin made a contented noise at that. The sound burrowed into Penelope and stayed there, glowing like an ember against the chill.

If Sydney and Eliza had been unimpressed with Melliton, they were gratifyingly delighted with Fern Hall itself. Penelope had put them in two of her brothers' rooms, filled with ancient toys and musical instruments and trunks of clothing from past eras. Sydney flipped through old primers, recognizing a few woodcuts done by Griffin's father. Eliza gathered up as much sheet music as she could find and carted an armful down to the parlor, where Penelope indulged them by picking out old tunes and carols on the pianoforte until it was time for dinner.

Between Mrs. Braintree's excellent table and her even more excellent spruce beer, they had a merry evening of it. Penelope returned to the pianoforte after dinner was cleared; she was horribly out of practice and struck countless wrong notes, but nobody seemed to mind. Eliza and Sydney pulled the most outrageous articles from the attic's dress-up trunks—faded brocades and velvets, lustrous waistcoats spangled with silver thread, ghostly lace that floated like cobwebs at collar and cuffs—and performed what they insisted was a gavotte, but which Penelope was fairly sure was a dance of their own devising.

Griffin mocked them with a fierce fondness as she sat on the bench beside Penelope, turning pages, the long warm length of her pressed up against Penelope's side.

If only they could have stayed like this forever: well-fed and warm, glowing with laughter, happy in one another's company. Like any other celebrating family. But the dark, cold night drew close at last, and they candled their way to bed.

Penelope got at least one wish: she woke the next morning to find the world outside frosted over with a light fall of snow. Enough to make everything sparkle, but not enough to delay the afternoon coach from London, and the arrival of Captain Harry Stanhope and ship's purser, John Flood.

They came up the road as a pair, matching one another's rolling stride, the leather straps of their seabags slung over opposite shoulders, their hands between them brushing but not quite daring to clasp. As always, the sight of that easy connection both pleased Penelope and made her envious, in some unnameable, uncomfortable way.

Penelope waved from the window, then turned to peer anxiously at Griffin. "Last chance to escape."

Sydney and Eliza had already gone trooping out into the woods behind Fern Hall in search of greenery—it would be a plausible enough excuse if Griffin wanted to chaperone the pair and keep them out of trouble.

The stern glance Griffin leveled at Penelope, however, was like an anchor for her seasick heart. "What kind of friend do you take me for?" she said. "I'm staying with you, as I promised."

The printer smoothed out her skirts, rose from the sofa, and marched toward the foyer.

Penelope squared her shoulders, wiped her clammy palms, and followed.

Harry flung open the door with a bang and wrapped his sister in burly arms. She hugged him tight in return, inhaling the cold, salt scent of him. "Welcome home," she squeaked, and when he let go she turned to John. "And welcome home to you, too, John."

John was taller than Harry, but shyer; he didn't embrace her, but he did take both her hands in his and bend down to buss her cheek. "Hullo, Penelope," he said. His eyes flicked to Griffin, who was standing at the foot of the stairs like she'd been planted there to guard them from invaders.

Penelope couldn't help a small smile, seeing how fierce Griffin looked. She turned, tucking John's arm into hers. He was always at his shyest around new people. "John, Harry, may I present my very good friend Mrs. Agatha Griffin?"

"Pleased to meet you," Griffin said, holding out a hand.

Harry, bless him, bypassed the hand entirely and wrapped her in a hug as warm as the one he'd given Penelope. Griffin's eyes boggled a little as he squeezed. "It's an absolute delight," he boomed. "Pen's told us so much about you. All good things, of course."

"Surely not, Captain," Griffin replied, a little breathlessly.

"You're calling my sister a liar?"

"I'm calling her brother a shameless flatterer."

Harry threw back his head and roared, his laughter bouncing off the stones of the hall. "I can see why she likes you. Now, I have to head to the kitchen—I have some excellent Highland spirits to bring to Mrs. Braintree—but don't you go anywhere. I want to hear all about you when I get back." He stomped happily toward the kitchen, and as usual the hall seemed suddenly smaller and emptier when he'd left.

Griffin blinked, slow to recover, as anyone was when meeting Harry for the first time.

John slipped his arm from Penelope's and stepped forward, hand out. "Don't mind him too much, Mrs. Griffin—the joke on board ship is that Harry has to take to sea because it's the only place he won't deafen everyone around him."

Griffin clasped his hand, her expression softening. "At least you'll never lose track of him, with a voice like that. That must be very reassuring." The words were innocuous, but there was a knowingness to her voice, just a hint of a certain hue, that spoke volumes.

John's gaze flickered back to Penelope, startled; Penelope smiled reassuringly. Her husband blinked twice. Then some unnamed weight shifted off his shoulders, and the smile he aimed Griffin's way grew by inches. "Not a chance," he agreed, leaning forward conspiratorially. "Harry clings to the ship like a burr, no matter the weather. He'd stay up there in a hurricane, if I let him."

They moved to the sitting room: Penelope took a seat on the sofa and John sat beside her, while Griffin took up her favorite position in the overstuffed armchair by the fire. Harry burst back in carrying brandy and eggnog, a maid following behind with a tray of mince pies.

Penelope took a pie and shook her head wryly when her brother poured Griffin a frighteningly generous amount of brandy. She took only the slightest sip of her own drink when John passed her a cup: the brandy was barely detectable in all that egg and cream.

She supposed it was wise to remain sober, at least until they had all gotten used to one another, but it still rankled for reasons she couldn't quite put words around. She bit rather aggressively into her mince pie.

Griffin smiled at Harry. "So how long until you two are back pursuing the whales of the northern seas?"

Penelope choked on a mouthful of mince. Beside her, John went still and spiky as an iceberg, visibly unsure where the conversation was tending.

Harry cocked a head, his smile bright, but there was something shrewd glittering in his gaze. "At least four months. The ship needs a few repairs, and that'll take time, and I've a mind to take a bit of rest, but after that . . . To be frank, Mrs. Griffin, we aren't quite sure ourselves. Decisions must be made. The northern fisheries are getting rather thin these days. And the bounties are hardly worth it—not when the country is bringing in so much seed oil to light their lamps and clean their wool." He looked across at John. "We've talked about heading to the southern grounds, to hunt for sperm instead of right whales."

"It would be a big change," John added.

"It would be a bigger profit."

"And a longer journey—by years, perhaps."

"But we'd not get icebound and have to sit idle and wait to see if we'd be crushed."

"We'd just have to risk storms and doldrums and a much greater loss if we were wrecked."

Penelope coughed. "I see this is already an old argument."

John rolled his eyes, smiling fondly. "You know what he's like when he gets set on something."

Harry harrumphed. "I *refuse* to risk losing the captaining of my ship, John. You've seen the numbers from this last voyage—we're butting up against the bitter edge of breaking even. Soon we won't be able to afford to provision a ship long enough to bring back any whales at all. And where will that leave you and me?"

Penelope broke in: "Have you talked to Michael about increasing the budget from the company coffers?"

"He won't have it," Harry said. "Said all the liquid assets are tied up at the moment, and he can't go moving things from one branch to another without a lot of pains and paperwork."

"Even when I offered to help him with the paperwork," John agreed, and sighed. "That's when he said he'd set me up as a clerk for one of his other enterprises, if the whaling was getting as dire as that." He looked across the room at Harry. "But I won't leave ship until the captain retires."

"And I'm not the retiring kind," Harry purred in response.

Penelope's face flamed.

"Gentlemen," Griffin interrupted. "Are you really going to argue about bank accounts on Christmas Eve? You haven't even given Mrs. Flood her gifts yet."

Harry slapped a hand to his forehead. "Damn if the lady's not right—skewered us right through the heart, sharp as any harpoon." He bounced to his feet and waved at John. "Come, there's at least two armfuls to bring down—maybe we won't make Pen open them yet, but we might as well pile them on the table to be admired, since Kitty did such lovely things with the wrapping of them." He bounded out of the room, John trailing after with one wry glance at Penelope.

Griffin shook her head. "I see why you might feel overwhelmed."

"Do you?" Penelope asked.

"Certainly. Harry's rather a whirlwind, isn't he?" Griffin rose and brought over the brandy, adding a healthy dollop to Penelope's glass of eggnog. "Are all your brothers like him?"

"More or less," Penelope replied. She took a sip of her drink and sighed, as the brandy cut through the thickness of the cream in just the way she liked. "Harry was only the second most talkative, until we lost Owen."

Griffin's mouth tightened. "That's right, you've mentioned losing a brother."

As Griffin had, too, Penelope remembered too late. She hid her face in her cup. "I imagine it's easier to lose one when you have six to begin with."

Griffin only shook her head and said gently, "Of course it isn't."

"No." Penelope stared into her drink, rolling the thick liquid around and watching it slide down the side again.

"Was Owen also involved in the family business?" Griffin asked.

Penelope's lips curved up. "Oh no," she said. "He was a poet."

Griffin sat straight up in her chair. "You have a poet in your family tree and you never *warned* me?"

Penelope's smile widened into a grin. "Well, technically Owen was a vicar—he held the St. Ambrose's living before Mr. Oliver did—but he was always writing and reading verse of some kind. He liked the Church because he said prayer was a kind of poetry." She leaned her head back against the chair, remembering. "His sermons were some of the most beautiful I've ever heard. Even if Harry always said it was just an excuse for Owen to get in an extra hour's talking on a Sunday." She smirked. "As I said, Harry was only second most talkative."

Harry himself now returned as if conjured, his arms weighed down with boxes and packages in brown paper and ribbon, John following hard on his heels. "Where do you want these, Pen?"

"In the window seat, I should think," Penelope replied. "We'll open them tomorrow after church."

Harry strode across the room and began arranging gifts to show to best advantage. John, blushing, went to help. They argued at great length and volume about which one to stack where, but if you ignored the words and the tone it was easy to see how their movements mirrored one another, as if they were merely two extensions of the same soul, rather than two separate people.

As if they had a little bubble of happiness, which wrapped around the pair of them, and left everyone else out in the cold. Penelope didn't know why it should suddenly bother her so much.

Griffin set down her glass with a *clink*, the sharp sound cutting through the deep burr of Harry's wind-roughened voice. "I was thinking about going over to Mrs. Stowe's," Griffin said comfortably. "Would you be up for a walk, Flood?"

Griffin had been right: the whole tangle of Penelope's loneliness and worry came loose with a single pull.

She wasn't alone. She had a friend. It was simple, but not small.

"I would enjoy that," Penelope replied. "I have a jar of blackberry honey to bring to Miss Coningsby—her favorite." She set her empty glass aside and rose from her chair. "Harry," she called in a louder voice, "Mrs. Griffin and I are heading out for a little while. Will you and John be alright on your own?"

Harry's grin was lightning-quick. "I think we'll rub along together just fine, thank you, Pen."

John's ears went red at the edges, and he kept his eyes downcast.

Penelope fought a fond urge to roll her eyes.

"Lord," Griffin said as soon as they were on the path, "they aren't half in love with one another, are they?"

"They've been like that since they met," Penelope said with a laugh. "They pass as brothers or friends well enough, but I know they enjoy not having to watch themselves so closely when they're home."

"I can imagine." Griffin's boots crunched on the frost, her thick wool skirts swirling around her ankles.

"Were you and Thomas like that? Lost in one another?" Penelope asked, because apparently she enjoyed torturing herself.

Griffin smiled wistfully. "At first, when we were young. When we were still a little unsure of how we felt about each other. But then we had a son, and we started the *Menagerie*, and we had to turn our faces back to the world." A robin trilled out from a nearby branch as they passed, then launched itself into the air in a burst of snow. Griffin's keen eye tracked it until it vanished against the winter sky. "I wonder, though, how things would have been different if we hadn't been able to marry. Keeping a secret love alight takes a great deal more effort, I should think. Like trying to keep a torch from being extinguished by the rain."

"Perhaps it depends on the couple," Penelope said. "Certainly Harry and John never seem to lack for fuel."

Griffin snorted.

"And Isabella and Joanna—well, they weren't like Harry and John, but they always seemed to sort of . . . drift toward one another. There was always a sort of pull between them, keeping them tethered. You only noticed it if you spent a long time watching, though—I'm still not entirely sure how many people in Melliton knew the truth, and how many just saw a very old, very deep friendship."

"Isabella and Joanna . . ." Griffin murmured. She turned her face up to the sky, her breath making clouds in the chilly space above her muffler. "That sounds more like what Thomas and I had," she said easily. "Our love was . . . comfortable. Oh, that sounds so tepid when put like that—but it didn't feel dull. Just—strong. Steady." Her lips quirked. "I miss that."

"Maybe you'll find it again someday," Penelope said. The words were soft, hardly more than a whisper.

Perhaps they were lost on the winter wind, because Griffin made no reply.

Night had fallen, the clock was about to strike eleven, and Penelope was knocking softly on Griffin's bedroom door.

Rustling and light swearing answered her. Then the door was pulled wide. Griffin stood, wrapped in a shawl, her eyes still sleep-softened even as they pinched at the corners. "Already?" she grumbled.

"We'll need to hurry to have everything ready by midnight," Penelope replied.

Griffin breathed a low curse, but Penelope only grinned in return. Anticipation thrummed through her veins and sizzled beneath her skin. This Christmas Eve tradition was one of her very favorite moments of the year, and she couldn't wait to share it with her friend. Especially a sleepy, grouchy Agatha Griffin wearing thick-soled boots and an expression of pure suspicion.

"Too much mystery," Griffin muttered as they crept down the stairs with only a single candle to guide them.

Eliza, Sydney, Harry, and John soon joined them in the hall. Voices were muffled and footsteps careful, to keep from waking the rest of the household. "Does everyone have their coins?" Penelope whispered, and was answered by a bobbing round of nodding heads. "Good—let's go." She shouldered her pack of supplies and the group slipped out into the night.

A cold moon had risen, silvering the trees and the long ribbon of the lane. Harry and John led the way in the snug shielding of their woolen pea-jackets, long tested by the Arctic climes they sailed. Griffin had wrapped her shawl over her head for extra warmth, leaving only her eyes free, and Eliza and Sydney were sporting two of the Stanhope brothers' cast-off felt caps from when they were boys. Nobody spoke: Penelope had cautioned them against it, for stealth's sake.

In a silent huddle, they slipped toward the Four Swallows.

They were not the first to arrive: Mr. and Mrs. Biswas let them into the darkened tavern hall, and helped Penelope begin emptying her pack. Mrs. Bedford was already setting out a bowl of her best cider, and Mr. Scriven was helping to cut slices of cold ham and bread and cheese to set beside Mrs. Biswas's curried pies. Before long Mr. Thomas, Mr. Kitt, and the Koskinens had all hurried inside, shutting the door carefully to avoid any noise.

"How long 'til midnight?" Mrs. Koskinen whispered.

"A quarter of an hour," Mrs. Biswas replied. By now she and Penelope had, with Griffin's help, wrapped green-dyed muslin around several lamps, and stretched long swaths over the windows. They fluttered lightly, seaweed-like. Mr. Koskinen brought out the guitar he played only once a year, and Mrs. Biswas handed small bells to Eliza and Sydney, as the youngest in attendance.

They waited, breathless, until the bells of St. Ambrose's rang midnight, and Christmas.

The whole group cheered. Spectral green lights blazed up as Penelope lit the muslin-masked lamps. Mr. Koskinen began singing a carol in an eerie minor key in his rich and resonant baritone. Eliza and Sydney kept time with the bells, a shiver of accompaniment. Mr. Thomas and Mr. Kitt bowed to each other and began dancing, singing along, as Mrs. Bedford handed round cups of cider and servings of bread and meat and cheese, then laughed as Mr. Scriven pulled her into a dance alongside the younger men. Harry and John were quick to make the third couple of the set, as easy on their feet as though the wooden boards beneath were the deck of a familiar ship.

Anyone passing by outside the tavern would have seen only an eldritch green glow, and shadowy figures flitting through it. Mr. Koskinen's guitar was imperfectly tuned, and he had a way of sliding his hands along the strings to make it wail in a way that always raised the hair on Penelope's arms in a most delicious way.

She watched as the realization dawned on Agatha Griffin's face, transforming it from wary puzzlement to sheer, mischievous pleasure. "It's the ghost Christmas," she said. "Jack Calbert's pirate treasure."

"The very same," Penelope said with a wild laugh. "Now empty your pockets!"

The pile of coins on the table grew and gleamed in the marine light, as they ate and sang and danced for a good hour. Then, as soon as the bells struck one, they hurried to snuff out the lamps and pull down the gauze and slip home as quietly as they could.

Mr. Biswas would pretend to discover the coins as a mystery when the tavern opened the next day, and the money would be distributed to those in sharpest need.

"It's Mrs. Biswas's family tradition," Penelope explained in a whisper to her guests on the walk back. "Been doing it a hundred years, at least—every Christmas Eve in the Four Swallows, at midnight. It's how the season always begins, for us." She flicked a glance at Griffin, whose grin was shining like the moon. "That's why people can never agree on the number of ghosts," she said. "There's always one or two who can't make it from year to year—times when Harry and John are at sea, or when Mrs. Bedford goes to visit her family on the coast."

"Did the ghost story come first, or did the feast?" Sydney whispered.

"Only the dead know," Penelope breathed, and chuckled when the boy shivered.

He rolled his eyes, scorning to be scared, but she'd had him for that moment and he knew it.

They doffed coats and hats and crept up the silent stairs. Penelope was stopped at her bedchamber door when Griffin put a hand on her arm. The candlelight on her face was stark and slanting, only one hawklike eye and the stern arch of her nose visible above the soft plane of her cheek. Half a smile curved the reluctant length of her mouth. "That was marvelous, Flood," she breathed in an undertone, low enough to set Penelope's veins buzzing. "Thank you for sharing it with us."

Penelope swallowed hard and nodded. Griffin vanished into the bedroom—just one room over, so nearby. The whole house was asleep, or would be soon enough. The sheets on Griffin's bed would be cold, and perhaps make her shiver as she slipped between them.

Penelope had heat to spare. Her heart was racing and her blood sang wildfire in her veins. She shut the door softly, leaned back against it—and bit hard into her clenched fist until temptation passed.

Chapter Nineteen

————————————————

Everyone in Melliton wore their finest for Christmas services. Mr. Koskinen looked uncomfortably scrubbed and ruddy, Mr. Thomas and Mr. Kitt were elegant in blue and bottle-green, and Mr. Scriven had trimmed his whiskers so fiercely that he was nearly unrecognizable to the general populace. Even Mr. Buckley the deacon, who normally abhorred any kind of fashionable show, had carefully brushed his black coat for the day. But even with everyone looking their best, Viscount and Lady Summerville were the most opulent, resplendent in ivory silk and green velvet and a ridiculous amount of fur.

Mr. Oliver's sermon touched the usual notes: Christian charity and faith and hope for the savior's birth. Penelope rather lost the thread, too busy staring at the way the winter light fell through the one window of colored glass that had survived the Puritans (because nobody at the time had wanted to be responsible for smashing the window showing the Abington coat of arms). But toward the end, a stir in the pews and a sudden tension in the air brought her abruptly back to earth.

"—such success in organizing support for our slandered Queen," Mr. Oliver was saying, "that it would be a shame for such zeal not to find a proper, pious outlet. Lady Summerville therefore desires me to announce the formation of a Melliton Auxiliary Branch of the Society for the Suppression of Seditious Libel and Mendacity."

A murmur of response ran through the congregation. Lady Summerville bowed her head like a royal accepting obeisance.

Mr. Thomas was whispering something urgent in Mr. Kitt's ear, while that gentleman sat stiff and nervous and unhappy in the pew.

Mr. Oliver continued: "This organization proposes to stem the rising tide of sedition, libel, obscenity, criminality, blasphemy, and impurity that threatens the peace and order of our fair village. The power of the press, which ought to be turned to the spreading of the Gospel and the bringing of divine light to barbaric mankind, has been perverted to strike at the very foundations of decent civilization. Men of humbler ranks have been poisoned against their natural protectors: greedy inflamers and agitators have stirred up trouble in much greater proportion than their numbers warrant. Such machinations are dangerous to us all, and their seedlings must be pulled up by the roots before they choke our better harvests. I look forward to assisting Lady Summerville in her work, and trust all good patriotic members of our hamlet will follow her most Christian example."

The sermon closed; the final hymn was sung; the congregation meandered out of the pews and away for the holiday celebrations to come. There was still a festive tone to the hubbub—but now a thread of unease ran underneath it, a trickling stream made up of sidelong glances and anxious whispers and people biting their lip to keep from speaking their mind. Mrs. Koskinen looked positively thunderous, already muttering objections in her patient husband's ear.

Penelope and Harry let the rest head back toward Fern Hall—Sydney was looking absolutely mutinous, and even John had a stony set to his mouth—and turned into the graveyard to visit their parents and Owen.

Owen Stanhope had been a thoughtful (if loquacious) vicar. His loss had come hard on the heels of their parents' deaths, and all the Stanhope siblings had reeled from the blow. One by one, they had set out for far-off horizons with fewer memories attached, until only Harry and Penelope had remained.

Then Harry had left, too.

"*Ave atque vale*," Harry read from his brother's headstone, as Penelope bent to place a sprig of holly on the grave. "What does that come to again?"

"'Hail and farewell,'" Penelope translated.

Harry snorted. "'Good day and goodbye'? Truly?"

"A very famous poet wrote it about losing his brother," Penelope offered wryly.

"A little pat, if you ask me."

"I didn't. I asked Owen, and this is what he picked."

Harry sighed. "It's like he was trying to find a way to keep talking from the other side of the veil."

Penelope put a hand on Harry's arm. "I miss him, too."

They stood a while, a little pocket of quiet amid the sounds of the holiday around them.

"I miss his sermons especially," Harry said at length. "What kind of nonsense was Mr. Oliver about this morning, do you think?"

Penelope's mouth went flat as dread took hold. "I think Lady Summerville wants revenge," she said.

"For the songs?"

"For that. For irreverence. For all of us who dared not to take her superiority seriously, and laughed at her." She bit her lip, sympathy welling up in spite of her anger. "She's a desperately unhappy woman, I think."

"Look at her husband—wouldn't you be?"

Penelope's irritation sharpened to a pinprick, and she pulled her hand back. "I don't think you or I are in any position to be particular about the state of someone else's marriage."

A much longer and more troubled silence followed. Penelope chewed harder on her lip.

"I consider John and me married, for whatever that's worth," Harry said at last. Very quietly, so only the snow would hear him.

Penelope's ire melted at this. "I know you do. And I know he feels the same. It's just—it's strange sometimes, to have spoken vows specifically so we could break them." She shifted her weight from one foot to the other. "Do you think Owen knew? About . . . about us?"

"About our deviant tastes, you mean?" Harry asked. He took Penelope's hand and tucked it into his arm. Warmth seeped through her gloves and sank into her grateful bones. "I think he had a very shrewd idea. I just think he didn't mind."

Penelope was shocked. "He was a vicar! How could he not mind?"

"I think he felt himself bound by a higher law than that of the crown, or even the Church," Harry replied. "Can you imagine any world in which Owen, of all the family, failed to love us?"

"Impossible," Penelope said at once.

"Exactly," Harry replied.

Penelope stared down at the headstone. Cool gray with chips of mica that glittered beneath the frost. It looked so cold, when Owen had always seemed so warm. Hair the same honey-blond as Penelope's—though his would never be streaked with silver, as hers was now. The memory of him seemed dimmer and dimmer every year.

Not his laugh, though. That stayed clear and immediate, as though the last time he'd ever laughed had lodged beneath her ear like a pearl bob. There'd been so much joy in it, a sound of pure delight and love and warmth.

If there was anything like a heaven—and Penelope had never been really convinced—but if there was, she was sure it was a place where such sounds were common.

This world had a ways to go before it deserved such laughter.

Beside her, Harry cast her a slantwise gaze from beneath the brim of his hat. "Have you never thought about coming with us on a voyage, Pen? We've never captained a hen frigate, but we could, if you wanted."

She snorted. "You think the best thing for a woman who prefers women is to spend years on board a ship packed full of men?"

"You'd be surprised," was the laconic response.

Penelope shook her head decisively. "There are no beehives at sea."

"Ah, well, that's true enough." Harry chuckled, and together they nodded farewell to Owen and turned back toward the road to Fern Hall. "But you aren't too lonely, here by the ancestral hearth?" His gaze was keen again, his mouth just a sliver away from a smile. "You're finding some use for that warm heart of yours?"

"My heart, maybe," Penelope said. She thought of Agatha Griffin, green-lit at a ghost Christmas; Griffin walking the bee circuit in her blue coat, grousing about poetry; Agatha Griffin, half smiling by candlelight. She sighed at the hopeless futility of all that yearning. "Other parts of me, sadly, have yet to be invited to join in the fun."

Harry chortled, as she knew he would.

Mr. Flood's coat was deep brown wool, and Agatha could imagine exactly how it would fit if she put it on. She knew she'd have to turn the cuffs up precisely twice to leave her hands free to work, and just how many inches of the fabric that fit his broad shoulders would drape down her more compact frame.

She couldn't seem to stop thinking of it. It kept her more

quiet than she might otherwise have been, on the walk back to Fern Hall.

Ahead of them, Sydney and Eliza were bent close together. Sydney's brow was still wracked with anger after that ominous sermon, and Eliza's anxious gaze occasionally flashed back to where Agatha and Mr. Flood kept pace a dozen yards behind the younger pair.

"Are you worried about them?" Mr. Flood asked, breaking the silence.

"I beg your pardon?" Agatha shook herself, and tried to bring herself back to polite attention. "We always worry about the people we love. Isn't it a mother's instinct where her child is concerned?"

"I wouldn't know," said Mr. Flood. "I ran away to sea at twelve, and I hardly remember mine. I do recall a distinct lack of worrying over me, though. Even though some of the trouble I found was . . . worth worrying over."

Agatha didn't want to pity Mr. Flood—it sat poorly alongside her determination to guard Penelope against the worries his presence stirred up. But there was a note in the tenor of his confession that gave her serious pause. It said, rather too plainly, that a lot of that trouble had been done *to* him, not *by* him. And that his mother hadn't cared.

"Perhaps some people don't worry enough, because the rest of us worry too much. We've used it all up," she said instead. She breathed in a lungful of bracing winter air. "What's the real reason you don't want Captain Stanhope to take your ship south to hunt for whales?"

Mr. Flood grimaced. "Too many answers to that. It's an extremely strenuous life, and neither of us is as young as we used to be. My joints are constantly stiff and sore, and I don't do half the work he does on deck, in all that cold." He jammed his hands into his coat pockets, and Agatha flexed her gloved hands in echo. Mr. Flood stared down at the road beneath his feet. "I'd rather see him retire than work himself into an injury, or worse—but he believes we can only be happy and safe as long as we stay on board ship."

"Captains do have a great deal more power at sea than on land," Agatha countered.

"Little kings of a wooden kingdom," John muttered, with a nod. "I think it goes to Harry's head sometimes."

"How unusual in a man," Agatha said dryly.

John's eyes flew open and he laughed. "Spoken like an experienced widow."

"Not that experienced," Agatha countered. "Many a wife feels the same, whether her husband is living or not."

Mr. Flood's mouth quirked at one corner. "You'll forgive the irony, but I don't actually have a lot of experience with wives."

"Of course you don't," Agatha said with a snort. "You sail off for years on end, stabbing hapless fish with long pointy sticks for money—but your very existence creates strictures people hold Penelope to account for, even if you don't. You have that wooden kingdom where the laws favor you: she has no such escape."

"Neither wives nor whales are as hapless as you're implying, Mrs. Griffin." Mr. Flood was frowning now, lightly, as if a stone had gotten into his shoe and he couldn't shake it out again. He paused in the lane and turned to face her square. "Let's be frank with one another. I'm sure Penelope has told you the truth about why she and I wed. Are you saying I should spend more time putting a polite gloss on our farce of a marriage?"

Agatha's temper roared up like a bonfire. "I am saying that she did you an immense kindness, and you ought to show that you are conscious of the debt!"

Ahead, Sydney and Eliza whirled round, blinking at the anger in Agatha's voice.

She clamped her lips shut, ground her teeth together, and marched on silently, head down.

Mr. Flood turned and followed, keeping pace with her. His hands slid out of his pockets and clasped behind his back. His head tilted up, squinting at the sky, which promised more snow in the evening to come.

Agatha watched him warily, afraid she'd gone too far in her friend's defense.

When Mr. Flood looked back at her, his eyes were clear, and frank, and shrewd as he said: "We always worry about the people we love."

And then he walked on, whistling, as though he hadn't just scoured every last bit of wax off Agatha's soul to reveal the true picture graven on the metal beneath.

Of *course* what she felt for Penelope Flood was not precisely friendship. It was longing, and protectiveness, and pride, and joy, all tangled up together. A good bit of wholesome lust as well, Agatha knew—and she'd focused on that because it was the most visible, and the most inexcusable.

But that was only the shading, not the scene itself. She knew what name to put to the entirety of her feelings, when she looked at the whole and not just each individual part.

Love, in a word. She ought to have realized sooner.

She *certainly* ought to have realized it before Penelope's husband did.

Merry Christmas, everyone, Agatha thought bitterly, and trudged unhappily toward the Hall.

CHAPTER TWENTY

Once home from church the party ate, and drank, and exchanged gifts as though their lives depended on it.

Flood had embroidered two new seabags for her brother and husband: sturdy canvas things, dotted with small bright bees and green leaves and a painstakingly stitched miniature Fern Hall. "Which was so reassuringly square and regular," she explained, "that even my haphazard embroidery skills could attempt it."

Mr. Flood looked immensely gratified.

Captain Stanhope went into paroxysms of delighted laughter on account of one particularly poorly embroidered bee. "The eyes!" he choked, shoulders shaking. "Look at the *eyes*! I can't stand it!"

Flood blazed red. "I can pick it out and try to fix—"

"Don't you dare," her brother protested, wrapping one arm around her and pulling her into an embrace. "I adore him. I'm calling him Clarence."

"Most bees are female," Flood reminded him, even as she blushed and ducked her head.

"I'm calling *her* Clarence, then."

Agatha had given Flood a new volume of poetry—one of the sonnets was about queen bees—and had received in return a very small, very beautiful pot of green glass. When she raised the lid and sniffed experimentally, she inhaled the scent of lemons and honey and just a hint of warm bread. It was sharp and sweet and strong and Agatha had to fight the urge to scoop it into her mouth and devour it like a sweet-toothed child snatching frosting from an untended cake.

Flood was watching her, smiling shyly. "It's one of Miss Coningsby's balm recipes," she said. "Do you like it?"

Agatha dabbed her fingers in and spread the balm onto the rough spots of her hand and the warm skin of her wrist; it sank in at once as that luscious scent swirled around her. "I love it," she responded softly. Her own pulse beat rather unsteadily beneath her scent-drenched fingertips.

Penelope's smile was so dazzling Agatha had to look away in self-defense—just in time to take note of Eliza and Sydney, gazing meaningfully at one another over a book of madrigals the girl had just unwrapped.

Sydney reached out and touched the back of her hand with just a fingertip; her lips curved teasingly . . . then Captain Stanhope's belly laugh rang out again and the two young people pulled away from one another.

Agatha quashed a sigh. It had been months, now. More than time to have a proper motherly talk with her son about how his courtship was progressing. A flash of memory warmed her and had her smiling softly. She'd resented her own parents' interference when she was his age; she had much more sympathy with them now, from the vantage of mature perspective.

Her mother would be laughing at her, Agatha knew.

Well, at least one Griffin could find happiness with the person they loved. Agatha was doomed to pine for the foreseeable forever, but there was no reason her son should do the same.

She managed to snag Sydney by the elbow as everyone else trooped to the dining room for dinner. "I have something for you," she murmured.

Sydney stopped and tilted his head. "You already gave me a gift."

"So I did, but indulge me." Agatha reached into her pocket and pulled out her silver wedding band. It gleamed hopefully in her palm when she extended her hand to her son. "You might like to take this as well. To keep handy. If you can think of someone who might be inclined to accept it." She smiled expectantly.

Sydney's lips tilted up, just as she'd hoped, but his smile gleamed much more falsely than the silver. "I don't believe I'll be needing a ring, Mum," he replied softly.

Her heart ached at his words. "You don't think Eliza would have you?"

His face tightened even more. "We've decided . . ."

Agatha waited the space of five whole breaths before her impatience got control of her tongue. "You've decided what?"

"We've decided not to get married." The words came out all in a rush, as if Sydney were trying to shove the incriminating sentence out the window before the constables came in and caught him with the evidence.

Agatha stood there, shocked.

Sydney tried to leave, but his mother's hand shot out quick as a striking snake and latched onto his coat sleeve. The ring tumbled to the wooden floor and chimed a protest.

"What do you mean, *not to get married?*" Agatha hissed through a clenching jaw.

"Mrs. Griffin?" Eliza stepped cautiously toward them down the hall. "Is everything alright?" She spotted the bright ring on the floor and bent to pick it up.

Sydney froze. Eyes wide, mouth flat, poised on the edge of a precipice, with a long fall threatening.

Agatha bit back a thousand different harsh words.

Eliza turned the ring back and forth, then raised her eyes to the Griffins, twin statues on the parlor threshold. After a moment, she held the ring out to Agatha—slowly, as though confronting some kind of wild beast liable to turn feral at any moment. "This is yours, isn't it, Mrs. Griffin?" Her smile was calm, poised, but the light in her eyes was just a shade too steely. She knew what she was doing, handing that bauble back.

Agatha closed her hand around the ring and felt the chill metal leach the heat from her palm. "It is mine, and was my mother's before that."

Eliza nodded. "You wouldn't want to lose it, then."

Sydney's eyes darted back and forth from his mother to his . . . His what? Beloved, but not betrothed?

Agatha's head spun, dizzy from the speed of revelations. "I had rather hoped to have a reason not to wear it much longer," she said weakly, then pressed her lips together and tried to resurrect some maternal fury. "I'd hoped you might be the one to wear it instead."

Eliza tilted her head. "But it would get tarnished, or dented, in the course of my work. I couldn't risk it." One quicksilver glance flashed to Sydney, and then her gaze was back to clash with Agatha's. "Something so precious is worth being thoughtful about. Once damaged, it might be impossible to repair."

Her eyes begged Agatha to understand what she was trying not to say.

Agatha could only shake her head. The conversation had gotten so beyond her she didn't know how to grasp it. There was a time for delicacy—and there was a time to heave delicacy aside like so much rubble and get right to the heart of the matter. "Sydney tells me you two have decided . . . *not* to get married."

Eliza nodded quickly, visibly relieved. "That's right, ma'am. We've been talking about it for a few months now."

Agatha's eyes narrowed. "*Just* talking?"

Eliza had the grace to blush.

Agatha's teeth ground hard. Foolish girl. Foolish, stubborn, *thoughtless* . . . She rode this new wave of anger, grasping gratefully at the invaluable clarity of rage. "Do you love my son, Miss Brinkworth?"

Sydney started a defensive reply, but cut it off at a sharp glance from Eliza.

The apprentice squared her shoulders to face Agatha, tucking her hands behind her back like a disgraced soldier at a court-martial. "I love your son dearly, Mrs. Griffin. I expect to love him for the rest of my life."

Agatha snorted. Such confidence meant nothing at seventeen. "Then why not marry him?"

Eliza's reply was quiet, and sure, and utterly devastating: "Because if I made that choice, I would lose the right to make too many other choices in my life."

Agatha's heart all but stopped beating.

"Marriage is a legal prison, from a wife's perspective," Eliza went on. Softly. Inexorably. "You've said so yourself. And I've read Wollestonecraft and Godwin and Wooler, among others, and I find myself strongly persuaded against the whole institution. Your son loves me enough to trust my decision on this. I would like to continue loving him—but I can't do that so earnestly if I marry him."

She bestowed upon Sydney a smile of such pure and profound affection that Agatha half expected the boy to keel over on the rug from the force of it.

Eliza's face when she turned back to Agatha was still composed, except for a slight tightness at the corners of her eyes. "I know this must be painful to hear, but I'm quite determined, and I hope that you can find it in your heart to understand in time."

Agatha could find no reply to this. After a moment, Eliza turned away and walked down the hallway toward the dining room. Her spine was straight, her step unhurried. Everything calm and collected.

It was the calm born of unsurprise. She'd known the argument with Agatha was coming. She'd prepared for it, and now that it was here she'd weathered it, and not let it sway her from her chosen course.

Agatha would have admired that if she hadn't wanted so badly to seize the girl by the shoulders and shake her until all her philosophical ideals fell to the floor like so many loosened hairpins.

She rounded upon her son, an equally appealing target. "What do you intend to do about this?" she demanded.

"Nothing," Sydney replied shortly.

Agatha choked. "That is unacceptable!"

Her son's frown deepened. "We talked about this, turned it over from every side. For *months*. She doesn't want to marry me. It's her choice to make. What kind of man would I be if I pressed my suit after she so firmly refused?" Sydney spread his hands, misery writ plainly on his face. "I love her. I'll take anything she chooses to give me—but not a thing more than that."

Agatha fumed at this, and fumed a little more when she realized he was using some of her own teachings against her. But there was one point yet to be made: "If you aren't planning to wed," she said, voice low and dark, "then the correct thing to do is to break off the affair entirely."

Sydney's long mouth twisted unhappily. "That's not what either of us wants."

"If your father were here—"

"He'd what?" Sydney cut her off. "Disinherit me? Throw Eliza out into the street?"

"We could find her another apprenticeship," Agatha blurted out, desperate. It was a mistake, she knew it at once, and she kept going, anyway. "Plenty of printers in London could use someone as talented as she is—Novello, for instance . . ."

Sydney's eyes blazed. "If you send her away, I'll go with her." His hands were fists at his sides. "I'll go anywhere with her."

"How about to her father?" Agatha shot back. "What will you do when he asks what your intentions are for his only daughter? What will you say when people start to whisper about you and Eliza—assuming they aren't already—when no wedding happens—and if there is a child—"

"There won't be," Sydney replied staunchly.

"You can't be certain—"

"If there is, we'll revisit the question then." One corner of his mouth turned up in grim amusement. "After all, we can always get married later on, can't we?"

Agatha felt like screaming, but had to restrain it to a furious hiss. "Of all the irresponsible—"

"*Enough*, Mum!" Sydney cried.

Agatha's mouth snapped shut.

Sydney huffed out a breath, fists balled at his sides. "I won't force Eliza to place her whole life in my hands if I can't do the same thing for her." He skewered Agatha with a furious glare, which reminded his mother far too much of herself. "You and Father taught me that honesty was a virtue—well, I'm telling you honestly: I love Eliza, and I'm not going to marry her, and there's nothing you can say to convince me what we're doing is wrong."

As Agatha gasped in outrage, he stomped down the hall and vanished into the dining room.

It was just past midnight, so farewell to Christmas Day. Penelope found herself fidgety—dinner had been a peculiar, tense affair, with half the guests at the table suddenly and inexplicably snappish and unsociable—and the first few hours of her sleep were punctuated by unsettling dreams. Running and running but going nowhere. Gravestones towering up as high as city buildings. Trying to write a letter, but watching the ink pour away from the paper as though it were blood being shed from a murdered body.

After this last, she decided a soothing drink was in order.

Apparently, she was not the only one in search of comfort. For when she stepped into the larder for milk, she found Agatha Griffin furiously slicing pieces of bread from a loaf. She wore a green robe and cream shawl, her salt-and-pepper hair hanging loose down her back and shaking with every movement. Penelope smiled at first—but her smile faltered, as she watched the abrupt, angry motions of Griffin's hands, and saw the light of the single candle outline the tight lines at the corners of her mouth.

Penelope cleared her throat softly. "I've got something stronger than bread, if you want it."

"Oh!" Griffin whirled around, knife raised—then fear

and fury melted away when she saw it was only Penelope. "Yes, thank you—the stronger the better."

Penelope strode to the shelves on the far wall. Mrs. Braintree usually kept a bottle near to hand—ah, yes, here it was. A short, slim bottle of deep amber. "I should give you fair warning," she said, "this is quite possibly the most dangerous drink in all of Melliton."

"What's in it?"

"Honey. Well, mostly honey." Penelope turned the bottle so its shoulders gleamed red in the candlelight.

A reluctant spark lit Griffin's eyes. "Only you, Flood, would try to comfort someone by offering them something dangerous."

"Is it working?"

"Give me a taste and we'll find out."

Penelope found two glasses, took a seat beside her friend at the long wooden table, and poured generous helpings for them both. Griffin sniffed at hers and reared back, blinking tears from her eyes.

Penelope grinned over the rim of her glass. "Warned you."

Griffin shot her a defiant glare and swallowed half the drink in a single gulp.

"Steady!" Penelope said, alarm flaring up within her. "This stuff's even stronger than that brandy you like."

"Good," Griffin wheezed around the alcohol fumes. She took one of the slices of bread and tore it apart with her hands, stuffing pieces into her mouth and chewing as if the bread had done her some grievous injury, and now she was finally taking vengeance.

Penelope sipped more cautiously at her mead, letting the fire of it roll over her tongue. She'd hoped it would sweeten her words, bring her something subtle and persuasive to say—but all she could find was a brief, blunt question: "What is it that's troubling you?"

"Sydney and Eliza." Griffin stared into her glass as if it could offer an oracle. "They've decided not to wed."

"Oh dear," Penelope murmured. "And they seemed to be getting on so well . . ."

"Oh," Griffin responded dryly, "they are."

Penelope frowned. "I don't understand."

"Sydney assures me that if they have children, they will reconsider the situation then."

For a moment she was puzzled—then Penelope gaped in horror. "Oh *no*."

Griffin toasted with the last of her mead. "Now you see where my head's been at all evening."

"That damn . . . nineteen-year-old!"

Griffin chortled bitterly. "Just so, Flood."

Penelope gravely poured another measure of mead for them both, and raised her glass in a toast. "To the follies of youth," she said. "Long may they last."

Griffin spun her glass round on the table, her shoulders bunched up tight, the gray in her hair turned molten silver by candlelight. "I was so ready to wish them joy," she said mournfully. "It seemed such a likely match. And Eliza is bright and kind and everything I could ask for in a daughter-in-law."

"Did they say why they aren't getting married?"

"I knew all that political talk would be trouble," Griffin muttered. "I just didn't foresee how." She looked up, her mouth a flat line. "They've been *reading*."

Penelope sputtered out a laugh. "Not that!"

Griffin remained unamused. "Eliza says marriage is a trap, and Sydney is unwilling to try to change her mind."

Penelope's laughter faded. "I sympathize, Griffin—really I do . . ."

Griffin's eyes narrowed. "But?"

"But . . ." Penelope sighed. "Do you think she's *entirely* wrong about marriage?"

Griffin's jaw clenched, and she took another long draught of mead. "No," she admitted. "Which is why it's so damned hard to argue with. But I've spent all night thinking it over, and I believe I know where to start."

"Tell me," Penelope said.

"My son is right that Eliza stands to lose the most if they married," Griffin said. Her hand began spinning her glass again, round and round on the old wood of the kitchen table. Her face had gone rosy, whether from drink or determination Penelope couldn't say. Griffin went on: "The problem is that Eliza also stands to lose the most if they *aren't* married. Her reputation will suffer far more than his, if people take note of their intimacy. And I don't know if she's told her family, or how they'll react." By now she was turning the glass so fast it was beginning to ring a little against the wood. "Because it's not only marriage that's the trap—it's being a woman. And I don't have a solution for that, either. But I have to do something. Ideals are all very well on paper, but in the real world sometimes one has to be *practical*."

"I'm not so sure."

"*What?*"

Griffin's tone was such a thunder crack that Penelope winced a little. She tucked her hands between her knees, squeezing hard. "I made a thoroughly practical marriage," she countered softly, even as her cowardly heart wailed a protest. "I thought it was the right choice at the time. But now . . . I am not so sure."

Griffin's head snapped up, her eyes widening.

Darkness and the warmth of the mead lured Penelope forward, into a confession she would probably regret in the cold, clear light of morning. "There are times when I think . . . there are some things that would be easier if I did not have such a knot in the fabric in my life." She took a breath, hoping it would steady her, but it was only a desperate gulp for air, a momentary respite and nothing more. Her stomach twisted, and in a burst of recklessness she blurted out the truth: "Perhaps if I hadn't married John, I wouldn't feel as though it were betraying him to love someone else."

"Someone else," Griffin said thickly. "Who, Penelope?"

Penelope was already starting to feel hot regret seep in through the cracks in her composure. She'd sink beneath it before too long. She shook her head as though she could shake the world away. "It doesn't matter," she said. Then she did something foolish.

She looked straight at Griffin.

Agatha Griffin's eyes widened.

Penelope's bravery crumpled, and she looked away again.

The silence stretched on for years.

Griffin's voice came slowly. "When I was younger, I thought kissing was something only girls did."

It was hardly more than a whisper, but it sliced through the night like an arrow and nailed Penelope to her seat.

Griffin continued, as Penelope held her breath so as not to miss a single soft word. "Plenty of us treated kissing like practice. For when we were grown up and could do it with men. It all seemed so innocent, really—holding hands, sharing clothes. Sharing a bed. Wrapping your arms around each other while you both dreamed. Kisses . . . and caresses." She fidgeted with the shawl on her shoulders, plucking at the fringe on the hem.

Her gaze flickered to Penelope, then away; Penelope shivered.

"When Thomas came courting—when I felt I had to grow up—I put all those feelings aside. They complicated things, and I wanted simple. Sure. But lately . . . Well, lately I have been thinking perhaps it's not something I'm going to grow out of after all."

Penelope remembered to breathe, and suddenly couldn't seem to breathe deeply enough to satisfy. She felt dizzy, disoriented. And not from the mead. "You're saying you could love women."

"Not just that." Griffin raised her head, and her eyes met Penelope's with a clarity that made the spinning world pause in its orbit. "I'm saying I could love *you*."

Penelope's heart was a firework, bursting into sparks in the middle of the night. The explosion propelled her forward, right into Griffin's arms.

Kissing, it turned out, was not something Agatha Griffin did by halves. Firm hands seized Penelope by the shoulders and held her in place, while Agatha's hot tongue slid hungrily between Penelope's lips. Penelope let her own hands tangle in the long waves of Agatha's hair, happy to let herself be devoured. There was no room for hesitation now, not a drop of reticence; only this wild, desperate entwinement.

Penelope's world split nearly in two: Before this kiss— and After. Nothing would ever be the same. She twisted Agatha's long locks around her fingers and kissed back as hard as she could.

Eventually, Agatha broke away. "My god," she gasped, "I've been wanting to do that for months."

"Then why stop now?" Penelope demanded, and reached out to pull her back.

Agatha caught her hands, amusement curling that long, beautiful mouth of hers. "A temporary respite, Flood," she said. "I don't want to get so lost to the world that the kitchen maid catches us when she comes to lay the fire."

Penelope sat back, chagrined. "Of course," she murmured. Chill air crept over skin heated by contact. It was good that one of them was thinking clearly, and making sure this would stay a secret. Penelope was no Isabella, with vast wealth and ancient bloodlines to protect her from gossip and the poisonous wagging of malicious tongues. She and Agatha would have to be careful. Discreet.

Just like every other time.

Agatha skated thoughtful fingers over the plane of Penelope's cheek. Aching, Penelope turned so her mouth could press against Agatha's palm. The scent of lemons from the balm she'd made as a gift speared through her, citrus sharpened and warmed by Agatha's skin.

Penelope throbbed hopelessly, and parted her lips to breathe in as deeply as she could.

Agatha's fingers slid lower, brushing teasingly across Penelope's mouth. Tingles like sparks flew up wherever she touched. "Come upstairs with me, will you?"

"Yes," Penelope replied. Instantly, and without question.

In all these long and lonely months, she'd never dreamed she'd have the chance to say yes to such an invitation. The word was honey-sweet on her tongue.

Agatha's eyes gleamed in the low light as she pushed up from the table.

They put the mead and bread away. Agatha grasped the candle in one hand and Penelope's hand in the other—just like she had in London. As if she feared Penelope might escape if she didn't keep hold of her.

Ha, thought Penelope fiercely, *not a chance*.

Agatha paused, candle raised, when they reached the twin bedroom doors. "Mine," Penelope whispered, opening the door and dragging Agatha in behind her.

"Why's that?" Agatha blinked.

"You were downstairs before I was," Penelope said. She shut the door and leaned back against it, hands still anxiously wrapped around the handle. "So my bed will have stayed warmer than yours."

"Ah." Agatha set the candle by the dressing table mirror, where it would give the most light. The fire had burned low and sultry in the grate. She tugged the cream shawl off her shoulders, draping it over the back of the chair. Penelope's eyes strained to trace Agatha's shape beneath the nightgown. Staring, but not ashamed to be caught this time.

The smile Agatha tossed back over her shoulder was wry and knowing. "Do you manage all your trysts so practically?"

Penelope licked her lips. "Why don't you share a few with me, and find out?"

Agatha let out a bark of laughter, then bit it back when the sound bounced too boisterously off the walls. "I'm glad to hear this isn't just about tonight," she said more softly. She took one step forward, and another, making Penelope's heartbeat skip from a trot to a canter. "It's been a long time for me, Flood."

Penelope gulped. "Does that mean you want to go fast, or slow? Because if you are out of practice, and want to move slowly, we can do that."

Agatha took another, very deliberate step nearer, putting her only an arm's reach away.

Penelope couldn't seem to get enough air no matter how rapidly she gasped for it. Her voice was thready with desire. "But if you're feeling impatient—or needy—or desperate— Lord knows I am—"

Agatha bent down and took Penelope's mouth, smothering the rest of her words.

The first kiss had been a surprise. This was a seduction. Agatha licked into her, breath and heat melting away the cold of the door at Penelope's back. One of Agatha's hands trailed up the long line of Penelope's neck and fingers threaded into her hair, pulling to tilt Penelope's head back. "No pins?" Agatha murmured.

"Prefer to keep it short," Penelope answered, half reply and half moan. "People only think I pin it up on account of how it curls."

"Handy," Agatha murmured. She tightened her grip, holding Penelope in place.

Penelope whimpered again, as pinpricks of not-quite-pain lit like stars in her scalp. She was slightly but inescapably in Agatha's control, and it made her whole body sing. Penelope's hands dropped away from the door handle, plucking at the ties of her own winter robe.

Agatha's mouth slanted harder against hers, little scrapes of teeth and long strokes of her tongue sending fire through Penelope's veins. Penelope reached out, tugged open the knot of Agatha's wool dressing-gown, banded an arm around her waist, and pulled.

Agatha's long body jerked forward and came up tight against Penelope's soft, plump shape.

They both shuddered at the contact. Agatha's free hand flattened against the door by Penelope's head. "Dear god, Flood," she groaned, a low tone that Penelope felt in every inch from throat to thighs. She wanted to rub herself against that sound—instead, she undulated and rubbed as much of herself as she could against Agatha, layers of warm

linen sliding and shifting between the creases and curves of
their bodies.

"I knew you'd be trouble," Agatha laughed, and took
Flood by the wrist to tow her inexorably toward the bed.
They scrambled together beneath the blankets, an absolute
tangle of limbs and cloth and racing, hungry hearts.

Penelope snuggled up against Agatha and pressed her
mouth to the base of her neck, just above her collarbone
where her night rail gaped obligingly. Agatha shivered. "Still
cold?" Penelope whispered.

"Still talking?" Agatha replied, in a voice equal parts
amused and strained. She shifted, sliding one leg in between
Penelope's, who sighed happily and hooked one thigh high
over Agatha's hip. Heat bloomed between them; Agatha
groaned again and pinned Penelope's shoulders to the bed
with eager hands.

With neither patience nor grace, they stripped one another. The rise and fall of blankets as they flung nightclothes
to the floor let in flashes of warm light to illuminate the
shapes revealed: the soft expanse of Penelope's belly, the
raindrop curve of Agatha's breast with a dark nipple puck-
ered by cold. Penelope raised her head and sucked happily
on that nipple, while her hands grasped their fill of Agatha's
solid hips. The hands on her shoulders flexed, pressing flesh
against bone; it was impossible to say who was holding on
more tightly.

On top, Agatha wriggled, pressed close but still eager to
get closer. Penelope gave a mischievous flick of her tongue—
making Agatha gasp—and slid a hand into the dark curls

between the other woman's legs. Agatha froze, panting, her sex slick and hot against Penelope's fingers. "Flood, please," she hissed.

"Please stop?" Penelope whispered teasingly.

Agatha shook her head, convulsive. "Please more."

"Anything you like," Penelope purred, and slid one strong, calloused finger into Agatha's cunny.

Agatha shuddered, arching her back, her long hair falling like a curtain around both of them, her hips working as Penelope toyed with her. Penelope flung the blankets back, the better to watch. She wanted to remember every bit of this—every sight and sound, each gasp and groan—because it was the first time, and whenever there was a first time, there would be a last time, too.

She shoved that thought aside; it could wait until the morning.

Agatha's hips rocked faster, matching Penelope's rhythm. Firelight shimmered on the lights and darks of her hair, swinging with every movement. Soon one finger wasn't enough; Penelope added a second, and thrust harder, feeling the sweet channel pulse and stretch around her fingers while her thumb strummed the bundle of nerves throbbing above. Agatha was making the loveliest sounds in the back of her throat—high almost-whimpers, desperate and needy—and when Penelope moved over to flick a mischievous tongue against her other, neglected nipple, Agatha tightened up everywhere and came with a choked, wondering cry.

Penelope kept her hands moving, keeping Agatha flying,

drinking in the sounds and the smells and the taste of sweat on skin.

And then Agatha clapped one hand over her own mouth, and sobbed.

Penelope froze for a moment in shock—then wrapped her arms around Agatha's shaking shoulders and pulled her down into an embrace. "It's alright, you're alright," she whispered, over and over, smoothing the wildness of Agatha's hair, pulling the blankets tight again around them both. "Everything's alright."

Agatha made a strangled noise; after a moment, Penelope realized she was laughing. Still crying, but also laughing, and scrubbing a hand over her eyes to clear the tears from them. "Oh, Flood," she said, "I'm sorry about that. It's just that . . . It's been so long, and here you are, and it was so, so *beautiful.*"

The awe and conviction in that one quiet word went straight to Penelope's head. She grinned, as her heart warmed with pleasure and triumph.

Agatha sniffled one last time, and pushed herself up. Her forearms were on either side of Penelope, their legs tangling together and sliding gently, unable to hold still. Agatha's gaze drifted down, and Penelope felt her nipples tighten beneath the heat of that gaze. One tear still sparkled in the corner of Agatha's eye—but then she smiled, and that curve of lips held so much naked carnal intent that Penelope went hot and breathless and trembling, all at once.

"Now then . . ." Agatha said, and bent her head.

And Penelope was lost.

The kissing had been marvelous. But it was nothing compared to what Agatha Griffin could do when she set her sights on a person's whole body. Her hands stroked and gripped and teased, her touch going from featherlight to almost bruising. Her mouth followed, hot and wet with the occasional light graze of teeth that made Penelope shiver and melt. By the time Agatha slid lower, settling her shoulders beneath Penelope's quivering thighs, Penelope was a gasping, writhing wreck of arousal and need.

She'd never felt so alive in her life.

Agatha grinned up at her, one palm pressing against Penelope's inner thigh to keep her spread wide. "God, I've missed this," she groaned. "You have no idea."

"Some," Penelope gasped. "It's been a while for me, too, Griffin."

"Well, then." Agatha slipped two fingers into her mouth, wetting them. "Let's not keep you waiting."

And then she was licking Penelope's cunny, open-mouthed, and thrusting those fingers inside her as deep as they would go.

It was rough and forceful and Penelope damn near screamed with the pleasure of it. She bucked up helplessly, one hand clutching at the sheets, the other slamming against her mouth to muffle the sounds that fought to escape from her throat. Agatha groaned ravenously against Penelope's flesh and the low sound set her off, every last quivering bit of her exploding in showers of sparks so bright she could swear she heard them sizzle.

Then she snapped back to herself, and it was only the rasp of her own panting breath.

Agatha slid back up for a kiss, long and slow and satisfied. Penelope groaned satisfaction into Agatha's mouth and pulled up the blankets again, her eyelids heavy and her brain starting to spin with drowsy delight.

Agatha nuzzled into Penelope's throat, and flicked her tongue against the pulse point where her neck met her shoulder. "I shouldn't stay," she murmured.

"Of course not," Penelope agreed. "You wouldn't want to risk anything lewd happening. Again."

Agatha sighed. "Nothing lewd about it, Flood." She raised her head; her eyes were serious, a little anxious.

Penelope's amusement turned to something more tender. "No," she agreed. One corner of her mouth hitched up. "Beautiful, as you said."

That made Agatha kiss her again, and then harder, which was precisely what Penelope wanted. But as soon as her hands began to wander, Agatha groaned in regret and pulled away. "I shouldn't sleep here," she said, slipping free of the blankets and retrieving her night rail. That damned garment, which was both too revealing and covered too much. Then the dressing-gown, of course, covering everything.

Penelope rolled to her side beneath the blankets and stretched, catlike. She would ache in the morning, she was sure. But it was all worth it, because Agatha's eyes ate up every movement even from across the room. A bolt of something bold lit up Penelope's core. "Do you know, Griffin?

I am prone to bouts of sleeplessness in the middle of the night."

Agatha froze in the act of cinching her robe tight. "That sounds so unpleasant, Flood."

"It's a curse," Penelope said happily. "All those hours—with nobody else awake—no one to hear anything…" She put her chin in her hand and contrived to look innocent.

Agatha snorted, but a flush had risen in her cheeks. She strode back toward the bed, footsteps beating the floor like a soft, hurried heartbeat. "And what if I tell you I want an uninterrupted night's rest?" she demanded.

Penelope widened her eyes. "Do you?"

"No," Agatha said, and kissed Penelope so soundly that all her impudence melted away into lust and longing. "At least," Agatha went on, in a sigh, "not yet. Good night, Flood."

Penelope grinned, nestling deep into the blankets. "Good night, Griffin."

CHAPTER TWENTY-ONE

It was an entirely frustrating thing to attempt to supervise two young people resentful of your intrusive presence, while trying not to make obvious calf's-eyes at the woman who'd fucked you senseless the night before.

After lunch, Penelope calmly announced her intention of taking an afternoon nap—with a twinkle in her eye that Agatha deeply mistrusted, but didn't dare call attention to in company.

Sydney dared to look hopeful, the worm. "Eliza and I were planning on going for a walk into town," he said.

"Excellent," Agatha said viciously, and earned herself a double glare by continuing, "I believe I'll join you. We ought to call on your grandmother." Mrs. Stowe and Miss Coningsby had been invited to the festivities at Fern Hall, but of course Miss Coningsby wouldn't come, and Mrs. Stowe wouldn't come without Miss Coningsby.

Judging by the gloomy look Eliza sent Sydney, which Agatha caught from the corner of her eye while they were donning cloaks and bonnets in the front hallway, a chaperone and a visit to elderly relatives were not how the couple had planned to spend their afternoon.

Too bad. If they were determined not to wed, Agatha would give them no quarter for temptation. There was simply too much at stake, for all of them.

They bid farewell to Captain Stanhope and Mr. Flood, stopped partway to town to bid a quick Merry Christmas to Mr. Thomas and Mr. Kitt, who shared lodgings on the outskirts of the village proper, and then made their way to the high street. All Melliton was decked out in furze and greenery, bright against the velvet of snow and the sparkle of frost. Miss Coningsby let them in with a shy hello, poured hot cider for everyone, and then vanished upstairs, overwhelmed by the unwonted number of people.

Mrs. Stowe was enthroned in the window seat, cocooned in shawls, only a bare few panes of glass separating her from her slumbering, snow-shrouded garden. She curved her gnarled hands around her cup of cider and smiled through the steam. "And a very merry holiday to you, my dears."

Sydney, bless him, lasted nearly a quarter of an hour before asking: "Can I show Eliza your beehives, Gran?"

"So long as you don't wake any of my bees," Mrs. Stowe allowed, and the two young visitors hurried to wrap themselves up again and tramp through the unblemished snow outside the window.

The two older women watched them, suspicions blooming from the mother and amusement from the grandmother. "Young Eliza seems sweet enough," Mrs. Stowe said. "Why do your eyes go all daggers when you look at her?"

Agatha flinched, hating that she was so obvious. "They told me they're not going to wed," she said.

"No accounting for taste," Mrs. Stowe said with a rueful shrug.

"They have every intention of carrying on as if they're married, though," Agatha added tartly. "They seem to think that's more ideal, somehow."

Mrs. Stowe considered this. "Maybe they're right."

Agatha gaped, shocked.

Her mother-in-law took another drink of cider. "Tell me something: Are you going to disown your son unless he marries her?"

"N-no," Agatha stammered, disoriented by the change of topic.

"Even if they have a child? Will you cast them out into the street to fend for themselves?"

The very image turned her stomach. "Don't be absurd."

"Then what do they really have to fear by not marrying?"

Agatha's mouth opened and closed for several moments. "People will be cruel," she said at last. It seemed the best summary of her fears.

Mrs. Stowe raised her brows quizzically. "Have you always been proper and prudent, where love is concerned?"

Agatha flushed to the roots of her hair.

"I thought not." Mrs. Stowe peered at her for a moment,

then broke into an infectious grin. "It's that Penelope Flood, I assume?"

Agatha gulped for air. This was her late husband's mother, talking about her new lover. Old defenses snapped up in her mind, almost audibly. "Thomas and I—"

Mrs. Stowe snorted, cider-steam billowing dragonish around her. "You and Thomas loved each other, yes, I'm well aware. I had *three* husbands, girl—do you think I don't know it's possible to love more than one person in a whole lifetime?" Her grin turned cheeky. "Maybe even in a whole night?"

Agatha didn't know *where* to put her eyes. If her face grew any redder she would spontaneously combust and get Agatha-ash all over Miss Coningsby's parlor rug. She'd never thought of Melliton as a hotbed of lust and debauchery, yet here was one of the village's revered, respected elders, casually dropping hints about activities that would make a Roman emperor blush.

But there was one vital question to ask: "How did you know about—about me and Mrs. Flood?"

Mrs. Stowe shrugged again. "People talk, dear. There's been rumors for a while."

Agatha was aghast. Panic bubbled up in her chest, hot and acidic. "How could they know, when I didn't?" she blurted. "We just—it was only last night—"

Mrs. Stowe waved this aside. "You've spent plenty of time together, and Mrs. Flood's tendencies are well known by this point. You might as well drop hints about Joanna and Isabella as tell someone Penelope Flood prefers women and expect them to be shocked by the news." She leaned forward and dropped her voice. "Now how Mr. Kitt feels about Mr. Thomas—that's a true secret . . ."

"Really?" Agatha breathed, then shook herself. "It's none of my business," she said mulishly. "But if people are spreading gossip about me, on the other hand—"

"Pssh, it doesn't have to hurt you any. People say the same kind of things about Miss Coningsby and me. It's not true in our case, but that doesn't stop them saying it."

"And it's never done you any harm?" Agatha asked skeptically.

Mrs. Stowe pursed her lips. "I wouldn't say never . . . But any harm has come from it, is because someone wanted an excuse to hurt us. If they hadn't a handy excuse, they made one up." She shrugged. "And the rest of the time, we get to live as we please. Isn't that the important thing?"

Agatha wasn't so sure. It nagged at her all the way until the end of the visit, as she collected a rosy-cheeked Eliza and a Sydney who looked far too innocent to portend anything good. Children always looked most angelic when they were up to the most trouble.

Agatha squinted around, trying to deduce from the tracks in the snow if they'd managed to slip out of the garden while she'd been distracted by Mrs. Stowe.

She didn't notice the handbill at first—it was only a creamy blot against the whiteness all around her. But then a gust of wind caught the edge and made it flutter, and Agatha found herself slowing to read the larger print, and then stopping altogether.

PUBLIC NOTIFICATION, read the largest line of type.

The Melliton Auxiliary Branch of the Society
for the Suppression of Seditious Libel and
Mendacity offers a bounty of
FIVE SHILLINGS
for information on activities or persons threatening
to undertake activities of a seditious, blasphemous,
or obscene nature. Anyone with such or similar
knowledge may apply to the Reverend Eneas Oliver,
JP, Squire Theydon, or His Lordship the Right Hon.
Viscount Summerville.

Agatha felt chilled in a way the frigid winter air couldn't account for. Her eyes ran over and over the text; her ears heard the tearing of paper, and the red of an soldier's uniform seemed to flicker like consuming flame at the edges of her vision. She forced herself to take a deep breath, in and out—and then, as her eyes ran over the text for the hundredth time she realized something new that snapped her back to alertness.

The typeface. Twenty-point Baskerville, with a chip in the lower serif of the capital *L*.

This handbill had been printed on Griffin's own press, right here in Melliton.

She fought the urge to spin on her heel, march straight down to the print-works, and demand to know when this job had been authorized. It would do no good: the shop and warehouse were closed up until tomorrow, a holiday break for the pressmen.

Tomorrow, she could go and make some sharp inquiries of Mr. Downes.

She balled her hands in her skirts to keep the hem clear of the snow—god, but she missed her old trousers—and hurried to close the distance to where her son and her apprentice walked with hands almost touching.

It did lift her furious heart to see how dismayed they looked, and how they moved slightly farther apart, when she closed the distance. The trio stomped silently homeward, snow crunching and frost grinding beneath the unhappy rhythm of their boots.

Anger and impatience were a volatile combination, especially when one was trying not to ruin a holiday. Agatha buzzed inside like an angry hive the rest of the day, through Mrs. Braintree's dinner and after, when Captain Stanhope and Mr. Flood regaled them with tales of the dazzling Arctic city of Smeerenburg. Eliza and Sydney were defiantly merry, dancing riotously to the captain's shanties until Penelope's boisterous brother threw up his hands and laughingly pleaded exhaustion.

They retired to bed. Agatha paced her bedroom floor, and noticed the gentle sound of a door opening, about an hour after everyone else had gone silent. A rumble in Captain Stanhope's usual key followed, harmonizing with lighter notes in Mr. Flood's softer tones. The door shut, and silence reigned again.

Agatha paced for another number of minutes, as many as she could stand. Then she slipped to the connecting door and tapped softly with one fingernail. The door opened at once, Agatha darted in, the door closed—and Agatha was backed up against the wall with her arms around warm, plump Penelope Flood.

Oh, an armful like this was worth any amount of trouble.

Penelope's mouth was hot and hungry. She wore her night rail, and a gray woolen wrapper against the chill, but she'd left the wrapper open so Agatha's hands could roam the rolling dips and valleys of her body. The shorter woman tore her mouth away on a gasp when Agatha's hand plunged into the neck of her night rail and cupped possessively around the soft weight of her breast. "Christ, Griffin," she groaned, warm breath against Agatha's throat. "What kept you?"

"No idea," Agatha groaned back. All her rage and frustration became mere kindling, and sent her blazing up now with love and lust and a need so sharp it was almost painful. She held Penelope tight and devoured her mouth until both women's joints gave way, and they slid down to the floor in a panting, grasping tumble of linen and limbs.

Penelope's knee landed hard on the bare floorboards and she cursed, then bit her lip and made a face. "This was easier when I was younger," she muttered.

"I know just how you feel," Agatha chuckled between kisses. And she did. A good hard fuck took a toll on a body at forty-five years of age. She could still feel last night aching in her muscles, and knew it would be even more noticeable tomorrow.

She couldn't wait.

Agatha remembered when she'd gloried in smooth, unlined skin and the dewy litheness of youth. Now everything had relaxed, and folded, and new spots seemed to show up without warning, as though she were a potato left too long unattended in a cellar.

But Penelope—she had folds in the same places, and creases, and skin that had slackened and gone delicate with age. She was round where Agatha was rangy, but her body also bore the marks of her years, and it was glorious to behold. Agatha tugged Penelope's hem up higher and higher, the better to see everything beneath, to learn it better than she knew her own body. Every freckle, every fold was somewhere to press wondering fingers, every roll was made to fit the greedy span of Agatha's palm.

Penelope's small teeth bit down on Agatha's earlobe, and what little remained of her patience went up in absolute smoke. "I hope you want it fast, Flood," she rasped, her voice all but choked from desire.

"And hard," Penelope replied, in an eager tone that sent lightning skipping down every one of Agatha's nerves. Penelope pulled back, grinning wickedly, with a light in her eyes that made Agatha catch her breath. "Can I show you something?"

"Anything," Agatha breathed. But she was still surprised when Penelope pulled a small box from her bedside table and opened it up to reveal . . . well, a respectably sized dildo made from sleek walnut. It gleamed cheekily in the candlelight as Penelope lifted it from the box's protective padding. "Good god, Flood, where on earth did you get that?"

"Believe it or not, this was a present from Harry after he made captain," Penelope said. "Nantucketers call it a he's-at-home. 'Every whaler's wife should have one,' he said." She patted the smooth surface with familiar affection.

Agatha narrowed her eyes and purred, "And you would like me to use it on you."

Penelope quivered visibly. "Yes, please."

The breathiness in her reply hooked under Agatha's skin and set her pulse to staccato. She took the wooden phallus in hand and rose to her feet. "On the bed, then," she said, putting steel into her tone.

It had been a guess, but it was a good one: Penelope scrambled to obey, flinging her wrapper over the nearest chair and stretching out on her side on the bed. Her bosom plumped up gorgeously against her arm beneath the night rail, and she winked when she caught Agatha staring. "There's oil in the box," she said with a grin.

Agatha retrieved the small jar of unscented oil and set it on the bedside table. Penelope rolled onto her back and flung her arms up over her head, arching so her nightclothes revealed even more of her ample curves beneath the linen. Eagerness was written in every panting breath, in the way her legs moved softly up and down against one another beneath her skirt.

Agatha felt heat sizzle along the back of her neck, and down her arms to her fingertips. It was warmer in here than it had been last night—Penelope must have stoked the fire in the hearth a little higher in anticipation. The warmth in the air, the untied wrapper . . . She'd done as much as possible to ensure everything was ready for when Agatha slipped secretly into her room in the night.

Agatha was strongly inclined to reward such thoughtfulness. Especially if it meant she got to fuck Penelope Flood good and hard.

She held the dildo regally, put all the command she could into her voice, and said: "Strip."

Penelope yanked her night rail over her head, while Agatha examined the dildo more closely. It had a good weight and feel against her hand, silken-smooth with a rope-like series of twists at the base that made it easy to grip and turn.

She wrapped her fingers around it and looked back at Penelope, who was now entirely, wonderfully nude and wriggling on top of the blankets on the bed. Her hand slipped down to her own sex, stroking lightly.

Agatha grinned wickedly. "Impatient, are we?"

"Yes, we bloody well are," Penelope responded tartly.

Agatha used her free hand to pinch the nearer nipple, and Penelope gasped. Agatha's own nipples went tight at the sound. "A little wider, if you please," she murmured.

Penelope's knees fell open, and she gulped for air.

Agatha put her free hand on Penelope's thigh, holding her in place, and bent low. She deliberately let her breath skate over the other woman's soft and quivering belly as she said, "Are you sure you're ready to be fucked already?"

Penelope squeaked. "Very," she said, her tone halfway a whine. "I may have started a little early. On my own."

Agatha snorted out a laugh. "How very naughty of you."

Penelope's hand worked faster, playing between her legs. "Are you going to punish me for it?"

"God, no," said Agatha with feeling, watching those strong fingers slide up and down her lover's beautiful pink-and-gold pussy. "Why on earth would I punish you for wanting?"

As Penelope watched with a burning gaze, Agatha poured a little oil into her palm and slicked it over the flared wooden head. She felt like a pagan priestess, clad only in linen and firelight, standing over a willing sacrifice. Penelope squirmed and licked her lips as Agatha knelt between her knees on the bed. She ran the head of the dildo up and down those glistening folds, making sure everything was properly slicked up for the purpose.

"Agatha . . ." Penelope pleaded.

"Patience, love," Agatha murmured, teasingly. She pressed one palm against Penelope's thigh to keep her spread, stroking the skin a little as she felt the muscles twitching and straining there. With the other hand, she slid the walnut dildo through her lover's dewy curls, found her opening, and gently pushed.

Penelope gasped, and breathed in, and whimpered.

Agatha pressed on, working the dildo in slowly but surely, feeling out the angles and learning by heart the ones that made Penelope's blue eyes go wide above her flushed cheeks. Those eyes flashed up at Agatha with clear avidity. "I thought you wanted it fast?" Penelope panted.

Agatha smiled and thrust the dildo fully home, all the way to where the grip on the base prevented it from moving farther.

Penelope's groan was delicious, low and resonant as a bell.

Agatha's whole body chimed in harmony. "Fast," she agreed, "but not too rough." She slid the toy back and forth, twice, just to hear Penelope sigh—then took both hands away and stepped back from the bed. "Now don't you move."

Penelope muttered half-serious curses in protest but clutched at the bedclothes and held still, as Agatha methodically stripped off her own night rail. And folded it. Carefully. One billowing bit at a time. As the hearth light flickered over her nakedness.

By the time she turned back to face Penelope, she was shivering a little—but what really shook her was the open, helpless hunger on Penelope Flood's face. "If you don't hurry," Penelope pouted, "I'm going to take matters into my own hands."

"Don't tempt me," Agatha retorted, but hurried back to the bed and grasped the base of the dildo again, pumping it sweetly back and forth.

"Mmm . . ." Penelope moaned teasingly.

But Agatha was done teasing. She gripped the flaring base of the wood and thrust hard.

"Oh!" Penelope gasped. Then: "Again! Please?"

Agatha complied joyfully, building up a steady, relentless rhythm of thrust and retreat, until Penelope's hips began rising up to meet her and drive the dildo in as deep as it could go. Agatha's greedy gaze drank in every toss of her head, the flush that spilled from her cheeks and down her throat and over the tops of that bouncing bosom. Her thighs were shaking now, legs splayed and straining, one foot arching up with toes spread as she fought toward the peak of pleasure.

Agatha leaned, down, breathing her words close into her lover's ear: "Go on, love—you know what you need."

Penelope let out a soft, choked cry, but her hand dove down between her legs and began stroking the aching flesh there. Agatha focused on the he's-at-home, fucking Penelope just as fast as she'd promised, until with a final cry her whole torso arched off the bed and she came in great, gasping waves.

As soon as she relaxed, Agatha bent low and buried her face between her lover's legs. The scents of heat and sweat and pleasure filled her mouth as she licked hungrily, suckling on the tender bud while holding the dildo in place to make sure Penelope stayed filled.

Penelope wriggled and writhed, but Agatha didn't know there was purpose to it until she felt Penelope's languorous tongue trace flickering fire against the inside of her thigh. The woman had twisted around until she could raise her head and lick at Agatha's cunt, echoing the pace of Agatha's tongue between her thighs.

Agatha moaned into the soft-sweetness beneath her mouth, and spread herself obligingly wide for Penelope's advantage. They devoured one another, Penelope newly sated, Agatha growing more and more needy as her desire built and roared through the ocean of her veins.

Penelope pulled her mouth away briefly, and there was the gentle chime of glass. Then her fingers were back, oil-slicked, one of them plunging deep into Agatha as that wicked tongue resumed its journey, the tip flicking against the tenderest, most aching part of her cunny and causing her to curse in startled delight.

Penelope laughed knowingly and added a second finger.

Agatha felt herself stretched to the brink; her eyes shut, her hands slowed, and she pulled the dildo free and set it aside on the bedclothes. Greedily, she pressed her cheek against Penelope's dewy thigh and gasped helplessly as sensations surged through her.

A third plunging finger, almost too much to bear—until the fourth was added. Agatha whimpered and keened breathlessly, shoving her hips back to take as much as she possibly could. There was nothing else in this world, just her heart and her cunt and the slick, solid pressure of Penelope's hand. Agatha begged for more in whispers, pleading desperately as she rocked back and forth, a torrent of senseless words pouring from her lips.

Penelope's low laugh skated over her inner thigh—and then a thumb pressed just *so* over the tight bundle of nerves buried in her folds, and all the striving and stroking and wonderful struggle of it burst like a glorious star behind Agatha's eyes.

Her hands on Penelope's thighs clutched tight and she rode that crest of pleasure until it faded and awareness of the world came creeping back.

Penelope's hand eased itself away.

Joints shaking, Agatha collapsed to her side on the bed with a wheezing laugh. She felt like she'd been taken expertly apart by pleasure and then reassembled by some hapless amateur, not sure what bits went where. "Good god, Flood, you'll be the absolute death of me."

"I hope not," Penelope murmured back. She went up on one elbow, eyes possessively roaming the long length of Agatha's spent form.

Agatha rolled slightly so their sides were pressed together, even though they were nose-to-toes and slightly diagonal across the width of the bed.

Penelope looped a hand loosely around Agatha's calves, curving one rough palm to fit them. "Stay with me tonight?"

Agatha sat up, hands clasping over her knees. "Could I? Won't someone talk?"

Penelope shrugged. "We can say you heard something moving in the wood and grew frightened."

Agatha snorted. "At least make it a ghost or specter or something, won't you? For the sake of my pride."

Penelope retrieved the he's-at-home, cleaned it, and patted it carefully dry.

By the time she'd tucked it back in its box and hidden the box away, Agatha had blown out the candle and tunneled under the blankets. The fire was down to embers now. Only the moonlight reflecting off the snow was left, a cool silver illumination that touched only the barest outlines of furniture and curtains. "Thank you for thinking to keep it warmer in here tonight," she murmured, as Penelope joined her and wrapped her arms tight around Agatha's waist. "Apparently the ghost frightened me so much that I had no choice but to fling my nightclothes entirely off."

Penelope cackled silently against Agatha's shoulder. "If you're worried, you could put them back on again."

"No joy," Agatha said, then wiggled so all their several bumps and valleys fitted perfectly against one another. Some part of her was only happy when skin to skin with this woman; she knew better than to lie to herself about that. And apparently most of Melliton already knew it, too. She grimaced. "Doesn't it bother you? The things people say?"

Penelope shrugged. Her voice was already growing slow and sleepy. "It's a small village. People always talk."

"But then you have to look them in the face, and *know* they know."

"And?"

Agatha shifted uneasily. "And how is that not terribly awkward, for everyone?"

Penelope shrugged again, less forcefully. "It might be, if that were the only thing they knew about me. It would feel more significant then. But they also know about the time my brothers and I stole Mr. Scriven's newest baby goat, and tried to keep it as a pet. They know how many months Mr. Biswas spent courting Miss Calbert before she agreed to become Mrs. Biswas. They know how many enemy prizes Mr. Kitt helped capture during the war, and what battle Mr. Thomas was wounded in." She shifted her cheek against Agatha's shoulder, as if hunting for the right spot to settle in for the night. "So the things they might not approve of, the things that make us different—they don't seem to stand out as much."

"Until they do," Agatha said.

"Until they do," Penelope sighed.

Agatha stared up into the darkness. "Mrs. Stowe said that if someone's looking for an excuse to hurt you, they'll find one, and that's all there is to it."

Penelope *hmmed* at this. "Sounds sensible."

"Sounds like London," Agatha countered. "Maybe the two places are not so different. Maybe the city is just several small towns, that all happen to be stacked on top of one another."

Penelope let out a puff of laughter, startled. "What?"

Agatha pursed her lips, warming to her theme. "If you live in town long enough, you find yourself meeting the same people wherever you go. You know someone who knows someone who knows someone, and it's like they're following you—when of course all it means is that you get invited to the same dinners and dances and such. And then you move to a different street, or you lose a fortune or gain one, or find a spouse or lose one . . ." She swallowed, thinking of the friends who'd just seemed to vanish after Thomas's death. "And suddenly you're in a whole new set of people. As though everyone's moving in carefully plotted circles—like a dance, rings within rings within rings."

"Who's calling the figures?" Penelope murmured drowsily.

"No one. Who could possibly?"

"No wonder it's all chaos, then." Penelope sighed, and shifted, and before long her breathing turned deep and even, the unmistakable rhythm of well-deserved sleep.

Agatha pressed her face into Penelope's hair, protectiveness like a tide washing through her. All at once she had so much more to lose than she'd started the holiday with. It would probably have been safer if she'd never gone to bed with Penelope Flood at all.

She couldn't dredge up even a single atom of regret. But she did make herself a silent promise, as the moonlight crept across the carpet: she would do everything in her power to keep anyone, in city or country, from hurting Penelope Flood.

Chapter Twenty-Two

Agatha dragged on her gray dress the next morning, fuzzy-minded, sore in unspeakable places. She washed her face with lukewarm water, and rubbed her winter-cracked hands with some of the balm Penelope had made for her. The scent of lemons and honey rose around her like a halo in the morning sunlight, and as her nose and mouth filled with that sharp summer scent, Agatha came to an abrupt decision.

She could, and arguably should, attach herself to Sydney and Eliza again. Hound them over hill and dale across the town. Trap them in corners of the house under an ever-waking and mistrustful eye.

But she wasn't going to.

She had business with Mr. Downes at the print-works. And while she could have tried to insist Sydney come with her, to give him grounding in the business he would some-day have to inherit . . . well, to be perfectly honest, she was tired. The amount of effort she knew she'd have to expend in getting him to accompany her did not seem worth the paltry reward of his sullen, silent companionship.

She went down to breakfast, and asked Penelope to walk out with her instead.

The sky had cleared again but the snow still lay glittering on the ground, sparkles dancing in the corners of Agatha's eyes whenever she turned her head. Icicles hung from eaves and branches like diamond spears. Sunlight glowed on the greenery over windows and doorways, and made red holly berries shine like rubies.

Agatha gloried in all of it, and stopped in one snow-shrouded hollow of the wood outside the town to kiss Penelope beneath the boughs until both their cheeks were flushed and rosy.

The steam press was hard at it again, pouring white smoke into the cold blue sky. It was toasty enough inside that Agatha and Penelope had to shed their coats.

"Mr. Downes!" Agatha called.

The print-works foreman looked up from where he was checking the latest proofs from the apprentices' compositing. "Mrs. Griffin," he said with a nod. "How are your holidays going?"

"Splendid," Agatha replied, "until I noticed a certain handbill that has lately gone up around town."

"Yes, I've meant to tell you about that," Mr. Downes hurried to say. His grin was proud and eager, not a whit of guilt about it.

"Did you not think to *ask* me about it before undertaking the job, Mr. Downes?" Agatha shot back, in her sharpest tone.

He paused, blinking. "I thought there would be no reason you would turn it down." He dismissed the apprentice, and turned to face Agatha fully, tugging his rolled shirtsleeves back down over his forearms. "It seemed like a good way to use up all the spare paper we had left when you cancelled that last run of the Widow Wasp."

Agatha's stomach lurched. So instead of printing seditious ditties, she was profiting off people making threats against Penelope Flood's friends and neighbors. She hadn't enjoyed being threatened by the soldiers; she wanted no part in making anyone else feel that same sick, powerless fear. "I appreciate your ingenuity," she said tightly, "but I must ask you to refuse any future jobs from Lady Summerville, or any other member of the Mendacity Society."

Mr. Downes' brows flew up like startled dragonflies. "Why, Mrs. Griffin?"

Agatha's eyes narrowed. "Because it's my press, not Lady Summerville's, and I have the right to say how it's employed."

"But . . ." Mr. Downes was sputtering now with bafflement. "But there was plenty of room in the queue . . . and the rates were good . . ."

"How good?" interrupted Penelope Flood.

Mr. Downes wordlessly turned to the ledger on the table beside him, and pointed to the line in the book. Penelope whistled.

Agatha's stomach twisted again. It was indeed a good

amount of money. Giving it back would be difficult, especially if they were to replace the lost paper on top of that sum. And especially considering the Mendacity Society would only use it to do more harm, if Agatha returned the funds.

"No more such jobs in future, Mr. Downes," she repeated. "On pain of dismissal."

He blanched, but he nodded obedience.

Agatha and Penelope wrapped themselves up again, while all around them journeymen and apprentices whispered to one another and avoided making eye contact. Agatha knew the instant their employer was out of sight, the discussion would begin. There was nothing she could do to stop it. There would be people who agreed with Mr. Downes, and people who were glad to see him scolded because of the one time he'd scolded them. It was a moment that could poison the air of a workshop for months, even years to come.

Unless: she gave them something else to talk about.

She turned on her heel and strode back toward Mr. Downes. "May I see that ledger again, please?"

Pale as milk, he handed it over.

Agatha ran her eye down the columns, tallying silently in her head, and came to a conclusion. It was tight, but . . . "We've been doing so much better these past few months, even with the Wasp cancellation," she said, and smiled. "I think a general pay raise is in order."

It was as if the entire room was holding its breath.

Agatha's smile widened. "Say, an extra shilling a month? And two shillings to you, Mr. Downes. For the overall excellence of your work, and that of the entire shop."

Mr. Downes' stiffness vanished, relief pouring off him like smoke. "Thank you, Mrs. Griffin," he breathed.

Agatha nodded, took Penelope's arm, and strode out into the winter world again. Just before the door snicked shut behind her, she heard the unmistakable sound of voices raised in excitement.

So what if she was buying their loyalty and goodwill? What else were employers *for*? And the quicker Lady Summerville's money left her hands, the better Agatha felt about not giving it back.

Her lover's frown, however, grew and grew as they walked by the snow-decked houses of Melliton. "What's wrong?" Agatha asked.

Penelope Flood, bless her, didn't beat around the bush. "Where do you suppose Lady Summerville got all that money?"

Agatha blinked. "What do you mean?"

"That was a great deal of cash to spend for those handbills," Penelope said, waving at one as they passed.

Agatha's hands itched to tear it down from the post— but there were too many windows around them, staring like pupil-less eyes.

Penelope waved at the vicarage, new windows misted over from the warmth within and frost without. "Mr. Oliver's new glass couldn't have come cheaply, either—not as quickly as they were replaced. And that's not even counting the bounties offered for information on—" her lips twisted painfully "—sedition, blasphemy, or obscenity."

"It does sound like a lot, when you list it out," Agatha muttered.

Penelope nodded sharply. "So where is she *getting* it all? Everyone knows Viscount Summerville's never had two pennies to rub together."

Agatha tucked Penelope closer against her side as they passed from the village and into the wood. "We know where the money comes from," she said. "She sold all of Isabella's statues."

Penelope's mouth gaped, then snapped almost audibly shut. "You're right," she said weakly—then cursed loudly enough to startle a raven into flight from a nearby tree. Both women flung their hands over their heads as snow flurries and icy droplets rained down on them both.

Penelope cursed again, low and bitter this time. "How *dare* she," she hissed. "How dare she put Isabella's work to such a use, when she knows Isabella herself would never have supported such—*cruelty*." She was shaking, her hands clenching shut and then flying open again, so bloody furious that Agatha was surprised the snow around her feet didn't melt and sublimate into steam.

"She's sold off nearly all of them, you said," Agatha murmured. She put a hand on Penelope's elbow, soothing. "The funds will run out, too, soon enough."

Penelope's mouth went flat. "Unless she's also sold the Napoleon snuffbox."

Agatha gaped.

Penelope's gaze was bleak and cold as the woods. "Her

statues were not small, but the snuffbox was even more valuable. It had rings of diamonds, and the highest quality enamel, and a portrait of the emperor himself." She kicked at a particularly grimy chink of ice. "She could fund the Mendacity Society for a decade with that kind of money."

"Damn," Agatha breathed.

Penelope wheeled to face her. "Do you still recall the name of that barrister you met? The one who told you where to find the dryad statue?"

"I can do better than that," Agatha promised. "I've already written to a few London art brokers about the Napoleon. They're sure to know who's been arranging those sales—it's a small, gossipy world and they'll be thrilled to be able to share what they know."

"Thank you," Penelope said. One corner of her lip tilted upward.

They walked on, but after three steps Agatha felt her heart sink as something else occurred to her: Joanna Molesey would be bloody *furious* if Lady Summerville had sold that snuffbox. And a furious Joanna was a dangerous Joanna.

Bad enough that the Wasp's popularity had caught the attention of the law in London. It wasn't fair, Agatha knew—but that had been little comfort when she'd been facing down soldiers in her own storefront.

Agatha had paid the price for Joanna Molesey's anger last time.

Who in Melliton would suffer, if she decided to sting again?

It was bound to happen: the Christmas holidays came to a close. Agatha and her family returned to London; Penelope yearned to claim a farewell kiss, but had to be content to squeeze her beloved's hand as she and the young folk climbed up into the stage.

After the coach had trundled off through the slush, Penelope trudged back to Fern Hall, where Harry and John flirted cozily as they sprawled on the hearth like two great mastiffs. Penelope sat in the armchair, tucked her legs beneath her, and began counting the hours until Agatha's next letter.

Bless the woman, it came swiftly.

My dear Flood,

My bed is far too big now for just one person. We must get you to London sometime—I'll be visiting Melliton next week, of course, but that's seven whole nights from now.

Imagine what we could get up to in seven entire nights . . .

And then followed a page of such dazzling and specific lechery that Penelope flushed head to heel. She was briefly worried the letter itself would burst into flame, or the chair beneath her catch fire from the heat that coursed over her skin.

Such a letter demanded revenge: Penelope sharpened a new quill, closeted herself in the study where no one would see, and wrote back three pages of even more explicit longings.

And so they went on, torrid promises flying back and forth, a game of wits that was both frustrated teasing and sensual fulfillment. Dreams recounted and embellished. Scraps of the most scandalous verses Penelope had found in her years raiding Isabella's library. One of Agatha's letters was simply a series of erotic woodcuts, some of which were old commissions she'd done and some of which she'd carved specially for Penelope—definitely the one where two tiny and *extremely* nude figures embraced, framed in vines and flowers, as a swarm of lazy bees bejeweled the sky around them.

The correspondence was punctuated by visits where Agatha and Penelope acted out as many of those shared fantasies as desire and physical stamina would allow. As the weather warmed and winter thawed into spring, they began walking the bee circuit again, finding time in the hollows and dells for a little discreet love play beneath the boughs and blossoms.

It would have been a halcyon time—were it not for the regular pricks and stings of the Mendacity Society, whose presence was becoming more and more of a goad in the town.

Harry was fined for swearing, then fined again when he swore before the magistrates; Miss Felicia Plumb was questioned at length about the origin of the lace on her attire—which it transpired she'd made herself, with months of painstaking effort; Mr. Koskinen was penalized for fishing on a Sunday morning. Mr. and Mrs. Biswas kept closer to each other than ever when they served customers at the Four Swallows in the evening, while Mr. Thomas and Mr.

Kitt were now careful to always have a third person seated between them.

As spring advanced, the whole country decked itself out in a festive mood for King George's approaching coronation. Agatha went exploring in Griffin's warehouse and brought out plates of antique ballads from the last coronation. Reprinting these was an easy way to keep the Melliton pressworks queue full, leaving no gap for Lady Summerville and the Mendacity Society to sidle into.

I feel like such a hypocrite, Agatha wrote after a few months had passed. *To spend so much of my time dreaming about you, while disapproving of Sydney and Eliza. They have put a little distance between them, to placate me, but their misery is contagious and we're all in a sad state. Sydney spends even more time out of the house than before—and Eliza, even though I appreciate her efforts and her skill at managing the contributors, spends far too many of her hours escaping into endless, anxious work.*

She showed me one set of etchings for the upcoming issue of the Menagerie: frock designs for the coronation Herbwoman and her attendants. White gowns in cream silk net, with crosswise garlands of green leaves and pink roses, also in silk. It put me strongly in mind of what you Melliton ladies wore to Brandenburg House, not even a year ago. And yet the same color scheme that spoke so loudly of support for the Queen back then is now a prominent feature of the coronation of her loathed royal husband!

I would venture to guess that the fashionable ladies

involved in this particular ceremony are too high in the
instep to be aware of the meaning of the color scheme.
Except that it appeared so often in the caricatures—and
there were plenty of high-born folk at Brandenburg that day,
punting down the river and cheering for Revolution and
Reform.

Perhaps all that rebellion was only a season's amusement
for them, as easily changed as a hat or a pair of gloves.

It pains me when I think back to that day. I was never
a reformer. I mistrust revolution—the people who call for
one never seem to consider how many people have to die
in them. But for one wild moment, I had hope that things
might alter for the better, simply because people decided they
should.

Looking back, I marvel at such naivete. Surely a mature
woman of nearly five decades should have learned this lesson
before now?

Penelope wrote back:

I know just what you mean. Lady Summerville, who was so
willing to lead us to parade on the Queen's behalf, has been
holding more and more teas and luncheons in support of the
King. Lady S seems to think that the actual ceremony will
somehow transform him from the decadent prince we know
he's been into the virtuous king he ought to be. As though
he will treat power any differently now that it's officially
his to wield. To my bafflement, this seems to be a common
opinion, which otherwise reasonable people are willing to

believe. Mrs. Koskinen turns almost purple every time
someone repeats it, and I can't blame her.

    It troubles one's sleep. And there are so many better
reasons for sleeplessness—for instance . . .

The heightened attention to royal feasting and finery was
a goad to the reformers among the Melliton folk. Talk about
corruption and the government spiked bitterly—though not
where any of the Mendacity Society could easily overhear.

Mr. Thomas was muttering darkly on just this subject
one evening at the Four Swallows. Harry egged him on, to
John's amusement, while Nell Turner played instrumen-
tal tunes on her guitar, perched on a stool in the front left
corner—Penelope was happy to be squeezed up on the back
bench beside Agatha, thigh against thigh, as the music and
the familiar arguments swirled in the air around her.

They all jumped when the door banged open. There on
the tavern's threshold stood a tall and slender man: dark hair
tousled by the wind, hands braced to either side, his form
framed portrait-perfect in the doorway.

Nell looked up and her finger slipped; one jarringly
wrong note marred the tune, until she recovered herself and
determinedly redoubled her volume.

The audience went quiet—not precisely silent, but conversations trailed away and benches creaked as people shifted
their weight. Eyes grew narrow, and a ripple went through
the crowd as people turned to make sure they had a view.

Agatha leaned closer to Penelope. "Who's this?" she
breathed in her ear.

Penelope's mouth pinched. "Mr. Turner," she replied. "Nell's husband."

"I see." Agatha quirked a brow and considered the new arrival. Her frown showed she didn't like the conclusions she'd drawn. "Odds that he's here to grab a quick pint and enjoy himself?"

"Rather slim."

"Thought so."

Mr. Biswas had been bending down in the far corner, listening to Mr. Painter complain about curried lamb pies not being English enough. The barman straightened now, and though he smiled, there was a challenge in it. "Mr. Turner," he said, loud enough to be heard over Nell's determined strumming. "This is a surprise."

Penelope leaned forward to whisper to Mr. Thomas. "I thought Mr. Biswas banned him from the pub. What's he doing back? Did he get barred from every tavern in all of London, too?"

"Doubt it—why would he go to so much trouble?" Mr. Kitt murmured back. "He only gets thrown out of taverns his wife is playing in."

Mr. Thomas had a pinched look as he added: "Mr. Scriven tells me he got dismissed from Birkett's for brawling. Apparently he'd written another play, and showed it to someone, and took it poorly when they didn't praise it to the skies."

The tall man stepped forward, into the tavern proper. He was smiling, a cheerful, self-satisfied expression that made Penelope clench her teeth. "I'm not here for any of your watered-down ale, my good host," Mr. Turner said, to a small chorus of scornful sounds. He held up one graceful hand with a small bag, and shook it so it jingled. "I'm collecting a subscription for a pair of special constables, on behalf of the Melliton Auxiliary Branch of the Society for the Suppression of Vice and Mendacity."

A surprised murmur flickered round the room. Special constables hadn't been used in Melliton for decades. Not since the last food riots, in fact.

Mr. Turner winked at Mrs. Biswas, whose face went wooden. "It's the duty of all good Englishmen to assist the Mendacity Society in their devotion to the law and the crown."

"Is Melliton truly such a hotbed of unrest and sedition?" Mr. Biswas said with a snort, though his mouth had gone flat at the mention of the Society.

Mr. Turner opened his bag and held it out. "There's an easy way to prove where your loyalty lies."

Mr. Biswas scowled, and folded his arms pointedly over his chest.

Mr. Painter stood up with his nose in the air. "Well, I for one certainly care about the safety and decency of our village." He sniffed. A trio of copper coins tumbled from his hand into Mr. Turner's sack. "One for me—and one for our local veterans, who so valiantly defended the Crown on land and sea." He gestured ostentatiously at Mr. Kitt and Mr. Thomas. "They should not be asked to sacrifice more than they already have."

Mr. Kitt started up, face thunderous, but was pulled

back to his seat by Mr. Thomas's hand on his shoulder. Mr. Thomas's face was a mask of grim disappointment, paler than his wont; Penelope knew he loathed hearing mention of his years in the army, especially among such a crowd.

Around the room Mr. Turner went, collecting subscriptions from tavern patrons. Some donated with an air of glee in the gesture. Others looked unhappy but handed over a few coins after hearing him tease the ones who refused. Mr. Kitt rose and stomped pointedly out the door when the bag came his way. Mr. Thomas only shook his head; he sat stiffly as if tied to his seat, but there was a wild look to his eye.

Mr. Turner passed over Harry, John, Penelope, and Agatha as though they weren't even there.

Just as he completed his circuit through the bar, and Penelope thought he might be almost done and would actually depart, Mr. Turner turned toward his wife in the musician's corner by the hearth. "And of course I'll be taking those, Mrs. Turner," he said, opening a hungry palm toward the coins Nell had collected in a small bowl at her feet.

Nell finished her song, drawing out the last notes as though taking a bracing breath. Then, without so much as a glance at her husband, she picked up the bowl, poured her tips into her pocket, and sat on her stool with her hands clutched around her guitar.

"Ah," said Mr. Turner. "I see you want me to ask properly." He bowed and with a flourish went to one knee before the makeshift stage. "Eleanor Turner," he declaimed, "most loving and generous wife, I ask you to help me show this town the power of true, humble charity, in service of your

Christian faith, and good King George." He held out the subscription bag, as though offering obeisance to a monarch.

Someone snickered. Agatha Griffin huffed out an irritated breath.

Nell didn't look at him. She didn't move. She looked, Penelope thought, like a woman who knew there were traps all around her, no matter which way she tried to run.

"No?" Mr. Turner asked, in a voice of wounded surprise. "Think of your neighbors, and how they will whisper of your miserliness. Think of the law, which mandates that those coins you hoard are mine to dispose of as I see fit." His voice sharpened; instead of a broadsword brandish, it now turned as sharp and intimate as a knife. "What will Arthur say, when I tell him his mother refused to honor his father in such a small request?"

Nell winced, as this struck home.

This was too much for Mr. Biswas. "Get out, Mr. Turner," he growled, making the people nearest him jump in startlement. "You've collected your subscriptions—that will have to be enough."

"I'll leave when my wife does, Mr. Biswas," Mr. Turner said, and put his second knee down. He stayed there, smiling at Nell, as behind him the audience murmured in mingled discomfort and fascination.

Nell sucked in a breath and began playing—halting notes on the guitar, attempting her usual verve but falling short. Penelope's heart ached for her; Nell was used to putting on a show for the crowds, but not like this. Not where the entertainment was her humiliation.

Mr. Biswas moved forward, but stopped when Mr. Painter aggressively cleared his throat.

Harry and John glanced at each other, and stood up in a single swift motion.

Mr. Turner had his back to Penelope's table, so he didn't see the two men move until they were next to him. Harry's stocky, sturdy body was fairly vibrating with suppressed anger, while John's height let him loom over Mr. Turner in a way nobody else in the room could have done.

Mr. Turner kept his eyes, liquid and soulful, fixed on his wife.

"Come now," John said in gentle tones, while Harry bared his teeth in an expression nobody mistook for a smile. "Let her be. We're all enjoying the music, Mr. Turner."

The man's hands clenched into fists on his knees. "This is private business, Flood, between a *proper* husband and wife—I'll thank you not to interfere."

Penelope's stomach twisted at the implied insult. She didn't dare look away from John, even as Agatha muttered outrage by her side.

John looked at Harry with a question in his eyes—Harry nodded, and together they reached out to seize Mr. Turner.

They hauled him to his feet—easy enough, for two sailors, either one of whom outweighed the man they held. Mr. Turner looked right at Penelope, and *smiled*—that same smug, pleased expression that sent a bolt of pure terror lancing through Penelope's gut.

Then he dropped.

It was so swift and total a collapse that Mr. Turner had

to have done it on purpose: his legs simply gave way beneath him. John let go of him in surprise, and Mr. Turner clutched at one arm and began shouting agony and assault.

It was a shocking performance, and half the crowd whistled and hooted in reaction.

Mr. Painter bounded forward, sweaty and florid, and after a moment Mr. Turner permitted himself to be helped slowly to his feet. Mr. Painter scooped the subscription bag from the floor, glaring at John, while Mr. Turner put on his best stoic air as he walked toward the door, calling out to be taken to the physician.

A few scattered hands clapped, and one by one the usual conversations slunk back into the room.

Penelope walked over to Harry, who was speaking to Nell Turner in low, careful tones. "Are you alright?" she asked. "Do you need a place to stay for the night?"

"I'll have to," she said. "He'll give me and Arthur no rest tonight if I don't." Her eyes were still fixed on the door, as if she expected her husband to return at any moment and harass her further. One hand crept protectively into the pocket where she'd poured tonight's tips. "I was there when Lady Summerville's steward asked him to take up the subscription," she said. "They promised him a cut of however much he brought in. An inducement to exert himself, they said." Something in her expression hardened, and her singer's voice burned low and hot, a note in the same key as the fury in Penelope's chest. "He was going to take everything I'd earned, and give it to people who already have more than enough."

"What do you want to do?" Penelope asked.

"What else?" Nell lifted her head, eyes bright as fire. "I'm going to sing."

She grabbed her guitar, moved to the musician's corner, and plucked the opening notes of "Lady Spranklin."

The audience shouted in recognition—cheers mostly, though a few dissonant notes were heard. John began stomping time, and Harry's voice was—of course—one of the loudest when he joined in as Nell reached the chorus. A few of Mr. Painter's friends harrumphed and left in a huff.

Mr. Thomas slipped away, too, shortly after, muttering something about seeing to Mr. Kitt.

Penelope resumed her seat beside Agatha on the bench. "Well, it could have been worse," she said, grasping for any sliver of comfort.

"It's going to get worse," Agatha promised darkly. But all the same, she squeezed hard and didn't let go when Penelope boldly slipped a hand over hers beneath the table.

Chapter Twenty-Three

Agatha and Penelope were sitting down to a late breakfast the next morning when they were interrupted by a knock at the door and the appearance of a very nervous Jenny. "Mr. Buckley and Mr. Painter, ma'am," the maid said, teeth worrying her lower lip.

Mr. Painter Agatha knew—and the dour, square-faced Mr. Buckley she vaguely remembered from church at Christmas. He was clearly in charge, leading the way into the breakfast room with his jaw set and his mouth at an unhappy angle. "Pardon the intrusion, Mrs. Flood. We're looking for Mrs. Turner, and we heard she was staying here with you."

Mrs. Turner was in the kitchen, helping Mrs. Braintree with her distillery. There was a moment where Agatha was sure she could see the words to explain this truth arranging themselves on Penelope's tongue.

But then the beekeeper stopped, put on a false, polite smile and said: "And what is it you want with Mrs. Turner?"

"I'm sorry to say we've been asked to bring her before the magistrates," Mr. Buckley explained.

Agatha's appetite vanished. She set her fork aside, tea and toast churning in her stomach.

Penelope, still smiling, sent her sharp little knife sailing through a piece of pound cake. "Whatever for?"

Mr. Buckley cast a nervous look at Mr. Painter, then back to the two women. "Her performance last night may have constituted a breach of the peace," he said. "The justices are holding a special session this morning to inquire into the matter."

"That sounds quite serious," Penelope said sympathetically. Another few stabs of the knife. "But—pardon me for asking—what does it have to do with the two of you?"

Mr. Buckley's dour expression doured further.

Mr. Painter puffed himself up like an irritable chicken. "We are special constables, of course. Appointed this very morning, by Mr. Oliver and Squire Theydon himself."

"Of course you are," Penelope said, so much honey dripping from her tones that Agatha's own teeth ached to hear it. The blonde woman dabbed at her lip with a napkin and rose from the table. "If you gentleman will wait outside, Mrs. Turner and I will be with you shortly."

Mr. Painter looked as though he wanted to argue this, but then Mr. Buckley seized him by the elbow. Nodding brusquely to Penelope, he towed his fellow constable outside, to wait in the lane.

Agatha waited until she heard the *snick* that meant Jenny had shut the door behind them. "What do we do, then?" she said to Penelope. "I take Mrs. Turner out the back and into the wood, while you stall and then eventually 'discover' she's run off?"

Penelope grinned, a sunburst of a smile that made Agatha's heart swell with joy. "I always knew you'd be a natural conspirator—but unless Nell wants otherwise, I think this is a problem we should face head-on." Her smile turned evil at the corners. "All three of us."

She walked down the hallway toward the kitchen, Agatha scrambling up from the table to catch up.

"She was singing the Wasp's ballads for half the evening last night," Agatha cautioned, balling her hands in her skirts so she could match Penelope's determined stride. "Those have already been labeled seditious libel."

"The printed broadsides, yes," Penelope returned. "But *singing* them isn't necessarily criminal. It all depends on how you argue the law."

"And how do you think Mr. Oliver will argue?" Agatha returned.

Penelope's hands clenched. "I intend to be there to find out."

They collected Nell, who went grim at the news but who was not surprised: "Breach of the peace—that's one of the ones they like to use against ballad sellers." She accepted Penelope's offer of help, and the three of them met the special constables in the lane.

Penelope walked arm in arm with Mrs. Turner, head high, an unaccustomed bonnet jammed over her curls. Mr. Painter went in front, huffing angrily into his mustache whenever the ladies behind walked too slowly for his taste.

Agatha went behind, dragging her boots in the dust.

It chilled her to leave the blue vault of the spring sky and step into the dead gray stone space of the vestry, musty with age, where the sunlight had to claw its way down through centuries upon centuries of pious dust. Mr. Oliver was sitting at a broad wooden desk, polishing his spectacles, and Squire Theydon was paging through the third volume of Burn's *The Justice of the Peace, and Parish Officer.* They both rose when the party arrived.

The ladies were now officially outnumbered. Agatha tried not to let her nerves show in her face.

"Ah, Mrs. Flood," said the vicar. "I wondered if you might come in person."

"You know I always want to see the right thing done, Mr. Oliver," Penelope replied. She dragged one of the heavy chairs over, and took a seat as close to Mrs. Turner as she could.

The vicar smiled beatifically. "Then let's not dawdle."

He proceeded to open the session with all proper oaths and forms, which ate up several minutes and caused Agatha's eyes to glaze over and her brain to turn into porridge. Even Mr. Buckley was looking a little dazed by the time Mr. Oliver finished the forty-three separate attestations of loyalty and honor to King George. He pronounced each one quite as seriously as if the monarch would magically know if he skipped one or two of them.

Mrs. Turner was sworn in, and the twisty legal arguments began.

It was, as Penelope had said, not at all settled if Eleanor Turner had committed a crime or not. It depended on so many interwoven details: whether the "Lady Spranklin" tune referred to Lady Summerville, a full catalog of the ballad's innuendoes—which were apparently something altogether else in legal terms than what Agatha understood them to be in everyday English; separately, whether the song was a public slander when sung, a libel when printed, or merely an insult delivered between private parties, whether performing the ballad counted as a new publication of that libel or not, how the character and context of the Four Swallows impinged upon all these questions . . .

Agatha found a lot of it impossible to follow—though Mrs. Turner apparently didn't, and was quick to cite certain statutes and cases in her defense, a few of which had Squire Theydon flipping through the pages of Burn like a card sharp shuffling a dodgy deck. This was clearly not the ballad singer's first time in front of a magistrate, but as the arguments went on and on and on, her voice grew higher and more frantic, and Penelope's polite posture turned more and more wooden.

Agatha squirmed in her seat, and felt helpless, and tamped down the desire to hit someone—anyone—if it would speed things along. Trial by combat suddenly seemed an eminently sensible system.

Mr. Oliver, too, was looking more than a little frayed at the edges. "I do think you might be reasonable, Mrs. Turner," he said with a long-suffering sigh. "I understand that the Four Swallows offers you gainful employment—though I do note that, as a churchwoman, you ought to be frugal enough to support your family handily on the salary your husband brings in, or to have him apply to the parish officers if you are in need of relief."

Mrs. Turner snorted, either at the uselessness of the suggestion or the description of herself as a *churchwoman*.

"Perhaps you might consider more wholesome subjects of performance," Squire Theydon offered. "My old nurse used to sing 'An Hundred Godly Lessons' to me before bedtime, and it always put me right to sleep."

"I'm sure it did," the singer muttered.

The good squire's brows beetled.

Mr. Oliver sighed. "It showed exceedingly poor judgment, Mrs. Turner, that you picked such a notorious piece to perform before an audience who had already been worked up into a froth by the evening's dramatics. I understand you are not the author of the slanderous song, and so are not originally liable for its harms where the law is concerned—"

Mrs. Turner, Penelope, and Agatha all breathed a little easier.

"—but I have to consider something more than the law: I have to consider what is good. For Melliton, and for the good householders of the parish. So if my fellow justice of the peace agrees with me . . ." Squire Theydon was already nodding. "Then I think it only fit to demand a surety for your future good behavior . . ." He licked his lips. "How does Burn put it, Mr. Theydon?"

"'*He*—' that's us justices, of course '*—he has a discretionary power to take such surety of all those whom he shall have just cause to suspect to be dangerous, quarrelsome, or scandalous; as of those who sleep in the day, and go abroad in the night; and of* such as keep suspicious company; and of such as are generally suspected to be robbers, and the like—'"

"Yes, thank you, Mr. Theydon," the vicar said. "I don't know about 'dangerous,' Mrs. Turner—but 'quarrelsome' and 'scandalous' certainly seem to fit. Let the surety be set at: ten pounds."

The singer gasped in horror. Penelope's hand flew to her mouth.

And Agatha—well, Agatha felt grim certainty roll over her like the tide. The sum was astronomical, far more than Mrs. Turner could earn even if she sang for a year straight. This was deliberate. This was meant to ruin her.

It was pure and petty tyranny, done for spite's sake.

"She cannot pay that, Mr. Oliver," Penelope objected. "You must know she cannot."

"Then she will be imprisoned," Mr. Oliver said pleasantly. "Until such a time as she has worked off her debt. With her child, of course," he said, nodding. "We are not monsters."

This was too much. Agatha rocketed up out of her chair as though someone had lit a firework under her seat. "The surety will be paid, Mr. Oliver."

Everyone swiveled to stare at her, even Penelope.

Agatha felt the heat rise in her cheeks, but barreled onward. "I will vouchsafe the sum on Mrs. Turner's behalf."

"You know the money will be forfeit if she errs again," cautioned the vicar.

Agatha almost laughed in his face, but managed to turn it into a cough and a demure widowly nod. "Mrs. Turner has been a successful composer of ballads for my press," she said. "I value her work and have every faith in her character."

Mrs. Turner blinked.

Mr. Oliver read out the closing ceremony for the session. Penelope was up as soon as he closed the book, nodding smartly and taking poor Mrs. Turner by the elbow.

Agatha clasped her hands behind her back—the better not to wrap them around Mr. Oliver's comfortable neck—and followed the other two women out of the vestry.

Sunshine and birdsong and a blossoming world, every sweet note and scent of it an affront. The three women walked down the road: Mrs. Turner's gait timid, as though she didn't dare draw more of the world's attention, Penelope's stomping louder than you'd think possible without her sturdy boots.

And Agatha, lagging behind. She made her feet hurry until she drew even with the other two. "I'll have Mr. Downes send the surety to Mr. Oliver by the end of today," she said, for lack of anything better to offer.

Mrs. Turner nodded, but anguish still clouded her features. "I don't know how I'll pay you back, Mrs. Griffin." Her mouth curved in a bitter twist. "I don't suppose I can consider this an advance on the next fifty or so ballads?"

"If you like," Agatha said, helpless to find any better response. "But I won't be holding you to that, if it causes you pain."

"Probably wise," Mrs. Turner went on. "I don't know when I'll find the time to write even the next one, now. It's just all so—impossible." She stopped, hands clenching her sides. "I can't escape him, not under the law. My husband's never laid a hand on me in anger. He just—he just *takes*, that's all. Whatever I try to hold back for Arthur or myself he swallows up, and asks for more." She wrapped her arms around her torso, holding herself together. Her voice lowered to a sadder register. "I wrote love songs for him once, you know."

Penelope smiled, and said: "I remember." Mrs. Turner looked at her. "They were more beautiful than he deserved."

They walked on. Agatha's eye was caught by a bumblebee trundling blissfully over the hyssop blossoms by the side of the road, rounder and larger than any of Penelope's honeybees. Her fuzzy legs were caked thick with pollen, almost full enough for her to carry back to the hive, where her sisters waited to help with the work—and where her brothers lounged in the doorway, like lazy lords, waiting to be attended . . .

"What if we could get you away from him?" Agatha asked.

Mrs. Turner's step faltered. "What's that?"

Penelope stopped dead in the middle of the road. "Griffin . . . By all the stars, Griffin, do you have an idea?"

"I might," Agatha said. "Look, Mrs. Turner, I'll have to ask her about it—but what if you moved in with Joanna Molesey?"

"The poet?" Mrs. Turner's eyes were wide as the sky around them. "I've never even met her."

"But you've been singing her ballads for months," Agatha countered. "And now you've landed in all this mess because of them." She flicked her skirts, shaking off the dust. "We could make a reasonable argument that she owes you some consideration for having put you in this position."

"We could tell her how much it would annoy Mr. Oliver if she helped you," Penelope said.

"And Lady Summerville," Agatha added. "*Especially* Lady Summerville."

Penelope began to laugh, stretching her arms out as though she could reach to the horizon.

"Joanna's an elderly woman, on her own for the first time in decades," Agatha went on. "Surely she's in need of a companion? One who is as quick-witted as she is, and who appreciates the sharper sort of poetry?"

"What do you think, Nell?" Penelope asked. "Would it work? Would it help?"

"Would I have to leave Arthur?" Mrs. Turner asked instantly.

Agatha grinned. "Let's write to her and ask, shall we?"

Joanna Molesey, it turned out, was *ecstatic* to thwart both Mr. Oliver and Lady Summerville, especially if it meant gaining a lively and musical companion. Before the end of the week Nell and Arthur Turner were safely ensconced in Gower Street, with promises that if Mr. Turner tried anything by way of the law, Mrs. Molesey would find the most ruthless solicitor London had to offer. Mrs. Turner and her son were safe.

Penelope and Agatha were insufferably proud of themselves.

The happy glow lasted until Agatha's return the following week. Penelope walked with her up the hill to Abington Hall, through the hollowed-out sculpture gardens (Penelope stole a kiss in every place where a statue had been). But when they turned the corner to the bee garden, they found it crowded with Lady Summerville and a half-dozen gardeners.

Abington Hall's mistress stood beneath the stippled shadows of a lacy parasol, though the winter sun could hardly pose a threat even to the palest complexion. She frowned at Agatha and Penelope's entrance, sniffing at their dusty boots and baggy trousers. "May I help you—ladies?"

Agatha noticed the slight pause, and bristled.

Penelope hurried to smooth things over. "We didn't mean to trouble you, Lady Summerville: we only came to see about the hives." She glanced around at the workingmen around her. "Are you planning some changes to the bee garden?"

"I am," Lady Summerville confirmed. Her smile was vulpine. "I am getting rid of it."

"What?" Penelope choked.

Lady Summerville waved delicately at the ancient medieval wall in which the boles were set. "I fancy a lawn and a prospect, so I am having this all knocked down and smoothed over."

Penelope looked around wildly at the growth of centuries: the lavender, the hawthorn and hyssop, the knobby apple tree that had been bearing fruit since Queen Elizabeth's day. And the bee boles, which had sheltered countless generations of loyal insects. "But—but you can't," she said weakly, breathless with the shock. Then, more firmly: "Those hives aren't yours to dispose of. Not according to your aunt's will."

"Perhaps not," Lady Summerville said sweetly. "She left you the hives specifically, if I recall."

"She did."

"But not their products, I think?"

Penelope looked at Agatha, who only shrugged, equally baffled.

"You've been harvesting honey and wax from them, have you not?" her ladyship went on, in that same sugary tone.

"I've been giving it to Mrs. Bedford," Penelope retorted hotly.

"All of it?"

"I took one jar to Mr. Scriven, last fall, when his throat was poorly," Penelope allowed. "But the hives—"

"From a legal standpoint, Mrs. Flood, that could be considered stealing."

And Lady Summerville smiled, as though she'd said something pleasant.

Penelope's blood was running painfully hot in her veins. "And what does the law call it when you destroy someone else's property for your own selfish gain?"

"Improvement," said Lady Summerville.

A seventh gardener appeared. With an ax. Which he placed carefully near the roots of the apple tree.

Penelope thought she might be sick. "You have no right to touch those hives," she bit out.

"Perhaps I don't," Lady Summerville allowed. "The will was so very clear, after all. But how do you think those hives will fare, when there are no more flowers here for them to feast on? Surely it is kinder to put them to the sulfur now, rather than leave them to suffer or to wander the countryside in high summer with no place to call home. I understand it would be difficult at this time of year for them to make enough honey to last through the winter."

Penelope thought of starving bees, and shivered. "Why are you doing this?" she asked plaintively.

The viscountess pressed a hand to her chest, as though Penelope's question had pained her. "Because you have chosen the wrong side, Mrs. Flood. You traipse about the countryside without a husband's oversight. You encourage the lower orders to follow the most vulgar customs, which ought to shame any God-fearing parishioner. I organized a very proper, ladylike procession in support of our Queen—and you exploited that day to gain attention for yourself, with help from your scribbling friend. You have defended indecency, encouraged the worst kind of irreverence for the law, and interfered with those who would keep Melliton respectable and Christian and pure. And now I must ask you to leave my grounds." She spun the parasol handle ever so gently, making the shadows pass over her face like birds fleeing a storm. "Before I have you removed for trespassing."

Mr. Oliver, poring over the Aeneid at the long table in his study, was quite apologetic when Penelope and Agatha stormed in to report this news. "My sister has rather objected to your friend's defense of Mrs. Turner, I gather," said the vicar.

Agatha's mouth set in a regretful, anxious line. Penelope clenched her jaw and rolled her eyes: this wasn't Agatha's fault. This was Lady Summerville's malice, unpredictable and merciless.

"I could perhaps offer you a sum equal to the value of the bees," Mr. Oliver went on. "In recompense."

Penelope slapped one hand down on the varnished wood. "I do not want *money*," she all but hissed. "I want to care for those hives. As your aunt wished me to do."

His brows peaked apologetically, like hands at prayer. "If my sister will not allow you on the estate, I don't see how it's possible," he said. "It is a question of following the law."

"To the point of absurdity?" Agatha scoffed.

Mr. Oliver sent her a scathing glance, then recovered his face. "If you and my sister cannot work out some compromise, Mrs. Flood, I'm afraid I will have to agree the hives must be destroyed. You know as well as I do that they will not survive once she has made her improvements to the garden."

Penelope ground her teeth so hard she feared they'd crack. "They can if they are *moved*."

But the vicar was already back among the Latins. "I will give you until Sunday to come to some mutual agreement."

Penelope stalked out of the vicarage, hands clenched into fists, arms stiff at the sides of her trousered thighs. Mr. Oliver, she knew, was expecting her to behave as she always had with him. He thought she'd be reasonable, biddable, and yielding.

He thought she'd be *good*.

She'd been good for years. Decades. Partly because it was her nature, partly because Mr. Oliver had stepped into Owen's vacant place. Sometimes she was still surprised to see his face at the pulpit in place of her sunny, softhearted brother. She'd been giving him Owen's share of deference, she realized now, expecting something like Owen's love and graciousness in return.

It had never happened.

It was never going to happen.

Rage and embarrassment at such a fundamental error thundered in her soul, and she turned from the road to strike one hand flat against the tall, sleek trunk of a mountain ash. "Damn him!" she cried, her eyes squeezing shut in shame.

In an instant, Agatha's arms were around her, turning her, wrapping her tight and holding her close. Penelope clutched at her beloved, shaking, burying her face in the familiar smells of sweat and skin and old, soft cloth. She felt stricken, like a wounded thing, even as she looked back and saw clearly that the blow had been struck years and years ago. She just hadn't felt it until now.

She had wasted too much time fretting over doing good. It was time to do what was *right*.

She let herself enjoy Agatha's embrace for one breath more, then pulled away and dashed the tears from her eyes. Agatha was watching her closely; Penelope met her gaze and said: "I have another conspiracy for you."

Agatha's eyes flashed, her lips curved in sly hope—and she saluted.

Together they marched to the Koskinen's farm, just below Backey Green. Mrs. Koskinen greeted them at the door, though her confusion was plain enough.

"We need your help, Emma," Penelope said, getting straight to the point. "How does one go about arranging for an action in secret?"

Mrs. Koskinen's face lit up, as her husband shook his head in resignation.

Small beer, it turned out, could be used in place of ink on a sheet of paper; it faded into near-invisibility, until the paper was held up close to a candle. Then the beer would burn, and the hidden letters reappear. "Nell and I would set up a batch of broadsides special," Emma said, as she poured them tea in her cozy kitchen, "and then hand them out the night before whatever it was we were planning." She shook her head. "I was thinking of approaching Mr. Biswas to help, now that Nell's gone."

"No need to wait," Agatha said. "It won't look too odd if I take over for a night or two."

"Then I can tell you who to give them to," Mrs. Koskinen said.

"Why did you never tell me this before?" Penelope asked.

Mrs. Koskinen's gaze was steady. "You were always good friends with Mr. Oliver," she said. "It seemed like too big a risk."

"Well," said Penelope after a moment. "I'm just impressed you were able to keep such a secret for so long, in this town."

Mrs. Koskinen's answering smile was proud and sly.

They would need only a few hands for the work: Harry and John were happy enough to offer help, and Mr. Thomas and Mr. Kitt were high on Mrs. Koskinen's list of reliable troublemakers. Agatha distributed code-marked ballads using the same system Nell had, and nobody was any the wiser. Penelope's list of equipment gave way to hasty preparations— wheelbarrows and makeshift bee veils and a truly alarming number of heavy gloves—and the next evening Penelope kept a careful eye on the sun as it sank, and the moon as it slowly but steadily rose in the sky like heaven's benediction on her plans.

Harry only grinned when she pointed out it was full, and would help light their way. "You sound like Mother used to, when her blood was up."

Penelope preened beneath the compliment.

They waited, in separate homes, while the bells of St. Ambrose's tolled eight, nine, ten. At half-past eleven, the conspirators all gathered behind the churchyard: Agatha and Penelope, Harry and John, and Mr. Kitt, all in dark clothes, lower faces masked, muslin veils bundled high on hats and heads. They looked oddly ornate and festive, as though the ancient Melliton dead had risen from their graves for an eldritch moonlit picnic among the headstones.

Silently, Penelope waved her friends to follow, and they crept up the long, high hill.

When the bells struck midnight, the sound covered the noise of the Abington Hall garden gate squeaking open.

The smoker hissed like a miniature dragon as Penelope wreathed all six hives in soothing pine-and-lavender smoke. Half the garden's plants were dug up already, she noted with affronted fury: the rows of strawberries and hyssop were gone, and the honeysuckle torn up by the roots and left stretched out on the ground like a bevy of lovesick maidens.

When the smoke had taken effect, Penelope waved the others forward, and they went about stealing the hives.

One slumbering skep went into the bottom of each wheelbarrow, a straw cover placed over its open base to protect the drowsy bees dozing in their combs. A board went over the top of the barrow, and another skep could be balanced on top of that, with twine quickly lashing it in place so as not to tip over on the journey.

The six hives were loaded up in silence, and the thieves wound their silent way back through the labyrinth and to the garden gate. Penelope caught Agatha's eye, and saw her grinning silver in the dimness. For one glorious, moonlit moment, Penelope's heart soared with triumph.

Then a shadow loomed in a window, and a cry went up from the house.

They were discovered.

"Go!" Penelope hissed.

Harry took off with the first barrow, bounding down the hill and into the woods, where it would take a bloodhound to trace him. Footmen and gardeners poured out of the Hall, carrying any handy weapons and shouting "Thieves! Burglars! Murder!" indiscriminately into the night. Mr. Kitt, steering the second barrow down the hill as skillfully as if it were a ship under sail, made it safely to the wood line, with Agatha and Penelope pelting after and ducking beneath the dark protection of alder and pine.

Penelope clutched the rough bark and turned frightened eyes upon her husband, who was doing his best with the third wheelbarrow. But he was so tall, and the barrow tilted more boldly forward in his hands, and as she watched with bated breath, the front wheel of the barrow hit a rock and staggered, dumping the top skep from its hasty ties and sending it bouncing over the ground.

Penelope would have rushed forward, but Agatha's hand clamped around her wrist and held her back.

Men, at least a dozen, poured over the crest of the hill. John scooped puzzled bees and broken comb back into the skep, and *shoved* the whole apparatus the last ten feet, to where his wife and her lover stood in the shadows.

Penelope lunged forward and dragged the barrow into the trees.

John waved at her to hurry, then took off running—but not toward them. Sidelong, parallel to the wood, pulling the muslin from his head and waving it like a banner as he made for the bright ribbon of the open road. "Never catch me!" he sang out, with the full force of his sailor's lungs.

The pursuers spotted him, sent up the cry, and turned as one.

"Come on," Agatha hissed, as Penelope's throat ached with unvoiced shouts and pleas. Each woman took one side of the wheelbarrow, and together they hurried it bumping down the track in the wood, toward Mr. Thomas and Mr. Kitt's house. There they found the others, sitting tense around the faint embers in the kitchen hearth.

Harry bounded up and wrapped one arm around them both. "Thank god," he muttered—but Penelope pulled back, heartsick, as he asked: "Where's John?"

"I don't know," she said, her fear clogging her throat.

"The barrow fell, and he got it to us, then drew the pursuit away," Agatha said.

Harry laughed, half knowing, half bitter. "He's too chivalrous for his own good, that man."

"Maybe they didn't catch him?" Mr. Kitt hoped.

"They'll catch all of us, if we're not careful," Agatha replied.

One by one, they split off: Mr. Kitt heading toward the Four Swallows where he'd spent the first part of the evening, and where Mr. Thomas had remained, buying rounds very visibly and giving them both something of an alibi. The others kept to the darkest spots, avoiding the open roads and holding their breaths, listening for the sounds of pursuit.

The hue and cry was just starting to spread through the town when Agatha and Penelope reached Fern Hall; Harry, who arrived a few minutes later, unusually pale and out of breath, informed them that the Four Swallows had been shouting about thieves and villains when he'd slipped past beneath the curtain of willows along the riverbank.

But by the time dawn rose, all of Melliton was awake and aware of the news:

John Flood had been taken by the special constables.

Chapter Twenty-Four

Mr. Oliver's difficulty was this: to properly charge someone with theft, one had to bring evidence he'd stolen something. And while the Abington hives were certainly gone, and Mr. Flood had been apprehended in the neighborhood at the time they vanished, nobody seemed to be able to find any of the hives at all.

They certainly weren't at Fern Hall, which the special constables and Mr. Oliver had walked around no fewer than three times, eyes peeled for stolen beehives tucked into an empty stall in the stables or hidden beneath a draping of canvas. But Penelope's leaf hive and her glass-topped skeps were the only bees present, and not even Mr. Oliver's palpable suspicion could make the stolen swarms appear out of thin air.

But John was not to be let off entirely. Mr. Oliver couldn't charge him with the felony—and six full hives' worth of bees and wax and honey would have doubtlessly earned a sentence of transportation—but since John's shouting had roused fully half the town from the sweet slumber of their beds, the vicar could certainly bring the full wrath of the law (or rather, the full wrath of Mr. Oliver) down on him for a breach of the peace.

To the horror of his captain and his wife, John was sentenced to spend an afternoon in the stocks. It was an archaic punishment, not much used in these more enlightened times—but Mr. Oliver was keen to make of John Flood an example in whatever way he could.

"This is all my fault," Penelope whispered.

She and Agatha were at Fern Hall. Mrs. Braintree had brought them some of her latest distilling to pour into their tea, but it hadn't stopped Penelope's hands from shaking. Agatha had wrapped her in blankets and cozied up beside her in the window seat—but Penelope couldn't shake the guilty feeling that had haunted her since she'd returned from visiting the jail with Harry.

"Nonsense," Agatha said, staunch and loyal. Not that Penelope had expected anything less. How could anyone be so lovely even when glaring? "They're being terrible, simply because they can. It is not in the least your fault."

It was shameful that this made Penelope feel better. Her feeling better was useless, because it did nothing whatsoever for John. The stocks were better than the pillory—if only just—but they were still dangerous. People died in the stocks. "Mr. Scriven says that some of the Mendacity subscribers plan to bring bushels of vegetables for the people to throw at him." Her mouth twisted. "For entertainment."

Because of who he is. Because of who he loves. They didn't have to say it aloud. It was written in Harry's unwonted silence, and the anxious clasp of Penelope's hands.

Mr. Oliver couldn't prove that, either—but he'd sent Harry away for the same reason, so many years ago. And now, with John, he had an excuse for a punishment he thought the man deserved—even if it wasn't what he'd been convicted of in the records.

Agatha's hands closed around hers. "They'll run out of vegetables eventually."

"Then they'll turn to bricks and stones," Penelope said grimly. "Whatever's handy. Because by then they'll be in a mood for throwing." She gulped at her tea, feeling the bite of hot alcohol burn down her throat. "And that's when it becomes dangerous. My god—I wish I could just *do* something!"

Agatha cocked a head. "Like what?"

"Like . . . like throw something back. Stand there facing them down, and defend my friend. My family." Penelope stared out the window. From here she could just see the edge of the red tile roof that sheltered her leaf hive. Worker bees clouded the hive entrance, guarding it against intruders and thieves, anyone who would threaten their queen and their colony.

What wouldn't Penelope give for a stinger of her own?

"The Romans used to use bees in war," she said grimly. "I read the accounts in Isabella's library. They'd throw whole hives over the walls of besieged cities before they attacked."

"I imagine that was very effective," Agatha said.

Penelope grimaced. "I wish we could do the same to

anyone who dares show up tomorrow, while John is in the stocks."

Agatha sat up straight. "Can't we?"

Penelope snorted. "We could, but someone would be sure to get stung—John, most likely, and that would defeat the whole purpose of defending him. And people have been known to die from being stung." She shook her head. "I couldn't live with myself."

"And you call yourself a beekeeper." Penelope's head whipped up, but the shock of the insult melted away when Agatha went on: "All you need, my dear, is bees without stingers."

"Bees without—" Penelope snapped her mouth shut, as the full force of the idea washed over her, brilliant as the dawn. "Griffin," she breathed, "you genius. If Pompey'd had you by his side, he'd never have lost to Caesar."

"I'll have to take your word on that."

Penelope laughed and dragged her into the apiary.

They did the circuit at record speed, hurrying through the twilight woods and across fields turned blue-green by the coming night. By the time they returned to Fern Hall they had half a dozen clay jars, with a little comb for sustenance, the jar mouths closed over with net to allow for airflow in and out overnight while the bees were sleeping.

Penelope herself lay awake until nearly dawn, clutching Agatha's arms against her waist, the warmth and strength of the woman like armor against Penelope's back. Penelope had a husband, if in name only, and she'd had lovers before—but this was the first time she'd had someone who felt like . . . What was the word?

A *helpmeet*, that was it. She'd always thought love was about feelings, and feelings were very fine things—but a helpmeet was all about *doing* something for someone. Putting in work, and effort, and support.

Until Agatha, Penelope had never had someone offer her that. And now she wondered that she'd managed to live so long without it. She smiled against the darkness in self-deprecation: clearly her greediness knew no bounds. Once she would have given everything just to love and be loved. Now she wanted love, and something more besides.

She'd be wanting everything, before long.

Morning brought a gray dawn, and a chill deep down in the pit of her stomach. Penelope dressed in her usual kit, gulped some tea and toast, and bundled up her jars.

Agatha waited by the door, in her blue coat and gloves. She helped Penelope pin on the bee veil—even though the veil shouldn't be necessary, they'd decided it lent a certain authenticity to the proceedings. "Are you ready?" she asked.

"No," Penelope admitted unhappily, making Agatha's lips quirk, "but we're out of time, so let's go."

The stocks were in the old Melliton barracks, a ring of squat brick buildings which had stood empty since the end of the war. Mr. Thomas had once been stationed here, before he'd gone on half pay. He was here now, standing far back against the wall, with Mr. Kitt very close by his side; Penelope couldn't tell which of them was holding the other up, but they both looked nauseous. A small crowd had already gathered: Penelope spotted Mr. Buckley and Mrs. Plumb, but also Mr. Downes, Mr. Scriven, and a gaggle of village children. Mr. Painter and Squire Theydon stood by a barrel full of what looked like moldy beetroots, knobby radishes, and spring potatoes that bristled with too many eyes.

Agatha's gaze took in all of this, but she said only: "Do you want me to come up there with you?"

Penelope shook her head. "Better if it's just me," she said. "Valiant wife defending her husband, and all that."

"Very romantic," Agatha replied, and gave Penelope's arm a supportive squeeze. Then she faded back to stand with Mr. Kitt and Mr. Thomas.

Penelope slipped through the crowd toward the stocks, just as John was led out. God, but he looked ragged: hardly surprising after the night he must have had. His wild eyes ran over the crowd—then stopped, as if snagged, on where Harry stood at the very front, brow thunderous, great arms folded. A look strung between them: anguish and faith and grim understanding, all mingled together.

It nearly broke Penelope's heart. Then hot steel flowed into the broken places. Her head came up, her breath came faster, and she wound around clumps of villagers until she was standing at her brother's elbow.

"Afternoon," she said to him.

He glowered in her direction—not *at* her, she knew, but at the general glower-worthiness of the whole event. The constables were fastening John's feet into the stocks now, two thick wooden pieces trapping him in a sitting position on the hard-packed ground. Harry's brow furrowed at this, then furrowed twice as deep when he took in Penelope's beekeeping garb, and the bag over her shoulder. "What's all this, Pen?"

She gave him a tight smile. "I'm here to uphold my marriage vows: mutual society, help—" she tapped the first jar, which buzzed in response "—and comfort."

For perhaps the first time in his whole life, Harry was struck speechless.

Penelope wished she had the time to enjoy it. She patted her brother's arm, and turned back to John.

Whatever office Mr. Oliver had to recite, he'd finished it, and retired to a safe distance. Penelope waited, hoping against hope that perhaps she wouldn't even need to—

But no, someone in the back called something foul, and someone else laughed. Mr. Oliver had his best vicarish face on, but there was a satisfied glow about him that Penelope resented.

A radish flew from the crowd and thunked against the wood by John's right ankle. He flinched, clenched his jaw, and then shouted a retort.

More insults came at once—they would have, Penelope knew, even if John had held silent in the face of abuse. This wasn't something he could stop: the point of this punishment was to make him a target, and everyone knew it. He was now a man people were officially permitted to do violence to.

Someone was bound to take advantage. There were people like that everywhere, even in Melliton.

Penelope had come today to stop those people from getting what they wanted.

She didn't want to wait for things to get worse, either. She stepped forward, ducking a little as more vegetables flew out of the crowd. A puzzled murmur rose up—you weren't supposed to get between the crowd and the person in the stocks. John's eyes widened, and his mouth went slack with surprise, as she stepped up right beside him, and turned.

Her breath froze in her chest.

It was vastly different standing here, the focus of every eye, the center of this circle of angry folk and the hollowed-out remnants of a war. For a moment the steel in her spine softened, melting beneath the heat of the mob's regard.

A flash of blue. Agatha Griffin, at the back wall, raising a hand.

Agatha Griffin, saluting. As one would to a general.

Just like that, Penelope could breathe again. Just like that, courage fountained up within her.

"Hello, everyone," she called, her voice echoing off the red brick around her. She grinned, enjoying the wave of surprise that rippled over the crowd, their anger breaking like a wave against the cheer in her voice. "I'll give you until the count of five."

"Until what?" Mr. Downes called back.

"Until you wish you'd left when I told you to," Penelope said. She pulled the muslin down, veiling her grin, and took the first clay jar out of her bag. "You all know I spend my time seeing to the beehives of the town," she said. "The bees know me quite well at this point. They're fond of me. They haven't stung me in years. I wonder . . ."

She shook the jar, and the first few rows of people took an automatic step back when it began buzzing furiously.

Penelope said, as loud as she could: "I wonder if these bees know not to sting any of *you*.

"One."

Mr. Downes was already making his way toward the entrance, his eyes wide and wild at the edges. Mr. Thomas had a hand over his mouth, and Mr. Kitt was laughing silently, eyes sparkling with vicious glee. Agatha, grinning, must have told them Penelope's plan.

Penelope grinned back. "Two."

Squire Theydon had pulled out one of Burn's volumes and was hastily flipping through it, even as Mr. Oliver grasped his arm and glared at Penelope in mute rage.

She shook the jar again. "Three."

One boy pelted out of the barracks, two other lads hot on his heels. The rest of the crowd shifted anxiously, muttering to one another. Knuckles went white on fists, and the soft mush of squashed vegetables squelched between tightened fingers.

Penelope raised the jar high. "Four."

Mr. Oliver dropped Squire Theydon's arm and started for her.

"Five!" Penelope looked the vicar dead in the eye, and hurled the jar to the ground at his feet.

It burst open in *spectacular* fashion, and a cloud of angry bees poured out.

The mob exploded into movement. People were running; people were screaming. Bees zipped every which way, bright gold and black against the earth and brick, all the more terrible for being so visible. The swirl of the crowd dragged Mr. Oliver away, until he had no choice but to turn and flee with the rest, legs pumping as he sprinted for safety, head clamped over his broad-brimmed hat. Penelope kept herself anchored with one hand on John's shoulder, as the crowd scattered itself to the four winds.

A strangled cry from her husband; Penelope looked down to see him waving away a furious bee, which buzzed aggressively around his head. "It's alright," she said on a laugh, crouching down so only he could hear her. "They're only drones."

"Drones?" he echoed, head swiveling to stare up at her.

"They're stingless. They won't hurt you. They won't hurt anybody." She grinned. "But don't spoil the fun just yet."

For the next few hours, she stayed by her husband's side. Every time someone approached, she would heft another jar in her hand and start counting.

Nobody lasted past three, after the first time.

It was almost anticlimactic, Penelope thought wildly. She'd made six bee bombs, and only gotten to use one. Later she could open the jars and let the unexploded bees find their way home again—but for now, best to keep all her ammunition intact in case she needed it.

But evening came on, and Mr. Oliver and the special constables returned to let John out. His punishment had technically been served under the law, after all.

Penelope considered a curtsey, but she was wearing trousers, and feeling more triumphant than polite. "Good evening, sir," she called instead. "I take it you've come to release the prisoner?"

The vicar fingered the key to the stocks for a moment.

"I should warn you," Penelope said, "if you dare proclaim my actions a breach of the peace, you'll have to say the same of everyone who came here hoping to throw something at my husband." She shrugged. "It might not hold up to a thorough examination, but any decent solicitor could make weeks of work out of it, I'm sure."

Mr. Oliver's face roiled with loathing, an expression so cold Penelope felt her triumph falter a little. There was open hatred there, such as she had never seen—and she knew, with a sinking in her soul, that this was the end of an old, old friendship.

Mr. Oliver tossed the key down to the ground. "You'll pardon me for being chary of coming too close, Mrs. Flood," he said, as Penelope bent to snatch the key from the dirt. The vicar's pale brows slashed down in his rage-reddened face. "You should also know, today's events will not be lightly forgotten."

Penelope straightened, key in hand. "I should hope not, Mr. Oliver. We went to so much trouble, you see. People ought to remember."

Penelope unlocked the stocks, and tossed the key back to the magistrates. Mr. Oliver and Squire Theydon turned and left without a word, as Penelope knelt to rub some feeling back into John's aching ankles. Harry, Agatha, Mr.

Thomas, and Mr. Kitt came striding up as soon as the justices were gone.

Penelope stepped back to let Harry take over. The captain bent down and clasped John's shoulder, the two men's foreheads pressing close in comfort and relief.

Mr. Kitt made a helpless noise in the back of his throat. Then another, hands clasped over his mouth. Sudden tears poured down his face, and he flung himself toward Mr. Thomas, whose arms embraced him without hesitation and held fast. The taller man murmured endearments, eyes screwed shut, face all but glowing with relief.

Penelope turned to Agatha, who sketched another salute. "My general," she said, a world of warmth in her voice.

They had precisely one night to bask in their victory. The next morning found handbills up all around Melliton—hand-lettered, not printed—declaring every beehive in Melliton subject to seizure by the magistrates. From humble skeps to Penelope's leaf hive to Mr. Koskinen's complicated octagonal glass structure, every home of every bee in the village was to be counted up and taken away as weapons. Anyone who wished to retrieve their hive was required to make application to the Mendacity Society, so that, as the handbill said, "such disorderly and dangerous creatures may be placed in the stewardship of those whose moral character has been sufficiently vouched for by the authorities."

Penelope felt these words like a blow, when she read them. Agatha's face went grim and she clasped Penelope's hands tight, but she had appointments in London, and so soon Penelope was facing down those dread sheets all alone. The handbills read like an escalation in a war; they made either painful surrender or heightened rebellion her only options.

That it was personally directed against her, she could not doubt. Mr. Oliver knew her well enough to know how best to wound. *Either you must give in*, the declaration meant, *or you must push back even harder, and be crushed beneath the wheel of the law.*

Penelope refused—*refused*—to have her choices so constrained, to so great a disadvantage.

She had tried flouting the law, and though it had been a success, she knew it did not suit her as a constant strategy. John was still looking a little haunted, which made Harry look rather feral in protective response. They would both be a while recovering.

Penelope herself had felt queasy and frightened, once the day's boldness had worn off. She wasn't sure she was meant to be a revolutionary. Open rebellion was really more in Mrs. Koskinen's line—and Mr. Kitt had come by and said Mrs. Koskinen had been speaking with the cottagers: offering to camouflage hives, tucking them deeper into the secret parts of the forests where the magistrates wouldn't find them, that sort of thing. Melliton had a fair bit of smuggling history, after all: people knew plenty of tricks to evade the eyes of the law. That was good, and Penelope would lend as much help as she was able.

What Penelope wanted for herself was simply this: to make such risks unnecessary, if she possibly could.

There had to be some other way, something between doing nothing and brandishing pitchforks in the streets. Something that put more pressure on the law than on the people fighting back against the law. She could hire a solicitor, as she'd threatened—but that would take time, and they hadn't enough of that.

Penelope wasn't good with violence. She was good with words. And knowledge. And letters.

And she was willing to be a little underhanded, for a good cause.

It was really quite simple, when she thought about it. Mr. Oliver knew her weaknesses—but in his irritation, he had forgotten that she also knew his.

She gathered a few things, and made her way to the vicarage.

Mr. Oliver was in his little Eden at the back, among his own hives. Plain skeps, no glass jars, because he thought the old ways were best. Penelope had always found it rather morbid to visit his hives, since she knew he'd be slaughtering them all at summer's end. It was one thing to know bees' lives were short, and quite another to end them all at once for convenience's sake.

She coughed a hello. The vicar waved to ask for her patience. He had one of the skeps tilted up, and was peering within it for something. He found it, eventually: a young queen bee, new and energetic. She squirmed in his fingertips as he gripped her at the waist, then raised a small pair of scissors toward her fragile, fluttering wings.

Penelope turned away before she saw the snip.

Some beekeepers thought clipping the wings of a queen kept a hive from swarming. The most words Penelope had ever heard Mr. Koskinen say at once had been a fifteen-minute impassioned explanation of why this was both absolutely untrue, and detrimental to both the queen and the hive.

Mr. Oliver replaced the poor clipped queen in her skep, and set the hive back onto its stand. "I am always disappointed that they turned out to be queens," he said. "Not kings, as Virgil calls them." His smile was sad, and fond, and for a moment Penelope felt as if she'd imagined their years of friendship.

His smile stayed sad. "What can I do for you, Mrs. Flood?"

Penelope put on her most polite tone. "I have come to speak to you about the beehives, Mr. Oliver."

He pulled off his gloves one at a time. "Then let us go inside, where we may be more official."

Penelope had once found the vicar's study a comforting place: it smelled of old books, and leather, and candles burnt late into the night. But now she only noticed how dark it was with the curtains shut to keep out the sun, and the books all crammed together on the shelves like captured creatures in a zoo.

Mr. Oliver sat in his favorite armchair, folding his hands on the shining surface of the table; Penelope took a seat in a spindly chair with a wobbly leg, and braced her feet against the moth-eaten rug on the floor.

"I imagine you have some questions," the vicar began cordially.

"Just the one," Penelope said, just as carefully cordial. "A great many Melliton folk depend on their hives as a supplement to their income, you know: Mr. Scriven, Mr. and Mrs. Koskinen, Mr. Cutler, many of the smaller farms and cottagers."

"I am well aware, Mrs. Flood. I am their vicar. Do you have a point?"

"Just this: are you truly certain you must take their hives away?"

He nodded piously. "They will get their hives back, if they deserve them."

"Some may lose a great deal of their work, in the time that may take."

The vicar steepled his fingers together and gave her a stern look. As if he were a teacher and she a recalcitrant student. As if they hadn't been friends for twenty years, trading thoughts on centuries-old poems. As if that time counted for nothing now. His voice was sweet and syrupy as cordial: "If those cottagers had been more prudent, they would not be in a position to suffer from the loss of one or two hives."

"Prudent enough to simply have more money, you mean?" Penelope muttered, and shook her head. "How can it be a fiendish crime to steal six hives from Abington Hall, but it's justice when you steal bees from half the people in the village?"

"It is justice when the law does it, Mrs. Flood." Mr. Oliver's cordiality slipped, and he scowled openly. "You said you had only a single question—that was two, by my count."

"Indulge me one more time," she said softly. "Is there

nothing I can say, to make you change your mind on this subject?"

He shook his head, pale hair floating on the air.

Penelope sighed. "Then I'm sorry, Mr. Oliver." She pulled out a sheet of paper, scribbled over with a spidery hand. "This is a letter from Mr. Oglevey, a London antiquary who specializes in art with certain . . . carnal tendencies. He was quite happy to tell me all about the deals he's brokered on behalf of Lady Summerville, for several high-quality works by the late and much-admired Isabella Abington. And *here*," she said, laying down another sheet, "is a list of everything I could find that Lady Summerville has spent money on since the founding of her virtuous moral society. Handbill printing, special constables' wages, informants' bounties—even the rectory glass, after your windows were broken during the Queenite agitation. I've spoken to every artisan and tradesman on the list, to confirm that the sums are accurate and verifiable."

Mr. Oliver's eyes were coals now, hot and luminous in the dimness. "What are you getting at, Mrs. Flood?"

Penelope leaned forward. "Simply this: what would the good people of Melliton think, if they knew the Mendacity Society was almost entirely funded by the selling of obscene art?"

The silence was *exquisite*. Penelope let it flow around her, thick and sweet as honey.

"There is nothing illegal about what my sister has done," the vicar said at last.

"Of course there isn't," Penelope said breezily. "Those statures were her inheritance, to dispose of as she wished.

But I remember when the will was read: She wasn't precisely eager to show them off to her friends, was she? Did she even tell anyone they now belonged to her?" She sat back, clasping her hands tightly in her lap to keep them from shaking. "It's not about what's legal or not legal, Mr. Oliver. It's about *what's right*. The Mendacity Society does exist to fight obscenity, does it not?" She tilted her head. "And if memory serves, yours is an auxiliary branch—imagine what the national organization would say if they were to find out . . ."

The vicar's teeth ground together so hard Penelope could hear them from where she sat. "Blackmail is a crime, Mrs. Flood," he sputtered.

"'Then bring me up on charges," she replied cheerfully. "But you'll need a second justice for that—perhaps Mr. Theydon, with his 'Hundred Godly Lessons,' could join you on the bench."

Mr. Oliver blanched a very springlike greenish.

Penelope leaned forward again. "Let the villagers keep their bees, Mr. Oliver. Or else you'll be at the center of the kind of scandal that gets talked about everywhere in England. Imagine your name in the hands of the caricature artists, or on the lips of every gossipy housewife from here to Scotland. I can hear the ballad lyrics now: 'Mr. All-Of-Her, the Vicar of Vice.'"

Mr. Oliver shook his head, as though he could shake off her threats so easily. Penelope waited, while he attempted to stare her down. But she knew his weakness, and it was this: he *must* be thought to be virtuous. It was as crucial a need for him as breath.

He made the only decision he could, and slumped heavily in his comfortable chair. "Very well, you harpy," he said. "You may have your bees."

"You've made a very prudent decision," Penelope said, and gathered up her letters. "In fact, since so many hives in Melliton are to be left in their proper place, I wouldn't be at all surprised if the Abington hives found their way back to Melliton."

"And just how will that miracle be accomplished?" Mr. Oliver asked bitterly.

Penelope only smiled. "The Lord works in mysterious ways, Mr. Oliver."

It was all she could do not to skip on the walk home. *This* was the kind of feeling she'd been chasing, that she hadn't gotten from the bee bombs. Not a single act of violence, sharp and sudden as lightning, but a shift in the way she moved through the world.

Penelope had gone up against Mr. Oliver, and she had won. The vicar would not forget this. She had taken back a little bit of ground for her own, and she intended to keep it.

It made her want to see what else she could have, if she were only bold enough to ask for it.

One hope came instantly to mind.

Chapter Twenty-Five

Y*ou ought to have seen his face!* Penelope's handwriting was rushed and flourished with triumph when she wrote to Agatha next. *It felt like I'd gotten back all the years of my life I'd spent worrying about offending him, or disappointing him, or being too improper, or too obviously myself. An embarrassment of riches, though not without some pangs of grief. I thought we were friends, and he thought he was my superior. We are not friends any longer—not that either of us will ever admit that aloud—but at least we are now something closer to equals, in both his eyes and my own.*

Perhaps it's not about overthrowing the whole towering edifice of bad government in one fell swoop. Perhaps you can thwart one small tyrant at a time, and get the thing done piecemeal. I don't have too much in common with the radicals at the Crown and Anchor, but I like to think they'd approve of the general tenor of what we've done.

Agatha smiled fondly, and traced her fingertips over the spikes and swirls of her beloved's handwriting. She could all but hear Penelope's voice in those words, as if touching the ink were like strumming the string of some instrument. The results set her heart singing like music.

Penelope was still buoyant when Agatha went down to Melliton three days later. She pulled Agatha into an embrace before she'd hardly stepped off the stage.

Agatha hugged her back rather anxiously as Penelope's arms tightened around her waist. The other woman was laughing, silently, joyously—but Agatha felt too many Melliton eyes on her to enjoy it as she wanted to.

"I've got something to show you," Penelope said, and as soon as they arrived at Fern Hall she brought out a small wrapped bundle. "Open it," she urged, with a knowing grin.

Agatha unwrapped the cloth to find—honeycomb? Mostly honeycomb, but an odd formation, some of the cells capped, others standing empty. They were misshapen because they'd been built around something else: a small enamel box, brilliantly colored, with a ring of sparkling stones and the shockingly familiar face of an ex-emperor . . .

"The Napoleon snuffbox!" Agatha gasped. "But where . . . ?" She poked at the comb that encrusted fully half the small object.

"Remember when John was captured, and he'd knocked over one of the Abington hives?" Agatha nodded. "Well, when I finally had a chance to repair it, I found this jammed into the straw of the skep. Waiting to be found until the hive was replaced. Isabella must have hidden it there for me to find, because she knew I'd get it safely to its proper owner."

She laughed. "It was the one place she knew where her niece would never go looking for it. I've already written to Joanna to tell her the good news."

"Aren't you going to clean it?"

Penelope wrapped it back up. "I thought Joanna might like to see it this way first. It's a little more poetic, don't you think, if the bees were helping Isabella hide it?"

"Poets." Agatha said it like a curse, but her heart wasn't in it.

Penelope's grin said she knew as much.

They changed into bee clothes and walked the circuit, feeling the heat rise off the earth as spring declined into full summer. Nell Turner's hives were thriving, though her garden had become rather overgrown in her absence. Mr. Scriven showed them his newest baby goats, two heartbreaking, mischievous bundles of black and tan.

The women bypassed Abington Hall and curved around down the hill.

Grass shushed in the breeze, bees and other insects buzzed from flower to flower, and the wheelbarrow full of beekeeping equipment clanked and thunked as it trundled over the packed earth of the road. Agatha rolled up her sleeves and opened her collar against the warmth—and as they walked through one of the shady, forested sections, Penelope dropped the wheelbarrow, stripped off her gloves, and pressed Agatha up against the cool white bark of a birch tree. "I've been wanting to do this for *months*," she said, kissing Agatha's neck, hands clutching at her trousered hips.

Agatha tilted her head back and sighed happily as Penelope's mouth skated over the pulse beating in the hollow of her throat. "I missed you, too, Flood."

"A week shouldn't feel like such a long time," Flood murmured, a nip of her small teeth making Agatha shiver with pleasure. "What if . . ." She nuzzled into the crook of Agatha's neck. "What if we never had to be apart?"

Agatha's fingers had slipped into Penelope's short curls—but at this question, they tightened.

Penelope's head bent back at the pressure, her smile sly, and her eyes wanton.

"How do you mean?" Agatha asked.

"What if you came to live with me, Flood?" Penelope went on. "Harry and John won't be staying past the coronation, and the house will feel so empty when they're gone. It's felt empty since Christmas, even with them here. Because *you're* gone. You should be here. With me." Penelope bit her lip. "I'm rambling, I know—how about I stop talking and let you answer the question?"

Agatha had forgotten how to breathe. Spending every day with Penelope Flood. Every *night*. No more empty beds, no more dull and solitary sleeps. To have someone again—not a husband, not something legal—but someone real, and loving, and true.

It was everything she'd wanted for herself, and it was going to break her to have to turn it down.

Because the truth was: "I can't, Flood," she said, through the iron bands tightening around her chest. "I can't leave

Griffin's. There is so much to do in London still. Eliza and Sydney need me too much."

The light went out in Penelope's eyes. She smiled, but she stepped back, her hands tugging at her cuffs and smoothing down the curls Agatha had been so glad to tousle. "Of course," she said with a laugh. Agatha feared Penelope was laughing at herself: it was such a small and brittle sound. "Not being a mother, I forget how it is sometimes. You have to put your son first."

Agatha nodded miserably. "It's not the answer I'd prefer to be giving you, Flood."

"I know." Penelope's smile began to crumble at the edges. She turned hastily away, taking up the wheelbarrow again and getting back on the road.

Agatha gulped a little and hurried to catch up. "Penelope . . ." she said.

"It's alright," Penelope said at once. "I'm just . . . I'd been hoping, that's all. But I suppose . . . you can only have one queen in a hive." She glanced over her shoulder, and her smile was almost back to normal. "I'll ask you again next summer. Maybe you'll be in a position to give me a different answer."

"I hope so," Agatha murmured, and fell in step beside the wheelbarrow.

The day was still beautiful, and before long Penelope was reciting pastoral poetry again, as always. She seemed to have shaken off the sting of Agatha's rejection entirely. The bees hummed sleepily in spruce-and-lavender smoke, there was plenty of honey in the skep jars, and everywhere they turned,

Melliton looked like a maiden decked out in her finest frock to meet a long-missed lover.

So why did Agatha feel so damn dismal?

Penelope barely waited until the household was abed before tugging on her dressing gown and slipping into Agatha's bedroom.

She nearly ran right into the woman, who'd been in the act of reaching for the door handle. "Penelope—?"

Penelope wasted no time. She all but yanked Agatha's mouth down to hers.

Agatha gasped against Penelope's lips, but something of the shorter woman's desperation must have caught her in its tendrils, because soon her hands were sinking into Penelope's short hair and her fingertips were almost painfully tight against Penelope's scalp. Her mouth opened, dark and hot and hungry as the kiss deepened. Penelope welcomed the little sparks of pain, as they kept her distracted from the larger cloud of hurt and worry that stormed in the center of her breast.

She'd known the affair was doomed from the start. This may not be *the* last night, but it certainly felt like *a* last night. Something had changed, and it was no use pretending otherwise. The sliver of hurt that had slid into her heart from today's denial was an injury that she would be a long while recovering from. If she ever did.

The fear made her move, had her backing Agatha up hard against the bed and following her down into the blankets.

Skirts tangled up knees and calves—Penelope tugged insistently at Agatha's hem, until she felt the other woman's hands close soothingly around her wrist. "Hold on," Agatha whispered.

Penelope froze, trembling.

Agatha gently worked the linen out from under them both, tossing her own nightclothes aside and then slipping Penelope's over her head. Penelope shivered in the chill air— it was supposed to be halfway to summer, but she felt as cold as winter in her bones.

And then Agatha tugged the bedclothes up around Penelope's shoulders, and over her head, and pulled the whole pile down to her long, soft self: blankets and sheets and Penelope and all.

Lack of sight descended on Penelope like sweetest relief. Everything was taste and touch and sound—the sweet weight of Agatha's breast beneath her hunting hand, the soft sigh warm from her lips, salt from the day's long walk in the sharp hollow at the base of her throat. Penelope tried to touch her everywhere, carving Agatha's shape into her memory: the curve of her hip and the softness of her belly, the long line of muscle in her calf. Agatha welcomed all of it, yielding softly to Penelope's grasp, tilting her head back on a gasp when Penelope's mouth began moving lower, spreading her thighs so Penelope could reach between.

She cursed when Penelope pressed hard where she was most sensitive, and arched up instantly into that stroking caress. Penelope was in no mood to be delicate, and soon was pumping two, then three fingers into Agatha's cunny, the scent of arousal curling around her like smoke and setting her own nerves afire like lines of powder. She sucked in a breath, sank her teeth into Agatha's shoulder, and thrust harder.

"Yes," Agatha breathed. And: "More." Her fingers scrabbled at Penelope's shoulders, and she pressed her heels into the mattress to better thrust her hips up off the bed, fighting to get as wide and deep as possible, to take more and more.

Penelope gave her everything—and nearly came herself when she felt Agatha tighten around her fingers and choke out a breathy, telltale cry.

Penelope fucked her higher and higher until Agatha's hand once more grasped her wrist, slowing her movements. She took Penelope's hand up to her mouth, and sucked gently on the fingers that had brought her to her peak. Her breath was hot, still panting, and her tongue swirled gratefully around Penelope's fingertips.

Penelope felt a moan tear itself from her throat, low and vibrant. She was shaking in the darkness, dripping wet, aching to be touched and horribly afraid she would shatter beneath Agatha's hands.

And somehow, Agatha knew—sensed it, perhaps, in the fevered press of Penelope's thighs against hers, or felt the trembling in her hands that had been so greedy and grasping before. She pulled Penelope down into her arms, cushioning her against her own body, arms banding tight. Penelope burrowed as close as she could, taut with fear and anguish and unsatisfied desire, while Agatha murmured words of comfort against her hair.

Penelope could only shake her head. Comfort was the last thing she needed. Comfort would destroy her completely. "I love you," she whispered against her lover's collarbone.

The heartbeat there jumped beneath her lips. "I love you, too," Penelope whispered.

And that was it. Four little words that broke her entire heart. Tears sprang to her eyes and she sat up, horrified, to dash them away.

"Penelope—?" Agatha said, reaching out to pull her back.

But Penelope only shook her head roughly, staggered free of the bed, and fled back to her own cold hearth.

CHAPTER TWENTY-SIX

Agatha was unhappy and sluggish when it was time to return to London the next morning. Last night had frightened her: there had been pain laced with joy in a way she was finding it hard to untangle in the clear and levelheaded light of day. Penelope had seemed almost herself at breakfast—except for the slight shadow that lingered in the corner of her eyes.

But as Agatha sat on top of the swaying stage, watching the hills and woodlands give way to the cobbles and walls and cathedrals of the city, she realized that Penelope's question had given her an opportunity. *I'll ask you again next summer,* Penelope had said.

That gave Agatha one year to get the London print-shop into shape. Three hundred sixty-five days to bring Sydney around to his responsibilities.

If she hadn't been surrounded by other travelers, she'd have rolled up her sleeves on the spot. As it was, she leaned forward, into the wind of the coach's motion, until her eyes watered and her cheeks went numb with the early morning chill.

The journeymen were hard at work already when she arrived. She could hear the muffled thumps even in the shop front, where Eliza was behind the counter showing young Jane the finer points of slicing the graver into the waxed ground. Agatha waved hello but didn't interrupt: instead, she dropped her things in her bedroom, and went straight to her desk to catch up on her paperwork.

She unlocked her desk, got out ink, paper, and quill, and began rifling through the stack of her correspondence.

On top was a letter from Penelope, talking about blackmailing the vicar. Then another, telling Agatha in more detail what the signs were of a hive about to swarm. The letter discussing Melliton's reaction to the Pains and Penalties bill. An earlier letter where Penelope had brazenly told her about playing with the he's-at-home while Agatha was away (she blushed and tucked that one hastily into her pocket for later rereading). More and more papers, every single one in Penelope Flood's sweetly looping hand: the Mendacity Society, Christmas plans, thoughts about the Crown and Anchor, stories from Penelope's childhood, anecdotes from evenings at the Four Swallows.

Nothing to do with Griffin's: no invoices, no editorial correspondence, no proposals from hopeful new writers or authors accepting an invitation to place a piece in the *Menagerie*. Agatha couldn't even remember the last time she'd sent one of those out. Not since . . .

Not since she started delegating the correspondence to Eliza Brinkworth. Somehow, during the past half year, she'd managed to offload most of the business of the London shop onto her apprentice. Who'd taken the burden up so ably that Agatha hadn't even noticed until now.

Agatha had unwittingly exiled herself from her own hive.

She slumped back in the chair, turning the revelation over and over. She'd been so focused on Sydney—on how to square his political leanings with the needs of the shop, on his frequent absences—that she'd overlooked a much better successor.

Eliza Brinkworth was more than capable of stepping into Agatha's shoes.

In fact—Agatha rifled through her older files—ah, yes, Eliza's apprenticeship had been set at five years, and would be complete at summer's end. Most journeymen changed shops at such a time, either to return to hometowns closer to family, or to start a shop of their own, or simply to see a little more of the world. But Eliza's father was in London, and she'd never mentioned wanting to start her own shop . . .

What if there was a shop ready and waiting for her? All it needed was for Agatha to step aside.

After all, like Penelope said: you couldn't have two queens in a hive.

She shoved up from the desk and strode impatiently down the stairs.

Young Jane had a good few inches of the wooden block carved away already—not terribly quick, but she was being careful to be precise. Agatha approved: quickness would come in time, with practice. "Jane, could I ask you to run to the Queen's Larder for a bottle of cider?"

Jane nodded eagerly at the reprieve and was off, summer sun winking brightly off the glass in the doorway as she departed.

"May I see you in my office, Miss Brinkworth?"

Once the door shut behind them, Eliza brushed her hands down her skirts and fidgeted in her chair. From the look on her face, she expected the worst.

Agatha could only grin, the anticipation getting the better of her. "My dear Eliza," she said, leaning forward and resting her forearms on Thomas's desk. "If you could change one thing about Griffin's—the way we do business, the type of work we do—what would you change?"

Eliza's eyes went wide, and she blinked several times, as if the sunlight had dazzled her vision. Then Agatha *saw* her brain engage with the problem, all the gears lining up and the machinery beginning to turn.

Good god, but young folk were glorious.

"We'd produce a lot more sheet music," Eliza said after a moment. "Regularly, both reprints and commissioned pieces, not merely the odd job or short run. More people are buying the new six-octave pianos, and the demand for music is growing. I'm good with music notation, and I enjoy it. We could afford to buy a font of type, if we were printing more of it. Also, Griffin's has plenty of plates in the warehouse from past years—older pieces, a few practice books, even one or two popular arias—we could add something in to each issue of the *Menagerie*, just like we do with the silk samples. It would take a bit of time away from the broadsides and the jobbing, at least initially—but I think it's a steadier market, and leaves us less open to . . ." she coughed ". . . certain legal complications." She bit her lip. "I'm sure you're going to ask what Sydney thinks about all this."

"Let's," said Agatha, and went to fetch her son from his compositing.

Eliza explained her idea again, at Agatha's request. Sydney's eyes lit. "It seems a very solid plan to me—do I get a vote?"

"Do you want one?" Agatha returned. "What I mean is: Sydney, do you really want me to leave Griffin's to you? Not just right now—but ever?" She took a bracing breath, as his eyes went wide with surprise. "I know we raised you with that expectation—Lord knows I've all but beat you over the head with it—but, well, I'd like to find a way to make you happy. Not just burden you with a duty that brings you no joy."

"I . . ." He swallowed—and bless him, he took a moment to consider before he answered. "I think what's been hard for me is the idea that I have to do it alone. You and Father had each other, and that seemed to work so well—but I . . ." He looked at Eliza, his heart in his eyes, then back at Agatha. "I can find us any number or kind of writers," he said staunchly, "provided I have someone to decide what's best to print. I have the energy—but *she* has the vision."

Agatha nodded. "I absolutely agree," she said. "So: how would you two like to take over—as partners?"

"Partners?" Sydney said, brightening.

Eliza's eyes went wide, and she gasped.

"Partners," Agatha confirmed. "We can have something legal drawn up with very little trouble. A proper contract, official and dependable." She tapped a finger on the counter meaningfully. "But something you could always dissolve later, if you two decide to—to part ways."

It was not an easy thing for Agatha to say, but she knew it was the right thing, and that helped her get over the awkwardness of it all. *My son, you have my blessing* not *to get married.*

Eliza's mouth hung open for half a minute before she whispered, "But ma'am . . . are you . . . What would you be doing?"

Agatha pursed her lips to keep from smiling too broadly and giving the game away. "I find myself more and more intrigued by your suggestion about sheet music. We could probably open a whole second shop for that—maybe with a little poetry and broadsides as well. But London rents are so very expensive . . . Perhaps we should look at premises nearer the other press-works, so I can still check proofs and keep the queue moving."

Light dawned in Eliza's eyes, as she caught Agatha's meaning. "Somewhere like Melliton, perhaps?"

Agatha nodded primly. "I know of a building near the high street that would do nicely." Mr. Turner would be happy enough to sell at any price, she was sure.

Eliza's grin had gone from a candle to a bonfire. "Do you think we could have it ready in time for Mrs. Turner's next batch of ballads?"

"We can certainly try."

Eliza squealed in pleasure, and clapped her hands over her mouth for a moment in sheer joy. She got hold of herself before too long, and schooled herself almost back to her usual semi-demure helpfulness. "Mrs. Flood will be happy to have you so close by, I'm sure."

Agatha's buoyant mood deflated a little. "I hope so. She asked me to—but I . . ." She paused, eyes narrowing at her soon-to-be-former apprentice. Who winked, the chit. "You know about Mrs. Flood and me?"

Eliza arched a knowing brow. "Did you two think you were being subtle?"

Agatha laughed until her sides ached.

Two days later, Agatha took the stage into Melliton. Even though she wasn't expected at Fern Hall for another few days.

She wanted this to be a surprise.

She left her things in the care of Mrs. Biswas at the Four Swallows, and went walking the circuit toward Fern Hall to find Penelope. It felt wrong, striding along the familiar roads and paths in skirts rather than trousers. The fabric of her dress caught on quite a few more briars and branches than she was used to; her light cotton hem was rather dusty and her petticoat a bit torn before long. No doubt Penelope's romantic soul would enjoy the idea, but not the reality, of Agatha showing up in tatters to beg for forgiveness. Penelope Flood was a pragmatist at heart, for all her love of poetry.

Just one more reason to love her, really.

Agatha walked as quickly as she could, but it wasn't fast enough to suit her impatience—so as she walked, she plucked flowers: columbine, hyssop, kingcups, dog roses, and more. Names and natures she'd learned from Penelope, along with all the local plants most beloved by bees. To this bounty Agatha added a long, twisting tendril of enchanter's nightshade—which, Penelope had said, referred to the witch Circe, who changed men into beasts. Agatha'd meant to ask more about that; she was curious about the full story.

If she could only find where the damned woman was!

She walked past the Turner place and up, across Squire Theydon's sloping fields to the small copse beyond: a shady, curving bowl of trees, with a small spring and a carpet of lily of the valley.

And there was Penelope. Brown coat, men's trousers, so beautiful and so very herself that Agatha had to stop and press a hand to her heart until she could breathe again.

No pointing apologizing if you were only going to faint before the thing was properly done.

Penelope didn't look up from the hive as Agatha approached, her hearing muffled no doubt by her veil and the joyous buzzing of three hives' worth of bees.

Agatha could relate: her own heart felt overfull of noise and wings. She had no idea how to begin, so she chose something utterly banal and said: "Hullo."

Penelope froze, then slowly pivoted. The smoker at her side puffed once as her hand clenched tight, and her eyes went very wide as she took in Agatha with her hem in shreds and her hands full of flowers and a lump the size of Wales in the back of her throat.

"Hello yourself," Penelope said in return.

And now it was Agatha's turn again. She had to speed things up, or at this rate they wouldn't get this mess sorted out before winter came and froze them where they stood.

"I made you something," Agatha said, and held up the flowers. She'd used the enchanter's nightshade to weave the various blossoms into a coronet, bright and blooming and fit for a fairy queen.

Penelope blinked, mouth opening and closing. She seemed staggered, as if Agatha were speaking a foreign language she only halfway understood. Her eyes never left the coronet. "Cowslips," she said. "I could quote you some excellent poetry about that."

Agatha sighed. "Go ahead: I deserve it."

Penelope was startled into a laugh.

"You said you can't have two queens in a hive," Agatha went on, "but that just means only one of us can be queen." She stepped forward, her heart hovering on the back of her tongue, ready to fly out from her lips. "I think it ought to be you. I came to tell you I'm sorry for yesterday—and to ask you if I could change my answer. To ask . . . if you'd like to share a home, and a life. With me."

She stretched out her hands, holding the coronet. She was proud of the way they barely shook at all.

Penelope raised a finger and almost touched one trembling

petal. A bee from the hive behind her beat her to it, diving into the bell of the flower, its velvet legs dusted with gold.

Penelope's face lifted, and now her smile outshone the sun in the sky above. "What if neither of us are queens?" she said, to Agatha's surprise. "What if we're only a pair of lowly worker bees?"

Agatha stared down at the coronet, as more bees found their way toward it, setting themselves in the flowers like tiny gems. "That sounds much less romantic than what I had planned."

"Is it?" Penelope set aside the smoker and moved forward, her gloved hands cupping the back of Agatha's. Heat crept up Agatha's skin at the touch. "Worker bees depend on one another," Penelope said. "They can't thrive or even survive on their own." One corner of her sweet mouth quirked. "I'd be no good without you, you know."

Hope struck like a kick to the chest. "Is that a yes?"

"Of course it is."

Agatha's heart gave a great leap, joy and gratitude and love all expanding infinitely, as if there was a whole second sky within her. She blew out a breath as the fear and tension of the past few days melted away. And here she was with stars in her eyes and her hands brimming over with flowers. "I still think you ought to wear the crown," she said. "I went to some trouble."

Penelope laughed, and bent her head, and blew gently until all the bees flew grumpily away. "We can take turns."

Her gloved hands raised the coronet and set the whole on Agatha's brow. It prickled terribly, but Agatha didn't care—

she was too busy pulling off Penelope's wide hat, the bee veil tangling between her fingers as she bent low for a kiss, catching Penelope's breathy laugh on her tongue. One kiss led to another, and another, and together they sank to the grass of the meadow, as the buzzing of bees played a lazy, loving counterpoint.

CHAPTER TWENTY-SEVEN

August 1821

The illustration of Queen Caroline's funeral was one of Eliza's finest etchings yet: a great black hearse, horses with plumes that drooped like willow branches, the tall, stern figures of the soldiery in black ink on the pale page. Agatha sold copy after copy as Mrs. Biswas read the account from the papers to the evening crowd at the Four Swallows. *"Some stones and mud were thrown at the military, and a magistrate being present, the soldiers were sanctioned in firing their pistols and carbines at the unarmed crowd."*

"Shameful!" Mrs. Koskinen cried, to a chorus of agreement.

Two people had been killed, as the massed crowd confronted the guard and demanded the funeral be allowed to pass through London proper, despite Lord Liverpool's forbidding it for fear of causing unrest. He'd been right to worry, it turned out. The crowd made its own riotous path. There had been wild, persistent rumors that the Queen had been poisoned: she'd kicked up a royal fuss in an attempt to attend her husband's coronation a month before, and to the public's eye the timing was something more suspicious than mere coincidence could account for.

All the contempt the people had expressed for her behavior vanished, and they once again rioted in her support.

To keep the Melliton folk orderly, Mr. Oliver had given a painfully patriotic sermon about kings and piety and respect for the crown—only to be shaken by the news that King George had not only gone to visit the Catholics in Ireland, with an eye toward their emancipation—but that George had at the same time enjoyed a cheery reunion with his mistress, Lady Coyningham, whose husband had recently been elevated to the Privy Council in return for the man's great kindness in overlooking adultery.

It was a great blow for a simple country vicar to take all at once, and Penelope thought he would be some time in recovering from it.

He would have no support from his sister: Viscount and Lady Summerville had let Abington Hall and were sparing expenses by moving in with his lordship's brother at his estate in Wessex. The Mendacity Society had rather flagged without its foundress—and without the support of the cash earned from the sale of Isabella's statues. The new Abington Hall tenant was set to move in at the end of the month, and was already the subject of several unlikely rumors and base speculations.

Harry and John had sailed off to the southern whaling grounds, with promises to write when next they made landfall.

Mrs. Biswas finished reading the description of the funeral, and the usual arguments broke out in the usual corners. Mr. Thomas and Mr. Kitt had their heads close together, reading over some piece about the navy. The new ballad singer began tuning her guitar, in preparation for a performance that would include Mrs. Turner's latest ballads and one or two still-popular works by the Widow Wasp.

Mr. Painter could be heard from the far side of the room, complaining as always that Melliton was growing too rude, too rough, and showed less and less respect for the law.

"Good thing, too," Agatha muttered, making Penelope snort into her ale.

The next breathtaking romance in
Olivia Waite's Feminine Pursuits series,

THE HELLION'S WALTZ

will be available from Avon Impulse
Summer 2021

ABOUT THE AUTHOR

OLIVIA WAITE is a former bookseller and *Jeopardy!* champion who writes historical romance, fantasy, science fiction, and essays. She is the "Kissing Books" columnist for the *Seattle Review of Books*, where she reviews romance both new and old with an emphasis on insightful criticism and genre history. She lives in Seattle with her husband and their stalwart mini-dachshund.

Discover great authors, exclusive offers, and more at hc.com.